THE
WRONG
WOMAN

THE WRONG WOMAN

A NOVEL

LEANNE KALE SPARKS

CROOKED LANE

NEW YORK

Copyright © 2022 by Leanne Kale Sparks

All rights reserved.

Published in the United States by Crooked Lane Books, an imprint of The Quick Brown Fox & Company LLC.

Crooked Lane Books and its logo are trademarks of The Quick Brown Fox & Company LLC.

Library of Congress Catalog-in-Publication data available upon request.

ISBN (hardcover): 978-1-64385-941-5
ISBN (ebook): 978-1-64385-942-2

Cover design by Melanie Sun

Printed in the United States.

www.crookedlanebooks.com

Crooked Lane Books
34 West 27th St., 10th Floor
New York, NY 10001

First Edition: February 2022

10 9 8 7 6 5 4 3 2 1

Chuck—for all your unconditional
love and unwavering support.
Your SM . . . finally.

PROLOGUE

A SERIAL KILLER'S MAIN objective is to kill.
It's a common misconception, perhaps true for some—maybe even the majority; he didn't know. Had never seen any research on the matter. And was not particularly interested in the answer. For him, it was more about the hunt. Finding the right target. Stalking the perfect prey.

Killing was simply the final step.

He likened it to preparing a nice meal. Discovering the perfect recipe. Gathering ingredients. Prepping, cooking. All steps leading to the pièce de résistance. Afterward, cleanup. Not a fun task, but essential. Necessary.

That's what killing was to him. The necessary cleanup after a big event. There was really no way around it. Like eating, killing was essential. Self-preservation. The hunt was the act that nourished him. Torture allowed him to feed the dark demon residing in his psyche—the one with a discriminating palate.

Then came the kill. The cleanup.

If the dishes were not washed, the pots and pans not scrubbed, the kitchen not cleaned—to keep with the cooking metaphor—it would only make it harder, even impossible, to continue to cook meals in the future. The man—the demon—would starve.

He looked into the woman's sightless eyes. Her blonde hair matted with red blood, cemented to her cheeks, and plastered to the back of her head. She'd been fun. Her trusting nature was almost a turn-off at first, until something sparked in her eyes—the eyes were always the first tell. The devastating aware-ness of danger moved through her body in a series of nervous quakes. Twitches. Hands into fists, ready to strike. Gaze fran-tic, searching for an escape. The anxiety coursing through her fueled his adrenaline rush, making her an infinitely more intriguing conquest.

Of course, there was no escape. He had already guarded against that.

And she'd fought him every step of the way. Boy, had he enjoyed that. The sheer audacity she could get away—could prevent him from taking what he craved—sparked fury and frenzy and desire. A futile attempt on her part, but enough to get blood rushing into his ears and his groin. Until she could no longer fight. Until the anger and will to survive he had seen in her lively blue eyes—again, always in the eyes—dimmed. Then came the cleanup.

Death.

Her eyes stared at him. They were void of questions and fear and appeals. They were empty. They saw everything—and nothing.

He dumped her next to a tree bordering the tenth tee. *Tak-ing out the trash.* He smiled at his own wit—one last cooking metaphor, perhaps—blew her a kiss, and walked away.

There was work to be done. The next time would be differ-ent. He would have to deviate from his well-ordered pattern. His next kill would be unique; his next victim, a message. The woman who had turned his world upside down.

Kendall Beck was going to regret the day she'd entered his life.

CHAPTER

1

JOHN SANDOVAL WASN'T the creepiest man Kendall Beck had ever met.

In comparison with the scum she usually dealt with as an FBI special agent, Sandoval fell somewhere between socially awkward and weirdly unpleasant, with an underlying "ick" factor. But that didn't stop the itch under Kendall's skin, alerting her to something menacing about the fifty-seven-year-old man.

"Mr. Sandoval, thank you for speaking with us."

Exactly forty-eight hours earlier, Kendall had been assigned to the possible abduction of five-year-old Emily Williams. No one knew exactly when the child had gone missing. Her mother, Kathy, had put Emily to bed at eight o'clock the previous night. When Kathy went to wake her daughter in the morning, the bed was empty. There was no sign of a break-in. Nothing was disturbed in the house. No sign of a struggle—although, if an adult had taken the little girl, it wouldn't have been much of a contest.

The sliding glass door, left open about a quarter inch, was the suspected entry and exit point of the kidnapper. Kathy admitted she had not set the alarm because her husband was due home in the wee morning hours following a business trip. This had become her usual practice after the husband had not entered the code quickly enough on a couple of occasions and had awakened the entire house with the loud shrilling.

Random? Coincidence? Kendall didn't like coincidences, and it was a stretch to think the one night Kathy left the security system off, a kidnapper would slip in undetected and steal the five-year-old. Which left someone who knew Kathy wouldn't set the alarm. Someone close to the family. Say—a neighbor who was very familiar with the Williamses and their habits.

Mr. Sandoval lived next door to the Williamses and had been at their home since before the police were called. He was very interested in the investigation and what the FBI was uncovering. Kendall's "spidey senses" heightened: she didn't like non-family members who inserted themselves into an investigation, eager to help, with theories and opinions of what happened. A good portion of the time, those people—*the interlopers*—were actually the perpetrators of the crime.

The furnace kicked on, and hot air whistled from the floorboards in the old house. The plastic covering on the windows rustled.

"So, do you babysit for the Williamses often?" Kendall asked, glancing around Sandoval's living room. She sat in a mauve wingback chair while Sandoval was on a cream couch splotched in what was supposed to look like mauve and seafoam green paint strokes. The same green was on the carpets. Puffy floral valances hung over the picture window. There was little doubt the house hadn't been updated since the eighties.

"I'm not sure I would say *often*, but usually once a week. Maybe twice, depending on what Scott and Kathy had going on." Sandoval's hands flexed over his kneecaps, eyes tracking Kendall's partner, Jake Alexander, as he wandered around the room.

"And you don't consider once or twice a week often?" Kendall turned to Jake. "Hey, Jake, how often do you and Felicia get a babysitter?"

"About once a month, if we're lucky." Jake picked up a picture, turning it over in his hand before passing it off to Kendall.

She studied the photo in the silver frame. Five-year-old Emily and her two-year-old sister, Sadie, were in a bathtub, surrounded by colored bubbles. Both girls—Emily with bubbles on both cheeks, Sadie with bubbles piled high on her head—had wide, happy grins. Kendall looked up and smiled at Sandoval. "And did Emily visit you any other times—outside of you baby-sitting her?"

"Uh, yes—" Sandoval's gaze was glued to the picture in Kendall's hands. Sweat broke out over his upper lip. "She liked to come over and help with the cats." He looked back up at Kendall. "She loves the cats."

"How exactly does she help?"

"Mostly just plays with them. Sometimes, if she's here at feeding time, she sets out the food bowls after I prepare them. Refills their water, things like that."

Kendall flipped the picture frame so Sandoval could see it. "Tell me about this picture."

Sandoval made a face. "It was one of the times they were over," he said, as if it was obvious and Kendall was an idiot for even asking such a stupid question.

Kendall raised an eyebrow. "You gave them baths?"

"Well, bubble baths—only sometimes—when Scott and Kathy were out at night and gonna be late getting back. Past the girls' bedtimes."

Kendall returned her gaze to the picture, raising a skeptical eyebrow. "And you took a picture?"

"Well—yes, they were being silly. And were very excited about the colored bubbles I found at the store. It was a fun night. Emily asked me to take a picture to show her mommy."

"And did you show Mrs. Williams?"

"I can't remember."

"But you printed it out and framed it?" Kendall leaned forward, setting the frame on the coffee table between them.

The picture faced Sandoval. He smiled at the photo. "The girls are very special to me. My wife and I weren't able to have children."

"And you feel . . . *close* to the Williams girls," Kendall said, making her voice more sympathetic, less interrogatory.

Sandoval nodded, eyes glassy.

"Like a grandparent?"

"Yes." Sandoval lifted his head, a sense of relief shining in his eyes. "Exactly."

"But you're not their grandparent."

He shrugged, deflating a bit. "I haven't done anything wrong."

"But you can see where this looks odd, right? You have framed pictures of naked little girls unrelated to you displayed throughout your home as if they *are* family." Kendall placed her elbows on her knees, leaning in. "And now Emily is missing. And you have been very concerned—almost overly concerned, if I'm honest, Mr. Sandoval. And I can't help but wonder if you're distressed Emily's *missing*—or *worried* we might find her. And what she'll say about who abducted her."

Sandoval bolted to his feet. Kendall fell back, trying to maintain her unfazed demeanor.

"I would never do anything to harm Emily," Sandoval spat. "I love that little girl. And I love her family." He dropped his head to his hands, a muffled sob breaking free.

Kendall stood, slowly. "Then you won't mind us taking a look around."

Sandoval glared. Kendall remained steady. "Do whatever you need to do," he hissed. "But Emily isn't here. And you're wasting time when you should be out looking for her."

Kendall didn't respond. Instead, she handed the picture frame to Jake. "I want to see if Sandoval showed Kathy this picture." *And find out if it disturbed her as much as it does me.* Of course, if Sandoval hadn't shown it to Kathy—well, that brought up a lot of other questions, most prominently, why not? Was he worried Kathy might react in the same manner she had?

Jake nodded. They had worked many cases together after she had moved back to Denver, and when it seemed appropriate to work as a two-person team, Jake and Kendall always gravitated toward each other. A sort of yin and yang thing—when either was going off the rails, the other was there to pull them back on before the train derailed.

"I surveyed the house on my 'trip to the bathroom,'" Jake said, using air quotes. "There's a bedroom that looks as if it's for a little girl. Double bed with pink sheets, dolls and such in a toy box. Mr. Sandoval takes his role as head babysitter very seriously."

"Text Brady that picture, see if we can get a search warrant based off it."

He cocked an eyebrow. "Pretty slim, Beck."

"I know, but if we take the sheets from the girl's room and find something, I don't want the court kicking the evidence because of improper search and seizure."

They wandered into the kitchen. Fruit-covered wallpaper with a matching border around the chair rail. Seams lifted and curled, exposing the dingy off-white walls underneath. As if it was barely clinging to life. Sandoval's wife had died of cancer in 1991, and like the rest of the house, the kitchen hadn't changed at all since she'd passed away.

"This is the same wallpaper my mother had in our kitchen when I was growing up," Kendall muttered.

"I weep for your childhood," Jake said.

"Hush, man-child, or I'll make you do all of the paperwork on this case by yourself." A sense of comfort and sadness swelled in her chest. She missed her mother so much, and cursed the sudden heart attack which had taken the vibrant woman's life. Pushing the rush of emotions aside, Kendall stepped past Jake and pointed to a structure at the back of the property.

"Garage," Jake answered.

"Anything in the basement?"

"You mean the hoarder's paradise? Not so far, but I could only see part of it from the top of the stairs. I'll send a couple underling agents down there to check since we have Sandoval's permission to take a look around the property."

Kendall pushed open the glass door. A whoosh of cold air hit her in the face. Winter was alive and well in Denver in February. Of course, the forecast called for highs in the sixties over the weekend, followed by four to eight inches of snow the next week.

She walked across the back deck and into the yard. The single-car garage backed up to an alleyway, prevalent in all the older neighborhoods in the area. A side door with a nine-panel glass window was covered in dirt, probably not cleaned since the house was new back in the fifties. She pushed on the door and it opened with a loud creak.

A four-door, burgundy Cadillac took up most of the space. Older model. The nose of the vehicle kissed the front wall. A rope, with a tennis ball tied to the end, hung from the ceiling and rested against the car's windshield. Kendall's father had done a similar thing in their garage to guide her mother in when she parked the car. Once the ball hit the windshield, the driver knew they were in far enough for the garage door to clear the back end of the vehicle. In this case, it looked as if it was also in place to let the driver know they were about to hit the wall with the front end.

Kendall walked to the back of the car. She had to side-step her way around the vehicle to get to the other side. Jake attempted to follow, shaking his head. There was no way he would make it around. He was built like a Mack truck, with thighs the size of boulders.

Kendall lifted her chin toward a button on the wall by the door. "Garage door opener, big guy."

As the metal slats folded and made their slow ascent, light filled the open space. Something rubbed against Kendall's leg. She yanked her foot away. A black cat looked up at her as if she was insane, or insensitive to its needs. A squeaky meow mocked her before it sauntered away.

As the cat reached a set of large plastic storage bins stacked on top of each other, it glanced back at Kendall and disappeared.

Kendall followed, only slightly worried about the cat crossing her path and the repercussions. Her mother would admonish her for not following protocol, to reverse the curse by walking in a circle and retracing her steps. She glanced up and checked her surroundings. Jake was walking toward her, and two other agents stood at the open garage door, discussing the classic caddy. Probably not a good time to show her crazy.

Instead, she peered into the dark space where the cat had wandered.

"Find something?" Jake asked, stepping up next to Kendall.

Kendall crouched. There was something pale colored on the floor, but the light didn't reach far enough to illuminate the area. "Not sure." She shined the flashlight from her phone.

Two small white and pink tennis shoes lay on their sides. The cat curled up beside them, rolling on its back as it snuggled into a pair of legs clad in Disney princess pajama pants.

"Shit!"

Emily lay on her stomach, face toward Kendall, eyes closed.

Kendall pushed aside the bins, desperately trying to reach the little girl. Jake began tossing the large boxes out of the way.

Emily's fleece pullover was dirty and too thin for the freezing temps. Kendall ran her fingers along the girl's neck while staring at her mouth, hoping to see white plumes of hot air being expelled.

But her skin was cold. Unnaturally cold. A knot tightened in Kendall's gut.

"No, no, no, Emily," she whispered, frantic to find a pulse. "Don't you dare be gone."

She pressed her fingers firmly into the soft skin and held her breath, willing the little girl's heart to beat against the pads of her fingers.

Once. Twice. A third time. A faint pulse tapped against Kendall's fingertips.

"Get EMTs here. Now." She shrugged her coat off and wrapped it as tightly around the girl as she could without moving her. As much as she wanted to grab Emily, hold her tight to her body, and run her to her mother, Kendall knew she could do more damage than good if the girl had any sort of head, neck, or internal injuries.

Jake tossed his jacket at Kendall while barking orders into his walkie-talkie, calling for EMTs. Kendall rolled the jacket and placed it carefully under the girl's head, careful not to lift it up too high.

Agents were moving around them. It felt odd, as if Kendall and Emily were in a bubble where nothing moved, but there was an insane flurry of activity around them. Never touching them. As if they were in an alternate universe, watching life carry on around them, but without them participating.

But this was a crime scene now, and Jake quickly shut everything down until forensics arrived. He looked down at Emily with a tight smile, then to Kendall, shaking his head softly.

They had worked many crime scenes together. No matter how many children they found—dead or alive—it never got any easier. And the need to make sure the most innocent of victims received justice was their sole objective.

Kendall stared back at him, her jaw clenched to the point of breaking teeth. "Go arrest that son-of-a-bitch Sandoval."

CHAPTER

2

ADAM TAYLOR STUDIED the photograph tacked to his cubicle wall, and scrubbed the two o'clock shadow along his jaw. In the photo, young Jenna Rose smiled back at him. Locks of golden hair framed her flawless face. She was leaning forward, elbows on her knees, palms supporting her chin, fingers gracing her cheeks. Her blue eyes shimmering like a swimming pool, her lips slightly parted as if she was flirting with the person taking her picture.

Adam wondered if that was true. Had she been smiling at someone she loved? Lusted after? Was hoping to get to know better? He would never know the answer to that question.

And he would never be able to ask Jenna about it.

Adam hadn't known Jenna Rose. Most of the people he met lately would never utter a single word to him, except from the grave. Looking at the picture once more, he sighed and again wondered if his chosen profession—a homicide detective with the Denver Police Department—had been the right move. If he had been anything else—doctor, lawyer, stockbroker—would he have met Jenna while she was alive? Spoken to her? Gotten to know her and her family under happier circumstances?

A fruitless road for him to venture down. For one thing, he was never going to be a doctor, lawyer, or stockbroker. Had never considered any of them for a minute during that period in high school when you started looking at life after graduation and deciding what to be when you grew up. No, Adam had been born and bred into the family business. Destined to be a cop. Same as his dad and uncles. Same as his brothers—well, except for Mark, always the rebel, who bucked the system to become a firefighter. It was in Adam's blood. Expected. And truth be told, he hardly had an inkling of reserve. Except in these rare moments, when he took time to really see the victims. Allow the senselessness to invade his mind, making his heart and soul heavy.

Here he was, staring at this gorgeous woman, barely twenty years old, who'd lost her life nearly four months earlier. Adam couldn't do anything to change that. Couldn't reverse the fact that she would forever be defined as a murder victim. But he could make sure she was afforded some justice, and the rat bastard who murdered her was found. Convicted. And lived the rest of his life getting the same treatment Jenna had received. Bent over a table or in the prison shower, getting the business end of a meat whistle shoved up his ass by men named Butch and Randall and Killer while he screamed and cried and begged for them to stop.

A little over the top, perhaps, but Adam was tired of seeing people die at the hands of others. Disgusted by men who took what they wanted without regard for the harm they were doing to the women they abused, raped, sexually harassed, or stalked. He could never understand the crippling fear that simply walking alone through a parking lot at night could evoke in a woman.

A rap on the doorframe—not really a door, just the opening to the cubicle, but who knew what the hell to call that—and Saul Chapman entered, landing in the chair across from Adam. About fifty-eight years old, Saul was in the best shape of his life. Once upon a time, he was the cliché cigarette-smoking, donut-eating, two-pots-of-coffee-a-day cop with a belly over his belt, grunting every time he moved an inch. Then he'd had a massive heart attack and turned over a new, healthy, svelte leaf, and he'd never gone back. Now he drank smoothies with grass and kale and other disgusting shit.

Adam bit into his powdered sugar donut without an ounce of regret.

"Got the surveillance footage back from the golf course." Saul scrunched up his nose at Adam's breakfast choice.

"How was it?" Security cam footage was often dark and grainy, thus rendered useless.

"It's a golf course, so a higher-end setup." Meaning the viewer could actually see what was going on in the footage, which was a bonus for law enforcement searching for the person who dumped a body on the tenth tee.

"Ready to view?"

Saul slapped his hands on his knees and stood. "Yep, the screen in the war room."

The war room. The conference room where investigators laid out all the evidence; tacked victim, suspect, crime scene, and autopsy photos to whiteboards; and commenced theorizing on the life and death of the unfortunate souls.

Adam followed Saul into the room. Fletcher Shelton, another investigator on the Jenna Rose case, and up on all the latest tech—more so than Adam, who wasn't bad, and Saul, who knew nothing—was sitting at the long table, laptop in front of him. He glanced up and gave the usual dude head-nod greeting. Adam returned it.

"Dark sedan," Fletch said, pointing to the projection of the security video on the whiteboard. "IT geek says it's a Taurus. I disagree. That's a Chevy Impala. Newer model, probably 2016 or so."

Adam wasn't that interested in the make of the car. He wanted to see who had murdered Jenna. On the screen, covered from head to toe in black, a man lifted a naked body—*he couldn't even be bothered to wrap her up*—from the trunk, walked over to the wooded area behind the tenth tee, and unceremoniously dumped her. After a long moment of staring down at the body of Jenna Rose, the man walked back to his car and casually drove away. No rush. No squealing tires. Calm as could be.

Adam thought about that for a moment. The killer's actions were quite telling. "This isn't his first time killing."

Saul let out a long exhale. "Doesn't look like it to me."

That wasn't good news—if there was ever good news in a murder investigation—but discovering they might be looking for a serial killer was the worst sort of news. That meant they needed to find this asshole before he took another life. If he hadn't already.

"Alright, let's go through what we have," Adam ordered. Fletch nodded, zooming in on the license plate. "We managed to get the plate number."

"Who owns it?"

Saul flipped a page of his notepad. "Vehicle comes back registered to a Harvey Bedlam."

Adam tried to quell the excitement. Yes, it was the first real lead they'd had in a few weeks, but this revelation didn't necessarily mean Mr. Bedlam was their killer. But, man, Adam hoped it did. He wanted to close this case. Finally get some justice for the pretty young woman who had nothing more to look forward to in life.

"Find out where Mr. Bedlam lives, and let's see when we can talk to him."

Fletch nodded and turned back to his computer.

"We need to go through everything again. See if we can find a pattern, or anything unusual, and run it through NCIC." The National Crime Information Center was an electronic clearinghouse of crime data, maintained by the FBI, where law enforcement could track crime-related information. Interlinked with federal, state, local, and tribal law enforcement offices, it was an important information-sharing tool between investigative agencies.

"If we're lucky, we'll find a pattern and nab this guy before we have to investigate another murder."

3

KENDALL LOOKED THROUGH the glass as Jake and Assistant District Attorney Tim Smith questioned John Sandoval. The older gentleman was still wearing the light blue sweater, but it seemed too big for him now as he sat, shoulders slumped. He had aged since Kendall talked to him in his living room just a few short hours ago. The lines on his face were deepened, his watery eyes rimmed with red, his hair in disarray from running his fingers through it so often. Gone was the smiling, grandfatherly gentleman Kendall had gotten to know over the last forty-eight hours. The man was haggard, fatigued—and scared.

The door opened, and fluorescent light flooded in from the hallway, temporarily blinding Kendall. She glared at whoever was coming into the room, prepared to tell the asshole to shut the door—then clamped her mouth shut. Her boss, Special Agent in Charge Jonathan Brady, sauntered in the room and closed the door behind him.

"Figured you'd still be at the hospital questioning our vic," he said.

Brady was a tall, good-looking guy. In his late forties, he was just starting to get streaks of gray through his dark hair. He had the physique of a twenty-year-old, hard in all the best places. Today's tie selection was the *Peanuts* gang in various stages of dance. Since Brady's wife died a couple years back, he had become "Father of the Year," wearing ties his kids picked out, just to show one of the many ways he followed his "family first" mantra. He had admitted to Kendall, in a rare unguarded moment, he had not always been there for his young family, instead succumbing to the demands of his career. All that changed when a drunk driver T-boned his wife as she drove through an intersection. She was in between dropping four-year-old Zoe off at a playdate and picking up nine-year-old Jet from hockey practice. The sudden death of Brooke turned Brady into a different man. Gone was the once good-natured guy. Now he was serious. And had zero patience for sarcasm.

Kendall's communication skills averaged about ninety percent sarcasm.

"Emily's father—Daddy dearest—wouldn't leave me alone with her and refused to stop answering questions for her." Kendall had understood. On the one hand, the girl had been missing for forty-eight hours. Scott Williams was distraught during that time. A mix of exhaustion and elation showed on his face. But there had been something else there too. Kendall couldn't place what she had seen in his eyes. "Emily didn't utter a word. Every time I asked her a question, she would look at her father, and he would come up with an answer lacking substance."

"That's not uncommon for a young victim," Brady said. "She went through a hell of an ordeal—I suspect."

Suspect—because, as of that moment, no one knew what Emily had been through. The girl had been mute since they'd found her in the garage. Hypothermic and severely dehydrated when they found her, she showed some signs of possible sexual abuse, but a more thorough exam was needed.

An exam Scott Williams would not consent to.

"Something's off," Kendall said, unable to put her finger on what was bothering her. "Williams won't allow the doctors to fully exam Emily. I mean, wouldn't you want to know? To make sure your daughter's okay?"

The eyebrows rose again, and the lines at the bridge of Brady's nose deepened. "Yes, I would, I suppose. But maybe he's concerned with her emotional state and isn't willing to put her through something he sees as more traumatic to her."

Kendall wasn't buying it. Mainly because she hadn't really gotten that vibe from Scott Williams. He acted as if he was concerned for his daughter—but also for what might be discovered. Was he just one of those people who lived happily with their head stuck in the sand? Was it easier to accept what had happened to Emily if he didn't know the extent of her injuries?

"He tried to hold Emily's hand, but she pulled it away from him. Very slyly, I might add. He put his hand on her leg, and she stiffened."

"Did she look afraid of him?" Brady asked.

"Hard to tell. She looked pretty zapped of energy . . . but I wouldn't say she looked scared of him."

"Well, if she was sexually abused, she may not want to be touched. Many sexual abuse victims don't want physical contact, even from loved ones."

"Yeah, I know." Kendall sighed and placed her hands on her hips, facing back toward the window. "I'm going to stop by the hospital in the morning, hopefully before Williams gets there, and see if I can get Emily to open up. Maybe she's just uncomfortable talking in front of her dad."

"Good idea." Brady nodded toward the occupants in the interrogation room. "What's happening here? Getting anything out of Sandoval?"

"Well, he hasn't lawyered up yet, so that's something," she said. "But he keeps denying he had anything to do with Emily being in his garage. Had no idea she was there. Did nothing to her. Loves her like a granddaughter. Would never hurt her. Yadda, yadda, yadda."

"Of course not—she was just found nearly dead in his garage hidden behind a stack of boxes."

The realization the little girl could have gone unnoticed had the cat not alerted Kendall made her gut tighten.

She stared at Sandoval. Tears streamed down his face. What was he upset about? Emily being injured? Or fearful of what might happen to him?

Was it possible he was telling the truth?

Kendall shook her head, hoping her thoughts would unscramble and become clearer. "Why now?"

"What?" Brady asked.

Kendall faced him, that nagging "something's not right" feeling under her skin making her itch. "Why would Sandoval kidnap her? I mean, if he was abusing her all this time, why the need to kidnap her?"

Brady rested his hands on his waist. "Emily's getting older. Maybe she told him she didn't want to do things with him anymore? Or she wasn't going to keep it a secret and was going to tell her parents?"

She glanced back at Sandoval. He was shaking his head to whatever Jake was saying. Something about Sandoval's reaction to finding Emily gave her pause. "It's just"—she faced Brady again—"he was genuinely happy she had been found. It didn't seem to register we discovered her in his garage, or the implications. He didn't ask to see her. Only asked if she was okay."

Brady frowned and shrugged. "He's a good actor. He could've been preparing for that reaction as soon as he saw you heading toward the garage."

"I guess." She didn't tell him she had been around the proverbial block with suspects and typically had a good read on when they were faking a reaction. "He handed over his laptop without hesitation. Provided the passcode to his computer and phone when asked. Don't you think we would've found some other photos? If he *is* a pedophile, he would've taken secret photos of the girls. Or had links to kiddie porn sites. Something. The man is damn near squeaky-clean."

Brady wrapped his beefy arms across his chest and continued to stare at Sandoval through the glass. "The man is an expert at covering his tracks. And his ass. He probably figured once Emily went 'missing,' we would start looking more closely at him, so he got rid of everything."

Again, good point. The computer and phone both came back clean through a cursory examination. It would take a while for the IT guys to go through the computer's history and verify if Sandoval attempted to delete files.

Brady glanced at her. "You got your man, Beck. One less sick bastard on the streets tonight." He lightly slapped her on the back. "We celebrate the victories while we can today. Tomorrow we hit the trail of another predator."

He left the room without waiting for a response, reaction, or affirmation. Kendall stared at Sandoval. She knew Brady was right. Sandoval checked almost all the boxes. Emily had been found in his garage, barely clinging to life. He had probably hidden her there, hoped she would freeze to death soon, and never be able to talk about what he had done to her. The below freezing temps in the uninsulated garage would have slowed down decomposition of the body and afforded Sandoval time to remove the body and get rid of it after the investigation had simmered down.

Prickles skittered below the surface of her skin.

Everything fit. Sandoval was her man.

So why did she still have questions?

4

Thursday,
February 20,
8:24 AM

"S HE'S AWAKE."
        Kendall looked up at the nurse on the opposite side of Emily's bed. The woman had blueish-black hair which looked like the tail of a horse and reached to her tailbone, which was fitting since she also sported a mouth full of teeth that would've made Mr. Ed proud. She was rail thin, and her scrubs—an assortment of stethoscopes and Band-Aids and syringes with sayings like "Listen to your heart", "Let's stick together", and "We call the shots around here"—hung on her frame and gave Kendall the impression that one good sneeze would cause them to fall off.

Emily's small fist rubbed at her eyes, an IV taped to the back of her hand. She looked so small—smaller than her five years. But when Kendall looked into her eyes, there was a depth of experience no child that age should ever have.

"Hi, Emily," Kendall said, her voice soft. "Do you remember me? I was here yesterday."

Emily's eyes went wide and just stared.

"My name is Kendall, and I'm sort of like the police. Your Mommy called us when you were missing, and we helped find you." Kendall showed the girl her badge. Emily reached a finger out and ran it over the gold eagle perched on the top. Kendall placed the badge in Emily's hand so the girl could get a closer look. "We're all so happy you're going to be okay."

Emily didn't acknowledge the statement, mesmerized by the bumps and curves of the badge. Or trying to pretend Kendall wasn't there. Kendall doubted talking to adults, especially unknown adults, was high on the list of things kids liked to do.

"I know you've been through a lot and are probably pretty tired still, but I need to ask you some questions about what happened. So we can get whoever hurt you and put them in jail."

Emily made no effort to speak, and Kendall wondered if her chapped lips hurt too much to open her mouth. She reached for the pitcher of water and placed the straw against Emily's lips. The child sucked down some of the water and moved her head away.

Kendall placed the cup back on the bedside table. "Do you remember the night you were taken from your bed?"

Emily handed the badge back without any acknowledgment Kendall had spoken.

"Hey, Emily? It's okay to be scared. And I know it's not fun to think about, but I promise nothing can hurt you here. Do you remember anything about that night?"

Emily looked down at her hands as she fidgeted with the blanket covering her and shook her head.

"Can you tell me anything about where you were taken?"

Headshake.

"Were you in the garage the entire time?"

Another headshake.

"Can you tell me who hurt you?"

The girl glanced at the door, then back at her hands, and shook her head.

Frustration rankled Kendall, and she inhaled. *Calm down.* This was a little girl who had been subjected to unknown— *and known*—horrors. After Scott Williams had left the previous night, doctors were able to exam Emily without parental interference. They had discovered vaginal tearing and repeated injury to her hymen.

Their conclusion: Emily had most likely been sexually abused for some time.

Kendall knew adults had a difficult time talking about this sort of abuse. Emily's mind was probably trying to figure out what the hell had happened to her, scared to even recall the events, let alone her feelings of her attacker.

The exercise was ineffective. Emily had rolled onto her side and stuck her thumb in her mouth. Kendall probably wasn't going to get anything out of the girl. Chances were good Emily was doing her best to block out the abuse in order to survive. No matter how much Kendall wanted to find the monster who had hurt Emily Williams, she wouldn't further damage the sweet child who had lost her innocence in such a brutal manner.

Kendall slipped her hand under Emily's and gave it a gentle squeeze. "Your mom and dad are on their way and will be here soon."

Emily's head jerked up. Her eyes grew large, and tears teetered on the rim of her lower lids. She shook her head again.

Maybe that was all the girl could do at the moment. Her only method of communication. Maybe her answers to Kendall's questions weren't actual denials, but the only way she was able to respond. The mind worked in mysterious ways, especially through traumatic events. Perhaps this was a sort of mental tick to protect herself.

Kendall glanced at the nurse and pointed to the door, letting her know she'd be in the hall. As she stepped away from the girl's bed, a random thought hit her. "Emily, did you run away from home?"

Slowly, Emily's head bobbed up and down.

Kendall stepped back up to the bed. "Were you hurt after you ran away?"

Emily shook her head.

The nurse stalled and Kendall saw her eyes widen.

"Did someone in *your home* hurt you? Is that why you ran away?"

Emily's head slowly lifted and dropped, along with Kendall's heart.

* * *

Scott Williams sauntered down the hallway, cup of coffee in hand. He faltered as Kendall stepped out of Emily's room, her eyes locked on him. At his side, his wife, Kathy, held tight to two-year-old Sadie's hand, practically dragging the little girl down the hallway. She swung the child up into her arms and tried to hand her off to Scott. The man tried to take the girl, but Sadie squirmed away from him, burying her face deep into her mother's neck.

Kendall no longer saw a man ravaged by pain. The look on his face was not relief that his little girl was alive. It was worry. Fear of what Emily had said. Fear of what would happen to him if his secret was exposed.

Sadie dropped her stuffed baby sloth. Kendall had yet to see the child without the plush playmate. As soon as it hit the floor, Sadie screamed, "Stop! Get Nala!"

Kathy struggled to squat with the child on her hip and grab for the toy.

"What are you doing in there?" Williams asked without slowing down to help his wife. "You are not to speak to my daughter without me being in the room, Agent Beck. She's frightened, and I won't allow you to further subject her to injury."

Red-hot rage blazed through Kendall. Emily had confirmed her father had been the one to hurt her. No, *brutalize* her. And the events that forced the girl to run away two days ago had not been the first time Scott Williams had sexually molested his eldest daughter.

"You won't allow *me* to injure her further?" The nerve of this man. After everything Emily had just told her Scott Williams had been doing to her for years, he was going to stand there puffed up with his indignation?

Brady stepped around Kendall and stood in between her and Williams. "Mr. Williams, we need to ask you some questions. If you could follow me, the hospital is allowing us to use their conference room for privacy." He gestured down the hall, indicating Williams should start walking.

Kathy stopped in the hallway behind her husband, eyes wide with confusion, Sadie wriggling to get out of her grasp. Williams lifted his chin, arrogance and defiance crackling in the air. "I will not. I'm going to see my daughter—see what kind of damage you people have done to her. If you have said anything to upset her, I'll sue the FBI."

Brady stiffened but managed to maintain a professional tone. "Mr. Williams, we will be asking you questions. Now, we can either do this in the conference room, or we can do this out here in the middle of the hallway. Either way—it doesn't matter to me. But the nature of the questions we will be asking are not the type of questions one usually wants an audience for."

Williams's nostrils flared. He stared at Brady, then swung his gaze to Kendall. "What did you say to Emily?" Without giving her time to respond, he looked back at Brady while thrusting a finger in Kendall's direction. "This is your agent's doing. She has filled my daughter's head with lies—she's behind any allegation Emily has made against me."

Why would he assume Emily had made an allegation against him? Kendall's blood pressure spiked. *Because he knows what he did to the child.* And he knows Emily told Kendall and Brady.

"No one had to suggest anything to Emily," she said. "Once she knew she was going to be safe from your abuse, she sang like a canary."

"That's a lie!" Williams's gaze darted back and forth between Kendall and Brady, before glaring at Kendall. "I have never abused my daughter. You put those thoughts in her head. You haven't liked me from the beginning." He cut his eyes to Brady. "I hadn't been home for five minutes after returning from a business trip when she started accusing me of harming my daughter. Implying the most vile things." Williams forced something Kendall could only assume was supposed to be a sob or a gasp of indignation. She rolled her eyes. "I had *just* discovered my daughter was kidnapped—"

"Mr. Williams—" Brady's hands went up in an attempt to get Williams to calm down.

"She's had it out for me from the start." Desperation laced Williams's voice. He took a step closer to Brady, a weak attempt at excluding Kendall from the conversation. Kendall had seen it used often; part of the "good ol' boys" club. "Please let me see my baby girl. Once I talk to her, I'm sure she will clear up this misunderstanding."

Brady looked at Kendall. She nodded. They'd already had this discussion. If Williams didn't cooperate and answer questions, there was enough to arrest him.

Kendall removed her handcuffs from the holder on her belt. "I need for you to turn around, drop to your knees, and raise your arms over your head."

Fear, incredulity, and anger simultaneously flashed through Williams's eyes. "I will not."

Kendall stepped closer and reached for Williams's arm, yanking until there was some resistance.

"Don't touch me," Williams hollered, stepping back. Brady took a step toward them. Williams threw the cup of coffee at him, forcing Brady to retreat, hands covering his face. Williams shoved Kendall away. Her shoes skidded across the polished linoleum floor, and she nearly tripped over her own feet. Williams advanced on her, his eyes dark and dangerous.

Kendall's hand balled into a fist at her side. She was shaking with anger. Her vision blurred at the edges but remained laser focused on the man coming toward her. She saw him clearly for the first time since the start of this investigation. All of his crying over his daughter, abducted from her bed in the middle of the night. Begging Kendall to find her. Offering to take out a second mortgage on his property so he could offer a monetary reward for information leading to his little girl's safe return.

All of it pure bullshit.

Williams grabbed Kendall's upper arms and shoved her back. She hit the wall hard, pain shooting through her shoulder blades.

Kendall's fist came from the right, connecting with Williams's jaw and knocking him on his ass. His hand went to his head, shock registering on his face. Visions of Emily—lying on the frozen floor of the garage, near death from hypothermia, the tears that ran down her cheeks when she told Kendall her father made her do things to him—darkened Kendall's sight. Something inside her cracked. She could almost hear it, like the branch of a tree snapping. Before Williams could make a move to recover, Kendall was on top of him, slamming her fists into his face. Blood exploded from Williams's nose, coating her hand, the red mirroring the rage in her sight.

Somewhere in the distance, beyond the low buzz in her head, a woman screamed. A baby cried. Slowly, voices became louder. Closer. The words began to have meaning.

"Beck! Goddammit!"

Someone grasped her arms and pulled her off Williams. He was curled into a ball, his arms covering his head, where blood was pooling. Red spots splattered the tile floor and wall behind him. Macabre artwork.

She wished she'd had more time. Should've charged him as soon as she saw him. Knocked him on his ass and beaten him into a bloody pulp until he confessed. The man deserved no less than excruciating pain for the rest of his life for what he had done to at least one of his daughters. Based on Sadie's reaction to him, Kendall was sure Scott Williams had been abusing her as well.

Brady stepped in front of Kendall, blocking her view of the sick asshole lying on the floor, writhing in pain. The sorry son of a bitch. "What the fuck is wrong with you?"

"Are you kidding? He attacked me," Kendall said.

Brady gave her a tight-lipped look that said he was not accepting her excuse. The threat against her had been over after the first punch—which was when she'd been justified in taking a shot at Williams. What came after could be construed as battery.

"He molested Emily." Kendall retucked her blouse, used her sleeve to wipe Williams's blood from her cheek, and glared at Brady. "She ran away two days ago after he repeatedly *raped* her."

"Beck—" Brady said.

"That's a lie!" Williams screamed, his voice high-pitched and cracking. "I would never—"

"Emily told me"—Kendall took a step toward the sniveling little asshole and shoved a finger in his face—"you lying piece of shit!"

"Beck!" Brady grasped her by the lapels of her jacket and walked her backward down the hall. Her back hit the release bar on the heavy door, Brady not slowing down until they were in the stairwell. "Get your head out of your ass—"

"But—"

"Now, Beck—before I fire your ass and force Williams to press charges against you."

"You're taking his side?"

"I'm trying to save this fucking case." Brady took a deep breath and loosened his grip on her. "You need to cool off, Beck. I understand you feel passionate about this, but your temper is going to work against us."

All the air slid from her lungs, and she sagged against the wall. He was right. Her little ass whooping, although cathartic, could destroy the case. She had to separate herself before she did more damage.

"You found her," Brady said, running his hand through his hair and straightening his tie. "Go home, write up your fucking report while everything is fresh in your mind."

"Yes, sir," she said, and moved past him to the stairs. It didn't matter she was on the tenth floor; the last thing she needed was to go back into the hallway, see Williams, and lose control again. She'd probably end up killing the bastard.

Brady grasped her arm as she passed him. "We'll talk later."

She nodded and continued down the stairs. Once outside, she inhaled deeply and closed her eyes, allowing the brisk winter air to send ice prickles through her lungs. So many rollercoaster emotions had rushed through her. Finding Emily in the neighbor's garage. Arresting Sandoval. Waiting for the doctors to finish their examination of Emily.

Discovering the truth.

Nearly sacrificing her career to beat the fuck out of the man who was supposed to protect his daughter from monsters—not *be* the monster—well, that seemed a small price to pay.

CHAPTER

5

KENDALL CAME THROUGH the door of the 1950s bungalow where she lived and dropped her keys into the tray on the table at the entrance. The home had been renovated several times over the years, but the same basic footprint remained. Her room-mate, Gwen Tavich, was adamant some things remain as they were intended. "It's part of the past that needs to be preserved," she'd say. Kendall didn't really give a shit about the architecture or the preservation of history, as long as she had a roof overhead, hot water, and a bed to crash in at the end of the day.

Sunlight saturated the room through the large picture win-dow, brightening the space and adding a comforting glow to the room. The window perfectly framed the snow-capped Rocky Mountains. They were beautiful. And inviting.

Maybe I should take a hike and clear my head?

Gwen sat on the couch, drinking a cup of coffee.

"Hey," Kendall said, hearing the pathetic tone in her head. She had spent the drive home mulling over her actions, and had gone from being angry to disgusted, to contrite.

"Well, that wasn't a very enthusiastic greeting," Gwen said with a chuckle. "What's wrong?"

"Brady" was all Kendall needed to tell her best friend, but she added, "and this piece-of-shit case."

"Color me shocked," Gwen said. "You can tell me all about it while I get ready for work." She stood and drained her cup.

Kendall unzipped her jacket, hung it on the coat tree, and faced Gwen, whose face paled a little.

"And this story will include why you have blood all over you?" Gwen asked. "I'm assuming that's not your blood?"

"Yes," Kendall said, "and no—not my blood." She hurried to her room, threw on a pair of sweatpants and an FBI hoodie, and tossed the blouse in the trash on her way out. She regretted the way she had lost her shit at the hospital. Not the best-played hand, and she knew better than to go off on a suspect that way. No matter how much she wanted to rid the world of scum, she never should've gone after Williams and endangered the case.

Gwen was in the kitchen. "Okay, tell me all about it."

"The little girl started talking today," Kendall said, leaning against the counter and wrapping her arms around her midsection.

"Was it the neighbor?"

"No." Kendall took a deep breath, and let it out in a long, loud whoosh. "She wasn't kidnapped at all. She ran away. From her Dad. Who's been sexually abusing her for a few years."

"A few *years*?" Gwen said on the tail end of a gasp. "But she's only a few years old!"

"I know! Makes you wonder how soon after she was born he started abusing her—the sick bastard."

"God, I hope they castrate him and feed him his balls."

"Yeah, well, that's not all." Gwen gave her a "what did you do?" look. "I sort of lost it with Williams."

"Kendall—" Gwen drew out in exasperation.

"He hit me first."

"You *hit* him?"

"Pummeled him is probably more accurate." Kendall shrugged. Part of her wished she could have a do-over and stop after the first punch. But there was also a part of her that wanted to finish the job she had started, and put Williams in the hospital.

Good and evil . . . Kendall had long reconciled that sometimes the line between the two was very tenuous. She often wondered if the only thing distinguishing her as a "good guy" was having a badge.

"Jesus, Kendall." Gwen filled a mug with coffee, added a shot of Irish whiskey, and handed the steaming brew to Kendall. "Are you going to be able to keep your job?"

Kendall shrugged her shoulders with a nonchalance she didn't actually feel. "I guess I'll find out when I talk to Brady."

* * *

Kendall stepped out of the shower, wrapped up in the large bath sheet, and slumped onto her bed. A chorus of *Bad Boys, bad boys, whatcha gonna do?* sang from her cell phone on the bedside table. The ringtone for her partner, Jake.

He had set it up one day without Kendall knowing, and as much as it annoyed the hell out of her, she also sort of loved it. Not unlike how she felt about Jake. She loved him like a brother, loved having him as a partner. But just like a little brother, he knew her soft underbelly and enjoyed poking it. A lot.

"What's up?" she said by way of greeting.

"What. The. Fuck. Happened?"

"What did you hear?" Jake hadn't been at the hospital, only Kendall and Brady. It'd be interesting to see what version of the truth was going through the rumor mill at the office.

"That Williams tried to resist arrest, attacked you, and then you exacted some vigilante justice on his ass."

"*Face*—not ass—but that pretty much sums it up."

"Fuck," Jake said, and let out a low whistle. "I can't believe you did that . . . *without me*. I mean, what the hell? I'm your partner, and you go off half-cocked on your own? Did you ever consider that *I* might want to take a shot at the prick? No, you didn't. You just thought of yourself. Always so selfish."

"Get your ass out of bed and come to work earlier, slacker."

"I was taking my kid to day care."

"It's always the same with you," she said, a grin sliding into place. "*I have to go to my kid's recital. I have to pick up my kid. I wanna have dinner with my family.* If you had your priorities straight and dumped that crap on your wife like every other good law enforcement officer does, you could be in the shit with me."

"Fuck you, old maid."

Nothing strengthened a bond more than telling a partner what a loser he was—and vice versa. It was their own special kind of love language. It had taken Jake's wife, Felicia, a few interactions to understand their relationship. It also helped her get past any thoughts that Kendall would ever have any romantic inclinations toward Jake. Another huge obstacle in law enforcement these days. Male law enforcement officers with female partners could cause even the strongest marriages to bend a bit under the devilish question *Is there more than just a working relationship there?*

Not that Kendall had romantic relationships. At least not since her fiancé had died a few years earlier. Life was easier without the heartache of romance.

"Don't do that shit again, though." Jake's voice was more serious. "We can't bring down the bad guys and get these pervs off the street, if you get your badge taken away."

"Yeah, I get it. I'm sorry and not sorry. The asshole deserved it, but you're right. Williams won't be the last sick fuck, and I can't put a dent in the population if I'm not an agent."

There was a pause, as if they were both reflecting on the last statement.

"So, heads-up," Jake said. "Williams bailed out."

"The fuck?" Kendall looked at the clock on her bedside table. Four thirty PM. "Already? I thought they'd be able to keep him at least overnight. Who the fuck is representing him?"

"Three guesses, and the first two are Ashley Simmons."

Kendall shook her head in disgust. "How a woman could represent a guy like that is beyond me."

"Yeah, well, you may want to be extra vigilant—you are not at the top of Williams's favorite people list. He was none too happy to learn his family is gone, and no one will tell him where they are."

"Screw him."

"He's even more pissed he can't stay at his house, since it's still a crime scene, and has to find other living accommodations. He's blaming that on you too. Just be on the lookout—he may be trying to locate you to exact some revenge."

"He can't find me," Kendall said. "My number is private, and Gwen's name is the only one on the house. She owns it, I just rent from her." Kendall put the call on speakerphone while she put on yoga pants and a sweater. "Has anyone let Kathy Williams or Sandoval know Scott is out?"

"Not yet."

"Okay, I already have a call in to Kathy Williams. She's supposed to be calling me back, so I can let her know. You call Sandoval. Also, make sure there are guards outside Emily's hospital room, and a picture of Williams. He is not to enter her room under any condition."

"Already done," Jake said. "But I'm serious, Kendall. Lock your doors. Scott is a loose cannon—he's lost everything and he's on the warpath."

The phone beeped with an incoming call. Kendall glanced at the screen.

"Hey, Kathy's calling. I'll check back in later." She didn't wait for a response before clicking over. "Kathy, thanks for calling me back. I wanted to apologize for what happened at the hospital this morning. I'm not usually that unprofessional, and I'm sorry if I upset you or Sadie."

"No, it's no problem," Kathy whispered into the phone. "Give me just a minute to get to another room."

Kendall could hear her murmuring in the background and then a door softly close. "Sorry, I couldn't talk freely in the kitchen."

"Where are you?" Kendall asked.

"The kids and I are at my parents' house."

"Scott made bail. I heard you got a restraining order against him, but that's just a piece of paper that will only help you after he's tried to come in contact with you—you understand that, right?"

"He's out?" Kathy cursed under her breath.

"Tell me about your parents' house. Is it safe there? It will be among the first places he goes to find you."

"Yes, it's safe. They live in Cherry Hills Village."

Swank neighborhood. Kathy's parents have money.

"The community is gated, and the property has security cameras that link to a home security company," Kathy said.

"Okay, text me the address. I'll see if I can get someone to sit on the house."

"Jesus—Emily's still in the hospital—"

"She's fine. We have a guard at her door. No one is going in or out that isn't a doctor, nurse, me, or you. Period. There is no way Scott will get to her. When is she due to be released?"

"Tomorrow."

"Good, get her back to your parents, and then don't go out unless absolutely necessary. Understand?"

6

K ENDALL STOOD AT the open door, watching Gwen back out of the driveway and head for the restaurant she co-owned with her fiancé. Kendall gave a final wave before closing the door.

Leaning against it, she inhaled deeply, absorbing the quiet of the house. "Alexa, play ABBA." It was her go-to music selection. Gwen—hell, everyone she knew—laughed at her music taste. "Big, bad FBI special agent takes down the nastiest of criminals while 'Dancing Queens' plays in the background," Gwen would harass her whenever Kendall played ABBA at home.

Kendall had hit the jackpot when she got Gwen as a room-mate her freshman year at Denver University. They were sisters from the start. "Gimme, Gimme, Gimme" flowed from the speakers around the living room. Kendall usually had the nights free since Gwen was always at the restaurant.

But tonight, the relaxing calm was turning into a suffocating cloud. All of the day's events ran through her head like a video on YouTube, resetting to the moment when Emily, so small and weak, divulged a secret Kendall was sure the girl had sworn to never tell.

Kendall flipped the light switch in the kitchen, grabbed a bottle of wine from the shelf, and poured herself a glass of cabernet sauvignon. What the hell had she been thinking, going after Williams that way? She hadn't been thinking, which was the problem. Professionalism was her strong suit—most of the time. But when she thought about Emily and how scared she must've been—enough to run away from home in the middle of the night in the freezing cold—it made Kendall's blood boil.

What was Brady going to do? Fire her? Suspend her? She couldn't lose her job. It was all she had.

There was a knock at the door. She crossed the living room and peered through the side window. Jan Gunnarson, her neighbor from across the street, stood on the doorstep.

She opened the door and stepped back. Neither one of them talked. She allowed him in and leaned against the door, pushing it closed with her butt. She took a swig from her wineglass, her gaze locked on Jan's eyes.

He stepped in front of her, took the glass from her hand, and downed the rest of the wine before setting it on the entry table behind him. One hand moved to her waist, the other grasped the back of her head. His lips pressed hard against her neck, his tongue licking along her jaw.

Kendall lifted her leg and wrapped it around him as he pressed her into the door. She had no feelings for this man but loved how he made her feel. He made her forget her troubles. And crave touch. But this was all there was. No emotions. No promises. No talking. Just a reprieve from the hell of the day. A lot of days over the past couple of years.

Kendall wasn't sure what Jan was trying to forget, or suppress. Nor did she care. This was her coping mechanism. How she banished the visions of children who were broken, beaten, molested, and raped. Their haunting cries. Their wide, pleading eyes. The worst were the kids with dead eyes and no tears left to shed.

Kendall led the way back to her room, both freeing themselves of their clothes. By the time Kendall slipped her panties off and tossed them on the floor, Jan was pushing her back onto the bed and crawling on top of her. She felt his tongue glide along her inner thigh, over her stomach and breast, and finally nuzzle her neck.

They never kissed on the mouth. Kissing was intimate. This was just fucking, and they never held back. The man was kind of an asshole, completely self-absorbed, with his bodybuilder physique and an ego the size of Texas. But when he went to work on her body, she gave in to him. All she wanted was for him to take away the hurt and pain. Make her feel nothing while she let an orgasm take her over the edge to a blissful oblivion.

They never spoke of forever. Or a future together. Although Kendall wanted a relationship someday. Someone to love and make love with—Jan was not that man.

And, thank goodness, he felt the same about her.

* * *

Jan dropped on top of her after the shudders from his own climax subsided. He rolled off the bed, got up, and walked into the bathroom. The water turned on, and Kendall figured he'd jumped in the shower. Why he couldn't shower at his own house was beyond her, but she had learned to let it go. He would be gone soon, and she could get the stink of sex with a man she didn't really like off her body too.

Kendall got up and fetched their clothes from the floor in the hallway, dropped them on the bed, and wrapped up in her robe. He came into the room and pulled on his boxers. He had a great body, but from the few conversations they'd had, he didn't have much going on upstairs.

Kendall's phone buzzed on her side table.

Brady.

Shit.

She swiped her finger across the screen and placed the phone to her ear.

"You know this thing you did at the hospital has to be dealt with." It wasn't a question.

"Yes, I know." She closed her eyes and hoped Jan couldn't hear her boss reaming her ass from across the room. Brady was not quiet when he was hot under the collar.

"I'm in DC tomorrow and won't return until Sunday. Be in my office Monday morning at eight sharp. Expect a suspension, at best, but there is only so much I can do if that twat, Williams, decides to press charges."

"The asshole deserved it."

She heard the ding of an elevator. He was probably leaving the office. "Possibly, but the state's attorney will not be pleased if you've destroyed his case." She heard the elevator doors open. They would lose the connection as soon as he got into the elevator car. "Monday. Don't be late, Beck."

Kendall slipped the phone in her pocket as Jan walked out of her room. She followed him down the hallway.

The front door opened. Her other best friend, Quentin, walked in carrying a load of takeout boxes from Gwen's restaurant. He halted when he saw Jan. His smile slipped into a frown.

Jan didn't acknowledge Quentin.

"Jan," Quentin said, making sure to enunciate the "J."

"It's pronounced 'Yaan,' simpleton," Jan responded, his face beet red.

Quentin gave Jan his best cheesy grin and walked past him.

"Your friend is rude," Jan said, pointing a finger at Quentin.

I shrugged, not willing to get in the middle of their pissing match. She was sure Jan expected her to say something to Quentin, perhaps even make him apologize. There was no way Kendall was going to prolong this stupidity.

Jan grasped the handle and opened the door, slamming it shut behind him, not saying goodbye. Didn't matter. He'd be back the next time he wanted to have sex. They'd been through this before. Many times.

Kendall turned to Quentin. "What'd you bring?"

"Why do you let him come here?" Quentin was like a brother to her—and about as protective.

She grabbed the bag from his hand and walked into the kitchen. "Not having this conversation with you, Q."

"But he's a condescending dick, Kendall." He grabbed two plates from the cabinet and set them on the counter. "How can you have a relationship with him?"

"I don't have a relationship with him—I have *sex* with him. That's it. I get mine. He gets his. He goes home and does . . . whatever, and I get to spend time with you." She dished the food onto the plates. "Win–win."

"It's wrong. He doesn't love you."

"Which is good, since I don't love him. Grab the wine and pour us each a glass."

"But don't you feel—"

Kendall put up her hand in front of his face to get him to shut up. She was tired of having to explain herself or her sex life to people who wanted to guilt her. "Enough, Q. I'm a big girl. He's a big boy. Quit being my moral compass and just be my friend. I've had a crap day, and I want to relax and enjoy some wine and food. If you can't handle that, leave."

She walked into the family room and sat on the couch, placing her plate on the coffee table. After a moment of what Kendall could only imagine was Quentin sulking, he got over himself and sat next to her. "Want to talk about your crap day?"

"Not particularly."

"Want to binge *Friends*?"

She smiled and warmth spread through her chest, releasing some of the anxiety that had a stranglehold on her lungs. Quentin knew her like only a true friend who had been around for years could know someone.

Leaning over, she kissed him on the cheek. "What would I do without you, Q?"

"God only knows. Starve, most likely." He picked up the remote and turned on the TV. The news was on, and Kendall prayed they didn't have a story about what had happened at the hospital. She could imagine a smug and arrogant Scott Williams standing next to his lawyer in front of a bank of microphones, expounding on the lack of decorum the FBI displayed during a time he had been suffering with the kidnapping of his daughter.

What came on, however, was worse. The talking head, in his dark blue suit with a pink tie, and overly white, straight teeth, tossed the story to a reporter in the field. In the background was Berkeley Lake Park, a recreational area in northwest Denver.

Numbness started at the top of Kendall's head and slid over her body like syrup running over a stack of pancakes.

"Ten years ago, Amy Carrington was found in the area just over my shoulder. The search for her ended in tragedy when her body was discovered in the lake. Carrington was the last known victim in a string of violent murders of young women over the preceding two years. So, what *exactly* happened to the serial killer known as the Reaper?"

Kendall's stomach twisted into a knot. Quentin stared at her, brows furrowed, frown deep. "Did you know they were doing a story on you?"

Of course she knew. She had been dreading the anniversary of the day she found Amy Carrington in the middle of the highway and helped the young woman try to escape a serial killer. The day Kendall was shot and left for dead. The day she first failed someone whose life depended on her. "It's not a story on me—it's on *him*. And all of the victims," Kendall said.

"Of which you are one—the only survivor."

Bile rose in her throat. Kendall was well aware of that fact. Although, in the scheme of things, she had gotten off a hell of a lot easier than his other victims. She'd only been shot. Not raped, tortured, and killed. She pushed the plate of food on the table away from her, her appetite gone.

Quentin opened his mouth, most likely to ask his question again, but Kendall halted him by pointing at the TV.

"When asked about what she believed happened to the Reaper, Kendall Beck, the only person to have survived the killer, and now an FBI agent, said this—"

They had caught Kendall outside FBI headquarters. Ambushed was more like it. She was wearing her FBI standard suit, and was on her way home after a grueling fifteen-hour day. Which was the only reason she could fathom for having stopped and answered the reporter's questions.

"I hope the snake slithered back into his hole and died," onscreen Kendall said. "It would be the best outcome for him, although I would love to meet him face-to-face now and be able to provide the justice he deserves."

7

Friday,
February 21,
12:05 PM

G OLDEN, COLORADO, WAS best known as the home of Coors
beer. One of the largest breweries in the world, the once-
family-owned business was now a part of the mega Anheuser
Busch conglomerate. But the brewery was still functioning in
Golden. People around the world could still enjoy an ice-cold
"taste of the high country." Adam's dad, a native of Colorado,
had always called it Rocky Mountain piss water.

Potato, potahto, Adam guessed.

The Bedlams lived in a small house in Golden. When Adam
had called to see if he could talk to Mr. Bedlam about the stolen
license plate, he was informed he was about two months too
late. Mr. Bedlam had succumbed to a long battle with throat
cancer and had died. Mrs. Bedlam, however, was available to
talk to Adam.

The brick ranch-style home had a cement porch nearly
spanning the front. A little dog—Chihuahua, maybe—had its
front paws on the windowsill, a sentinel surveying the yard. A
mat at the door announced, "All are welcome here." After too
many years in law enforcement, Adam wonder if Mrs. Bedlam
actually meant *everyone.* There were some pretty shady people
in the world, just waiting to take advantage of an older woman
living on her own with an open door policy.

Adam rang the doorbell. The little dog's bark was even more high pitched, and he raced from the window to the door and back to the window.

"Muggsy!" A yell came from behind the door. "Knock off that racket!"

The door opened, and a woman with short white hair with streaks of black answered. "Stupid dog," she was muttering to herself. When she saw Adam, she smiled. "You must be Detective Taylor."

"Yes, ma'am."

She opened the screen door, and stepped aside. "Please come in."

The little dog sniffed Adam's legs and shoes, and looked up at him with suspicious eyes before backing away in another series of barks.

"Hush up, you silly mutt." Mrs. Bedlam shooed the dog away and ushered Adam into the living room, gesturing for him to take a seat on the couch. The room was bright, with plenty of light coming in through Muggsy's window. It was also littered with children's toys. Mrs. Bedlam quickly picked up a few and deposited them in a large basket. "I watch my grandchildren when my daughter and her husband work. My daughter is a yoga instructor and a barista at a little coffee shop in town—it does pretty good business for such a small town, but then we get a lot of tourists."

She was rambling. Adam was used to that. People, no matter if they were guilty of something or innocent, always wanted to provide too much information because they thought it made them look as if they were cooperative. Adam just let her go. She wasn't really a suspect, so he wanted her to feel at ease.

"Her husband works for the airlines as a flight attendant. When he first told me what he did, well, I thought he might be not of the heterosexual persuasion, if you know what I mean." She gave a little wink. Adam wasn't sure if nodding would be construed as confirmation he understood what she meant, or that he agreed all male flight attendants were gay. He opted to do nothing, just to be safe.

"Cassidy—that's my daughter—she told me I was behind the times, that not all men who are flight attendants are gay, and even if they were, it wouldn't matter because it's okay to be gay. I never thought it wasn't, mind you, but it wouldn't have surprised me if Carl was gay. My late husband, Harvey, always thought Carl was a little light in the loafers—if you know what I mean—but Cassidy just says he's 'sensitive.'" She took in a conceding breath.

The dog jumped onto the couch next to Adam and stared as if Adam were sitting in his spot. Adam wondered if he should move.

"Muggsy," Mrs. Bedlam said, and snapped her fingers. "Get to your bed." She pointed to a large pillow on the floor in the corner of the room.

"Muggsy?" Adam asked. "As in the basketball player?"

Mrs. Bedlam beamed like a proud parent. "Yes, my husband's favorite player. I think it was because Harvey was also on the vertically challenged side, if you know what I mean." She gave another little wink. "Would you like anything to drink, Detective?"

Adam drew out his notepad and pen from the inside pocket of his jacket. "No, thank you."

Mrs. Bedlam reached for a wineglass from the side table next to her and took a sip. Adam tried not to look at his watch but knew it couldn't be much past noon.

"Just a little tipple," Mrs. Bedlam said and tittered. "I don't have the grandkids today."

Adam nodded as if in agreement, unsure of what else he should do. Clearing his throat, he said, "I understand you had a license plate stolen off your vehicle last year."

"Oh, yes, off the Silverado. My husband's truck."

"Can you tell me when you first noticed it was missing from the vehicle?" Adam asked.

"Well, I didn't. It was my husband's truck. But I guess it was around August of last year. Actually"—she took another drink of wine and leaned closer, as if divulging a dark family secret—"it was the last time he drove. The cancer was getting so bad, and the treatments were horrible, and he was just not in a good place health-wise to be operating a truck of that size. He was either driving too fast or too slow—there was no in between. Have you ever been around someone who has cancer?"

"Uh, no ma'am." Adam's head was spinning trying to keep up with Mrs. Bedlam's tangents. "So, you say he noticed in August the license plate was missing?"

"I wouldn't say *he* noticed it first. It was really the police officer who pulled him over."

"Do you have any idea how long the license plate had been missing before the cop stopped him?"

"No clue. It could've been a week or a month."

"Where did your husband usually park his truck when he was home?"

"In the street. My car was always in the driveway on account of he had too much junk in the garage. Once he passed away, my daughter and son-in-law helped me clean it out so I could park my car in there. I hated leaving it in the driveway. You never know what someone might do."

"Like steal your license plates."

She snapped her fingers and pointed at him. "Exactly!"

"When did your husband pass away?"

Her gaze drifted to the fireplace to a picture of Mrs. Bedlam with a man, each with an arm around a young child. It couldn't have been taken much before his death. The man was gaunt, with sunken eyes, no hair, clothes hanging off his frame. A Christmas tree was behind them. "December thirtieth." She smiled and looked at Adam. "At least he made it through Christmas," she said before taking a final sip of her wine and setting the empty glass on the table. "Of course, he was in and out of the hospital during the final three months. Ended up bringing him home so he could die here with his family and friends around him. In the house he and I bought when we first married."

So, no way in hell Mr. Bedlam could've been responsible for the death of Jenna Rose. Aside from being about a foot shorter than the man in the video dumping the body at the golf course, there would've been no way Mr. Bedlam had the strength to lift or carry Jenna, let alone torture and kill her.

"Do you know a woman named Jenna Rose?" Adam asked.

Mrs. Bedlam looked up, her head cocked to the side. "Nooo," she drew out, as if searching her memory, "doesn't sound familiar."

Adam closed up his notepad and replaced it and the pen in the pocket. "Thank you so much for speaking with me, Mrs. Bedlam."

They both rose and she followed him to the door. Muggsy barely lifted his head. Adam felt a little slighted. He thought he and Muggsy had developed some sort of friendship, at least enough to warrant a tail wag or an escort out of the home. Chihuahuas are fickle dogs. Adam much preferred his Lab. Bruno would eat this dog for breakfast. Adam chuckled. Not really—Bruno would more than likely run and hide at the sight of the feisty little runt.

"Which coffee shop did you say your daughter works at?"

"Bump and Grinds," Mrs. Bedlam said with a straight face, but quirked up her eyebrow when Adam snickered.

He cleared his throat and found his professionalism. "Thank you so much for your help."

Adam swung by the Bump & Grinds Coffee Shop and had a brief conversation with Cassidy Campos. A carbon copy of her mother in nearly every way, including her need to go down rabbit holes of unrelated information, Cassidy confirmed her father had been very ill during the last three months of his life, not able to walk from the bedroom to the living room without assistance. Checking the computer, she provided a printout of the hours she had worked the week Jenna Rose's body had been found. Not that Cassidy was anywhere close to resembling the person on the video who had dumped Jenna's body—having inherited being vertically challenged from her father. Paul Campos also confirmed in a text exchange with his wife that he had been on his way to Charlotte the night in question.

Thanking Cassidy, Adam headed back to Denver. At least he could strike three names off the list of suspects in the Jenna Rose case. Unfortunately, that didn't leave anyone else to consider.

8

Monday,
February 24,
6:54 AM

KENDALL TUCKED HER blouse into her slacks, grabbed her suit jacket from off the bed, and headed out to the living room. She wanted to get into work well before her meeting with Brady. Sleep had been elusive at best, and anxiety laden at worst. Several times she got up and went into the bathroom, thinking she might hurl from nerves. The idea she could take something to help her get to sleep crossed her mind, but she hated how even melatonin made her feel groggy the next morning. If she managed to keep her job, she would come home and take the melatonin. With a glass of wine. Or three.

After filling her travel mug with coffee, she headed for the front door. Her keys weren't in the bowl.

"Damn," Kendall muttered. Gwen must've been so tired when she got in, she forgot to put the keys in the bowl. She hadn't seen or spoken to her roommate since Saturday, when Gwen asked to use Kendall's vehicle because hers was having "issues." As she left for work, Gwen promised Kendall the Jaguar dealership would have her car done on Monday.

Gwen hadn't been home in two nights. Not unusual. She usually stayed at her fiancé's on the weekend. Now Kendall was going to have to risk waking her roommate to retrieve the keys from Gwen's purse.

Slowly, as silently as possible, Kendall twisted the door-knob and opened Gwen's bedroom door enough to slip inside. The light from the hallway illuminated the room enough for Kendall to locate Gwen's purse. Her gaze swept the quiet room.

Too quiet. Too still. She glanced at the bed, expecting to see the lumpy form of her best friend. But Gwen wasn't there. And by the look of the made bed, hadn't been there all night.

"Fuck!" Kendall pulled the cell phone from her front pocket and hit the speed dial for Gwen's phone. One ring. Two rings. By the end of the sixth ring, the call went to voicemail. After the beep sounded, Kendall said, "Hey, where are you? I need my car. I have a meeting with Brady this morning, and since my ass is on the line, I can't afford to be late."

She clicked "End," and pressed "Speed dial" again, hoping the reason Gwen wasn't answering was because she was driving home and couldn't find her phone inside her purse. Again, the voicemail message filled Kendall's ear. She ended the call and dialed Gwen's fiancé, Ty Butler. No doubt Gwen had spent the night at his place and was on her way home.

But the call went to his voicemail.

Kendall checked the time. She could kiss her hopes of being early right out the door and was in serious jeopardy of being late if she didn't leave the house soon. Not willing to risk it, Kendall opened the Uber app on her phone and ordered a car.

She would deal with Gwen later.

Her stomach churned, and for the first time, Kendall allowed herself to consider what was going on. It was not like Gwen to be this inconsiderate. Gwen was time conscious to a fault. Everything—no matter how mundane—went into her calendar with at least two notifications for each event. And she knew Kendall had to work today, even if she didn't know about the meeting with Brady.

Had something happened to her? Had she been involved in a car accident?

Sweat broke out over Kendall's skin, and she wiped her brow. She flipped the lock on the deadbolt, stepped onto the front porch to wait for the Uber, and shut the door behind her, locking it. She tried Gwen's phone again, leaving another message to call back and let Kendall know she was okay. Then she tried Ty's phone and left a brief message to call her. Bringing her contacts up, she hit the speed dial for Quentin.

A black Toyota RAV4 pulled into the driveway with the distinctive Uber sticker in the front windshield. The driver rolled down the passenger side window and said, "Kendall Beck?"

Kendall waved at the man as Quentin answered the phone. "Hey," she said, and slid onto the back seat. She took the phone away from her mouth and confirmed the address of the FBI field office with the driver, then returned to Quentin. "Have you heard from Gwen this morning?"

A pause. "Why would I?"

"You wouldn't. I was just wondering." Kendall glanced out the window. "She didn't come home last night, and I can't get a hold of her or Ty. She has my SUV, and I need to get to work."

"I'll come get you," Quentin said.

"No need—I called an Uber."

"Oh, you should've called—I would've swung by and gotten you."

Quentin had been a permanent fixture in her life since they had met at a new resident mixer back in Fredericksburg, Virginia, ten years earlier, both having moved there from Denver. Kendall was at the FBI Academy in Quantico. Q had moved to Virginia for a job with some computer gaming company. She had leaned on him extensively during those years until she moved back to Denver.

She sighed. "Yeah, I know, but I need to get there now, so I called an Uber. I wasn't sure if you were close to leaving for work or not. Can you pick me up after work and give me a ride home?"

"Of course. What time?"

"Good question. Depends on how my meeting with Brady goes this morning." A humorless chuckle escaped her chest. "I might be out of a job and need to be picked up within the hour."

*   *   *

Despite the departure from the original plan, Kendall was at her desk a full fifteen minutes before the start of her meeting with Brady. She had spent the time booting up her computer, going through emails, and checking her phone every thirty seconds to see if either Gwen or Ty had tried to contact her. And every time there was nothing, the knot in her gut twisted a little tighter.

Glancing over the top of her cubicle, she could see Brady walking through the bull pen. As he approached her desk, he motioned for her to follow him to his office. Once they were both inside, he dropped his briefcase beside his desk and hung his suit coat on the hook. "Close the door," he said, and sat in his desk chair.

He grabbed a file from the upper corner of his desk and opened it, perusing the contents as she took the chair opposite him. Even though she had worked with him for a while, being around him was somewhat intimidating. Especially since he literally held her career in his hands at the moment.

Flipping through the documents, he released a heavy sigh. He leaned back in his chair, placed his elbows on the armrests, and steepled his fingers under his chin. The excruciatingly long, assessing look he gave her felt as if minutes of her life were ticking away.

"Well, this is a shit mess you've gotten us into. And let me be clear—this isn't just about you—you've brought scrutiny on the whole unit with your serious lack of judgment."

"I know, sir, and I apologize."

"Beck, what the hell were you thinking?"

"I—I just lost my head for a moment. Seeing that poor little girl, so small and so scared, hearing her tell me what her father had done to her—how the only way she could get away from the abuse was to run away—and then watching him act all concerned for her when he came down the hallway." She inhaled deeply and let it out. "I just lost it. Did you see how the other daughter cringed when the mother tried to pass her to Williams? There is more abuse going on in that house."

Kendall knew she was rambling, very uncharacteristically.

Brady's eyebrow raised. "Jesus H, Beck. This is what we do. We deal with kids who have seen the very worst in adults—many times at the hands of those who are supposed to be caring for them. We don't beat the shit out of the abusers. We turn them over to the justice system and let them mete out punishment. Or did you forget that part of your job?"

"No, sir—well, yes, sir, I temporarily forgot that part. But it won't happen again."

Brady's gaze was captivating, and Kendall could see the wheels turning. She knew he trusted her instincts, but that trust had taken a major blow when she'd attacked Williams.

"Look, Beck, we've all been there. And, while I agree it was a well-deserved ass kicking, that shit cannot happen. It *will not* happen in my unit. Understand?"

"Yes, sir."

"Play down the beating in your report, but don't leave it out. I want to see it on my desk before you leave for the day, which should be soon. Lay low for a few days—consider taking some vacation time."

"That won't be necessary, sir. I have my shit stored."

He glanced up at her. "Think about it." He turned his attention back to the paperwork in front of him and signed something. "Get the fuck out of my office, and don't ever make me call you back in here for something like this again."

"Understood. Won't happen again."

"Better not. I won't be your buffer with the higher-ups next time. I haven't spent years storing up favors to blow them on you."

9

Kendall had Quentin drop her off at a rental car agency. There was no telling what condition her SUV was going to be in when they finally found Gwen. Chances were good she had hit ice and ended up in a ditch somewhere, unable to call for help. Gwen's phone was going straight to voicemail, which told Kendall it was turned off. So, either Gwen didn't want to be bothered, or her battery was drained.

Quentin drove out of the agency parking lot, headed back toward Kendall's home. He was instructed to work his way out from the house, in a circular pattern, seeing if the SUV was parked in front of a home, in a parking lot, or off an embankment. If he found anything, he was to call her immediately. This sort of thing wasn't in his bailiwick, but Kendall didn't have any other option. She needed help, and Quentin was there.

Kendall drove straight to the restaurant. Snowflakes drifted and swayed with the wind but didn't seem interested in sticking to the roads. For the time being, anyway. The snow was flirting with them now, but the storm was coming. She parked in the employee lot and entered through the kitchen. Ty was behind the grill, yelling obscenities at his sous chef and line cooks. They glanced at each other with wide questioning eyes. Kendall had seen Ty let loose on his staff before, and the staff would let it roll off their backs as part of the job of working in a busy kitchen at one of the most popular restaurants in the city.

But from the looks on their faces, Ty was unleashing hellfire that was quite possibly unwarranted.

Did he and Gwen have a fight? Kendall left the kitchen and wove through the dining room to the bar. Gwen would sit there so she could watch everything happening in the dining room, bar, and hostess station. Grabbing the attention of Dave, the bartender, Kendall gestured for him to come to the end of the bar where she stood. "Hey, is Gwen around?"

He wiped the bar with a rag and straightened a pile of coasters. "Haven't seen her. Check with Sandra—she's been trying to call her. With the Jag's track record of being in the shop more than on the road, maybe it broke down again."

A customer waved from the other end of the bar. Dave scooted toward the man.

Kendall had a sour taste in her mouth. Gwen wasn't driving her Jaguar. She was in Kendall's SUV. And while it was possible the vehicle had broken down somewhere, why hadn't she called Kendall to let her know? Or Sandra?

The door from the kitchen swung open, and Sandra came through, head glued to her phone, her gaze lifting randomly to make sure she wasn't running into anything. Kendall met her at the hostess station. Before Kendall could open her mouth, Sandra asked, "Where's Gwen? Is she here? Did you bring her?"

The fire in Kendall's gut flamed to a raging inferno. "No, I was going to ask if you'd heard from her. I've been trying all day."

Sandra lips pursed. "She's not here, Kendall." The hostess interrupted them, and Sandra excused herself to take care of a customer complaint. Kendall returned to the kitchen. Something wasn't right. Strike that—*nothing* was right.

And she had some questions for Ty.

He glanced up at her when she came through the kitchen door. No smile, no shit-eating grin. No questioning look. Not a grimace, sneer, or frown of annoyance. *Nothing.* There was that word again. But the *nothing* was beginning to turn into *something.* And Kendall could feel it was something bad.

She pointed to Gwen's office on the right and started walking toward it.

"Martin, take over for a few. I'll be back." Ty was wiping his hands on his black apron as he entered the room. "What's up?" His voice was a mix of casual irritation.

"What do you mean?" He couldn't be that obtuse. "Where the hell is Gwen?"

"I don't know."

"What do you mean, you don't know? Jesus, Ty, when was the last time Gwen didn't show up for work?" They both knew the answer to this, so she didn't wait for one. "No one seems to know where she is or be able to reach her and you just *don't know?*"

"I figured she was with you."

At a loss for words was an understatement. Kendall cocked her head to the side.

"Well, she's not. I haven't seen her since Saturday afternoon, when she left home to come here." Kendall took in a steadying breath. Losing control and flying off the handle at Ty was not going to help find out what had happened to Gwen. "When was the last time you talked to her?"

"Saturday night. She called to tell me she wasn't coming over. She wasn't too happy that I didn't make it into work. Said she had a migraine and was going home."

"What time was that?"

"Around midnight."

Midnight on Saturday night. Almost two days had passed since then. "Ty, she never came home on Saturday night. She wasn't there all day yesterday either."

"She's probably at her mom's."

"Then why didn't she call and let me know?"

"Jesus, Kendall, she doesn't have to clear her schedule with you."

Was he serious? His lack of concern was more than a little disturbing and was bumping up against her last nerve.

"She has my SUV, Ty."

"Look, Kendall, you know she's been killing herself with this damn place." He gestured toward the kitchen, his brows tightly knitted together. "Maybe she cracked and took off for a few days on her own. Did you check her mom's? Or the cabin?"

"How are you so cavalier about this, Ty?"

"Because I don't think there's anything to worry about. She's been joking with us forever about just up and running away one day. Maybe she finally decided to do it—get away from everyone and everything—and doesn't want us to bother her." He tapped his finger against his chest. "The best thing I can do for her is to run the restaurant until she gets back. I'm just trying to respect that and give her space and time to cool down."

He was back behind the grill before she could utter another word.

Dismissed.

Kendall no more believed Gwen had left without telling anyone than she believed Ryan Reynolds would dump his wife, Blake Lively, and marry her.

Ty was busying himself, avoiding the issue—Gwen's biggest complaint about her fiancé. Ty had stopped talking, and in Kendall's extensive experience interviewing people, she knew she wasn't going to get any more out of him.

Time to shift gears and get the police involved.

10

QUENTIN PACED AROUND Kendall's living room, anxiety rising with each passing minute. After he had driven all over hell and high water, they'd met back at Kendall's house to regroup. There was no sign Gwen had been home.

Ty had seemed genuinely surprised Gwen was missing, but oddly distracted by having to run the restaurant by himself. Kendall had put off talking to Gwen's mother, not wanting to worry the woman unnecessarily. But too many hours had passed without a word from Gwen. Kendall placed the call and prayed Gwen would answer, and they could all have a laugh about how Kendall went off the rails.

By the time Kendall disconnected the call with Darla Tavich, it was clear something was not right. Kendall sent text messages to Gwen's brothers, asking if either of them had spoken with Gwen, and both stated they hadn't received anything from her since their last text check-in two weeks ago. Finally, Kendall decided she needed to call the police and report Gwen missing.

Officer Travis Warren's five o'clock peach fuzz on his upper lip was only visible when the sunlight hit it at just the right angle. Otherwise, the kid looked as if he was a twelve-year-old playing dress-up with his father's uniform. Every time he asked Kendall a question, he nodded his head as if he understood, but gave the impression he believed she was overreacting.

It took every ounce of restraint Kendall had, after the hours on hours of worry for her best friend's safety, not to launch across the coffee table and beat the ever-loving shit out of this rookie. Her need to handle things with violence lately should probably concern her more—she would have to deal with that, once they found Gwen.

"Sooo"—Officer Warren dragged out the word as he looked over his notes—"you and Ms. Tavich are roommates and have been since college." He lifted his eyebrows in some sort of knowing manner as if he realized just what type of roommates they were. Kendall was getting a little tired of Officer Warren's need to fulfill his girl-on-girl porn fantasy.

"Is there a question?" Kendall asked. Quentin gave her a subtle elbow to the side, indicating the statement came out as being too close to the exasperation Kendall was feeling.

Warren kept his nose in his notes. "And you loaned her your car, and she hasn't brought it back."

Again, no question. Kendall shifted in her seat, irritated she was allowing this pipsqueak to get under her skin.

"And you checked with the family and friends regarding her whereabouts, and no one has seen or spoken to her since midnight Saturday." He flipped a page in his notebook and glanced at his watch, calculating the time. "And you do understand that adults are free to come and go as they like."

Officer Travis Warren was a prick.

"I am aware," Kendall said. She wanted to remind the little shit she had been an FBI agent when he was still in diapers, but she needed his help.

"Look, Ms. Beck, I understand you're worried about your friend, but the police don't get involved in domestic disputes of this manner. If Ms. Tavich wants to leave you—your home—and not let you know, she has every right." He closed his notebook and let out a long sigh. "My advice is to give it some more time. Chances are, after she cools down, she'll get in touch with you. She's probably staying with someone you don't know." He gave her a sympathetic smile. "Someone she may not want you to know about."

"Wait." Quentin sat forward. "Are you trying to suggest Kendall and Gwen are lovers?"

This was going nowhere, and Kendall knew this asshat police officer wasn't going to take them seriously and certainly wasn't going to submit a missing person's report. There was only one thing left that would get action—and hopefully lead to finding Gwen.

"I'd like to report my vehicle stolen."

11

Tuesday,
February 25,
7:42 PM

ADAM LOGGED OFF his computer while sliding his arms into his coat. He glanced over the top of the cubicle walls to see who was left in the squad room. Two other detectives were gathering their things.

The race was on. No one wanted to be the last person in the squad room at the end of their shift, and it looked as though all the other detectives were either running down leads on their various cases, or on "detective time"—code for leaving the department building without any reason other than not wanting to be the only person there. Adam looked to be about two steps ahead of the remaining cops, ensuring he wouldn't be the "last one"—and therefore, the guy the boss called on to do menial shit, or catch a case that just came down.

Turning on his heel to escape the four-by-four cubicle, a box was thrust into his chest.

"Going somewhere, asshole?"

Dread passed over him as he stared at his ex-girlfriend, Sheri Colburn. It was unfortunate she also worked in the department, albeit in forensics. Even more unfortunate they'd had a nasty breakup which had spurred whispers, jabs, and filthy looks from almost everyone who worked in the building. Apparently, Sheri had been nice enough to spread her version of their relationship and parting of the ways, which had not been favorable to Adam.

"Hello, Sheri," Adam said as sweetly as possible, forcing a smile on his face. "What can I do for you?"

An obnoxious snort came from her, along with the most condescending grin. "There is not a damn thing you can do for me, limp dick, except take back the crap you left at my house."

Adam glanced into the box. A photo of the two of them sat atop what looked to be remnants of T-shirts and underwear that had been torn to shreds. Sheri was smiling happily in the photo. Adam had been transformed into a large penis, drooping over with a sad face at the tip.

He took comfort in the fact she had at least made the penis large.

On the verge of making some smartass retort, he thought better of it as one of the detectives walked past them. That left Adam and one other guy, and Adam was desperate to get away from his boss. And Sheri.

"Thank you." He kept smiling, which was apparently the wrong thing to do, because his happiness—contrived or not—pissed her off.

She glanced around the squad room, and smiled maliciously before fixing her gaze back on him. "Oh, I'm sorry. You're trying to leave, and I'm preventing you from doing that. How rude of me." Her bottom lip protruded, and she frowned; all the while her eyes were lit up with the excitement of a child on Christmas morning.

The other cop sauntered past them with a smile on his face. She made a tsking sound, which was impressive since he didn't think that sound could be made with a forked tongue. "Do accept my apology."

She turned on her heel, and he counted to ten before making a move to leave. No sense in taking the elevator and risk having to ride down with her, so he headed for the door marked "Stairs." Three steps from freedom—

"Taylor!" The boss's voice boomed through the empty space, making it feel as if a bomb had gone off. "Get your ass in my office."

Adam's shoulders dropped along with his heart. *So close* . . .

And not for the first time, Adam questioned his sanity in dating a woman he worked with, especially when his colleagues had warned him about that particular coworker.

No point in crying over shredded underwear.

Adam stood in the doorway of Lieutenant Dale Underwood's office. "Sir?"

"Lou" glanced up, took Adam in, and then returned his attention back to the paper on his desk. "What the hell is going on with the Jenna Rose case?"

"We finally got the security video from the golf course parking lot. We hoped it might lead somewhere, but the license plate came back as stolen."

"No way the plate was reported stolen to cover the unsub's tracks?"

Adam shook his head. "Owner was two steps from the grave when Jenna was murdered. No way he could've done it." Adam took a deep breath. "Afraid there might be some more bad news. It's possible this guy has killed before."

Lou rubbed the bridge of his nose and exhaled. Even his expirations sounded perturbed. "Are you telling me we may have a serial killer on the loose?"

"I'm not willing to go that far. At the present time, it's really more a gut feel. I have Saul and Fletch taking a look at possible correlations to other unsolved murders to see if there are any similarities."

"Well, shit fire, any more good news you want to spread?"

"No, sir, I think that about covers it."

"Fine." He shuffled a stack of papers. "Got a stolen vehicle case for you."

Adam stilled. "I don't do stolen vehicle cases."

"You do if I say you do. This may turn out to be nothing and should only take a minimal amount of your time—just needs to be checked out."

Adam dropped the box of deconstructed personal items onto the empty chair and stepped closer to the desk to retrieve the sheet of paper the lieutenant held out.

"Some FBI agent has lost her vehicle and her roommate. It probably won't amount to anything, but as a professional courtesy, we're going to check into it for her." He peered at Adam, no emotion on his ruddy face. "Got a problem with that?"

"No, sir," Adam said. Except he had a big problem babysitting some FBI agent who couldn't keep track of her vehicle or her friends.

Adam tossed the paper on the top of his box and turned to leave.

"Taylor," the boss said, "I don't want to hear about your *gut-feel* serial killer murdering someone else. Find him before he finds another victim. Do I make myself clear?"

"Crystal," Adam said, and headed for the elevator now that he was sure he wouldn't run into his ex. He stepped into the car and pressed the button for the parking garage, still stewing over his latest assignment. There were more important things he needed to be doing. Like finding a serial killer. Or clipping his toenails. "Thanks a lot—" he glanced at the name of the reporting party—"Kendall Beck, Special Agent."

12

Wednesday,
February 26,
8:30 PM

ADAM DREW UP alongside the curb and took in the bungalow. The lawn was well manicured, with a simple flower
garden curving artistically from the side of the house around to
the front porch and lining the walkway. The FBI must pay well
if Kendall Beck was living in one of the hottest "everything old
is new again" neighborhoods, where historic homes were gutted
and given a modern update with all the fancy bells and whistles.

Adam's house was similar to this, except his wasn't in the
right neighborhood and wouldn't net him a huge payoff if he
ever sold it. And, unlike all the houses in Agent Beck's bour-
geoisie neighborhood, where expensive architects were brought
in and contractors did all the work, Adam had done most of the
updates on his home with his own two hands.

Being a detective with the Denver Police Department did
not net him enough to live in the upscale neighborhood.

He climbed the front steps of the house and rang the doorbell. Shuffling sounds came from the opposite side, and then
the deadbolt slid back, and the door opened. A tall, slender
woman, brunette hair pulled up in back, intentionally chaotic,
and wearing yoga pants and a sweatshirt, stood in the doorway.

"Can I help you?"

"Are you Kendall Beck?"

"I guess that would depend on who's asking."

Adam moved his jacket out of the way to reveal the badge clipped to his belt. "Adam Taylor, Denver PD. I'm following up on a report of a stolen vehicle. Are you Ms. Beck?"

The woman stepped back. "Yes, please come in, Detective." She led the way to a family room just off the foyer. A big window looked out onto the yard. In front of it was a large chair and matching ottoman. Along one wall was a leather couch that sat across from a fireplace with a flat screen TV mounted above the mantel. The furniture was expensive, but comfortable. The home was decorated but still retained the coziness a bungalow promised.

She sat on the sofa and pointed to the large chair. Adam sat down, taking his notepad out of his pocket and clicking his pen. "Okay," he said, referring to the copy of the report the lieutenant had provided. "When was the last time you saw your vehicle?"

"Saturday afternoon."

"And can you tell me what was happening at that time?"

"I had been working a case and had just come home. Gwen asked if she could borrow my SUV."

"And Gwen is?"

"My roommate, Gwen Tavich."

Adam nodded.

"She had to take her car into the dealership for some type of servicing or another. Anyway, she took off to work, and I haven't seen or heard from her since."

"Do you loan her your vehicle often?"

"Just every time her car is in the shop for repairs—which is a lot of the time."

"You didn't need your car?"

"No, I didn't have any plans for the evening, so I let her take it."

"And about what time was it she left for work?"

"Around three thirty."

"Where does she work?"

"She owns The Oyster Grille. It's a restaurant not far away."

"Yeah, I know it." Meaning, he'd seen it when he had driven by it, but didn't have the coin—or the desire—to drop in the haughty joint.

"Does your vehicle have a GPS tracking system?"

"Yes, but it's showing the vehicle is sitting in the restaurant parking lot. I guess I'll need to have that checked when I get it back."

"Have you verified Ms. Tavich's vehicle is still in for servicing?"

"Yes, they left a message the car was done. When I called back, they told me it's still there. They also said they had not spoken to Gwen, only left messages for her at home and on her cell."

He showed Kendall a picture of Ms. Tavich he'd printed off from her driver's license. "And this is Ms. Tavich?"

"Yes."

"Okay, Agent Beck. I think that's all I need."

He got up, shook her hand, and walked to the front door.

"Can I bring up something unrelated?" she asked.

"Shoot."

"The officer who took the initial report?"

Adam glanced at the report and cringed. He couldn't stand the arrogant little shit. "Not a fan of Officer Warren?"

"Not so much." She chuckled, but the humor did not brighten her sad eyes. "He would benefit from not jumping to conclusions too early in an investigation."

"Rookie," Adam said by way of explanation. "But not an excuse. I'll talk to him."

"Not necessary, and really, I'm not usually one to tattle on someone." One corner of her mouth lifted in a near smile. "It's a nice distraction, though."

Adam got it. Easier to focus on Warren and his shortcomings—which were many—than sit and mull over what might have happened to her friend. "I'll be in touch if I hear anything. You do the same."

When he got into his car, he started it and headed toward home. The only suspicious part of this case was that Ms. Tavich had taken off in her roommate's vehicle. But even that wasn't a huge red flag. Sometimes people just leave. And some are ass-holes and take other people's belongings with them.

Adam would make sure the vehicle was listed with dispatch as one to look out for. Chances were good the case would be closed by the next day, and he would just have paperwork to file. Chances were also good he would never see Kendall Beck again.

13

Friday,
February 28,
6:24 AM

RINGING ABRUPTLY WOKE Adam from the best dream he'd had in months. Too bad he had no idea who the nameless, faceless chick was giving him a blowjob in his slumber. He hit "Talk" on his cell phone without seeing who was calling. Didn't matter. He was already pissed at whoever it was.

"Taylor," he grumbled into the receiver.

"Detective, this is Officer Young—"

"I'm not fucking on call!"

"Yes, sir. I realize that, but I found a vehicle that was reported stolen a couple of days ago."

"Fabulous. I'm sure the owners will be ecstatic to get it back. What does this have to do with me?"

"The vehicle is related to a case you're working."

Adam rolled onto his side and rested into his elbow. "Which case?"

"The vehicle belongs to Kendall Beck."

Kendall Beck . . .

The FBI agent who lost her SUV and roommate.

"All right, I'll get there when I can."

"Yes, sir . . . it's just . . . well, the vehicle was found with the engine running and the driver's side door open."

Adam sat up in bed. "Anyone in the vehicle?"

"No, sir."

"I'm on my way. Have someone get me a large, strong coffee."

By the time Adam rolled to a stop and put his car in park just outside the cul-de-sac on the east side of Rocky Mountain Lake Park, darkness was making way for the early dawn. Checking the dashboard clock, the green light screamed it was only 6:24 AM. An ungodly hour to have to be up and focused.

The city was seeing warmer temps lately, but in Colorado, residents knew there was no way to accurately predict the weather. Earlier in the week there had been snow. And though it had already melted, every day was an exercise in layering clothes to keep up with the fluctuating temperatures. Adam inhaled the cold mountain air and watched his breath turn to a white cloud as he exhaled.

"Coffee?" Adam asked Officer Young as way of introduction. The cop reached inside his patrol car, grabbed a large paper cup from a carrier, and handed it to Adam. He took a tentative sip to check the heat level. "What do you have?"

"Call came in of a suspicious vehicle around zero five hundred. I arrived at about zero five thirty, found the vehicle running, lights on, driver's door open. I called in the plates and they came back to a"—Officer Young flipped a page in his notepad—"Kendall Beck, vehicle reported stolen by the owner. I was informed you were the investigating officer. I made a cursory search of the immediate area around the vehicle and inside, but found nothing suspicious."

"Other than it was left running with no one around." Adam walked toward the SUV parked half on the asphalt, half on the mile-long trail that wrapped around the lake. Prior to the 1900s, the lake had been a watering hole for travelers along the Overland Trail. At the opposite end from them were football and baseball fields and playgrounds for the young families now populating the neighborhood.

"Yes, sir, other than that." The young pup either didn't have a sense of humor or was still so new he didn't put it on display for the upper ranks. Adam vaguely remembered being that green . . . it had been so many years ago.

"No sign of anyone at all?" Adam checked the inside of the vehicle. On the floor behind the passenger seat was a black purse. He reached into his coat pocket, pulled out a pair of latex gloves, and retrieved the purse, placing it on the driver's seat. He fished on the inside until he found a wallet. Inside was Gwen Tavich's driver's license and cell phone. He pressed the button to turn it on, and a red battery icon blinked, indicating the phone was dead. He dropped it back into the purse and returned the purse to where he had found it. "You checked the rear cargo of the vehicle?" Adam asked, hitting the rear hatch release button and walking to the back of the SUV.

"Looked through the window and didn't see anything." Young cleared his throat and tugged at his collar. "Didn't want to disturb more than I needed to before you got here, sir."

Adam nodded. The kid was doing fine and didn't need to feel self-conscious around Adam, but telling him so would make the kid even more self-conscious, so Adam left it alone, happy he had moved beyond youth and inexperience. He wouldn't want to go back to that time.

He loved being a detective—and thrived when there was a homicide. Not that he ever wanted someone to die so he could do his job. It was just a fact of life, and he relished putting murderers away and getting justice for the families of the victims. "Who called in the vehicle?"

"Resident of the apartments, Emil Washington."

"And what was Mr. Washington doing up and out at this hour—what time did he find the SUV?"

"Zero five hundred. According to Mr. Washington, he was on his way to Walmart to get diapers."

"Where is Mr. Washington now?"

"At his apartment with his wife." Young pointed to the building off to the east of the lake. "Number 205. He knows someone will be coming to talk to him and is waiting to go off to work."

"Okay, I'll head over there now. Get some more people out here and search the area around the lake in case Ms. Tavich is injured. Call me if you find anything."

"Yes, sir."

Adam crossed the parking lot and placed a call to Saul. "Up and at 'em, princess. I may need your help tracking down our lost restaurant owner."

Saul grumbled something of an acquiescence and asked for the address. The door to the apartment building was locked. Adam pressed the button for apartment 205.

"Yes?" A man's deep voice came over the intercom.

"Mr. Washington?" Adam asked.

"Yes."

"I'm Detective Adam Taylor, Denver Police Department. I'd like to talk to you about the vehicle you found this morning. Can you buzz me in?"

"Yes, of course. We're on the second floor, stairs are to your right when you come in."

The buzzer sounded and there was a loud click, disengaging the lock. Washington stood in his doorway about halfway down the hallway. Adam showed him his badge as he got closer.

Washington was average height, around five feet ten, but stocky and built like a house. His hand dwarfed Adam's when they shook hands. He stepped back to allow Adam into the apartment. "Come on in."

Off to the left was a decent-sized kitchen. Empty bottles filled the counter next to the sink, with more flipped upside down in the drying rack. Cannisters of formula were stacked in the only corner Adam could see from his vantage point. The living room was straight ahead. Baskets of laundry sat on the floor next to the couch, some folded on the coffee table. A baby swing, playpen, worn leather recliner, and large-screen TV were the only other things in the room.

"I understand from Officer Young you called in the vehicle?" Adam asked.

"Yes."

"Why did you feel it was necessary to do that?"

"It looked odd, sitting there with the door open, running." He spread his hands open across his body. "Just didn't feel right."

"What were you doing out at that time of the morning?"

"I had to run to Walmart to grab diapers."

Adam raised his eyebrows. "Pretty early to make a run to the store."

"The baby's sick—we wouldn't have made it through the day with what we had on hand. Didn't want my wife to have to take the baby out to get more later, so I got up and went before going to work."

"And what do you do?" Adam asked, jotting down notes.

"UPS driver."

That would account for the odd hours, Adam guessed.

"When did you first see the vehicle?"

"As I was pulling out of the parking lot. But I didn't call it in until I got back, and it was still sitting there, running. Door open. I mean, at first I thought it was some drunk taking a piss, but when it was still there when I returned, I thought maybe the dumbass had fallen in the lake."

"And you didn't feel the need to check?"

"Not my department." He glanced toward a closed bedroom door with a pink wooden sign that declared it was Olivia's room. "I was already in trouble for not stopping on my way home last night to get diapers. No way was I going to dawdle and get the wrath of my wife. She's been up most the night with the baby."

Adam wasn't a father, but had nieces and nephews. He'd seen how the sweetest woman could turn into a barracuda when caring for her children.

"You mentioned you thought there was someone perhaps by the lake. Did you see anyone?"

"No, but we get people driving into that cul-de-sac all the time. At all hours. But I didn't see anyone—near the vehicle, anyway."

Adam looked at him, waiting for him to explain.

Washington shifted on his feet. "I saw a guy walking in the park as I passed on Forty-sixth."

"Can you describe him?"

"No, he was bundled up. Wearing a black jacket, dark pants. Ski mask. Couldn't make out anything else."

"Height? Weight? Just estimates."

Washington closed his eyes. "Tall—maybe six foot. Couldn't really tell weight 'cause he was wearing a coat but didn't appear overweight, if that helps."

"Why do you think it was a man? Could it have been a woman?"

Washington shook his head. "Doubt it. There's just a way guys walk, you know—you can tell when it's a dude, most of the time."

"Okay, Mr. Washington, thank you for your time." Adam handed him a business card. "If you could have your wife give me a call when she has a chance today, I'd appreciate it."

Washington was immediately defensive. "Why do you need to talk to her? She didn't see the vehicle. She's been in the apartment for two days without leaving."

"I understand. I just need to verify the times with her. It's routine—I'm required to dot the I's and cross the T's."

Washington nodded, but his eyes narrowed and darkened. Adam got it. The man was a good Samaritan, of sorts. Adam didn't want to tell the guy he needed to cross him off the suspect list when Washington was trying to be helpful and could just as well have left it alone.

Adam moved to the door. "And if you think of anything else—no matter how small and insignificant—give me a call."

14

KENDALL DROPPED HER bags next to her desk and slumped into her chair. She had slept like crap the night before. Tossing and turning, her brain refused to shut off and instead showed her every horrific potential Gwen was facing. Closing her eyes was a dangerous proposition most nights—she had seen some disgusting shit over her career with the FBI—but when her best friend was missing, those visions made her physically ill.

And panicked.

Not a feeling she had often. Not since she'd been in college, when she'd picked up a woman on the side of the road and was chased—hunted down, more accurately—by the man who had kidnapped her. Weaving through the streets, Kendall had been desperate to get to the police department. She'd gotten out of the car and made a mad dash toward the police station. The bullet had pierced her back, and she'd hit the icy asphalt.

She didn't remember much about that night. Most of the memories were disjointed, and she knew, from talking to investigators, they were often out of sequence with the actual events.

Kendall had never experienced pain like that in her entire life up to that point. But it was the overwhelming fear that ravaged her body. Paralyzed her. Fear she would die. Fear she had failed the young woman she'd promised was safe.

"Beck," Brady bellowed from the doorway of his office.

Kendall snapped back to reality. Pushed back the memories. Revisiting them was dangerous. And pointless.

She inhaled deeply, grabbed her cell phone off the desk in case Gwen called or texted, and walked across the bull pen to her boss's office.

Brady barely looked up at her from behind his desk. "Close the door and take a seat."

Kendall did as she was told. She should probably feel more nervous than she did, being summoned without knowing what the hell was happening, but she had little motivation for the job. Worry for Gwen wracked her body and mind, and overrode any trouble she might be in with her employer.

"Just got word from the prosecutor—Williams's attorney may be setting up an insanity defense. She wants a psych eval. Which means I want you digging into Williams's past to see if there is anything we can learn about him. We need to get a jump on what his problem might be."

Kendall nodded.

Brady leaned back in his chair, the intensity of his gaze drilling a hole through her. "What the hell is up with you, Beck? This case could make or break your fucking career. Thought you might be a little more enthusiastic to block whatever bullshit is coming down the line from Williams and his scuz lawyer."

So much shit . . . but how much of it was she willing to tell Brady? "Sorry, boss. Have some personal crap going on right now."

"Worse than potentially getting canned or thrown in jail for assault if this case goes in the shitter?"

"My roommate, Gwen, is missing." She stopped there before the emotions coming up her throat made an entrance and she burst into tears. The weight of the stress she'd been under the past few days was catching up with her, along with virtually no sleep and an alarming lack of nutrition.

Brady slowly sat forward, his eyes still boring into her, but softer. Something akin to sympathetic. Damn near kind. "Explain."

"She went to work on Saturday and hasn't been seen since." She sat back in the chair, remembering how Gwen twirled the keys to the BMW on her finger as she left the house that afternoon, big smile on her face. "She borrowed my SUV, went to work, and—" Kendall shrugged, unable to say again that Gwen was just gone. She knew it happened all the time. People just left. Disappeared without a trace, either intentionally or by force. She swallowed back the rush of anxiety and bile coming from her empty stomach.

"Did you report it?"

She nodded. "As much as I was able to—you know the drill—grown woman where there's no evidence of foul play is not going to be investigated. I reported my vehicle stolen and dropped that I was an agent, so they sent a detective over to talk to me. Not holding out much hope they'll actually do anything, but they have the vehicle and Gwen's description in the system. That's about all I can hope for right now."

"Did you talk to her family?"

"I was at her parents' house last night, trying to keep her mother calm while seeing if Gwen had said anything to her about needing to get away. But Gwen would never talk to her mother about her problems. That would put more stress on her mother, and Gwen avoids that as much as possible since her father's stroke."

"What's the boyfriend got to say about all this?"

"He states he hasn't seen or talked to her, but he's being squirrelly. Basically shrugged it off—was more pissed he had to run the restaurant on his own because Gwen wasn't there."

"They having issues?"

"No."

"Would you know if they were?"

What the fuck? "Of course. She's my best friend. We talk about everything." She glared at him. The asshole. Intimating she wouldn't know what was going on with her best friend.

Brady exhaled while wiping his hand down his face. "Get the hell out of here, Beck. You're not going to do me any good today. You're too distracted."

"No—Brady, please—let me work today. I'll look into Williams. I need to think of something besides Gwen, and I can't be in that house, wondering what the hell is happening to her."

Brady was shaking his head but hadn't told her no.

"I can handle this, boss. Just let me get some things squared away with Williams and this case. I need to talk to Kathy now that we know what really happened. Maybe she has some insight into her husband—something we can use to nail the asshole and get a slam-dunk conviction."

The silence was deafening in the room, but it was Brady's death glare that made Kendall suck in her breath and hold it. "Fine, but don't make me regret not kicking you out the door—or firing your ass."

She got up and opened the door before he changed his mind. "Beck."

So close . . .

She glanced over her shoulder at him.

"I hope Gwen's okay."

Kendall rushed out the door before emotions bubbled to the surface. The last thing she wanted was to start crying—especially at the office. She might never stop.

When she got back to her desk, Jake was there with a cup of coffee from Starbucks and something wrapped in a napkin. Kendall grabbed the coffee from his hand and took a drink.

"What was that all about?" Jake nodded toward Brady's office.

"Why didn't you come in and find out?"

"Fuck, no, it looked way too intense. Besides, I was worried I had missed a meeting, and no way in hell was I walking in late."

"Chickenshit." Kendall sat down and turned on her computer. "Where the hell have you been?"

"Daddy–Daughter Donut Day at Ciara's day care."

Kendall smirked and shook her head.

"Don't be bitter." He edged the napkin along the desk toward her. "I brought you a jelly." He practically sang the last words.

She tried to maintain her aloofness, but the jelly donut was calling to her. Actually, it was her stomach calling, reminding her she had once again skipped a meal. She took a huge bite, powder sugar clumps landing on her chest and in her lap. Her tongue darted out, lapping up a glob of raspberry jelly before it rolled down her chin and onto her shirt.

"So, you gonna tell me what your meeting with Brady was about?"

"He wants us to dig into Williams some more in case his lawyer goes with an insanity defense."

Kendall's cell phone buzzed with an incoming text. She grabbed the phone and quickly checked it. *Please let it be Gwen.*

Any news? the message from Q read.

Her heart sank. She quickly typed "no" and tossed the phone on the desk. The remainder of the donut sat on the napkin, but she had lost her appetite.

"What the hell is wrong with you?"

She wrapped the donut back up in the napkin and pushed it away. "Gwen's missing."

"What does that mean?"

She explained the circumstances.

"Holy craziness, Batman," Jake said when she'd finished. "What can I do to help?"

"That's just it—there's really nothing to do except hope she calls or comes home soon." Kendall let out a long exhale. She needed to get her mind off Gwen and the possibility she might not be in a position to call or come home. "I'm going to go talk to Kathy Williams and see if she can give us any information about her husband."

"Want me to tag along?"

Kendall shook her head. "No, it might be better one-on-one, just between us girls. I need you to start going through all the background info we have on him, and see if we can find people to talk to who know something about Scott Williams. Similar to the questions we asked previously, but let's ramp it up a bit. Last time, we just wondered if Williams was involved. Now, I want people to know—and start dropping info."

"On it," Jake said, and walked out of her "office." "Hey, if there's anything I can do about Gwen—"

"I'll let you know."

15

ADAM CROSSED THE parking lot of the apartments. The sun was shedding light across the sky in gorgeous shades of purple and pink. It should've been soothing. A sign of the city waking from slumber to start a new day. But Adam had a feeling this day was not going to be bright and happy—especially for Kendall Beck.

Or Gwen Tavich.

Officer Young and Saul were standing in a circle of people about two hundred feet down the trail from the abandoned SUV. As Adam drew closer to the group, he could see a body lying on the cold asphalt. No one was kneeling next to the person. CPR was not being administered. The determination the person was dead had been made.

"Is it Tavich?" Adam asked Young.

The officer nodded his head. "Looks like the picture on her driver's license."

"Damn," Adam muttered under his breath. In his line of work, dead bodies were just a reality, and the shock had worn off a long time ago. But he still hated it when there was hope of finding a missing person alive, only to have that hope dashed.

Death was never pretty, even when it was routine.

The officers broke apart and made way for Adam. "Where was the body found?"

Young pointed to the lake. Past the dormant grass, beyond the bulrushes, large rocks spanned the edge of the lake. A space between the lake's edge and the rocks created a crevasse. "She was found facedown in that small area. We dragged her out, but it's clear she's been deceased for some time."

Adam removed a pair of latex gloves from his pocket and slipped them on as he squatted next to the body for a closer inspection.

Young stood over Adam. "Must've committed suicide," the young pup said with more authority than he had.

Adam looked up at Saul, who just shook his head and yawned. Adam searched the woman's head as much as he dared. He was not about to mess with the medical examiner's body and risk the wrath that would surely ensue. But Adam would love to see if there was an injury to the back of the head, which might explain how Gwen Tavich ended up facedown in the lake. "Drawing your conclusion from what?" Adam asked.

"Car abandoned, engine running. No one around."

"Suicide by drowning? Not the typical way to off one's self, but I guess there's a first time for everything."

Saul snorted.

It wasn't Adam's intent to embarrass the young cop, just to get him to start thinking like an investigator. Sometimes first impressions were correct, and the mystery was simply explained. But investigators couldn't afford to rely on instinct only. Too many people had been convicted through an investigator's gut feel, only to be found innocent through DNA and other means after they had sat in prison for many years.

A black SUV entered the cul-de-sac, parked, and a woman stepped out of the vehicle. After signing in, the medical examiner made her way toward them.

"Fran," Saul shook her hand. "Thank God, you're back."

She was short, with a pixie cut (according to Sheri; Adam knew nothing about haircuts other than short, spikey, long) and had only recently returned from maternity leave. A bright, bubbly personality, which was odd for a person in her occupation, but her eyes told a different story. They had a knowledge only people who work with the dead and witness the depravity of humanity have.

"Not a fan of Nestor?"

"You mean"—Adam pushed nonexistent glasses up his nose and changed his voice to a high-pitch nasal tone—"*Dr.* Watson?"

She snickered. "Yeah, he has a bit of an air about him, but he is really a decent guy."

"A bit of an air? I assume by that you mean total twat waffle."

"Well, he's nice to me."

"Everyone's nice to you," Saul said.

Adam tipped his head toward the man next to him. "This is Officer Young. He found the body."

"Yes, sir," Young said. "I know Dr. Ward."

"Nice to see you again," Fran said. "*Nice* being a relative term and all." She stepped toward the body of Gwen Tavich while pulling on latex gloves. "What have we got here?"

Young explained how he came to find Ms. Tavich facedown in the lake. "Do you think she drowned?"

"No way to tell until I can get her on the table."

"Why don't you run your theory by the doc?" Adam said with a straight face.

Fran looked at Young, and cocked an eyebrow when he concluded his hypothesis.

"Suicide by drowning?" Fran glanced at Adam and shook her head. He knew she was calling him a shit in her head. She smiled at Young. "Not the typical way to off one's self, but I guess there's a first time for everything."

16

KENDALL DROVE UP to the gatehouse and gave the guard her name. The gates slowly swung open, and she made her way through the Cherry Hills neighborhood. Kathy Williams's parents obviously had a shit-ton of money. Their neighbors were professional sports figures and descendants of Molly Brown. Kathy's father was the CEO of some tech company. He had stated, if there had been a ransom demand, no amount of money would be a problem. They only needed to tell him how much, and he would secure the amount. Of course, that had been when they considered Emily might've been kidnapped and were waiting to see if a ransom demand came in. Kendall almost wished that had been the outcome.

Mature Pinion pines lined the lane leading to the circular driveway. She parked her rental car and approached the mahogany and glass double doors at the entryway and rang the doorbell. Deidre Merkle, Kathy's mom, answered the door. They had met during the initial investigation. Deidre had been a fixture at her daughter's side almost the entire time. As usual, her almost shoulder-length white hair was perfectly coiffed without a hair out of place. Kendall wondered if hair became tame and more manageable with the amount of wealth one had. It would explain why Kendall's hair was only submissive when pulled back in a ponytail.

"Hi, Mrs. Merkle. I'm here to see Kathy. She should be expecting me."

"Yes, Agent Beck, come in. Kathy is in the kitchen."

The tiled foyer was open to the second floor. Deidre Merkle led Kendall through a family room with a large stone fireplace that took up almost an entire wall. A leather sectional couch sat in a semicircle around the fireplace. Off to the side, on a glass and wood console table was a large flat-screen TV tuned to cartoons. As Kendall passed by, she almost missed Emily curled into a corner of the couch, eyes glued to the TV, a stuffed bunny in the crook of her elbow. The little girl didn't look up as they walked by, and Kendall wondered if anything was registering with Emily.

Or had the impact of the horrors she'd faced for so much of her short life finally caught up with her?

The thought of Emily never being able to get past this part of her life and have a normal childhood made Kendall's blood boil. If it was the last thing she did, she would make sure Scott Williams paid for the hell he'd put his daughter through.

The kitchen was empty when they entered. Mrs. Merkle stopped short and glanced around, something akin to panic distorting her features. The squeal of a baby eased the woman. Just outside the kitchen, at the end of a wet bar, stood a highchair.

Mrs. Merkle gestured to Kendall to go ahead. "I'll bring some coffee for you."

Kendall nodded. "Thank you." She approached Kathy Williams and her daughter, Sadie. Along the wall behind them was a large fish tank. Various tropical fish swam slowly by, the black background highlighting their brilliant blues and bright yellows.

Kathy looked up, hair drawn up in a messy bun, bloodshot eyes with dark circles under them. Her clothes hung from her frame, and Kendall wondered if the woman had lost weight since they'd first met almost two weeks ago. She glanced at the child in the highchair.

"She loves to look at the fish while she eats," Kathy explained. "Although, I'm not sure it really makes it easier to feed her."

Mrs. Merkle came up behind Kendall and placed a mug of coffee on the bar next to her. "Why don't you let me finish feeding Sadie, and the two of you can talk in the solarium?"

Kathy nodded and handed the bowl of food to her mother. Kendall followed Kathy around the corner and down the hall to a room with heavy wicker furniture. Floor-to-ceiling windows looked out over a perfectly manicured lawn with flowers and bushes planted to look as if they had naturally grown along the winding path. Except there was nothing in the yard that wasn't planned. Kendall was sure there was a master designer on the payroll who maintained the property, digging up dead flowers before anyone in the house noticed, and replacing them with plants in full bloom. The magic of lots of money.

To their left, glass doors opened to an indoor swimming pool. The house oozed as much money as the rest of the neighborhood.

Kathy sat on a loveseat and curled her legs under her. Kendall took the chair across from her, setting her coffee on the table between them.

"How is Emily doing?"

"As well as can be expected, I guess." Kathy sighed heavily and rubbed the bridge of her nose. "She's seeing a therapist, but it's just too soon to know how that's going. So far, she just colors and shrugs whenever the doctor asks anything about her father, or why she ran away."

"It takes time."

"I just can't believe I didn't see what was going on right under my nose."

Kendall didn't ask, but she hoped to hell Kathy was seeing a therapist, as well. This was a whole different level of injury. "Abusers know how to manipulate their victims. And when the abuser is a parent—it makes it incredibly difficult for the child to turn in that parent. The abuser convinces the child they are providing love—natural and beautiful and special—and if the child were to tell the other parent, that parent would get angry and not understand."

Kendall sat forward in her chair, wanting to reach out and hold Kathy's hand, but trying to remain professional and distanced. "The abuser may even tell the child they will get into trouble and be sent away."

"Yes, I've heard it all from the therapist. But I'm her mother! I should've seen something. Known instinctively that my child was being hurt. There had to be signs that something wasn't right—"

"You did, though. You told me you'd been worried about Emily's behavior before she disappeared. She had started talking back and was uncharacteristically irritable."

"And now I know why. But why didn't I sense something more back then? I should've taken it more seriously."

"Except Scott convinced you that you were being too sensitive and blowing it out of proportion. He had control of the narrative, and it was easy for him to make excuses to divert attention from what was really going on."

"And I believed every word out of that asshole's mouth." Tears streamed down her face. "I should've protected my girls."

Kendall let her cry it out, not wanting to argue with a mother who just needed to blame herself for what she perceived as her biggest failure to date. Nothing Kendall said was going to make the woman change her mind. After a moment, when Kathy took a shuddering inhale and swiped the tears from her face with her sleeve, Kendall asked, "Is there anything in Scott's past which would explain why he was doing this?"

"It's possible," she said with a shrug. "I know he had a rough childhood. He never talked about it—would shut down if I asked questions. From the bits and pieces I did pick up, I think he was physically abused."

"Do you know who might have abused him?"

"No. Like I said, he was pretty close-mouthed about the subject."

"Did he elude to any sexual abuse?"

"He never said anything directly about the abuse, so I guess there's a chance."

"I know his parents are both dead now, but did he grow up with them?"

"Just his mom. His dad wasn't in the picture. Left when Scott's mom was pregnant with him."

"Any siblings?"

"No. I mean, I don't think so. If he does, he has no contact with them." She closed her eyes. "Why is all this necessary? Who cares what happened to him as a child?"

"Depending on the jury, some may sympathize with him because of his circumstances growing up. Empathize with a child who turned into an abuser. The defense will say there are mitigating circumstances beyond Scott's control—a learned behavior from his own upbringing that he was never able to put aside."

"What he did to *my* girls is inexcusable. It shouldn't matter if he was abused. It doesn't give him carte blanche to do it to his own children."

"No, it doesn't." Kendall took another sip of coffee and rose from her seat. "And I will do everything in my power to make sure he pays for what he did to Emily and Sadie. It's the only reason I came over here today. The more information we have about him, and where his defense may go, the better the prosecution will be able to combat it."

Kathy nodded and stood, leading Kendall back through the family room to the foyer. Emily was in the same position she had been in when Kendall arrived. It was eerie to see a little girl so withdrawn and quiet.

"Hi, Emily," Kendall said. The little girl didn't acknowledge her. Didn't move at all. Just continued to stare at the television screen. "Can I ask you a question?"

Emily didn't answer, but coiled tighter into a ball in the corner of the couch.

Nope. Kendall sighed. She wasn't going to get anything from her today. Kendall stood and followed Kathy to the foyer.

"Has she said anything?" Kendall asked.

"Not much since she told you about what Scott was doing to her." Tears flooded Kathy's eyes, but she swiped them away, cleared her throat, and squared her shoulders. She was trying to be strong for her daughters, Kendall could see that, but she also knew that at some point in the near future, Kathy was going to fall apart. "We've set up for the therapist to come by the house daily to work with Emily."

"Good." She gave Kathy a small smile. "I'm going to have to try again with Emily, though. Let me know when the therapist thinks I can ask a few questions."

Kathy nodded and opened the door. Kendall turned to her. "You have my number. Call if you think of anything." She grasped Kathy's wrist and gave it a squeeze. "Or if you just need to vent. I'm a great sounding board."

"Thanks." Kathy mustered a smile. "Oh, and that knockout punch—thanks for that too."

17

IT WAS LATE afternoon when Adam finally called Kendall Beck and asked if he could stop by and update her on the case. She had agreed. He was driving to her house, not looking forward to providing the information she was no doubt dreading. Even though she was a law enforcement officer and used to the horrors of human iniquity, she was also human.

His cell phone rang, and Saul's name popped onto the screen. Adam hit the hands-free button. "Yeah?"

"Was able to check the security cam at Walmart," Saul's voice came out over the speakers. "Mr. Washington was telling the truth. He entered the Walmart, purchased diapers and some type of juice or something, and left. Times match his statement."

Adam pulled up to the curb in front of Kendall's house. "Okay. I got off the phone a few minutes ago with his wife. She backs up the husband's story, so I guess we can cross his name off the suspect list."

"Where are you now?" Saul asked.

"About to drop the bomb on Kendall Beck."

Saul sighed. No cop liked this part of the job. "Good luck with that."

"Thanks."

Adam rang the doorbell. The lock disengaged, and Kendall Beck stood in the doorway. Her hair was down, her eyes piercing. Still wearing her fed uniform of dark suit, white blouse, nondescript facial expression. Adam was glad he wasn't being interrogated by her. He'd probably confess to killing Kennedy.

"Detective," she greeted him, and stepped back to allow him inside. She skirted around him and into the living room, pointed to the chair he had sat in the last time he was there, and sank into the couch.

Adam entered and looked around the room. The underlying feeling of calm surrounded him. The home was inviting. Charming. Happiness resided there.

And he was about to destroy it all with one statement.

"We found Gwen Tavich's body."

There was no lead-up. Not necessary, especially with another law enforcement agent. He knew it was better to get it over with and not beat around the proverbial bush.

He watched as the words slowly sunk in. Her face paled, and her breathing became ragged. She was staring at him so intently, as if she was expecting him to tell her it was a joke played at her expense. Adam waited for the meltdown, anticipating uncontrollable sobbing, but it didn't happen. She was wringing her hands so tightly he marveled that her fingers hadn't already popped off. But other than that, she appeared in complete control of her emotions.

Kendall swallowed, her eyes glassy, and cleared her throat. "Where?"

"Rocky Mountain Lake Park."

"What can you tell me?"

"Early this morning, your vehicle was observed by a resident of the apartments near the lake. When police arrived, the officer found the driver's door ajar, engine running, but no one in or around the immediate vicinity. A search of the area uncovered her body. She was already deceased." He paused and took a deep breath, sorrow twisting his gut. "I'm very sorry for your loss."

Staring at the floor, or her shoes, or nothing at all, she asked, "How did she die?"

"The ME couldn't say on scene. We'll have to wait for the results of the autopsy." He placed his forearms on his knees and leaned toward her. The time for consolation on his part was over. Now came the hard questions, and as much as he hated to think any law enforcement officer would commit murder,

Kendall Beck needed to clear herself of this crime before he provided any more information.

"Does that area hold any significance for Ms. Tavich?"

Her head slowly wagged from side-to-side. "Not that I'm aware.

"It's not far from here."

She nodded. "We've been there a few times to take a walk around the lake, but it wasn't something we did on a regular basis. Most of the time we forgot it was even there."

"You said the other day, the last time you spoke to or saw Ms. Tavich was on Saturday afternoon before she left for work in your vehicle?"

"Yes." She swiped the tears from her eyes and sat up straighter. The anguish he had seen vanished, her gaze steely with just a hint of sorrow. In the blink of an eye, Kendall Beck had become the model of fortitude. He was taken completely off guard. Her demeanor was all business. Gone was the gentle grief threatening to turn into sob-filled mourning from a moment earlier. Now there was stoicism, which seemed out of place.

"It didn't concern you she hadn't come home—or called—until you discovered she hadn't returned by Monday morning when you needed your vehicle?" He was aware they had covered this ground in the earlier conversation, but that had been an information-gathering session. Now, Ms. Beck was on the hot seat, and he wanted to see if her story remained the same—rehearsed, even—or changed at all. Any could mean she was covering something up.

"No, not really. It wasn't uncommon for her to stay at her fiancé's house on Saturday nights after they closed up the restaurant, and spend the day with him, and her family, on Sundays. Sunday was typically the only day she took off."

"That seems odd for a restaurant owner." He looked up at her and smiled, trying to soften the question: "I've always heard owning a restaurant was a twenty-four seven job and owners rarely took time off?"

"Sunday was her only exception. The restaurant didn't open until after noon, and she has an excellent manager who can handle it for one day. Ty was there on Sunday nights, so Gwen could go to her mother's for a family dinner."

"And did she go to her mom's on Sunday night?"

"No, apparently they'd cancelled the dinner earlier in the week because one of her brothers was unable to make it."

"And she didn't let you know this?"

Kendall blinked rapidly for a moment. "No. I had no idea."

Adam let that hang for a moment. From the look on Kendall's face, she seemed to be wondering the same thing Adam was—why hadn't Gwen let Kendall know the plans had changed? Especially since she had Kendall's vehicle?

Or was Kendall stalling so she could come up with a plausible answer?

The front door opened. Her eyes shifted to it, and she stood.

A man sauntered into the room. Early thirties, dirty-blond hair, tall, medium build, abruptly halting when he saw Adam. His eyes swung over to Kendall, and he was across the room and by her side in a flash.

"What's going on?" he asked, placing his arm protectively across her shoulders. Adam wondered if it was for Kendall's benefit or his.

"It's Gwen—she's dead," Kendall whispered. Tears rolled slowly down her cheeks.

"What?" The man turned so he faced her. "What are you talking about?"

She rested her forehead against his chest. It was comfortable but not intimate. They were close, though—that much was clear.

The man turned his head toward Adam, his eyes wide. He had gone about as white in the face as Kendall. His eyes dropped to the gun holstered at Adam's side.

"What happened?" he asked, his voice soft, a note of disbelief coming through.

"I'm very sorry for your loss, Mr. —?"

"Novak. Quentin Novak."

"And how do you know Ms. Tavich and Ms. Beck, Mr. Novak?"

He gently caressed the woman's head. "I've known Kendall since we lived in Virginia—going on eight—maybe nine—years now. I became friends with Gwen after Kendall moved in here." He paused. "But we were all close friends." His voice trailed off.

Interesting, he's already comfortable using past tense when talking about a woman he'd just discovered moments earlier was dead. Adam filed the information away for more consideration later.

"Can you tell me the last time you spoke to or saw Ms. Tavich?"

"Um, Saturday night. I stopped by the restaurant to pick up food for Kendall and me."

"Did you talk to her or just see her while at the restaurant?" Adam watched him closely, trying to get a feel for him. He genuinely seemed distraught. If he was acting, he should be on Broadway.

"Both. We talked for a just a few minutes. Saturday nights are busy."

"What did you talk about?"

"She was upset that Ty—her fiancé—hadn't come into work. Apparently, he wasn't *feeling well*. Again." He rolled his eyes. "Gwen was ranting about how unreliable he had become lately."

"Anything else?"

His face was about five shades of red, his gaze darted nervously to Kendall. "No, that was all."

Hold the phone. Was there a secret between them? Was he hiding something about Kendall? Or *from* her?

She just smiled at him, giving his hand a conciliatory squeeze.

"Can you tell me where you were last night, Mr. Novak?"

"I was home," he responded, as if this should be a foregone conclusion.

"Anybody with you who can verify this?"

"Thousands, actually. I was playing *World of Warcraft* for most of the night."

Adam jotted down the information into his notes. "Home all day?"

"Got home from work at around six. Talked to Kendall on the phone for a bit and started gaming until around three in the morning."

"And where do you work?"

"Advanced Information Systems Solutions. I'm a software engineer."

Adam fished a business card from his jacket pocket and handed it to Novak. "If you could just provide contact information for you and your employer, along with a log of your time playing *Warcraft*, and email it to me, that would help eliminate you."

Novak scrunched up his nose as if the card was made of shit and he didn't want it all over his hands.

"I'll give you some time and show myself out," Adam said, took two steps away, and stopped. "I'm sorry, Ms. Beck, but where did you say you were last night?"

"You can't seriously believe Kendall had anything to do with this?" Novak asked. "They're best friends. Roommates."

Kendall laid her hand on Novak's forearm and looked at him. "It's all right, Q. He has to ask." Turning to Adam, she said, "Here."

"Can anyone confirm this?"

"Not really," she said, but didn't look the least bit concerned by her lack of a sufficient alibi. "I did some work on a case, so I was remotely logged into the computer. I can get a copy of the log for you. But no one else was here. I set the security alarm before I went to bed around midnight, and didn't turn it off until this morning when I left for work. I'll see if I can find some sort of verification of that, as well, and send it to you."

"Can you provide contact information on Ms. Tavich's fiancé and her family?"

Kendall released Novak, walked to the table behind the couch, and wrote on a notepad. Tearing the piece of paper off, she handed it to him. "Her parents live here, but her brothers live out of town—Colorado Springs and Fort Collins. I'll forward their contact information to your phone."

"Okay, thanks. That's all I need for right now."

"Please call me if you find out anything . . . anything at all. Or if you need any other information." She offered a slight smile, but the tears sitting on her lower eyelids made it clear she was barely holding it together.

He nodded and walked to the front door as she followed close behind.

"I'm very sorry for your loss, Ms. Beck. I'll be back in contact with you to go over things more thoroughly. In the meantime, if you think of anything, please feel free to contact me. I don't mind middle-of-the-night phone calls."

She smiled and gave him a half nod. "Will you be talking to Ty?"

"I'm heading over there now," he said, peering into her eyes. "I can't stop you from calling him, but I would really appreciate it if you didn't give him advance notice of my visit."

"I won't contact him, I promise."

Adam glanced back inside. "He's pretty protective of you. I didn't mean to upset you with my last question. It's more about eliminating you as a suspect than it is making an allegation."

"I understand, Detective. He just doesn't know how these things work. Don't worry about him—he's upset about Gwen."

Adam stepped off the porch and started toward his car.

"Detective?"

He stopped and glanced back at her.

"Will you be informing Gwen's parents of her death?"

"Yes."

"Will you please let me know when you do? I'd like to be there. She was their only daughter, and the baby of the family . . . it's going to be really hard on them. I just want to be there for support."

"Yes, of course. I'll let you know when I'm heading over there."

Tears spilled over and ran down her cheeks. "Thank you," she said, although it was barely audible.

Adam nodded and walked to his car. Sliding behind the wheel, he took a gander at the address Kendall had provided for the fiancé. There was a reason it was cliché to believe the spouse or significant other was the perpetrator. It was typically true.

And that's where this investigation needed to start.

Time to see what Tyson Butler has to say.

18

KENDALL STOOD UNDER the showerhead and let the hot water stream over her face, washing away the tears. There was something pressing on the center of her chest, a heaviness not allowing her to breathe, threatening to stop her heart from beating.

Gwen's dead.

The words felt foreign, unreal. Untrue. They had to be. Kendall would get out of this shower, walk into the kitchen, and Gwen would be there. Chastising her for being so gullible. Falling for such an obvious prank. Kendall would explain—sarcastically, of course—how she would have to be an idiot to believe something so stupid. And they would laugh like they did on so many occasions.

But as hard as Kendall tried to convince herself that would happen, the harsh reality was pounding through her head on an endless loop. *Gwen's dead . . . Gwen's dead.*

She was gone, and Kendall would never be able to talk to her again. Tell her she was more than a best friend. She was a sister. Sanity. The person who had helped Kendall get through the most difficult time in her life. A time which paled in comparison to the pain and sorrow and fear she felt at the prospect of facing life without Gwen beside her.

She slid down the tile and sat on the shower floor. Everything was numb. Her forehead rested on her knees while she continued to wish away all the pain flooding her heart and soul. A sob that had been building since Detective Taylor first told her the news, finally broke free of her chest and flooded the enclosed space. She pounded on the river pebble floor until her hands ached, and then she pounded some more.

There was a light rapping at the bathroom door. Kendall sucked in a breath and halted her sobs.

"Kendall?" Quentin's voice was low and soft. "You okay? You've been in there a while."

She took in another ragged breath, trying to get air around the large lump lodged in her throat. "Yeah, I'll be out in a sec."

She listened to his footsteps as they shuffled across the wood floor until they were out of the bedroom and down the hall. She hoisted herself up, turned off the water, and grabbed a towel off the hook. Wiping the condensation from the mirror, she stared at the reflection. Red, puffy eyes. Pale face. A frown she couldn't lift into a smile no matter how hard she tried. This face—*this feeling*—she remembered it from so long ago, but somehow it felt as if it was yesterday. The day she'd stopped in the middle of the road to help Amy Carrington. The day her world stopped spinning and reversed direction, throwing her off balance for such a long time.

It was Gwen who'd kept Kendall from falling so far into the depths of anguish she'd never recover. Gwen who first suggested Kendall turn the tragedy into a way to help others, prevent anyone else from having to experience the hell she and the other victims had been through. Find the bastards who victimized people and force them to face judgment in whatever form it took. Prison. Death. It didn't matter as long as justice prevailed and there was no way they could ever hurt another person again.

Kendall threw on a pair of sweatpants and a T-shirt, smoothed her wet hair back into a ponytail, and headed into the kitchen. Quentin was taking bowls out of the cabinet and setting them on the counter.

"Hey." He had a lopsided smile, but not nearly his usual bright liveliness. "I picked up some sandwiches and chicken noodle soup from the deli around the corner. I know it's supposed to be for when you're sick, but I figured soup is comfort food, and you probably need a little of that right now."

Kendall walked behind him, wrapped her arms around his waist, and rested her cheek against his back. "What would I do without you, Q? I can't imagine having to go through this without you here to prop me up."

"Where else would I be, Kendall? You know I'll always be here for you, no matter what."

She smiled and stepped back so he could fill the bowls with the soup. She wasn't hungry, but she was cold. Internally. Her blood had turned to ice the minute Detective Taylor stated Gwen was dead. There was no expectation of feeling warmth again for a very long time, but the soup might provide a short reprieve.

They ate in silence. It was nice not having to fill the void with idle chatter. Quentin knew her, knew her moods. It had been that way from nearly the very first time they met. He was one of her best friends. The only best friend she had left. He was her family, and she was going to do whatever was needed to make sure nothing happened to him.

No one else could leave her. No one else could die.

19

Saturday,
February 29,
9:13 AM

K ENDALL PULLED INTO the circular drive of Gwen's parents'
home. Detective Taylor was leaning against his car, waiting for her.

"Detective," she said as she approached. "Thanks for calling
me."

He pushed off his car and smiled. He was taller than her—
around six feet, with black hair and dark eyes. Fun to look at,
and she might have been interested if her best friend hadn't just
been murdered. Although the circles under his eyes and dark
scruff along his jaw were an indication he hadn't been getting
much sleep.

"Adam. And not a problem. Oddly enough, I'm not a fan of
having to make these calls on people. I'm grateful you're here
to help them."

She half-heartedly chuckled. "You mean you're glad I'm
going to save you from having her mother fall into your arms
sobbing uncontrollably."

His eyes jerked over to hers, and his mouth opened in what
she could only assume would've been a protest. Kendall put up
her hand. "I get it, Adam, and I completely understand. Dealing
with victims' families has got to be the worst part of the job."

He nodded and glanced down at his feet while they moved
slowly toward the front door of the house. He didn't seem any

more anxious than she was to relay this message to Gwen's family.

"A little background on the Tavich family," Kendall said. "Gwen's dad had a stroke a while back. He can't do much for himself—can't walk, get out of bed, speak. He has around-the-clock care, but it's still pretty hard on the family. Darla, Gwen's mom, especially. Her world has been turned upside down."

"Gwen's the youngest?" Adam asked.

"According to her brothers, Gwen's the *baby*." It was a subtle distinction Gwen always made. Her brothers often forgot Gwen was a grown woman with a successful business. It tended to be a sore spot. "Did you talk to Ty?"

"Haven't been able to connect with him. Left a couple of messages to call me back, stopped by his apartment building and the restaurant—nothing."

Kendall stopped and turned toward him. "So, he has no idea Gwen is dead?"

"As far as I know." He lifted an eyebrow. "Unless he does, and that's why he's nowhere to be found and not answering calls."

"Well, hell—" Kendall fished her phone out of her pocket and was about to hit the speed dial for Ty when Adam gently grasped her wrist. She looked up at him.

"Maybe wait until after we tell the family." He glanced up at the big house. "If you do manage to get a hold of him, the conversation might take longer than you want to have standing in the driveway while the family waits on you to come in."

He was right. Ty could wait.

20

THE DOOR OPENED immediately after Kendall rang the bell. A tall man, dressed in jeans and a wool sweater, and with a quizzical brow, took in Kendall, then Adam, before returning his gaze to her.

"Hey, Nick," Kendall said.

"Kendall, what's going on?" The tone was cool with a hint of wariness.

"Can we come in?"

The man stepped back allowing them to enter, then closed the door behind them. The foyer had a circular staircase that elegantly sloped up to the second floor. In the alcove under the stairs was a gorgeous baby grand piano. The floors were white marble, the light fixtures gold, and huge framed art canvases graced the walls. Adam wondered if this was a home or a museum.

"Nicolas Tavich, Adam Taylor." Kendall gestured toward him. "Adam is a detective with the Denver Police Department." Kendall looked at Adam. "Nick is Gwen's oldest brother."

They shook hands but Nick Tavich kept his gaze firmly fixed on Kendall, waiting for further explanation. "Where's Gwen?"

"Are Noah and your mom here?"

A curt nod proceeded him walking through French doors into a long living room. Sitting on a white couch opposite a crackling fire was a petite woman, hands folded neatly in her lap. Adjacent from her was a man who could've been a carbon copy of Nick Tavich, except he was in running pants and a North Face pullover. He stood as soon as they entered the room.

"Hi, Noah," Kendall greeted him, giving him a one-arm hug before moving onto the couch beside the woman and planting a kiss on her cheek.

Noah returned to his seat. Nick gestured at another chair for Adam to take. Nick remained standing, his elbow resting on the fireplace mantel, his stern gaze never leaving Kendall.

"Darla, Noah, this is Detective Adam Taylor. He's been investigating Gwen's disappearance."

"Have you found her?" Nick asked.

"Yes," Kendall said.

"Well, where is she? Is she okay? She's not with you—is she hurt? What hospital is she at?" Nick rapid-fired questions at both of them.

"Nicolas," Darla Tavich said in a calm and level tone. "Please let Kendall speak without interruption. I'm sure she will answer all our questions." Mrs. Tavich looked at Kendall. "Go ahead, dear."

Kendall took a deep breath and exhaled, her fingers wrapping around both of Darla Tavich's hands. "Yesterday, the police found my SUV at Rocky Mountain Lake Park. No one was inside, so the police checked the area. Gwen was found in the lake." Kendall took a shaky breath. "I'm so sorry—but she's dead."

Kendall choked on the last word, her head dropping to her chest.

Darla Tavich's hand went to her mouth. "No." Tears rimmed her lower lids, then rolled down her face. "Not my Gwen. It can't be!"

Nick stepped in front of Adam. "What the hell happened to her?"

Adam stood, forcing Nick to take a step back. Grief did weird things to people, so Adam was going to give the man a moment to check himself. "We don't have much information at the moment. The medical examiner will be performing the autopsy this morning. That should shed some light on what caused her death."

"Oh, Christ," Noah groaned at the mention of the autopsy. The idea that his baby sister was about to be sliced open had to be tough to consider—especially on the heels of learning she was dead.

"Well, you must know something—" Nick's arms flew over his head, and red flooded his face and neck.

Adam knew it was the pain the man was going through, but he could feel the violent anger coming through Nick Tavich's pores. "The investigation is just beginning."

"Nick," Kendall said, standing but still holding Darla Tavich's hand. "Your mom needs you and Noah, right now."

Noah moved to the couch to sit next to his mother. Nick glared at Kendall for a long moment. Kendall dropped Darla's hand and stepped out of the way. Nick passed her, Adam keeping his gaze on the man in case he needed to step in. Not that Kendall would need it. He was sure she had the same, if not better, training as he did. And she had a dangerous job taking down sex slave traders. It was doubtful Nick Tavich posed much of a threat to her.

But Adam wasn't taking chances. Finding out a loved one has died turned even the most docile people crazy.

Nick sat next to his mother on the couch. She placed a hand on his arm, but he didn't acknowledge her. Jesus, the guy was really starting to get under Adam's skin. He got that tensions were high, but Nick Tavich's anger crossed a threshold, as far as Adam was concerned.

"Can you tell me the last time you spoke to Gwen, Mrs. Tavich?" Adam asked.

Darla Tavich cleared her throat. "It was Saturday during the day."

"Did she seem upset?"

"Yes—she had to get off the phone with me because the dealership had sent a tow truck to pick up her car. She was very frustrated with the situation. I told her she needed to get a different vehicle, but she didn't want to hear it. She told me she would call me back—but I guess she got busy." She looked away, and Adam could see the woman was wishing she had initiated calling her daughter back. Thinking if she had maybe it would've changed the course of the events which had taken her daughter from her.

If that wasn't an official stage of grief, it should be, because everyone did it. At some point, typically after someone close dies unexpectedly, people believe they are God and may have pissed away the only chance to save a loved one simply by doing one thing differently.

Adam had so far been lucky not to lose anyone close to him through violent crime, but he understood the need to take some of the blame as a part of the acceptance of death. "And what about you?" He pointed at Nick and Noah.

"I haven't actually spoken to Gwen in a couple of weeks," Noah said.

"What does that mean, 'actually spoken'?"

"The three of us—Nick, Gwen, and I—have a group text on Friday nights. Just to check in, stay caught up with each other. We all live in different cities."

"And did you text on Friday night, February twenty-first?"

"Yes."

"Anything unusual about the texts?"

Noah glanced sideways at Nick, but Nick was looking down at his feet. "Uh, no, not really."

"'Not really'?"

"Yes, not really," Nick responded through gritted teeth. His eyes were dark, his lips a thin white line across his face. Adam wondered if this was a normal state of being for the man, or if he was unusually belligerent. "We texted like we always do, and there was nothing particularly unusual about the discussion. Is this really how you plan to find who killed my sister? By drilling down on stupid text messages between us?"

Adam maintained eye contact with Nick. "At this point, yes."

"It's sometimes the most insignificant things that can blow an investigation wide open," Kendall said softly. "One statement or action that means absolutely nothing in the whole scheme of things, but can end up being a piece of the puzzle which breaks the case." She gave Nick a supportive, non-condescending smile.

Nick provided a curt nod before looking away. Adam was in awe. Agent Beck was pretty good at diffusing powder keg situations.

His phone buzzed in his pocket. He took it out and glanced at the text message from Fran Ward, the medical examiner, explaining they would be commencing the autopsy on Gwen Tavich in an hour. He turned the phone so Kendall could see it. She nodded at him in understanding.

"I'm truly sorry for your loss." He tossed a couple of business cards on the coffee table. "If you think of anything, please give me a call. I'll have more questions for you after I have information regarding the time and cause of death."

"I'll walk you out," Kendall said.

At the front door, Adam turned to her. "The questions are going to get a lot more probing after the autopsy. I get the feeling there was more going on here between them than big brother Nick wants me to know about."

"They are both very protective of Gwen. She's the baby"—she caught herself, and her eyes dropped to the floor—"*was* the baby." Inhaling, she raised her head and plastered on a smile. "I'll talk to them, see what I can find out."

"Thanks. I'll call after the autopsy and let you know what the ME finds."

21

THE MEDICAL EXAMINER'S Office was in a nondescript building. Adam had been surprised the first time he attended an autopsy there. He wasn't sure what he'd expected—possibly a large neon sign with a swooping arrow pointing to the building, proclaiming "Death done here"—but the single-story, gray stucco seemed too ordinary for what happened on the inside.

Through the brown metal double doors, Adam strolled down the wide cream-colored hallway with industrial gray flooring. After taking a deep cleansing breath and readying himself for the unique and horrible sights and smells he would be greeted with, he entered the autopsy suite. Three stainless steel beds were evenly spaced in a row down the center of the room. On the center bed was the body of Gwen Tavich.

Fran was bent over the handwashing sink at the end of a row of three deep commercial sinks—most likely not all that different from the ones he would find at Gwen Tavich's restaurant. Except he doubted the ones at the restaurant also had scales above them in order to weigh organs.

"Detective Taylor, glad you could make it." Fran's gray scrubs still fit snugly around her belly, a sign of her recent pregnancy. If she was anything like Adam's sisters-in-law, she was probably self-conscious about retaining the added weight now that the bulk of it had been expelled in the form of a baby. He wanted to tell her the added weight still provided a healthy glow, but wasn't sure that was within the realm of professionalism. Her black tennis shoes screeched along the floor as she took a few steps forward. "I'd shake your hand, but I'm all scrubbed up and ready to go." She gestured toward Ms. Tavich. "Shall we proceed?"

Adam stepped toward the end of the table, close enough to see what was happening, but not so close that if he hurled, he would contaminate the evidence. A lesson he'd learned from his partner when he first became a detective; the partner had subsequently been banned from all autopsies. Adam suspected his partner's vomit fest was self-induced with a specific purpose—which he had achieved.

Tapping a pedal on the floor, Fran began providing the basic specifics of Gwen's autopsy, beginning with name, weight, and the entire "dating profile" list of particulars. "X-rays reveal fractures of the sternum and ribs, specifically ribs one, two, and three. No other anomalies are present on the X-rays."

A thin rail of a man, with blond hair tied back in a ponytail and wearing the same gray scrubs and black shoes as Fran, walked into the suite, scrubbed up, and worked his hands into gloves while walking toward the table. Toby, Fran's assistant, picked up a clipboard with the anterior and posterior drawing of a female.

"There is the presence of debris in the victim's hair—dead leaves and twigs—apparently from being in the lake. No petechiae apparent in the eyes. Bruising evident on the right cheek, looks to be approximately two to three days old. No other bruising on the face or neck."

Toby was marking up the picture while Fran spoke.

"Now, the breasts are a different story. Redness around both areolas, along with black charring of the skin consistent with an electrical burn."

Adam stilled for a moment. *What the fuck?* Adam had assumed she'd drowned.

"No other outward injuries to the anterior." Fran tapped the pedal to stop the recorder. "Let's roll Ms. Tavich onto her side."

Fran stared at Gwen's back, her fingers lightly running over the skin. "Marks covering the entirety of the back—appear to be random."

Adam stepped beside the doctor. Barely discernible cuts marred Gwen's entire back. "What caused that?"

"I can't be sure," Fran said slowly as she continued her probe of various cuts. "If I had to guess, I would say they were produced by a razor, or a scalpel perhaps. A very thin blade. What's more interesting is that it appears they were all done at various times. Some appear to be newly made while others are on the brink of being healed. Seem fairly deep too. If Ms. Tavich had survived, she would most likely have had permanent scaring from this."

Adam took out his phone and snapped a couple of pictures of Gwen's back. Fran tapped the recorder and provided details regarding the cuts and stated no other marks were evident on the posterior of the body. She and Toby gently rolled Gwen onto her back.

Fran turned to Adam. "I'm about to begin the tedious aspects of the show, so if you want to bail, now is your chance."

"Yeah, I think I'll head out. Any idea of the cause of death? I'd assumed she drowned in the lake."

"I doubt it, but I can't be sure. I'll let you know what I find out after I complete the autopsy."

"Okay, thanks."

She pointed to a bag sitting in a chair by the door. "Ms. Tavich's personal effects, if you could make sure her family receives them, please?"

"Absolutely."

Adam left the building and placed the bag on the passenger seat of his car. *So, Gwen Tavich didn't drown.* That meant there was a high probability she was killed somewhere else. But where? And by whom?

Seemed like a good time to track down and question Gwen's fiancé, Tyson Butler, and see if he could shed some light on the mystery.

22

DARLA TAVICH HAD moved from the living room into the four seasons room, where it was not only more comfortable, but brighter. Given the dark news, and the plunge into grief and depression providing an oppressive gray heaviness to the house, any bit of light was welcome. Sunlight bathed the room, bouncing off the white furniture and walls, adding much needed heat to the day. Kendall laid a tray with the china tea set Darla loved—the one Gwen had given her for Christmas a couple of years ago—on the table.

Dropping a sugar cube, some milk, and pouring the tea, Kendall asked, "How are you feeling?"

"I'm not quite sure." Darla stuffed her tissue into the sweater's wristband, just the way Kendall had seen her mother do a million times. "I—I'm exhausted. Just thinking about all the unanswered questions. Why would someone do this to my Gwen? What do we do now? How will we ever live without our baby girl?" She leaned closer to the coffee table, grasped the handle of the teacup, and slowly brought it to her lips. "So many plans to be made, and I don't want to do any of them. Usually when I feel overwhelmed, I call Gwen and she helps me. I just can't imagine life without her."

"No decisions have to be made today," Kendall said, placing a consoling hand on Darla's shoulder. "Today is just about letting it all sink in. I'm still trying to get used to the idea that Gwen won't be at the house when I get home tonight."

Kendall slowly swirled the spoon around in her own cup of tea until all of the sugar had dissolved, concentrating too hard on the motion of the liquid. Desperate for the surge of raw emotions to pass over her.

"I know you two were like sisters, and you will miss her as much as we will." Darla squeezed Kendall's hand and smiled.

"She was."

"I'm most sad at the way things were left between her and her brothers."

"What do you mean?"

"They had some sort of disagreement and decided to cancel the Sunday family dinner."

Interesting. Kendall hadn't known about any discord between the siblings. Which was curious, because it was something Gwen normally would've shared with her. "Do you know what the disagreement was about?"

"No, they don't talk to me about any of the important stuff. I guess they think I'm too old and fragile to handle anything." She sighed and took a sip of tea. "With Robert's condition, they just don't want to burden me with anything. I'm a lot stronger than they give me credit for." Her mouth curved into a slight frown and she shook her head. "They love me and take such good care of me and Robert—I really shouldn't complain."

Kendall wanted to ask more questions, but the doorbell rang. Darla started to stand, but Kendall placed a hand on her arm to stop her. "I'll get it." Gwen's killer was still at large. No way was Kendall going to allow Darla to walk into a possible ambush. The killer could be going after family members because of some business deal gone wrong with Robert's company. They just didn't know enough about the murder to establish a motive, so everything was on the table.

And everyone a suspect—no matter who they were.

"If that's Susie, let her in, dear. Anyone else, tell them I'm lying down."

Kendall nodded. She didn't even need to open the door to confirm it was Susie. The Taviches' longtime neighbor was from Texas originally, and hadn't lost her accent or her big hair. She was possibly one of the nicest people Kendall had ever met.

"Hi, Susie," Kendall greeted her as soon as the door was open.

"Hi, sweetheart." A friendly smile was on her face—Kendall had actually never seen her without one—but her eyes were red and puffy from crying. She lifted the casserole dish she was holding. "I made chicken and dumplings."

Kendall took the dish from her and stepped back. "Come in. Darla's in the sunroom."

She gave Kendall a one-arm hug as she moved past. "Thank you so much for being here. This is going to be so hard on them all." Tears welled in her eyes and rolled down her cheeks. She swiped at them, put her smile back in place, and walked toward the sunroom.

Kendall swallowed down the grief swamping her. It was strange being in the house. She had spent so much time here, so many weekends and school breaks when she was in college. Kendall and Gwen didn't always like staying in the dorms— that novelty wore off after the first month as freshmen—so, until they got an apartment together at the start of their junior year, they often spent time at the Tavich home.

But Kendall had never been here without Gwen. And her loss was unbearably apparent. So many things were going to change because of Gwen's death. Would she remain as close to the Taviches as she had been for the last twelve years? Or would the connection slowly thin out until it broke or just disappeared, neither side knowing how or when it occurred? Or why. Just that it had.

Kendall shook the thoughts from her head. She wouldn't let that happen. She owed it to Gwen to make sure her family still functioned as close to normal as possible. Which meant Kendall would need to be here when they needed her. And maybe sometimes when they didn't think they did.

She walked into the kitchen and set the casserole on the kitchen island. Noah was standing at the sink, filling the coffee carafe with water, staring out the window. He turned to her when the glass casserole dish clinked against the counter. "Hey."

"Hey, you okay?"

"Yep, just making coffee."

Water poured over the top of the full carafe and down the drain. "You need some help with that?" Kendall pointed at the carafe.

He let out a humorless chuckle. "Maybe." He turned the water off and drained some of the overflow from the pot. "What's that?" He gestured toward the casserole.

"Susie's chicken and dumplings."

Noah moved across the kitchen to the coffee maker and poured the water into the reservoir. "I should've known she would be the first over—with something wonderful to eat."

"She's in with your mom."

"She's a good friend. Mom's going to need all the support she can get." He scooped the coffee into the filter, and hit the brew button. Turning toward her, he leaned against the counter. "This just makes no sense. Who would do this?"

"I don't know." She had been asked this by victims' families for so many years, but had never felt the desperate panic of uncertainty flowing through her veins, chilling her. This time it was personal. It was Gwen. And a gut-wrenching fear she would never find out who had done this grew inside her. Unable to give Gwen's family the solace of knowing her murderer would never see the light of day.

She took in air and held it for a moment, treading carefully, knowing she needed to ask questions without it coming off as an interrogation. But if she was going to give Gwen's family the closure they needed, she was going to do what she did best— investigate. "When did you talk to her last?"

"It was—Jesus, over a week ago? Friday? We had our usual weekly text check-in." Noah looked down at his feet. "It didn't go well."

"What do you mean? What happened?"

The coffee maker beeped. Noah grabbed two mugs from the cabinet and filled them. "Nick was upset at Gwen. Sometimes those two are like oil and water." He sighed. "Or maybe they are just too much alike." His Adam's apple bobbed as he swallowed and pushed a mug across the counter to her. "*Were* too much alike."

Kendall pulled out one of the bar stools and sat. "Why was Nick upset?" She took a tentative sip of the hot liquid, hoping it would provide some sort of soothing warmth to her cold body. She doubted anything but time would snap the arctic chill inside of her.

"Nick doesn't think we should be paying people to look after Mom and Dad when Gwen is right here in town."

"What do you mean? Like the home health nurses who take care of your dad?" Kendall refused to believe Nick would deny his father the care he needed so he could remain in his home after his stroke. No one wanted Robert to be in a nursing home, but there was no way Darla could take care of him on her own. There was too much involved, especially with him on the ventilator.

Noah shrugged. "I think it was more the addition of household help he had a problem with." Noah placed his empty mug on the counter. "Look, Kendall, I don't want to give you the wrong impression. Nick wants my mom and dad taken care of; it's just—well—sometimes Gwen was not as forthcoming with information on the finances as we would like."

"But you all agreed she was the best to handle that stuff." Kendall remembered how difficult it had been on the family when they learned the devastating effects of Robert's stroke and how he would be confined to a bed for the rest of his life, unable to breathe without aid of a ventilator. "And to have round-the-clock care."

"True, and we do still agree that's best. And we don't think Gwen was doing anything wrong or intentionally being secretive, but she doesn't always like when Nick asks her to explain where, and how much, money is going out." He dragged his hand down over his face, looking ten years older than he had when Kendall had arrived that morning. "I guess Nick's last text was somewhat prophetic—he may have to take over the family finances."

He pushed himself off the counter. "I'm going to go check on Dad. We need to tell him about Gwen, but want to wait for the doctor to get here in case he has medical issues once he learns Gwen is gone."

Kendall nodded. "Do you know where Nick is?"

Noah pointed to the backyard.

23

T HE THIRD FLOOR of the police department, where all the detectives were located, was quiet on Saturday when Adam arrived. He hung up his jacket, tossed his cell phone on the desk, and dropped into his chair. He had spent the entire ride from the morgue with the window down despite the cold weather. It was always the smell that lingered. Got caught up inside the nostrils. And the smell conjured up memories of the body he had just seen on the cold metal table.

Not just a body. Kendall Beck's best friend. Darla Tavich's daughter. Adam picked up the phone and called the desk sergeant.

"Clifton," the gruff voice coughed into the phone by way of greeting.

"Hey, it's Taylor. Is there an open conference room?"

Adam heard the clicking of keys on the computer. "Jesus, Taylor, you plan on taking up all the conference rooms? You're lucky we don't have a rule that you have to solve a case before you get another conference room."

Adam bit his tongue, which prevented him from telling the desk sergeant to shove his opinions up his ass. Although, the fact he was running two major murder investigations and had virtually no leads in either case was worrisome.

"Case name and number?" the sergeant asked.

Adam rattled off the information. He brought up DL license information on everyone involved in the case so far, and printed out their pictures, along with the snaps he had taken at Gwen's autopsy. Then he gathered his files, collected the items from the printer, and flipped on the light in what would be his home until this case was solved. He taped the pictures onto the white-board, adding names and other pertinent information under each. When he sat down at the table, he stared at the board. Too much white space. Not enough information.

He emptied the bag of Gwen's personal items onto the table. A ring with a black pearl surrounded by tiny diamonds, Adam assumed it was her engagement ring. A necklace with a sterling silver heart pendant, an emerald in the center. A day planner. He flipped through a few pages but couldn't understand any of the notations. It appeared Gwen had a distinctive shorthand he hoped Kendall would be able to decipher. Gwen's purse. Adam flipped it open: wallet with ID, credit cards, and twenty-seven dollars in cash.

And Gwen Tavich's cell phone. He plugged in the charger, pressed the screen, and it lit up.

Notifications of phone calls; several from her mother, Kendall, and both of her brothers. He scrolled through the list again, searching for one name. Ty Butler, the victim's fiancé, had not tried to get in touch with her since the last time she'd opened her phone. From the time listed on the last call, that had been for a call from Gwen's mother on Sunday morning at around ten.

His own cell phone buzzed. He swiped his finger across the screen. "Taylor."

"Adam, Fran Ward. I have some preliminary information on the Gwen Tavich case."

Adam slid a notepad close to him and clicked his pen. "What did you find?"

"No evidence of lake water in the victim's lungs, so my ear-lier assumption she hadn't drowned was correct."

Lake water in her lungs would mean Gwen had been breath-ing and taken water into her lungs. Gwen had died before being placed in the lake. "So what killed her?"

"Cardiac arrest as the result of electrocution. As I mentioned during the autopsy, the victim had electrical burns around her breasts."

"You said also that her broken ribs were due to chest compressions. Is it possible the person was performing CPR and when that didn't work, tried a defibrillator? Could the defibrillator have caused those burns?"

"Not likely. That's not how defibrillators work."

Adam mulled that over. So how on earth had Gwen Tavich received enough of an electrical current to put her into cardiac arrest? And what the hell was going on resulting in burns on her breasts?

"I've seen injuries similar to this before," Fran said. "They are usually a result of engaging in electrophilia."

Adam wrote the word down. "Which is?"

"The use of an electrical stimulus to become sexually aroused. Akin to autoerotic asphyxiation, except instead of depriving the body of oxygen, an electric shock is administered. However, this is the first time I've seen it around the breasts."

"I'm almost afraid to ask where it's normally found."

"Mostly in males around the genitalia and anus."

Adam squirmed in his chair, uncomfortable with the idea of being shocked through his favorite playmate.

"To do it to the breasts is like playing with fire—extremely dangerous."

"How so?"

"The stimulus is too close to the heart. In our victim's case, the electric shock—or shocks, as I believe it would have to have been more than one, and most likely in rapid succession for it to cause death—would cause the heart to go into fibrillation. Fibrillation is a heart rhythm problem, causing the heart to beat erratically. The ventricles quiver and stop pumping blood, essentially becoming useless."

"Is this something Gwen could've done on her own?"

"Yes. Most deaths caused by electrophilia are caused by men administering the electric stimulus to themselves. Perhaps, in those cases, if someone else had been there, the chance for survival, while still slim, would have been increased. However, I find it hard to believe that Ms. Tavich did this to herself, died of cardiac arrest, then drove herself to the lake."

"Could she have tried to get herself to the hospital while being in cardiac arrest?"

"Doubtful. If she had been able to function, I would've expected her to wreck her vehicle long before she decided to stop at the lake. Better likelihood she died while the electric shock was being administered."

"Okay. Anything else?"

"Still working out time of death but will let you know when I have a good feel for it."

"Thanks, Doc." Adam disconnected the call, sat back in his chair, and stared at the photo of Gwen Tavich on his murder board. Had she been exploring a little kink and it went horribly wrong? With who? Her fiancé? Someone else? Was her relationship with Kendall closer than he had originally thought? Had whomever she'd been with panicked and dumped the body to avoid getting into trouble?

Or had this been an intentional murder? He stared at the cuts on Gwen's back. Someone had taken their time slicing into her while she was still alive. The doc had said Gwen's injuries were consistent with receiving chest compressions. Had someone caused Gwen to go into cardiac arrest and then brought her back from the edge of death, just to do it over and over again?

If so, that was a clear case of murder.

He picked up his cell phone from the table and grabbed his coat and keys from his cubicle.

The most likely suspect in any murder is a spouse or significant other. Tyson Butler was done avoiding Adam. There were too many questions, and all of them were starting to center around Gwen's fiancé.

24

Nick was sitting in the sun, cigar burning, more than a couple fingers of scotch in his glass. The half-empty bottle of Macallan 25 sat on the table next to the ashtray.

"Mind if I join you?" Kendall asked, standing next to the adjacent chair.

"Be my guest." He waved toward the open chair. For a moment they both just sat in silence. Kendall had known this man for a few years. He was intimidating, much like his father. Not that Kendall had ever felt apprehensive around him, but she knew from Gwen that he had made an art form of bullying people. When Gwen was a child, it had worked in her favor. As she grew to an adult, Nick turned his blustering toward her and was not happy when his baby sister stood her ground and fought back. But Kendall was seeing a new side to Nick since he'd learned of Gwen's death. Annoyed, tense. Uneasy. The sorrow was there, yes, but he was also on edge.

"My wife wanted to come down from Fort Collins, but I told her no. It probably hurt her feelings, but I just can't handle her and the kids right now. She wants to comfort me, but I don't want to be comforted. I don't want to be told everything will be okay—it won't, and I don't want her to lie to me and tell me it will." He took a long drag off the cigar and slowly pushed the smoke from his lungs. "I'm a selfish bastard—just like Gwen said I was."

"Gwen loved and respected you. Envied the life you have with Sasha and the kids. She never saw herself as becoming a mother because of the demands of the restaurant."

"The restaurant," Nick snorted. "That place stole so much of her time and energy. For no apparent reason that I can see."

Kendall knew Nick had never believed the restaurant was as important or demanding as his job teaching chemistry at Colorado State University. It was strange to hear him actually express it. And a part of Kendall was suddenly offended for Gwen and wanted to defend her in her absence. But to what end? Kendall needed Nick talking, not fighting with her over his sister's choice of career.

It didn't really matter anymore. Gwen was gone.

"Noah said the three of you texted on Friday a week ago, and you were upset."

His eyes narrowed, and his gaze shifted sideways over to her. "You going to question me like I'm a suspect, Kendall?"

"Would you prefer the questions come from me and the information be passed to Detective Taylor by me, or would you like for him to draw his own conclusions from your answers?"

Nick took another long drag from the cigar and nois-ily exhaled the smoke. Exasperation flowed from and swirled around him, mixing with the cigar smoke and creating tension in the air between them.

"Yes, we texted a week ago Friday. We all decided to forego the Sunday night dinner here at the house. I have a lot going on—tests to grade, the necessary work of molding the minds of future chemists so that cures can be discovered and the world can be eradicated of some of the diseases that plague it."

Nick always did think highly of himself. Not without merit—he was a genius with chemical compounds, just not with interpersonal skills. Odd he wasn't giving her the full story, though. Noah had said Nick was upset at Gwen, and that was what led to the decision to skip the monthly family dinner. Was he intentionally trying to hide the fact that he and Gwen had been at odds? Or was he not able to confront the truth that he would never be able to right things with his sister?

"And that was the last time you had contact with her?"

There was a long silence, and Kendall wondered if he had even heard her question. He took a large gulp of the expensive scotch, set the glass on the table, and added more spirit. "No. I called her on Saturday."

"You talked to her on the phone?"

"Yes."

"What about?"

"Nothing of import."

Patience was waning, and Kendall was already tired of the half answers. "Are you going to force me to pull teeth to get answers from you? Because you either tell me what was going on, or you tell Taylor, but your refusal to cooperate is sending a really lousy message."

He took a final drag from the cigar and mashed it out. His body was rigid, and he wouldn't look at her. "During our texting session, Gwen made it clear she was upset at me for not coming home enough. She never understood the importance of my position and that I can't just up and go somewhere whenever I want. I have a family. Responsibilities. I was frustrated, she was frustrated; Noah just wanted us all to get along. We decided to skip the family dinner. It was a decision made in haste in the heat of the moment."

Swirling the Macallan in his glass, he took a sip and let the liquid sit in his mouth before swallowing. Was he savoring the spirit as it was meant to be? Or buying time while he came up with a version of the phone call which wouldn't make him look as if he'd been angry with Gwen the day of her disappearance?

"I wanted to apologize and set things straight with her, so I called her. We talked and got things sorted out. Then the subject of finances came up. It is a sore spot between us, and I'm sorry to say, we argued over how much she was spending of my parents' money on unnecessary luxuries."

"Such as?"

"The cook, when there is only one person to cook for—and Gwen could have food sent from her restaurant for free. The country club membership, when Dad can't golf, and Mom rarely ever goes to the spa anymore. The driver who takes Mom to get her hair done once a week—"

"And to her doctor's appointments," Kendall added defensively.

"Yes, which Gwen could've—*and should've*—been doing. All a waste of money."

Kendall inhaled deeply through her nose. As much as she wanted to argue Gwen's side, there's was little reward in doing so. Kendall needed information—not a win. "Did she give you an explanation as to why she felt it necessary to continue to pay for these things?"

"So Mom wouldn't have to make drastic changes to her life any more than she already has since Dad got sick. And I agreed with her on most things. But it's just not feasible to maintain Bronco season tickets just so Noah can go to a game every once in a while. She swore Dad would never want to give those up. Would want to pass them down and keep them in the family." He shifted in his seat to face her, grasping one of the arm rests. "But that's just it. Dad can't really make those decisions, and Gwen can't unilaterally decide what is and isn't a necessity."

"So how did you end things?"

His shoulders slumped and his voice dropped. "She hung up on me. I tried to call her back, but she wouldn't answer, so I left her a voicemail. One I wish I could take back."

"What did you say?"

"It's inconsequential." He grabbed his glass and the bottle of scotch and went into the house before she could clarify.

Kendall sat for a few minutes, mulling over the information in her head. Money, especially excessive amounts like Gwen's family had, tended to override common sense. And familial bonds. Kendall had seen it time and again. Even the most loving families lost their fucking minds over inheritances. It was a sad but true fact of life. Blood was thicker than water, but not Dom Perignon.

But could Nick have been angry enough at Gwen, and what he considered as her squandering the family fortune, to hurt her?

Or kill her?

25

THE SUN WAS setting when Adam parked in a spot down the street from The Oyster Grille. He had passed by this restaurant a few times over the past couple of years, with its all-glass front. When he and Sheri had been dating, she had dropped a few not-so-subtle hints about wanting to try the place out. Adam had checked the prices of appetizers and decided he didn't want to use an entire paycheck to eat tiny food whose names he couldn't pronounce, on odd-shaped plates.

A young lady dressed in a smart yet simple little black dress, with her long black hair slicked back into a ponytail, reached under her reception desk for a menu. A smile lit up her face. "One for dinner?"

"No, I'm looking for Tyson Butler. Is he here tonight?"

Her smile faltered just a bit, her gaze inadvertently going to the kitchen. "He is—he's cooking right now. Is there something I can help you with? Or perhaps you'd like to leave your name and number, and I can let him know you stopped by and have him contact you when he's free?"

Yeah, if only that would work. So far Tyson Butler had been doing his level best, as far as Adam could tell, of avoiding any conversation or answering any of the voluminous messages Adam had left on his voicemail. Adam pulled his badge from his belt and showed it to her. "I'm afraid I'm going to need to talk to him right now. It's extremely important."

The young woman's eyes widened. "I'll see if he's available."

"Thank you. I appreciate that."

The woman walked away and entered the kitchen. Within a couple of minutes she returned. "He'll be right with you." She didn't wait for a response from Adam. She turned her back and began shuffling through the menus.

Ten minutes later, a large man, roughly six feet tall, with a muscular build, strode from the kitchen, wearing black pants and a black chef's jacket, the top button undone so the collar flopped over to one side. According to his driver's license information, he had just turned forty.

"Tyson Butler?"

Adam could feel Butler's inquisitiveness, but not fear or apprehension. Adam had become pretty adept over the years at reading people and their mannerisms. Butler was relaxed yet curious.

"Yes, how can I help you?" His eyes caught sight of the badge, and his demeanor shifted just slightly.

"I'm Detective Taylor with the Denver Police Department. I'm wondering if I can ask you some questions?" He clipped his badge back onto his belt and reached to shake Butler's hand.

"What about?" Butler squared his shoulders.

"Is there someplace more private we can talk?"

He nodded and walked back to the kitchen. "Martin, I'll be a while longer—hold down the fort."

A younger guy, wearing a white chef's jacket, glanced up at them as they passed by the grill. Adam wondered if there was an industry distinction between the different-colored jackets.

Butler led Adam into a small office and closed the door behind him. "What's so important you have to bother me while I'm at work?"

"You're a difficult man to get in touch with, Mr. Butler. I've tried calling and left several messages for you to call me back."

"I'm a busy man. This restaurant doesn't run itself."

"Gwen Tavich is your partner. Doesn't she help?"

"Gwen's not here."

"Is it her night off?"

He shifted his weight and wrapped his muscular arms across his chest. "No."

"Well, I assume you called to find out why she wasn't here?"

Butler's lips flattened. "No."

"Odd." Adam stroked his chin and watched Butler for a moment. The man was definitely tense, but then again, most people tensed up when talking with cops, even if they'd done nothing wrong. "That doesn't strike you as weird?"

He shrugged. "I'm not sure where it's any of your concern how I run my business. So, what's your point, Detective?"

"You seem rather dispassionate about your business partner and fiancée—to the extent of not returning calls from a law enforcement officer who is inquiring after her."

"Kendall already talked to me about Gwen. We agreed she just needed to get away for a bit. Take some time for herself. Since Kendall's with the FBI, I figured she had things under control."

Adam was calling bullshit. "Yeah, she's with a different agency than me—we investigate different crimes."

The lines on Butler's forehead deepened and his eyebrows scrunched together. "What crime are you investigating?"

"When was the last time you saw or spoke to Gwen?"

"Why?" His left eye twitched.

"Mr. Butler, this will go a lot faster if you could refrain from answering a question with a question. I promise to address your concerns if you'll just indulge me for a moment."

His eyes narrowed. Adam tried not to focus on the constant twitch in Butler's eye, but it was distracting. And it was alerting him that Butler was as nervous as a hooker in a confessional.

"Last time you spoke to Ms. Tavich?" Adam repeated.

"She called me last Saturday night from work."

"What time was that?"

"Uhh . . . it must've been about midnight. She called to tell me how the night went and to let me know she wasn't coming over to my place."

"Did you have plans for her to come over?" Adam already knew the answer to this, but Butler's answer might reveal more than he intended.

"Yeah, but she said she had a headache and just wanted to go home. So I told her I'd see her the next day."

"And you didn't see or hear from her after that phone call?"

"No, I went to bed."

"Why weren't you at work last Saturday night?"

He darted his eyes over to Adam. "What?"

"Well, you are the head chef, correct? Why wouldn't you have been at work on the busiest night of the week?"

"I told you: I didn't feel well. Gwen had Martin, our sous chef, handle the executive chef duties."

"And do you do that often? Have him take over for you?"

"He's my replacement on night's I take off."

"And how many nights do you take off a week?"

"Usually only one . . . sometimes two. Not more than that, though." He squared his shoulders.

"And did you see Gwen on Sunday? Or talk to her?"

"No." He lifted his chin. "All right, I've answered your questions. Now, tell me what this is all about. Why all the questions about Gwen and me?"

"I'm sorry to have to tell you, Mr. Butler, but Ms. Tavich is dead."

Butler stumbled back and hit the door. "What are you talking about? That can't be."

"I'm afraid it's true, sir. I'm very sorry for your loss." Adam felt bad for the guy, but he wasn't here to comfort him. He had a job to do. A job that entailed observing Butler's raw reactions.

Butler's hands went to his head and he shook it back and forth. "No, no . . . not Gwen. Please, not Gwen." He looked at Adam, his eyes glossy, and Adam would swear they were begging him to take back those words. "How did it happen?"

"We aren't sure of the specifics. Her body was found in a lake not far from where she lived." Adam tempered his voice, offering a hint of sympathy. "Mr. Butler, do you know of anyone who would want to harm Ms. Tavich?"

His eyes widened for a split second. He immediately looked away, staring at the floor. "No. I have no idea why anyone would kill Gwen. Why? Who do you think did this?"

"We don't know—that's why I'm asking you questions."

"I didn't have anything to do with it." The words were sharp, his voice elevated, and his eyes flamed.

Odd response. Usually people try to come up with a name or two of someone who may have had a beef with the victim.

But this—this was instantaneous defensiveness. Not a normal reaction until there has at least been a hint of an accusation. Mr. Butler was feeling guilty about something. Adam just needed to figure out what.

"Were either of you having any issues with anyone at the restaurant? Former employees who might be carrying around a grudge? Any customers giving her a hard time?"

"No, no, there was nothing like that going on." He looked up, eyes still wide. "Did you talk to Kendall?"

"Yes, she was my first stop. Do you think she could have had anything to do with it? Were there any issues between them?"

"No, no way. Gwen and Kendall were like sisters. Add in Quentin, and you had a girls' night out." He let out a humorless chuckle.

"Do you think Mr. Novak could do this?"

"Shit, have you met Quentin? The dude has no balls— he wouldn't have the sac to hurt anyone, let alone kill them. Besides, Quentin loves Gwen as much as he loves Kendall. That's how it works."

"Left you on the outside. Did that piss you off?"

He snorted. "Quentin's all right. I don't have any issues with him. He's just an easy target for jokes. Dude's quiet, but he's cool. I was happy to have some type of male presence around the girls—such as it was."

"I don't know—Novak seems like he might be able to hold his own. He looked like he was in pretty good shape."

"Yeah, he's got some muscle to him, but he's never thrown a punch in his life, as far as I know. He's all brawn without any street smarts."

Something was off . . . *What the hell am I missing?*

He reread his notes in an exercise of futility. "You spoke with Gwen around midnight? Were you at home at the time?"

"Yes." There it was again, that damn eye twitch.

"Leave at all after the phone call? Go anywhere? See anyone?" Adam stared Butler straight in the quiver. This guy had great facial tics that were telling a compelling story, if Adam could just fit the pieces together.

"No, I was there all night." Double twitch. *Interesting.*

"Was anyone with you? Can anyone verify you were there all night and didn't leave?"

The twitch was running amuck, along with eyes that had turned to slits. "No. I was home alone. No one was there with me. And I resent the implication, Detective."

Nice overreaction, Mr. Butler.

"I apologize if you think I was inferring anything. I'm simply trying to ascertain if you had anyone who could corroborate your statement."

Ty's eyes shifted away, and he took a deep breath. His shoulders dropped. "No." He shook his head. "No one can corroborate I was home all night." The man looked defeated—or maybe guilty—but of what, Adam couldn't be sure.

"And how were things between you and Gwen?"

"Fine." The answer came too fast. Something was there.

"Did the two of you engage in any type of sexual games?"

"*What?* What the hell kind of question is that?"

"I have to ask. Due to the way Gwen died, there are some questions as to types of sexual arousal she was engaged in."

"What the fuck are you talking about?"

Adam usually didn't like to give out information to a potential suspect, but he couldn't see any way of getting the answers he needed from Butler without providing some facts.

"According to the medical examiner, the cause of death was cardiac arrest brought on by electrical stimulation. It's possible Gwen was engaging in a type of sexual stimulation through the use of electrical application to her body."

Butler gave Adam a look of disbelief—or disgust—Adam wasn't sure which. "You think Gwen died because of a sex game gone wrong?"

"It's where the evidence is leading."

"And you think I'm going to talk to you about my sex life?"

"Mr. Butler, in any investigation, the people closest to the victim are the ones we look at first. Since this seems to be associated with a sex act, I'm naturally going to ask her long-time boyfriend and fiancé about it. Is there a reason you don't want to answer these questions?"

"Yeah, it's none of your damn business what Gwen and I did in the privacy of our bedroom."

"It does if it's the cause of death." Adam paused. He needed to get Butler off the defensive as much as possible in order to get anything out of him that would move the investigation forward. "It's nothing to be ashamed of, Mr. Butler, and I can assure you I'm not making any judgments. But I do need you to answer my question, no matter how uncomfortable it makes you."

"You can go to hell."

"Did something happen on Saturday night between the two of you?"

"What are you insinuating?"

"Perhaps Gwen did come over. You engaged in sex, things got out of control, and Gwen died as a result. Maybe you panicked—which would be understandable. You took Gwen to the lake and dumped her there. It wouldn't be the first time someone acted uncharacteristically and lost it." Adam took a deep breath and held up a hand in defense. "I know I might if I was in that situation."

Butler stared at Adam, his nostrils flared, his eyes wide. "Am I under arrest?"

"No, we're just having a conversation."

Butler reached for the handle and opened the door. "Get the fuck out of my restaurant."

Adam sighed and dropped a business card on the desk. "If you think of anything, give me a call." He stepped up to Butler. "But we're not through."

Tyson Butler was lying. And Adam was determined to find out what about and why.

Adam walked out to the front of the restaurant to the hostess area.

"Can you tell me the name of the manager and let him know I would like to speak to him?"

The hostess scrunched up her nose as if Adam had let loose an offensively stinky fart. "Sandra Bennett is the manager, and *she's* busy with customers, so you may need to wait a few minutes."

"Not a problem." Adam glanced over at the bar. "Can I order food in there?"

"Yes, sir. We serve our full menu in the bar as well as the dining room."

He gave her a two-finger salute, walked into the bar, and plunked down on a black velvet stool.

"What can I get for you?" the bartender asked, placing a cocktail napkin in front of Adam.

He probably shouldn't, being on duty and all. *Fuck it.*

"Beer."

"Any preference?" The bartender peered at Adam, probably assessing whether or not Adam had enough money to afford the overpriced alcohol served in this joint.

"Give me your favorite craft on tap."

"You got it," the man said. "Would you like a menu?"

Adam considered it for a moment. It might take a huge chunk out of his grocery fund for the month, but he had seen the steaks being prepared in the kitchen and was dying to sink his teeth into one. *What the hell—at least I'm only paying for one meal.* "Why not?"

The bartender smiled and passed a menu across the bar to him. Jumping straight to the entrees, Adam found what he was looking for—a New York strip. His stomach rumbled in appreciation of the choice and anticipation of the feast. Then his eyes took in the price, and his wallet actually laughed.

He flipped the menu over. A selection of sushi. *Nope.* He hated raw fish. Sheri loved the shit—which should've told him something about her—and was hellbent on getting him to try the crap. When he told her the reasons he wouldn't, she became very animated about how he was an idiot, some other stuff about sushi wasn't always raw, blah blah blah. He would tune her out at that point because he just didn't care. He wasn't eating sushi. Period. End of story.

The spicy pork ribs on the appetizer menu would satisfy both his stomach and his wallet, so he ordered them.

He pressed the speed dial for Saul, and when the man answered, said, "Find anything linking Jenna Rose with any other murders?"

"Other than very basic shit—no. A few young women have been murdered in the area over the past few years and the cases remain unsolved, but so far, that's all that's linking them. It's going to involve a little more digging to find the needle in the haystack. If there is one."

"Keep looking. It's a long shot, I know, but I'd rather be sure it's a dead end. The alternative is not a road I want to go down. Especially now we have the Tavich murder to work."

Saul grunted. Adam always took that as acquiescence, but was equally sure Saul was casting aspersions on Adam's birth under his breath. Adam's motto: *Ignorance is bliss.*

"Speaking of the Tavich murder"—he could hear Saul shuffling papers—"I've got background checks on all the major players so far."

"Anything stand out?"

"Nope. Gwen Tavich didn't have so much as a parking ticket."

"What about the fiancé?"

"Got into some trouble when he was young—nothing very exciting. DC and DUI during college. Clean since then."

Disorderly conduct and driving under the influence. Not unusual for young males.

"Any evidence of domestic violence?"

"Not that was reported. Fletch has a couple of names of former girlfriends he's left messages with, but Butler and Tavich had been an item since their senior year in college."

Adam shifted in his seat to get a better view of the restaurant. A woman in a smart black suit approached the hostess stand. The hostess pointed at Adam. The woman nodded and then continued to speak to the hostess.

"See what you can find out about the Tavich family—specifically her two older brothers. One has a quick temper. Also, get financial records for Tavich, Butler, and the business." Saul grunted again, and Adam ended the call.

"Here you go, sir." The bartender slid the beer glass toward him. "Local brewery, makes a great stout aged in bourbon barrels."

"Thanks." Adam took a drink and was pleasantly surprised.

"Detective Taylor?"

The woman in the smart suit stood next to him, her hand outstretched. She had a smile on her face, but her eyes were red and puffy. "Sandra Bennett. I'm the manager."

Adam put the beer down, wiped his hand along his pants, and took hers.

"Ty told me about Gwen . . . I just can't believe it." She swiped at new tears forming along the rim of her eyelids before they had a chance to fall.

"I'm very sorry for your loss."

Ms. Bennett glanced around the restaurant. "I haven't told the staff yet."

"I'm going to need to question everyone. Is there a way you can send them over to me as they get off and before they leave the restaurant?"

"I can do one better. We are in the process of closing early, so as soon as I get the last of the customers out, the staff will be at your service. If I can just ask that you not tell them until I can tell everyone at the same time?"

"Of course." Adam was once again thankful for not having to be the one to drop a bomb of horrendous news on people. "I'm a little shocked Mr. Butler would want to lose out on all the profits you pull in on a Saturday night. According to him, this is the busiest night of the week."

Her smile faltered a bit. "Yes, well, Ty took off right after he told me about Gwen, so he doesn't get a say in how I run the restaurant—especially tonight."

There didn't seem to be much love lost between the head chef and the manager. But there was a whole lot of animosity, at least at the moment.

Adam extracted his notepad from his jacket pocket and clicked his ballpoint pen. "When was the last time you saw Gwen?"

"A week ago Saturday. I worked the early shift—opened for lunch and got off around eight that night, when things started to slow down."

"Is that your usual shift on Saturdays?"

"Yes, until today. Ty asked me to close the restaurant tonight. God knows he doesn't know how to do it."

"He doesn't stay until closing?"

"No, he stays through the rush and then lets Martin close the kitchen down and prep for the next day. When he deigns to come into work, that is."

"How was Gwen last Saturday night?"

"Normal. Irritated with Ty for not coming in, but that was becoming commonplace lately. Ty has been out sick more than he's been here."

"Was he always like that?"

"No, just over the last few months. When I first started here, he and Gwen were a force to be reckoned with. Once the restaurant started to make a name for itself, things seemed to shift."

"Do you know why?"

"No."

"Were Mr. Butler's absences causing issues or tension between them?"

She huffed out a laugh. "Them. The staff. It had a trickle-down effect. It was sad to see. Gwen works—worked—so hard to create a happy environment where staff felt like family and people enjoyed coming in. It was fun. And it helped tremendously with employee retention."

"So, if last Saturday was the last time you saw Gwen, who has been running the restaurant?"

"Me. And, to his credit, Ty has stepped up. He's been here more in the last week than he has in the previous three weeks combined."

Interesting. What had changed with Ty in the last three months? Had something happened between him and Gwen? Had they been on the outs, and he was avoiding her? Or were they at odds about how to run the business?

"Where did you think Gwen was?"

"I thought maybe something happened with her father or—god forbid—her mother. I asked Ty if he knew where she was. He said he didn't, but figured she just needed some time away from the restaurant. I asked him if she was at her parents, but he shrugged. I guessed that perhaps he didn't want to betray a confidence—you know, an *if Gwen wanted me to know, she would've told me* sort of thing—so I let it go. Figured Gwen would get in touch with me when she could. It made sense to me, somewhat."

"Meaning?"

"Gwen is extremely conscientious. It's odd she would just be gone without telling me what the plan is."

"Did you bring that up with Ty?"

She shook her head. "I figured this was what I was hired to do—manage in her absence. And if she was gone, she had a good reason for it. She's here the majority of the time—this business can be exhausting—and she never takes any real time off. Even on days off, she was doing work from home. Payroll, other administrative things."

"So, you accepted Mr. Butler's theory for Gwen's extended absence?"

"Yes, but I still tried to get in touch with her." She looked off over Adam's shoulder, her eyes glazed over. "Now, I wish I'd been a little more firm in demanding where she was. Maybe I should've reported her missing. Something."

Adam leaned into her just enough to get her attention. "Just so you know, Gwen's roommate, Kendall, tried to file a report. Even she couldn't get us to list Gwen as missing. She had to report her vehicle stolen, and even then, it was a long shot that anyone would look very hard. Unfortunately, vehicles are stolen every day, so they aren't a priority. And as much as family and friends are sure a loved one would never leave without telling them—it's the case more often than not. It makes it very difficult to report an adult missing without some sort of evidence of foul play." Adam paused for a second to let that sink in.

Ms. Bennett gave a slight nod of understanding, but Adam guessed she still felt as if she could've saved Gwen if she had done something. Not unusual—hindsight being twenty–twenty and all that.

Adam redirected the conversation. "Did you question Mr. Butler about it after you initially asked him?"

"I tried to, but he would get irritated with me. He told me Gwen was fine and not to worry. It wasn't until Kendall came by to talk to Ty that I finally decided he might be right."

"Why do say that?"

"Well, I figured if Kendall bought Ty's explanation, I had no room to question it. Kendall and Gwen have been best friends since college. Maybe Gwen had done something like this in the past—before I knew her."

"How long have you been here?"

"Three years."

Plausible, Adam guessed. But then again, there would've been some sign over the past three years that Gwen Tavich was prone to just taking off, wouldn't there?

"You said Mr. Butler left through the back?"

"Yes, there's an employee parking lot."

"Is there a security camera back there?"

"Yes."

"Would I be able to see the footage from last Saturday night."

"Of course. After the employees have gone, I can show you. The computer is back in Gwen's office." Her gaze darted to the front of the restaurant. "I'm sorry, I need to help close the restaurant, and smooth over some ruffled feathers of customers upset at being asked to leave."

Adam turned back to his beer and took another long drink.

"Can I ask you a couple of questions?" Adam asked as the bartender delivered his food. Adam laid his badge on the bar for the man to see.

"If you don't mind me working while you do."

"Did you work last Saturday night?"

"Nope. Dave was here."

"Dave?"

"Collins. We alternate weekends."

"That's a great idea."

"In Dave's case, it's a necessity. His family has a ranch up in Wyoming. He goes up there every other weekend to help out. I guess his dad has some medical issues, and so all the kids chip in to keep things running."

"And Gwen was okay with this arrangement between the two of you?" As soon as the bartender quirked up an eyebrow, Adam realized his mistake in using the past tense in reference to Gwen.

"Uh, yeah . . . it was her idea. She approached both of us with her proposal, and we jumped at the chance."

"Pretty good boss?"

"Awesome boss. I don't think I could ever work for anyone else. I hope I never have to."

Adam raised his beer and took an extraordinarily long draw, feeling like a shit for not letting the man know his worst fear was about to come true.

26

KENDALL SANK INTO the deep cushions on her couch, dropped her head back, and closed her eyes. She had spent the entire day at the Taviches as they tried to come to terms with losing their only daughter. They sat, cried, and remembered. And made plans to say goodbye.

"Here ya go, K."

She opened her eyes to a nearly full glass of red wine hovering just in front of her face. Quentin stood behind the couch, waiting for her to take the glass from him.

"How do you always know what I need?" She took a larger gulp than was customary.

"Well, it could be that I've known you for more than a few years now." He came around and sat next to her. "But it's more likely I thought, 'What would I want waiting for me when I got home from having to tell my friend's family she is gone?'" Quentin took a drink from his glass. "I came up with a big-busted, naked blonde in my bed or a glass of wine. I went with the wine."

"Good call." She clinked her glass against his and took another long swallow.

"So, how was it?" Quentin asked, his voice soft.

Semi-rolling onto her side so she could face him but still nestle into the cushions, she said, "About how you'd expect. I dropped the bomb, tried to console them. Detective Taylor asked some questions and then left. I stayed behind and we called a bunch of family and friends, and cried. A lot."

"Were there a lot of people there?" Quentin asked.

"A few, mostly from her mother's side of the family, since they all still live in the area. I took off when I knew Darla wouldn't be alone, and Nick and Noah would be staying."

He dropped his hand on her knee and squeezed. When she'd first moved back to Denver, some people, including Gwen, thought Q and Kendall were dating. But it never went any further than her knee, leg, or arm. Nothing intimate. Always just good friends.

"Sorry I made you go through that alone." His head dropped, his finger running around the rim of his wineglass. "You know how I am, though. I just never know what to say, and I get uncomfortable and make stupid jokes and then make everyone around me miserable." One side of his mouth quirked up in a smile. "You remember Derek Simmons's funeral."

Kendall chuckled—which was somewhat of a miracle and something only Q could've elicited from her at that point— recalling the memory.

Derek Simmons had been a neighbor who they hung out with sometimes. He would pop over for a beer every once in a while. Nice guy. Moved to the area from Saskatchewan and knew not a soul. Celebrating a promotion and substantial raise, he decided to buy a Porsche, test how fast it would go, and wrapped himself and the car around a large tree. He died instantly.

Quentin, Kendall, Gwen, and Ty had gone to the funeral. In an attempt to calm his nerves, Quentin had had one glass of wine too many at the reception that followed, and had ended up cracking inappropriate dirty jokes with Derek's father—the Reverend Doctor Blaine Simmons.

"I don't think, however, that will excuse you from the funeral. Your presence will be required, if for no other reason than I will need you to keep me from completely falling apart."

He leaned his head against hers. "You got it. I'll always be there for you, K. Always."

"Thanks for sticking around and waiting for me to get back. I was dreading walking into the house and it being so quiet. That's what I'm going to miss—hearing her voice. All the laughter that filled this house when she was here. How will I ever deal with the silence, Q?"

"Day by day. Like you deal with everything life has thrown at you. A little bit at a time until you can take on a little bit more."

Hot tears rolled down her cheeks, and for a split-second she wondered how she could still have any tears left. Her heart hurt. Ached more than the gunshot she had survived. And she was sure the pain would never go away. She had lost her friend. Her sister. Life was never going to be the same from now on. All the truth in her life would become a lie.

"I was thinking I could stay here tonight—that way you won't be alone," he said, his hand running comfortingly over her hair. Q was one of only a few people who had ever seen her cry. He was also the only one—save her father—who she would allow to comfort her.

"Really?" She reared back and looked at him. Relief washed over her like a warm tidal wave. "You don't mind?"

"Not the first time I've slept on this couch." He patted the throw pillow next to him.

"Might be the first time sober," she said.

He tipped the bottle of wine and refilled both wineglasses. "Not if I can help it."

Pizza was ordered and eaten in front of the TV. Sorrows temporarily drowned out by one mindless sitcom after another. Kendall dozed off just before midnight, begging sleep to reach her.

And suppress the nightmare vision of Gwen, floating face-down in a lake.

27

MOST OF THE Oyster employees had worked the previous Saturday night, but so far, no one remembered anything out of the ordinary. Melissa Martinez was the last of the waitstaff Adam needed to interview. If she was five feet tall, it was because she was standing on her tiptoes. She provided the standard response he had gotten from the previous employees—didn't notice anything off—but she was wringing her hands so tight, Adam was concerned she would worry them clean off her wrists.

"Is there anything you want to tell me?" Adam asked. "Even if you think it's insignificant, it might lead to something helpful."

"Well, it's just—I don't know if it really matters, and I don't want to get anyone into trouble—but I did see *something*—well, heard something, but—"

"Last Saturday night?"

"No, earlier in the week. Must have been Wednesday night after closing."

"What happened?"

"So, Ty wasn't working, and Martin was in charge of the kitchen that night. He was all sorts of pissed off for most of the night. Slamming things. Cussing at the waitstaff. It was really bad. Gwen finally came back and threatened to kick his ass out the door if he didn't get his shit under control and act like a professional."

"And did he? Settle down?"

"In a quick hurry, but you could tell he was still on the hairy edge of losing it. We all treaded carefully around him for the rest of the night."

"Why was he in such a bad mood?"

"Um, well, Ty has been taking off a lot of nights and Martin has to take over for him and do Ty's job."

"Did Martin say anything to Gwen after she threatened him?"

"Not then, but later. I was putting stuff up before going home and I heard him screaming at her in the office."

"Could you hear what was being said?"

"I'm surprised the entire city couldn't hear him. Martin told Gwen he was tired of filling in as the head chef and only being paid a sous chef salary."

"How did Gwen respond?"

"I don't know—she lowered her voice, probably to calm him down—she had a way of being able to do that with employees and irate customers—but I couldn't hear her. I left because I was worried they would come out, and I didn't want them to think I was eavesdropping."

Which was exactly what she'd been doing, but Adam was happy she had.

"Were there any issues you know of after that?"

"I didn't work again until Saturday night, but Martin seemed his usual slightly grumpy self." She quirked her mouth up on one side. Adam understood. He had waited tables in high school, and the kitchen staff always seemed to be in a perpetual bad mood.

Adam thanked Melissa and went in search of Martin. He entered the kitchen, half expecting to find the man had left out the back, like Butler. Instead, Martin stood in front of an open fridge. He glanced over his shoulder at Adam. "I thought I would go through all this in case Ty decides to close the restaurant for a few days."

"He's lucky to have a diligent employee who thinks of those things."

"Don't know what it'll be like with Gwen gone. I doubt Ty will step up. The place will fall apart in six months with him running it. He better hope he can get Sandra and me to stay on, or this will go down the shitter in a quick hurry."

"You don't get along with Mr. Butler?"

"I did until a few months ago. Then he changed. The restaurant seemed—I don't know—less of a priority to him."

"How so?"

"He got into running marathons, would train all the time for them. And he was always going out of town to compete in marathons all across the country. I swear, if he didn't come back and show off all his medals, I would've thought he was cheating on Gwen. When he was here, he acted like he hated the place."

"You don't think he was cheating on Gwen?"

"No. I mean, I think they had their issues, but they still seemed to be doing okay."

"Did you ever see any of their issues?"

"Not really. They were never really into PDA in front of the staff. Lately, though, Gwen was getting tired of his shit, but she never said anything to me. Just a feeling I got when she would tell me he wasn't coming in—again."

"I heard you were upset on the previous Wednesday night, and Gwen threatened to send you home. Any truth to that?"

He exhaled while wagging his head back and forth. "No—I mean, yes, I was upset—but it was nothing."

"But you were pissed off?"

"Yes."

"About?"

He sighed and placed his hands on the stainless steel countertop and leaned into them. "Look, I don't mind working as a head chef on Ty's nights off. But it's becoming a full-time job, covering for him. Ty's gone more than he's here. I just felt like I was being taken advantage of. I mean, if I'm responsible for the kitchen, I should be compensated for it."

"Did you argue with Gwen about it?"

"Yeah—well, I yelled, and she let me get it out, so it wasn't really an argument. And then she calmed me down. She was really good at stepping in and making peace between all of us. Anyway, we talked and came to an agreement."

"Which was?"

"On nights I'm in charge of the kitchen, I get a higher hourly wage."

"And you were okay with that?"

"Yeah, I mean, at the rate things were going, I figured Ty was going to leave, and I'd get the job—and his pay—when he did." He ran his hand through his hair. "I was just biding my time."

The young man was probably considering what life was going to be like working for Butler and not Gwen. From what Adam had learned of Gwen from the employees, she had been a unique and caring boss. Adam could see why he felt an air of unease running through the place once the news of her death sunk in.

"You worked last Saturday night?" he asked.

"Yes."

"But Mr. Butler wasn't here?"

"No, he was home 'sick.'" Martin included air quotes and a roll of his eyes.

"How late did you work that night?"

"I clocked out at one fifteen in the morning after completing the prep for the next day."

"You always do that the night before?"

"Yeah, I like to. Allows me to sleep in on Sunday."

"Was Gwen still here?"

"Of course—the woman is a machine. It's rare anyone was here after her. She made a point of making sure the staff was safely out of the building before she left."

"Considerate boss."

His shoulders slumped. "You have no idea."

"So, Gwen was still here when you left?"

"Yes, she said she was going through some emails before she left. It'd been a wicked busy night, and she'd spent most of the night working in the dining room, especially after Sandra took off."

"Any idea what time she left?"

"No."

"Okay, thanks for your help." He left a business card on the stainless steel prep table. "Call me if you think of anything at all."

"Yeah, okay." He picked up the card and shoved it in his back pocket. Adam walked to the swinging doors leading to the dining room, to look for Sandra Bennett.

"Hey," Martin called after him, "I did ask if she wanted me to stay until she was done, you know, and walk her to her car. She told me not to worry, that she'd be fine." He ran his hand through his hair. "I wish I would've stayed."

Adam gave him an understanding head nod. He felt bad for the guy if what he said was true. Adam would need more than Martin Griffin's word to clear his name from the list of suspects.

After the employees had all taken off, Sandra Bennett showed Adam back into the same office where he had been earlier with Ty Butler. Sitting in front of the computer, she pulled up the security cam footage. They watched the footage from the front of the restaurant, but nothing unusual happened. Then she switched to the camera that monitored the back of the building. Just as Martin had said, he'd left the restaurant after he clocked out at approximately 1:17 AM. When Gwen pushed open the rear door and emerged, Sandra sucked in her breath and tears welled in her eyes. Adam checked the time. 1:41 AM. Gwen maneuvered Kendall's SUV out of the small parking lot and turned right onto the street.

Sandra backed up the video and watched the same scene again. "That's odd."

"What is?"

"She turned right."

"Why is that odd?"

Sandra looked up at him. "She lives to the left."

28

Sunday,
March 1,
8:45 AM

A FTER A NIGHT of tossing and turning, Kendall drained the last of the coffee Quentin had made before he left that morning, and started another pot. It was too early to reasonably start drinking alcohol, but that didn't ease the desire to add a bit of bourbon to her coffee. Or just drink it straight from the bottle.

Black coffee in hand, she climbed the stairs to the attic loft Gwen had turned into her home office. When Kendall had first moved back to Denver and in with Gwen, Gwen offered to share the office space with her. Sweet gesture, but even if Kendall had wanted to work from home, the things she wrote on her whiteboard would be too heinous to share with Gwen.

Nestled into the corner where the roof sloped and the brick was exposed was a white corner desk. The chair was also white but had one fuzzy pink pillow to help ease lower back pain. The top of the desk was clean and organized, with a desktop computer taking up a good portion of it. A basket held smaller glass cups containing pens, paper clips, sticky notes, and push pins. Everything was in its place, and there was a place for everything. Gwen was known to have a panic attack if things were in too much disarray, which was why she rarely ventured into Kendall's room.

Next to the desk was a filing cabinet that looked more like an antique dresser. Kendall opened the top drawer and smiled.

The files were uniform and alphabetized. Toward the back was a file with Kendall's name on it. She pulled it out and dropped back on her ass, gasping when she saw the photo staring back at her.

"Mac," she whispered, running her finger tenderly over the face of the man with chiseled features and dark, dangerous, sexy eyes. In the picture, Kendall's hand rested on Mac's chest, the diamond engagement ring shimmering in the studio light. They had been so happy—or so she'd thought. But a month before they were set to say "I do," Mac had taken his life, leaving Kendall to pick up the pieces and figure out what had gone so wrong.

He was the first man Kendall had truly loved . . . and would be the last. She was cursed. It was just better to be alone than to have to face heartache. Death sucked. And Kendall was tired of losing the people she loved most in the world.

She thumbed through the rest of the photos in the folder, memories swamping her. So many photos of her and Gwen. The two of them in barely there bikinis on some beach in Cabo San Lucas, margaritas in hand, sombreros on their heads. But it was the width of the smiles that tugged at Kendall's heart. They'd had so much fun on that trip—what she could remember of it. Those were the best times, when they went away and were able to just be themselves. Gwen would let loose and have fun.

And, man, was she fun. One memory stuck out most from that trip, Gwen dancing on the bar and singing karaoke. And the guy they had been hanging out with during the week—*Dave? Dan? What the hell school was he from?*—had dared Gwen fifty bucks to give him and the other, mostly male patrons a show.

When Gwen was done, Kendall asked what had possessed her to do it.

Gwen shoved the fifty, a few twenties, and some singles into her bra. "Easiest hundred dollars I've made in a while, and I didn't have to have sex with any of them to get it. I just had to dance, which I love to do anyway—not usually on top of a bar, but what are ya gonna do?" She tossed back a shot of tequila and grinned.

Tears rolled down Kendall's face and dropped onto the picture. She grabbed a tissue from the box on the top of the cabinet, and dabbed the photo until it was dry. Closing the file, she placed it to the side. She had no right to any of the other files Gwen had, but figured Gwen would want her to have this one.

And Kendall needed to hang onto whatever she could to keep Gwen alive. It wasn't hard now, but she knew from experience that death had a way of making it difficult to recall the face of a loved one years after they'd passed. A lesson she was continually learning from her mother. It had been a few years since Marlena Beck had died, and Kendall struggled to hold onto her memories. They had not been a family who took a lot of pictures. There was too much work to be done on a ranch.

The Bad Boys theme music cut through the silence. She swallowed down a sob before answering. "Hey, Jake. What's up?"

"You okay?" Jake asked.

"Not really."

"Is it Gwen?"

Kendall could count on one hand the times she had been emotional in front of Jake. "Yeah," she managed to choke out. "They found her body in Rocky Mountain Lake Park."

"Oh, man, Kendall." His voice was quiet and soft—two things Jake never was. "I'm so sorry."

She nodded—why, she had no idea. Not like he could see her over the phone. But it was the only thing she could manage to do. She inhaled a ragged breath, exhaled, and cleared her throat. "What's up?"

After a brief pause, Jake said, "I talked to Williams's coworkers. Most people I spoke to have never had any issues with him. He took more than a passing interest in interns, but nothing more than the other males in the office."

"You said 'most'—was there someone who didn't get a warm fuzzy from him?"

"One woman says he always asked about her young daughter—she assumed it was because she was only a couple of years older than Emily—and always wanted to see pictures of her. Never thought too much of it until his arrest, but she definitely got a creep vibe from him."

"Interesting. Check with HR and see if there were any complaints from interns or other female employees. Get a list of the interns over the years, in case someone had an uncomfortable encounter with him."

"Got it," Jake said. "But going after adult women isn't really part of the pedophile profile."

"Except interns are usually young—some still in their late teens—and maybe he's not picky as long as they look younger than they are."

"Long shot."

"Still need to know."

"Yeah, got it covered." There was an almost uncomfortable pause until he spoke, his voice soft and low. "Let me know if you need anything, okay?"

A swell of emotions crept up her throat. "I'm good."

"I know, but just in case you're not. I'm always here for you. No matter what. No questions asked. No judgment. Got it?"

"Got it." She swallowed over the lump in her throat. "Thanks, Jake."

"Anytime, partner." He ended the call and Kendall was grateful he hadn't heard her cry.

Closing the drawer, she opened another containing the business of running the restaurant. Bank statements, ledgers, receipts: if there was something going on at the restaurant, the answers were in these files. Somewhere.

Kendall swiped the tears from her cheeks and blew her nose. She grabbed the Accounts Receivable file and plopped down into Gwen's desk chair.

It was going to be a long day.

Surveying the top drawer for a legal pad and pen, Kendall's hand brushed against something small and hard. She pulled the drawer out as far as she could without dumping it into her lap. A small mahogany box with a gold latch sat at the back of the drawer. She'd seen the box before. A year earlier Ty had presented it to Gwen when he'd proposed to her at a Sunday family dinner.

Gwen had been so happy. And Kendall had been thrilled for her best friend and the man who adored her.

She lifted the latch and opened the box, expecting to find it empty. Kendall's heart kicked into overdrive. Inside, nestled in the white velvet was the princess-cut diamond engagement ring.

What was it doing in here? What did it mean that it was in the box and not on Gwen's finger?

But the question which bothered Kendall the most, made her heart drop into the fiery pit of her stomach: *How had she not noticed Gwen was no longer wearing the ring?*

KENDALL ANSWERED ADAM's call on the fourth ring. "Hello?"
"Kendall? It's Adam—Detective Taylor."

"What can I do for you, Adam?"

Jesus, she sounded tired. He wondered if she had been able to get any sleep, and then figured the answer was no. Even if she'd managed to close her eyes, the constant grief of losing her friend and the myriad questions regarding what and how and why most likely made for a fitful night.

Adam had been there. He knew this exhaustion well.

"I was wondering if I could stop by? Bring you up to speed on the case so far. I've got a few questions for you."

"Uh, yeah, that's no problem." She sounded distracted, and Adam could hear the shuffling of papers in the background.

"I'm not disturbing you, am I?"

"No, I could actually use the break—I've been trying to go through the papers Gwen kept here for the restaurant. My head hurts and my eyes are starting to bug out, looking at all these numbers." She let out a long sigh. "When would you like to stop by?"

"I can be there in ten minutes."

"Okay, I'll put on fresh coffee," she said on a yawn, and then told him goodbye.

When he knocked on her front door, she yelled for him to come in. From the living room, he could see her in the kitchen.

She came out carrying two mugs of coffee and handed one to him. "I assume you take it black?"

"Yep." He took a sip. It was strong, which shouldn't have surprised him since Kendall was in law enforcement, and there was virtually no way to do the job on weak-ass coffee. "Talked to the elusive Ty Butler last night."

"Really?" She sat on the couch, and he took his usual chair, which felt a mix of odd and somewhat comforting. He felt an uncommon bond with Kendall—not romantic or anything. But like they were both cut from the same cloth. Siblings without any relation. "And how did that go?"

"He seemed genuinely surprised Gwen was dead, but I've seen many a killer provide an Oscar-worthy performance when confronted." He gave her a rundown of his conversation and how Ty left the restaurant right after he heard the news. "One thing that caught my attention was the manager, Sandra, says Butler told her he thought Gwen had just needed to get away."

"Yeah, he told me the same thing."

"Is that something she would do?"

"Not the Gwen I know—not without telling someone. She would never leave the restaurant in a lurch. And would especially not want to worry her mother."

"Sandra said you seemed to accept Butler's version. In fact, Butler said you both agreed Gwen needed some time away."

"No, I just didn't have the time to sit and listen to his bullshit. I've been questioning people for many years. He was at that point—you know the one. If he knew something, he wasn't going to tell me. So I left and decided to report Gwen and my SUV missing. Figured the cops might have better luck getting something useful out of him."

Adam relayed the information about the tension with Martin.

"Money is a powerful motivator," Kendall agreed. "Especially if someone feels they're getting the short end of the stick. I know Martin lives with his mom still. I would think he'd want to make enough money to get his own place."

"If he saw Gwen as an obstacle to achieving his goal, could he have gotten mad enough to kill her?"

She shrugged. "He doesn't seem the type, but we both know once a level of rage is achieved, anyone can do anything."

True statement. Even the most laid-back person could build up a lethal tantrum.

"But you haven't ever noticed him being violent?"

Kendall snorted. "Have you ever been in the kitchen of a restaurant? They are notorious for being assholes and yelling at the waitstaff. They could put a line of expletives together that would make you and me blush—and cops can cuss with the best of them. I've seen both Ty and Martin lose control, but it never really amounted to being violent. Loud and uncalled for? Yes. But violent and aggressive—enough to kill a person? I never saw that."

She had a point. People could yell and scream and be assholes, but it didn't always equate to being murderous.

"Did you find anything interesting in Gwen's business files?"

"Not really—at least, not in any of the documents—but I just started."

"But?" She was leaving something out. "Something besides documents catch your attention?"

"The killer didn't steal Gwen's engagement ring," she said. "I found it in a ring box at the back of her desk drawer."

Well, that was unexpected news.

"Wait—" Adam grabbed his phone and brought up the picture of the ring he'd found in Gwen's personal items. "I thought the black pearl ring was her engagement ring."

"How do you know about the pearl ring?" Kendall asked.

He flipped the phone around so Kendall could see the screen. "It was in her personal effects."

Kendall pointed at the picture. "That was an heirloom passed down to her when her grandmother died."

Adam mulled the information over. "So, the killer didn't steal the engagement ring."

"Nope, it was in the back of her desk drawer."

"Could she have been waiting to take it in to a jeweler to get it sized or something?"

Kendall shook her head. "No, that was done months ago."

He placed his mug on the coffee table and sat back, letting the news percolate. "Did she and Butler break off their engagement?"

"Good question." She looked a mix of sad and embarrassed. "I have no idea what was going on."

Adam took a deep breath. He was not looking forward to the next line of questioning, but it had to be done. "I heard back from the ME." He paused to see if she stopped him. She was a professional, but she was also grieving her best friend. Sometimes it was best not knowing all the gruesome details of someone's death.

She nodded for him to proceed.

"Cardiac arrest brought on by electrocution."

Her face paled. "What?"

"Apparently, some type of electric current passed through her breasts and caused her heart to stop pumping blood."

"What the hell does that mean?"

Time to drop the bomb. *In for a penny, and all that crap.* "Do you know if Gwen and Ty engaged in unusual sexual practices?"

"Like what, exactly?"

"Electrophilia?"

Her eyebrows furrowed. "Which is what?"

Adam read the explanation from the ME as they both squirmed in their seats—Adam still uncomfortable with the subject; Kendall, most likely not wanting to delve into her best friend's sexual proclivities.

"Pffftttt." Kendall exhaled loudly, then chuckled. "I can't say no for sure, but I would be drop-dead surprised if they were into any of that. Ty may have wanted to shake things up in that area of the relationship, but I can't see Gwen going that far. Some mild bondage, perhaps, but"—she waved her hand at his notes, her nose scrunched up—"no way."

"Did Gwen talk to you about her sex life?"

"No, not really. What are you thinking?"

Adam leaned forward and picked his coffee mug up, taking a drink before proceeding. "They were messing around, didn't fully understand the ramifications of the situation—"

"Gwen has a heart attack, and Ty freaks and dumps her body?" She leaned back into the couch and stared at the ceiling in contemplation. "I can see that more than I can see him intentionally killing her." She lifted her head and gazed at him. "I mean, I know there was some tension between them lately.

But that's to be expected, I guess. Sometimes it can be hard to work with the one you play with."

Adam leaned forward. "What kind of tension?"

"The business was booming, and Gwen had thoughts of expansion. Ty wanted to keep it small. I think they argued about it, but it was normal disagreements. I never got the feeling it was causing serious trouble."

She ran her fingertip around the rim of her coffee mug. "Although, I guess I don't really know what was going on with her these days. Apparently, she was upset enough at Ty to stop wearing her engagement ring. And I never even noticed." She glanced up at him under a lock of hair that fell across her forehead. "Some friend I am, huh?"

Adam wasn't getting into this type of conversation with her. He was the last person who should be waxing poetic on interpersonal relationships. He was clueless. And not a good emotional cheerleader.

He was really good at asking questions and investigating murders.

"Why do you think she didn't tell you?" he asked.

She looked down and away. "I've been pretty self-absorbed in this case I've been working—a child abduction that turned out to be a runaway from a molester."

The thought turned Adam's stomach. He hated working cases involving kids. No way would he be able to work them day in and day out like Kendall.

"Knowing Gwen, she wouldn't want to worry me when I needed to focus all my attention on finding the victim." A small, sad smile played across her lips. "That's just the sort of person she was."

30

D AVE COLLINS WAS a tall, clean-cut guy with dark brown hair and biceps which stressed the fabric of his white dress shirt. The large box of liquor he placed on the bar was lifted with ease, as if it were filled with cotton candy, not sixty-plus pounds of expensive hooch.

After leaving Kendall's, Adam made his way to The Oyster to interview the bartender.

"Anything happen out of the ordinary on Saturday night?" Adam asked.

"Uh, let me think . . . still trying to wrap my head around Gwen dying." He snapped his finger and pointed at Adam. "Yeah, yeah, there was something. Gwen had to kick a drunk out of the bar."

"And that was unusual?" That sort of thing happened frequently at the bars Adam went to.

"For this place, definitely."

"So, what happened?"

"One of our regulars, who usually handles his liquor better, started getting obnoxious with the waitstaff. Gwen finally stepped in when he turned his drunk ass on the customers." Collins shook his head and laughed. "It was sort of comical— for such a petite woman, Gwen has balls the size of an elephant. She got up in his face and talked real low, so only the people directly around them could hear, and told him there was a cab waiting outside to drive him home, courtesy of the restaurant, and that he had better leave before she called the police."

Collins placed two bottles of vodka on the shelf opposite Adam. "That only made the poor sap start blubbering about how he would behave better, and please don't kick him out forever—don't remember the exact words, but you get the idea. When Gwen told him that her decision was final, he stood up, towering over Gwen, and told her she'd regret banning him. I grabbed his arm in case he tried anything, but Gwen?" He faced Adam and whistled, a smile on his face. "She stood her ground."

"Sounds like you admired her?"

"Dude, I have mad respect for her."

"Do you have a name to go along with the regular?"

"Uh, Jimmy something . . ." He tapped his finger on the bar. "Bell," he exclaimed. "Jimmy Bell."

"So, I'm assuming Mr. Bell left without further incident?"

"Yeah, I escorted him to the door and put him in the cab myself."

"Seen him since?"

"Nope."

"Things calm down after that?"

"Yeah, but it caused quite a frenzy in the bar. Everyone loves drama, right? And there was no shortage of customers reliving the harrowing experience of witnessing a drunk get angry and thrown out. I swear, you would've thought ol' Jimmy had whipped out a gun and started aiming it at people, the way the stories morphed throughout the night."

"And no doubt still are as they're recounted at dinner parties where no one can challenge them on the veracity," Adam added.

"Exactly."

Adam closed up his notepad and slid a business card across the bar to Collins, pointing to it. "Think of anything, no matter how minor, give me a call."

"Will do." Collins slipped the card into his breast pocket.

Adam walked through the bar and was approaching the door when Collins called out to him. Adam turned as the man jogged up to him.

"Hey, I remembered something that happened earlier in the night."

"What was that?"

"Gwen and a friend of hers, Quentin, were having a heated discussion in the bar. He was waiting for a to-go order, which isn't uncommon—he and Kendall are always getting food to go—but, man, was he upset."

"Do you know what about?" Adam recalled Novak being squirrelly when Adam spoke to him at Kendall's house.

"No, but he was getting loud enough that Gwen was glancing around the bar to see if anyone was getting annoyed. Luckily, there weren't many people in here at the time, and no one was really paying attention to them. Once the food arrived, Quentin pulled himself together and left."

"What did Gwen do?"

Collins chuckled. "Rubbed her forehead and asked for the bottle of migraine meds we keep behind the bar."

"Okay, thanks." Adam shook the man's hand and left.

So, Novak was having a heated discussion with Gwen the night she disappeared. Could whatever they were arguing about have pushed him to kill Gwen?

31

Monday,
March 2,
8:32 AM

ADAM SWIVELED HIS chair and faced the murder board for Jenna Rose. Leaning back, he steepled his fingers and tapped them against his lips. His gaze traveled over the crime scene photos first, then the autopsy pics. Jenna had been raped. Sodomized with a pistol. The .22 caliber hollow point lodged in her spinal column. The shot had paralyzed her first and then, eventually, killed her. But that wasn't the photo that stumped him. Something about Jenna Rose's back seemed off.

The autopsy report had concluded the marks on her back were due to scratches, possibly from being dragged over the rough landscape around the trees on the tenth tee. But the determination wasn't ringing true to Adam.

He pulled up the video from the golf course. The killer removed Jenna from the trunk. Carried her across the parking lot, over the closely cut grass, and dumped her under the tree. Then he stood there, looking at Jenna, before turning and walking back to his car.

He dumped her.

Adam jumped up, grabbed his coat and keys, and headed out the door. With any luck, Fran was not armpit deep in a dead body, and he could get her take on the marks. Fran hadn't performed Jenna Rose's autopsy—Jenna had been murdered while Fran was still on maternity leave. And it wasn't that

Adam didn't trust her replacement; it was more he didn't really know the man. Nestor Watson had been on loan from Grand Junction while Fran was gone. He was an odd sort of guy, not personable at all. One of those doctors who instantly believes anyone who didn't attend medical school is an idiot, and therefore needed to slow his speech for simpletons. Complete with inane hand gestures.

Adam was not a fan of Dr. Watson.

Fran was in her office, staring at her computer, eyebrows squished together, her fingers racing over the keyboard. Adam tapped on the doorframe. She glanced up but said nothing. Adam had been here before. Best to just let her finish whatever she was doing. Interrupting her while in the middle of a thought would likely bring wrath down on him. And he needed her help.

The tapping ceased, and her gaze swung to him, a broad smile on her face. She exhaled and said, "Hey, Adam, what can I do for you?"

"I'm stumped on the Jenna Rose case and could use a second look at something, if you have the time."

"What kind of second look?"

He handed the autopsy pic over to her. "Dr. Watson said these were scratches, most likely caused by being dragged along the ground."

She picked up the picture and glanced at it, then typed on the computer. "Rose is the victim's last name?"

"Yes."

"And why don't you believe those are scratches?"

"According to video surveillance at the scene, her body was dumped, not dragged."

"Could've been an animal who dragged her after the killer left."

"But wouldn't there have been some type of bite mark or something? Besides, her body was found where it was dumped."

Fran was ignoring him, her attention on the computer screen.

"I see what you mean," she drew out each word. She waved him over. "Come take a look."

Adam rounded the corner of the desk. The autopsy photo was easier to see on Fran's twenty-seven-inch monitor. She had also apparently zoomed in to get a closer look. "If these were scratches, I would expect to see a sort of feathering effect. Some lines deeper than others, creating a variation on the colors—the deeper ones being darker—you get what I mean."

She didn't wait for him to respond. She used a pen to point to specific marks on the screen. "Some are perfectly straight lines. But even the ones that aren't straight"—she pointed to a few lines that were curved in almost a semicircle—"they're clean. These are marks made on purpose, with a razor or sharp knife."

"Why?" Adam asked out loud.

Fran looked up at him with a sweet smile. "If I do your job, do I also get your pay?"

"Rhetorical question."

"Oooo, such a big word."

"It's Dictionary dot com's word of the day. I hoped I'd be able to use it in a sentence."

"Happy I can provide the opportunity. It's nice to see you're still trying to improve your station in life."

Adam laughed. This was a common theme between them. Fran was the most down-to-earth, nonpretentious doctor he had ever met. He had told her that once, and she had responded she'd have to work harder at being pompous in the future.

He took the picture from the desk and headed for the door. "Thanks, Fran."

"I'm here to serve."

He smiled and waved a goodbye, but she was already typing furiously on the keyboard, eyebrows knitted together.

32

MORNING CAME WAY too early, and Kendall could've stayed another hour under the covers. She forced herself out of bed and headed straight to the shower. Nothing was going to help the dull ache that was her constant companion these days. But a nice, long, hot dousing might release some tension, and that was better than nothing. Somehow the warmth and the mindless act of washing her hair relaxed her, and she was able to mull over information in Gwen's business files.

She dried her hair, dressed, and walked out to the kitchen. Grabbing the stack of reports she had gone over the previous night, she sifted through them while waiting for the coffee to brew.

Something wasn't right—she just couldn't put her finger on what. The balance sheet from the previous month showed a deduction of ten thousand dollars, but there was no explanation of why the money was withdrawn or what it had been used for.

Filled mug in hand, she headed into the living room and searched for the bank statements that coincided with the recent withdrawal. The statement from the previous month showed the deduction reflected on the balance sheet. The bank statement for the loan, however, didn't show the amount being deducted. She grabbed the statement for the next month, but no withdrawal for that amount was listed there either, nor were there any withdrawals equaling that amount. She went through the previous month and found the same. No withdrawal.

Finally, a statement two months prior listed a deduction for ten thousand dollars. Dialing Adam's number, she waited while it rang.

"Taylor."

"It's Kendall." She could hear the buzz of a busy office in the background. "You at work?"

"Yes, just got in. Interviewed the bartender working the night Gwen disappeared." He told Kendall about a drunk getting belligerent with Gwen and having to be escorted off the premises. "What've you been up to?"

"My ass in financial reports. There's a reason I didn't get any sort of math degree. Me and numbers are not always friends."

Adam laughed, which made her smile. He was a good guy, and she liked him. Not as anything more than a friend. Although, the number of male *friends* she was acquiring was starting to alarm her.

"Well, I found something interesting, but it creates more questions than answers, unfortunately. Back in September, ten thousand dollars was withdrawn from the business account. That money was not listed on the ledger until November, two months later. It shows as a short-term loan paid out one day and repaid the next."

"Odd."

"That's what I thought, but there's more. I remembered seeing a withdrawal for that amount recently, and went back through the ledger. Sure enough, there's a ten-thousand-dollar withdrawal, but this time the description is blank. Not a single notation as to what it could be. I went through the bank statements, and it was withdrawn on the date listed in the report, but I don't see anything showing it was repaid—if it was another short-term loan."

"And I'm guessing there is nothing that states who borrowed the money back in September?" Adam asked.

"Not that I could find, and I don't remember Gwen mentioning any purchases or expenditures equaling that amount during that time."

Adam exhaled, long and loud; the exhaustion in his voice had been evident the entire conversation. "Okay, I'm going to need all those reports."

"I'll box everything up. I'm also going to put in a call to Gwen's business accountant and see if he can shed some light on this."

"Good idea." Someone was talking to him in the background, but Kendall couldn't make out what was being said. "And thanks for going through all of that," he said when he came back on the line. "I share your dislike of crunching numbers. Tedious fucking job."

"Which is why we are in law enforcement and not accountants."

"True. I've got to go—they have the security footage from around the lake ready for me to go through."

Speaking of fucking tedious jobs. "Have fun with that." She disconnected the call and punched the number for Oren Mitchell, Gwen's accountant. She was told he was out of the office, and put through to his voicemail.

"Hi Oren, this is FBI Special Agent Kendall Beck. I'm Gwen Tavich's roommate—I don't know if you remember me. I need to talk to you as soon as possible—it's of utmost importance." She provided her number and ended the call.

This case was getting more confusing with each passing minute. She just wondered if this had been a random killing—or at the hands of someone close to Gwen.

Someone like Ty.

33

ADAM WAS ABLE to talk the IT guys into sending the video to his laptop so he could sit in the Tavich war room to view it. A comfortable chair was imperative. Access to a pot of coffee was also paramount, considering the amount of time he was most likely going to be staring at video footage consisting mainly of raccoons searching for food, and cats searching for other cats in heat for a little springtime action.

The biggest plus of being in the conference room was not being in the cramped closet the video guys hung out in. It was small, dark, and reeked of sweat and cigarettes from the days when it was acceptable to give your colleagues lung cancer from secondhand smoke.

Adam was glad he hadn't been part of the department during that time. While there were plenty of windows, not one of them opened. And no matter how many times the worn industrial carpets were cleaned and the walls were painted, the stench of cigarette smoke still pervaded the bullpen.

Adam checked his notes before bringing up the first video. One of the residents along the street facing the park took his dog for a walk around the lake at ten PM. He'd only gone less than a quarter of the way around before turning back and heading home. No one was parked in the semicircle or the small parking lot where the SUV had been found. Another neighbor, Ted Marks, whose house directly faced the lake and parking lot, told officers he routinely checked the park when locking up and going to bed each night around midnight. Again, no cars at the lake.

At least that narrowed down the time line a bit. Adam had a starting place. Midnight. Luckily, Mr. Marks was into high-tech gadgets, including a nice security system on the front, sides, and back of his house. Adam fast-forwarded the video of the front yard, with a slightly visible lake in the background. At 4:08 AM, a vehicle slowly rolled down the street and into the cul-de-sac dead-ending at the lake. A dark BMW SUV came to a stop.

A person in dark clothing, head covered, got out and went to the back of the vehicle. A large object was hauled out of the cargo area, and Adam could make out the distinct figure of a body. Gwen had been dead long enough at that time for rigor mortis—stiffening of the muscles after death—to have come and gone, making it easier to handle her body. If handling dead weight, even someone of Gwen's small stature, could be considered easy.

The killer probably knew rigor mortis was temporary. A doctor? Someone in the medical field? Or just a killer who knew what he was doing?

Could this be the same person who had murdered Jenna Rose?

Adam pushed that thought to the back of his mind and concentrated on the Tavich case. Ty Butler was probably not a serial killer, but it was looking more and more like he was involved in the death of his fiancé. So this was less likely to be a serial murder and more likely to be a crime of passion or, at the very least, a sex game gone wrong and a sloppy ass-cover.

The killer lumbered down the path, but eventually went out of the camera's range. After a few minutes, the figure reappeared. He walked straight past the vehicle without stopping, making his way across the large expanse of grass. Adam checked the map of the area tacked up on the wall. Forty-sixth Street ran the length of the park on the south side. He checked where other videos had been retrieved. Two people along Forty-sixth had video doorbells and had submitted their footage.

The first one Adam checked required him to back up several times before he could make out the ghost figure walking through the park, heading west. The other security footage from a house on the corner of 46th and King streets, showed the black figure cutting the corner of the yard and heading down King. That's where Adam's luck ran out. No one on King Street had security systems on their homes.

So either the killer had to have parked a vehicle in the neighborhood surrounding the park in order to get away. Or he lived close by.

Adam picked up the phone and dialed an extension. "Officer Young? Detective Taylor. How would you like to earn your stripes in a homicide investigation?"

"What do you need me to do?" The kid sounded enthusiastic enough. Of course, that might change once he heard the shit assignment.

"I need to see if anyone parked a car in the days preceding Gwen Tavich's body being dumped at the lake. Specifically the blocks from Forty-fourth to Forty-sixth, between King and Federal. Think you can handle that?"

"Yes, sir. Thanks for thinking of me."

"Yep." Adam hung up. He opened up Google maps on his computer and typed in the address for Ty Butler. The apartment building was south of the lake. Five miles away. A bit of a hike. But then again, Butler had been running marathons the previous few months. Probably wasn't even a challenge for him.

Despite what Kendall had said about Butler and her claims she couldn't see Butler killing Gwen, Adam was not as convinced.

Circumstantial or not, the evidence was stacking up against Mr. Butler.

34

Tuesday,
March 3,
10:37 AM

A DAM LEANED BACK in his chair and stared out the glass
walls of the conference room. Out of the corner of his eye,
he could see the one person he was not in the mood for—Sheri
Colburn. Her eyes were narrowing with every step she took.

"Shit," he muttered under his breath, and sat up. He prayed
she was over making a spectacle of herself, and perhaps they
could be professional toward each other.

"Well, hello, Detective Asshole," she said, stepping into the
room.

Optimism smacked down, once again.

"Hi, Sheri, how are y—"

"Save it for someone who cares, dickweed." She tossed a file
onto the table. "The cell phone records for Gwen Tavich."

He sat up quickly and lunged for the papers. "Already?
Damn, that was fast."

"Well, the people at AT&T like me." She snatched the
Snickers bar he had just bought from the vending machine.
"You, not so much." She ripped open the wrapper and took a
bite. "Thanks for the candy bar," she called over her shoulder as
she sauntered away with his mid-morning snack.

Adam sighed, opened the file, and pulled out the call history for Gwen Tavich's cell phone for the past month. Quickly
scanning the dates, he looked through the phone calls for the

night she was murdered. All the calls fit with the information he'd received from her friends and family. All except one.

A call came into her cell phone—and was answered—at 2:17 AM, but only lasted a minute. Another call from the same number at 2:19 AM.

"Son of a bitch." Adam dialed the number, but he already knew who was going to answer it.

"Butler," came the greeting from the other end.

"Mr. Butler, this is Detective Taylor. I need to meet with you to go over a few more things. Can you come down to the station?"

35

Dr. Beverly Clarkson was a very petite woman with mousy brown, shoulder-length hair she wore down. Her bohemian dress swept the floor, and Kendall caught a glimpse of the Doc Martin sandals she was wearing. She shook Kendall's hand with as much vigor as a limp, wet noodle, her hands cold and clammy. Her voice was soft, which Kendall figured was a good thing when working with children. When she got to Jake, her eyes grew a little larger.

"I didn't realize you were bringing your partner, Agent Beck," she said, her comment directed at Kendall but her eyes firmly affixed to Jake.

Jake gave a tight smile; irritation lingered in his expression. No one liked to be talked about instead of talked to.

"He's here to observe," Kendall said.

"And I promise to stay back so Emily isn't anxious with me here," Jake added.

Clarkson stared a moment longer, then straightened her back. "Best if you can stay as much out of her sight as possible. She's still very intimidated having men around, as you can imagine."

Jake nodded. "Not my intent to cause any further harm, Doc."

Emily lay on her stomach on the floor, working on a coloring book, being careful not to color outside the lines of the cat lazing in a tree. Her hair was combed, and she tapped her foot on the carpet. Way more animated than when Kendall had seen her a few days earlier. She guessed the sessions with the therapist had been doing Emily some good.

"Emily," Kathy said. "Agent Beck is here. Can you sit up and say 'Hi,' please?"

The girl glanced up at Kendall, put her crayon down, and sat cross-legged. "Hi." Her voice was flat, her gaze on the picture she'd been coloring.

"Hey, Emily," Kendall said, lowering herself to sit near the girl so she could be on the same level, and not an imposing adult figure. Jake stayed on the periphery of the room, behind Emily so he wasn't in her direct sightline. The girl was skittish enough around adults, thanks to her father. They didn't need to add to her anxiety. "I like your picture," Kendall continued.

"Thanks." Emily smiled at her. "Mom says we can get a cat when we move to our new house."

"Wow, that'll be fun. I lived on a ranch, and we always had cats around when I was growing up."

Emily's face perked up. "Really? I wish we could have a ranch with lots of cats. But not dogs. Maybe an otter, though."

Kendall couldn't help but laugh at the youthful exuberance of a child who was probably fighting every day to get back to some semblance of normal in her life.

Dr. Clarkson smiled her approval and sat adjacent to them, also on the floor. "Emily, Agent Beck has some questions to ask you. Remember, we talked about this yesterday?"

In an instant, Emily's demeanor shifted. Her head dropped to her chest. Her fingers twisted in the material of her sweater. "Yes." Even her voice had dropped to a whisper. It made Kendall wish she could strangle the life out of Scott Williams for the pain and horror he had inflicted on such a sweet little girl.

Dr. Clarkson turned her attention to Kendall. "If I feel she is becoming too stressed or upset, I'll ask you to stop and maybe revisit this another time."

Kendall nodded her agreement. "Understood." She turned her attention to Emily.

"Emily, why were you hiding in Mr. Sandoval's garage?"

Wrinkles creased her little forehead. "Just 'cause."

"Just because? I know you went over to visit him a lot, huh? Did you go over to visit him that night?"

She grimaced and nodded her head.

"Then why did you go to the garage and not the house?"

She picked up her crayon to color the picture. Kendall opened her mouth to repeat the question, but Dr. Clarkson put up a hand to stop her, then lifted one finger, indicating Kendall should give Emily a minute.

Finally, Emily said, "I went to the house and knocked on the door on the side like I always do. But Uncle Sandy never came to the door."

"So you went to the garage?"

She nodded. "The kitties are there."

"And why didn't you go home when Uncle Sandy didn't answer the door."

She stopped coloring but didn't look up from the picture. "Daddy was coming home from his business trip."

Out of the corner of her eye, Kendall could see Kathy's hand cover her mouth.

"So you went to Uncle Sandy's to get away from your daddy?"

Emily's response was a barely discernible whisper. "Nothing bad happens at Uncle Sandy's house."

Kendall's heart clenched for the little girl. Sneaking out of her house, going to the one place she felt safe, and being forced to find refuge in the frigid garage to get away from an abusive father. It never got any easier. No matter how many times Kendall interviewed children, the feeling of little pieces of her soul withering away never dissipated. But she had a job to do, and as distasteful as it was to push Emily to talk about the worst thing that had happened in her short life, there was just no other choice.

Scott Williams had to pay, and this was the only way Kendall could ensure he spent many years in prison.

Kathy was hard at work worrying her bottom lip with her teeth, eyes glassy. Kendall was certain Clarkson was going to make her cut the interview short, but the woman gave her a head nod.

"Hey, sweetie," Kendall said, "I know this is hard, but I need you to tell me where you were when your daddy hurt you. Can you remember? Was it in your bedroom?"

"At first." She ripped the paper wrapper off the crayon, discarding the pieces on the carpet. Then she picked each piece up and tore it into smaller pieces. "I would cry and that made him mad because Mom might hear and come and yell at me for what we were doing."

A stifled cry came from where Kathy sat on the couch behind Kendall. "But then he took you somewhere else?" Kendall asked.

Emily nodded her head, still not looking at Kendall.

"Do you know where it was?"

Emily looked at her mom, then quickly away. "The secret room."

Kendall glanced over her shoulder at Kathy who frowned, shook her head, and mouthed, "No idea."

"Do you know where the secret room is?"

Emily nodded again. Kendall took a deep, steadying breath. Interviewing children was not for the faint of heart. Or the impatient. It took time and calm and understanding to get an abused child to speak about the worst thing to ever happen to them. It was unfair to make a child relive the atrocities, but it was necessary to build a case and send the bastard away. And let the other convicts mete out justice. Convicts were scum, but even they had a code of honor. To them, hurting a child was the worst offense to be imprisoned for, and it came at a high price to the asshole who was convicted of a sex crime against a child.

"I know this is hard, and we're almost done—I just need to know where the secret room is?"

"In the basement."

"I know where she means," Kathy said in a low voice. Kendall shifted so she could see her more easily. "It's not really a secret room. It's a storage room."

"No, it's not!" Emily jumped to her feet. Dr. Clarkson was at the girl's side in a flash, placing a protective arm around her. Emily's face was bright red, and her body quaked.

"It's okay, Emily." Dr. Clarkson glanced at Kendall. "I think we have to be through for today."

Kendall nodded and touched Emily on the arm. "Hey, Emily, you did great. Thank you so much for talking to me. I know it's hard to talk about these things, but you did an amazing job. You're a very strong girl, and I'm really proud of you. I'm going to go, and I promise the next time I come, we won't have to talk about any of this. Okay?"

The little girl sniffled and nodded.

"Maybe you'll be able to show me your new kitten."

That produced a slight smile, which Kendall figured was a huge win, all things considered. She got to her feet and motioned for Kathy to follow her and Jake to the front door so they could speak in private. The good doctor was speaking in a singsongy voice to Emily as they left, comforting the girl as much as was possible at that point in her recovery.

Once Kendall reached the door, she turned to Kathy. "Tell me about the storage room."

"We never went in there because the room's filled with boxes and things, and we didn't want the girls to get hurt if they played in there."

"Why would Emily call it a 'secret room'?"

"It does have a lock on it, so that might be why she thinks it's secret. And we told them it was off-limits—like most of the basement." She rolled her eyes. "It was basically Scott's man cave down there."

Had Scott Williams told Emily it was part of their secret, and the girl morphed that into the *room* was secret. Kendall didn't know, but she wanted to take another look around the basement of the Williamses' home.

"Are you planning on moving soon?"

Kathy glanced over her shoulder toward the kitchen. "Hopefully." She looked back at Kendall. "It's not easy moving back home with parents when you've had as much time away from them as you had with them."

Kendall huffed out a laugh. "I can imagine." She and Jake stepped outside, and she turned back to Kathy. "I know all of this has been just as hard on you. Stay strong; it will not get any easier the closer to trial we get."

"I wish there was a way he could be convicted without Emily having to testify."

A pang of remorse made Kendall's heart hurt. This family had been through so much already. "Me too."

36

KENDALL ENTERED THE Denver PD, walked up to the bulletproof glass window, and flashed her badge at the officer on desk duty. "Agent Kendall Beck to see Detective Taylor."

Officer Travis Warren gave her a salacious smile. *The little shit actually winked.* "Is Detective Taylor expecting you?"

Fuck my life. She stared at him for a moment, face blank. "Yes. He is."

Warren picked up the phone, pushed a few buttons, and then talked to someone on the other end. He glanced up at her as he replaced the receiver, and pointed toward the door next to him. It buzzed loudly and the lock disengaged. He swiveled in his chair to face her as she came through the door.

"Just down the hall, first left. Detective Taylor is in the first interrogation room but wants you in the observation cave. Door is marked."

She nodded and took off down the hall.

"It's nice to see you again, Agent Beck," Warren called after her.

Prick. She was tempted to flip him off, but there were too many other people around.

She cleared her head. Time to focus on priorities. Adam had called her as she was leaving Kathy Williams's temporary sanctuary with her parents. He was questioning Ty again and wondered if Kendall would like to sit in on it. He'd come across an inconsistency in Ty's story. That intrigued her—and worried her—so she decided to see what Adam had.

And how Ty responded.

The observation room was small and dark, with only one window which looked into the interrogation room. Ty sat at the small metal table facing Kendall, unable to see her through the one-way glass. He looked calm, as if he was happy to be able to help in the investigation. She doubted he knew Adam had evidence against him, though.

Kendall almost felt bad for Ty. She'd always gotten along really well with him. Something had shifted in his relationship with Gwen over the past few months, but she was finding it hard to believe he would do anything as drastic as killing her, especially in the heinous manner in which she was murdered. But people never failed to surprise Kendall. Sometimes it's the person you think you know best who ends up destroying your life.

"Good afternoon, Mr. Butler. Thank you so much for coming in today. I just have a few questions that need clarifying." Taylor pressed "Record" on the tape machine.

"Anything I can do to help, I'm happy to do. I want you to find this bastard for what he did to Gwen." Ty looked upset but still calm. Still believing Adam considered him an ally, not a suspect.

"Great, I appreciate it." Adam shuffled through his file and pulled out a police report. "Now, you stated the last time you spoke with Gwen was on Saturday night around midnight—is that correct?"

"Yeah, she called me from the restaurant," Ty said, nodding his head.

"You didn't talk to her after that?"

Ty sat up straighter in his chair and rubbed his hands along his thighs. "Uh, no . . . no, I'm sure it was midnight."

"Well, that's curious." Adam placed a document on the top of the file. "You see, records indicate Gwen received a call at 2:17 and then again at 2:19 that morning. How do you explain that?"

"Maybe it was a wrong number?" Ty fidgeted in his seat, his eyebrows drawing together. He wasn't looking at Adam.

The sound of her own breathing reverberated off the walls. *Oh, this was so bad.* Her chest clenched tightly. Her mind tried to make sense of the information, but things were getting fuzzy.

She didn't want this to be true. Ty couldn't have murdered Gwen.

Adam leaned in a little closer to Ty, as if they were buddies and he was going to tell him some big secret. "Here's the problem with that: I called the number. And guess who answered?" He paused for a second. "You answered, Mr. Butler."

"You don't know it was me," Ty roared. His face twisted and his nostrils flared. A light sheen of perspiration covered his skin, and his top lip was quivering.

"But I do. You see, when you answered, all professional, you gave me your name. You remember that call, don't you? I asked you to come down here and talk to me. Now, would you like to explain to me why your cell phone called Gwen twice that night, after you say you didn't speak with her?"

Adam sat back in his chair and crossed his arms over his chest. He had the upper hand and wanted Ty to know it. Kendall had done that maneuver herself, many times. It was a great feeling, knowing you controlled the situation. At that moment, though, Kendall would've given anything for Adam to be wrong.

"Maybe I accidentally butt-dialed her. I keep my phone in my pocket. It could have redialed the last number I called." Now it was Ty's turn to sit back, although he was anything but the picture of calm and composed he'd been when the interrogation started.

"Your butt have a minute-long conversation with Gwen, as well?" Adam leaned forward, his forearms on the table. "Tell you what . . . we'll get back to that. Were you and Ms. Tavich still engaged?"

"What the hell—of course we were." His voice wavered.

"Then maybe you can explain why the engagement ring you gave her was in a drawer in her home office?"

His eyes bulged, but he recovered quickly. "She said it was loose—didn't want it to fall off. We were both busy and couldn't find time to get it to the jeweler."

Kendall's skin tingled. *Bullshit.* Gwen had taken it to the jeweler right after Ty had proposed. The ring fit her finger perfectly. Why was he lying? Had he even noticed she'd taken it off? Or had they broken up?

Kendall couldn't believe Gwen would've ended her engagement—or relationship—with Ty without talking to her. No matter what they were going through in their professional lives, Gwen would've talked to Kendall about something so monumental.

"You know I can check your story pretty easily, right?" Adam asked.

Ty glared at him. "Am I under arrest?"

"No, just having a chat to clarify some things."

"Then I'm not answering any more of your questions." Ty pounded his index finger on the metal table with every word he spoke.

"Thought you wanted to help, Mr. Butler? You said you wanted to find the bastard that did this to Gwen." As Adam spoke, he tossed crime scene photos onto the desk. Kendall was too far away to see them, which was perfectly fine with her, but judging by the way Ty gasped and immediately looked away, they must've been of Gwen's body.

Ty covered his face and rocked back and forth in his chair. "Man, don't show me that shit. I don't wanna see her that way!"

"She didn't deserve this, Mr. Butler. She didn't deserve to die this way. Come on, man. Help me. Tell me what happened?" Adam's voice was low, soft. Sympathetic.

Ty raised his head, his eyes instantly narrowing. "What are you thinking? That I did this? That I killed Gwen?"

"I don't know, Mr. Butler—you tell me. Did things get heated between you? Was she upset? Did things go too far? Let me help you, man. Tell me what went wrong that night."

Ty stared at him, shook his head, and smirked. "Lawyer."

"Come on, Mr. Butler, don't do this. Help me. Help Gwen and her family find some peace."

Ty stood up, momentarily towering over the detective. "Arrest me or I'm leaving. Either way, the next time you want to talk to me, contact my attorney." He was out the door before

Adam could react. But it didn't matter. The fact he'd lied—and continued to lie—about talking to Gwen after two in the morning, and the bullshit with the engagement ring, was not proof he'd murdered her.

Far from it.

But it produced a molten lava ball in the center of Kendall's chest, and she couldn't help wondering what the hell had happened between Gwen and Ty that might've pushed him to that extreme.

37

O REN MITCHELL'S CALL came just as Kendall was walking
into her house.

"Ms. Beck, I'm returning your call. What can I do for
you?"

Kendall sat in the chair, her purse slipping off her shoulder and onto the floor next to her feet. This never seemed to
get easy, even when it was someone she didn't know. But this
was Gwen, and every time she opened her mouth to speak the
words, she had to swallow down a sob lodged in her throat.

"Thank you for calling me back. I'm afraid I have some bad
news. Gwen Tavich was killed this week."

Oren audibly gasped. "What? How?"

"I'm sorry, I can't really get into specifics while the investigation is ongoing." Kendall slipped out the notes she had taken
regarding the discrepancies in the restaurant's financial statements. "I was going through the books for the restaurant and
had a couple of questions."

"What would you like to know?"

"I noticed there was a withdrawal of ten thousand dollars
in September of last year, but it wasn't noted in the ledger until
November, where it shows as a short-term loan. Can you tell me
about that?"

Mitchell sighed. "Yes, that caused a great deal of anxiety
and discourse between Gwen and Ty. Unbeknownst to myself

or Gwen, Ty withdrew the money. Gwen confronted him about it, and he returned the money in November."

"Do you know why he needed the money?"

"No, Gwen never told me, and I didn't feel it was my place to ask. She had me record it as a loan that was paid in full."

"There was also another ten thousand taken out last month. I haven't been able to find it listed anywhere either. Was that another loan?"

"I have no idea, Ms. Beck. As soon as I realized the money had been taken from the account again, I emailed Gwen."

"How did she respond? Did she know about the withdrawal?"

"I don't think so. I received a response that simply said she would take care of it and get back to me."

"When did you receive the email?"

Kendall heard the tapping of keys on a keyboard. "At 1:28 Sunday morning."

Right before she left the restaurant, never to be heard from again.

38

Thursday,
March 5,
11:52 AM

MOURNERS MILLED ABOUT the front of the church, even though the temperatures were hovering around freezing despite the sunshine. So many people had attended Gwen Tavich's funeral; Adam felt cheated he was only getting to know her in death.

He had spent the majority of the service looking to see if anyone seemed out of place. Killers were known to attend the funeral of their victims, getting some sort of thrill at the pain and suffering they had caused loved ones. Psychologists believed often it was as powerful as the act of killing.

Ty Butler was also at the funeral, sitting with the family. Of course, they had no idea the police suspected him of anything. But if they were paying attention to the body language between Butler and Kendall—which they most certainly were not, their focus on honoring Gwen—they would've seen the two were excessively uncomfortable being near each other. Neither looked at the other. Spoke to the other. Or sought to console the other.

A man, another feeb, maybe Kendall's partner—Adam could tell the way all law enforcement officers could spot each other—sat behind Kendall and grasped her shoulder. A petite brunette sat next to him and offered Kendall a sympathetic smile when she turned to greet them.

Down a slope at the back of the church, Quentin Novak stood along a fence, a plume of smoke circling his head.

"Mr. Novak," Adam greeted him. "I didn't know you smoked."

"Quentin." Novak crushed the end of his cigarette against the post. "I rarely do. Kendall gave me enough shit when we first met, it was just easier to quit than deal with her constant harassment. Haven't had one in a couple of years. But, this—" he gestured back toward the mourners—"this is too much."

"I hear ya. There has been many a day I wish I hadn't quit smoking," Adam added, hoping to find some common ground between them. He needed something to smooth over the fact he was about to ask the man questions which could be considered offensive, especially today of all days. It was bullshit. Adam had tried smoking in high school to look cool, but couldn't get past the disgusting taste cigarettes left in his mouth. "Hey, you mentioned the other day you'd been to the restaurant the night Gwen went missing."

"Yeah, to pick up food for Kendall and me."

"And you spoke to Gwen about Ty not being there."

"Yes."

"I got the feeling the other day there was something else, but you were reluctant to say in front of Kendall."

Novak pushed his sunglasses up his nose and inhaled deeply. "That's true."

"Well, Kendall's not here, so spill the beans."

He stilled for a moment. "I was upset about something that happened at work. I was talking to Gwen about it."

"I heard the discussion was loud and angry."

"Yes, but not at Gwen. She was always my sounding board— someone I could vent to about . . . *things*."

Adam waited for him to elaborate, and when Novak still said nothing, asked, "What happened at work that was so upsetting?"

Novak rubbed the back of his neck. "I was able to solve this glitch we've been having in a game we produce—it's been a pain in our asses for months now, thought we might have to remove the game from the servers because people were complaining so much about it and we couldn't figure out a way around. Anyway, I figured it out, took the solution to one of my coworkers, and we decided to double-check the solution after we got back from lunch, and before we took it to our boss. Well, the fuckstick screwed me over and took it to the boss while I was out. So, not only did he get the credit for it, but the five-hundred-dollar incentive to anyone who came up with a viable solution."

That was it?

"Why wouldn't you want Kendall to know about this?" Adam asked. "You seemed to want to keep this from her when I questioned you about it."

"The truth is, this happened about a week before . . . before Gwen died, and I had already talked to Kendall about it. Twice. She told me I needed to get over it. I guess I didn't want her to know I was still so upset about it and taking it to Gwen." He dropped his gaze and shuffled his feet before looking at Adam again. "Seems less important, given what's happened."

Quentin squared his shoulders and glanced up the hill toward the church. "It's clearing out. I guess I should go check on Kendall."

"Yep." Adam put his hand out. "Thanks for answering my questions. I'm very sorry for your loss."

Novak gave him a slight nod and sauntered up the hill, making a beeline for Kendall.

Adam wasn't sure if he had a good enough read on Novak to believe him. There was virtually no way the story could be substantiated. But then again, there was really no reason to believe Novak wasn't telling the truth either.

39

JAKE AND FELICIA each gave Kendall a hug as she stood outside the church following Gwen's service. Felicia told Kendall she'd have Jake drop off a casserole—lasagna, Gwen's favorite—later in the day. Kendall thanked her, although to her it sounded more like a mumbled affirmation that was barely understandable.

Ty hadn't stayed long after the service. They had scarcely acknowledged each other the entire day. It was too hard for Kendall to feel bad for him. There were so many questions. And while she didn't truly believe Ty had killed Gwen, something was not right. Ty was lying and being secretive, which was enough for Kendall to harbor some bitter feelings toward him. Kendall would move heaven and earth to find out who murdered her best friend. She expected Gwen's fiancé to do the same. But Ty was too shrouded in secrecy and his own issues for her to be able to cross his name off the list of suspects—or for him to assist in uncovering who murdered Gwen.

Unless Adam was right, and Ty acted guilty because he *was* guilty.

"Hey, Kendall." Gil Brandt, Kendall's neighbor, gave her a hug. "I'm so sorry about Gwen. How are you doing?"

"I'm hanging in there," she said, a lump in her throat. It was getting easier, keeping the grief in check. But today she was forced to fight back the tears. Nonstop crying was physically exhausting.

"Well, if you need anything, please don't hesitate to call Cindy or me. We're happy to help with anything you need."

"Thanks, Gil. I appreciate it." Kendall tried to keep her emotions from spilling over.

"I'm sad the restaurant won't be around either," he added almost as an afterthought.

Her head shot up, taken by surprise. "What?"

"Well, I mean, I know it's still going to be a restaurant, but it won't be the same without Gwen and Ty running things. There was something magical about the two of them working together in that place. They were the perfect balance. I'm not sure I can go back in there, you know, with new owners."

Kendall's heart stopped. "What are you talking about, Gil?"

"I guess I assumed you knew. Ty put out feelers for interested buyers last week. It took me back a bit, so soon after Gwen's death and all. But I guess he needed to do something with it. Still, it will never be the same."

"Do you know if he found someone to buy it?" She was dizzy. Slightly disoriented.

"I think so, but I'm not completely sure. A friend of mine knows a guy who has a couple of restaurants in Telluride and Aspen. I guess he was putting in a bid on it."

"Huh," she said. Someone tapped her on the shoulder. Another one of Gwen's relatives she had met at one time or another over the years whom Kendall didn't remember. "Thanks, Gil. I'm sure I'll be seeing you around."

She gave the woman a hug but was unable to concentrate on anything except Ty selling the restaurant.

Less than a week after Gwen had been found dead.

Kendall was discovering there was a whole lot she didn't know about the people she was closest to in her life.

40

THERE HAD BEEN no burial for Gwen Tavich. Winter in the Rockies meant no bodies would be actually placed in the ground until the spring thaw. There was a gathering for friends and family at the Tavich home, but Adam was neither. And Kendall had enough support to get her through the remainder of the day. The best thing Adam could do was find a murderer—or two.

Walking into the squad room, he glanced around for Saul. In the Jenna Rose war room, Fletch caught his eye and waved him in.

"Was just about to call you," he said.

"What's up?"

Saul disconnected a call he was on and placed his cell phone on the conference room table. "We think we've found a connection between Jenna's case and some unsolved murders."

"It's tenuous at best," Fletch said.

"Well, it's something, at least," Saul agreed.

Adam drew in a calming breath. "Someone want to clue me in on this flimsy link?"

Saul sat forward in his chair, arms on the table. "We started looking at cases where the victim had been sodomized by a gun—"

"—found jack shit—" Fletch said.

"Then we widened the net and searched for victims who had been sodomized with any sort of object—"

"Jackpot!" Fletch bellowed.

Saul grimaced his displeasure at being interrupted.

Adam wasn't interested in how they provided the information—just that they did. "And?"

"And so far we think we have five victims, including Jenna, who were defiled in a similar fashion. I just called down to records to get the files pulled on these other four vics."

Adam grabbed a chair and sat down. "So, how are they connected?"

"All of them died from injuries sustained from being sodomized—"

"Practically fucking impaled—" Fletch clarified, which caught the exasperation of Saul again.

"—with a foreign instrument."

Adam nodded. "Lay it out for me."

Fletch picked up a dry erase marker and approached the whiteboard, ready to add the vics' information to the murder board. Saul shuffled through his notes. "Isabelle Kenyon. Nineteen. Cause of death: exsanguination. A screwdriver was found lodged into her uterus. Coroner determined the instrument had also caused severe injuries in her anus."

Saul glanced at Fletch to see if he was caught up before continuing. "Jessica Coen. Eighteen. Same cause of death. Instrument: glass bottle, believed to be a beer bottle. Only vic where the murder weapon was recovered—at least parts of it."

Adam ran his hand through his hair. The cruelty of people was incomprehensible sometimes. "Just one bottle did enough damage to kill her?"

"ME believed there were at least two bottles used." Saul looked at Adam. "One for each hole. Also stated the majority of the injuries were from the glass breaking inside the victim."

"She bled to death also?"

"Yes." Saul waited for Fletch to finish writing. "Next up, Amy Carrington. Twenty. Died from excessive blood loss from what the ME states was a broken handle of a broom. Naturally, the asshole used the broken end to penetrate her, again uterine and anus."

A chill ran through Adam like a Nordic wind. Four young women. Their lives extinguished before they'd had a chance to really live. Dying in what had to be excruciating pain. There was not a hell savage enough for the evil son of a bitch who had done this.

"And, finally, Megan Southerland. She's the youngest at sixteen. ME couldn't state the murder weapon definitively, but injuries were consistent with a crowbar."

Saul took in a long, deep breath and exhaled slowly. "The bastard rammed that thing inside that poor little girl so hard, it perforated her intestines and stomach."

"Jesus," Adam muttered. He stared at the board. The unusual deaths did link the first four women, that was true. But Jenna had been sodomized by a gun. "I can see where you're going, but it's slim. The change in how he killed them is definitely the weak link."

"Perhaps," Saul said. "But hear me out. All five of the women were injured and those injuries were severe enough that they all bled to death. All the injuries were to their . . . private parts, the murder weapon a foreign instrument. He used a different weapon on each of them."

"But in the first four deaths, he basically impaled them with the weapon. With Jenna, he used a gun, shot her."

"But it's pretty damn close."

"And," Fletch turned toward them, his back against the whiteboard, "he may have gotten bored with 'sticking it to them'—so to speak—and wanted to try a new method."

Adam and Saul peered at Fletch with the same distasteful look. Fletch shrugged. "Just sayin', is all. But"—he pointed the marker at Adam—"that's not all that connects them."

"What else?"

"All of the victims were young, blonde, with blue eyes. Killed somewhere—crime scene unknown—and transported post-mortem. And all were dumped in a place where they would be discovered quickly." Fletch turned back toward the whiteboard. "Isabelle was in a park by her home. Jessica, in the Evergreen Nature Center. Amy, on the campus of the Colorado School of Mines—no, she was not a student there. And last, Megan, who was found by cyclists at the entrance to Red Rocks."

"And Jenna, at the golf course," Adam said. "How recent are we talking on these murders?"

"Well, that's the interesting part—and potentially the worst part. There's a seven-year gap between them. Isabelle Kenyon died in April, 2007. Jessica, August, 2008. Amy, February, 2010. And then the gap: Megan was killed May 2017. And Jenna, last year."

"So, we had a serial killer who went on hiatus and has now returned to kill again. Where was he for seven years?"

"Probably prison," Fletch said. It was the most likely explanation.

Saul rubbed at the growth along his jaw. "But he would've had to have been convicted of something other than murdering young, blonde, blue-eyed girls, or all of these cases would be solved."

"Dude has a predilection for raping young women," Fletch said. "Maybe he was up for rape. Got caught before he offed someone."

"Not likely," Adam said. "He may have started his career as a serial rapist, but once he started killing them, he wouldn't have gone back to just raping them. Serial killers don't revert back to where they started." They get more sadistic and twisted, pushing the boundaries of what will get them off.

"Won't hurt to check any rapists convicted of similar proclivities," Saul said. "It's a long shot, but best to check all the boxes."

Adam agreed. There was nothing worse than finding out a killer had slipped through law enforcement fingers because of an assumption based on zero fact when it would've been just as easy to check out even the flimsiest lead.

"Some of these cases are in other jurisdictions—one in Evergreen, another in Golden," Fletch said.

Adam stared at the whiteboard. Five victims. "Maybe there are other victims in other areas of the state we just haven't found yet."

CHAPTER

41

Friday,
March 6,
10:05 AM

Ty BUTLER SAT next to his lawyer, one of the top criminal defense attorneys in the city, Ashley Simmons, looking immensely perturbed he was forced to answer questions.
Which just pissed Adam off. Even if Butler was innocent, he
had no right to be put out. He was supposed to have loved
Gwen. It seemed inconceivable he wasn't cooperating more to
help clear his name and find the real killer.

And it was looking less and less like he was innocent.

"Mr. Butler, did you withdraw a large sum of money from
the business account last September?"

Butler glanced at Simmons, who nodded that Ty could
answer. "Yes, I took out a loan, which I paid back in November."

"Did Gwen know about it?" Adam never looked away from
Butler. At some point, even the most skilled criminal gave
something away. And Adam was going to make sure he didn't
miss anything Ty Butler was going to expose.

"Yes, she did."

"At the time you took the money out? Or was it when you
repaid the loan?"

"That's irrelevant," Simmons said. "They were equal business partners. Mr. Butler had every right to take out a loan
against the business. The loan repayment was satisfied."

"It matters if there was contention between the victim and Mr. Butler regarding the withdrawal," Adam said.

"I told her when I paid it back."

"What about this most recent withdrawal, Mr. Butler?" Adam spoke only to Butler, ignoring the lawyer's statement.

Butler shifted in his seat but kept his mouth closed tight as he glared at Adam.

"Mr. Butler, did Gwen know you took out another ten thousand dollars last month?"

"Yes, she knew," Butler said through gritted teeth.

"And when did she find out?" The men were in a visual standoff, their eyes locked onto the other's, neither one looking away.

"It makes no difference when she found out, Detective," Simmons said, attempting to draw Adam's attention from her client.

It didn't work. Adam continued to stare at Butler. "It makes a huge difference if he took the money out without Gwen knowing. It would've been the second time that happened, isn't that right, Mr. Butler? The first time she found out from the accountant, Oren Mitchell. What happened when she found out this time? Did you fight about it? Things go a little too far?"

The attorney leapt to her feet. "We're done here. Ty, don't say another word. We're leaving." She tossed her legal pad into her briefcase and shut it. Adam watched Butler and Simmons walk out of the room, the lawyer's high heels clicking on the tile. After another minute or two, Adam walked into the observation room.

"Well, that went about as well as I expected." He crossed his arms over his chest and glanced at Kendall. "Did you see or hear anything noteworthy?"

"I'm not sure. I need to mull it over, I guess. Seemed pretty defensive, though. I mean, if he really believes he has the right to borrow money from the business whenever he wants, why would he get so pissed? And why would his attorney be so bent out of shape?"

Adam shrugged. "All good questions that unfortunately lead to the conclusion he did something wrong, and both he and his attorney know it."

"It just doesn't seem to fit his personality or the crime." Kendall leaned against the wall directly across from Adam. "Ty has a temper, and I've seen it in action in the kitchen. And his line cooks know not to push him too far."

"Sounds like a guy who could lose it and kill someone in the heat of the moment," Adam said.

"Except I have never, ever seen him get mad like that and direct it toward Gwen. He hardly ever used profanity around her and definitely never directed at her. It was the one thing we used to laugh and joke about. How Ty's momma would knock him into the next week if she ever learned he had uttered a curse word in Gwen's direction. That was not the way she'd raised her boy."

"You weren't around them all the time, though, Kendall. Maybe that's something he kept strictly out of the view of others. Maybe he only lost it when she was at his house or something. You know abusers can go for years with people thinking they're great and wonderful pillars of the community because no one knows what goes on behind closed doors."

"Yeah." She nodded. "I know you're right, but it just doesn't seem possible."

"That's because you're too close to both of them. You don't want to see the worst in someone you've called a friend for so many years." He dropped his arms to the side and took a step toward her.

"Nice psychobabble bullshit, Detective."

"Yeah, well, I've been hanging around this chick who thinks she knows something about human nature just because she's a big bad-ass FBI agent. I guess it's rubbing off on me a bit."

"I seriously should kick your ass for calling me a chick." She passed by him and knocked him off balance leaving the interrogation room, forcing a low deep chuckle from Adam.

42

Saturday,
March 7,
11:07 AM

JIMMY BELL WAS proving to be elusive. Adam had gotten tired of following dead-end leads to find the man and had asked Officer Young to hunt him down. Young was proving to be quite a valuable asset, and Adam wondered if he should ask the boss to requisition the kid as a sidekick.

Cape optional.

Adam stared at the murder board in the conference room, hoping something would jump out at him. So far all he knew for sure was Gwen and Butler were having issues stemming from the growth of the business, and Butler was finding interests other than being a chef and business owner. Did that equate with murder?

No, but all the lies were definitely a red flag. There was no reason to lie about the phone calls, unless he had something to hide.

There was a knock on the door. Young stood in the doorway looking like a kid who found money and bought out the candy store. "I have some updates for you."

"Well, come in, my young padawan."

He took the seat opposite Adam. "First, the canvas of the area around the lake where the body was found turned up nothing. No one I spoke to remembers a car being parked along the side of the road or in front of their house the week prior to Ms. Tavich being found."

So the killer had been on foot.

"Also, I wasn't able to find any other security footage that showed someone walking down the street the morning of the twenty-eighth. Not many people had cameras, and those who did, the quality was extremely poor."

"Well, it was a long shot, but thanks for checking it out."

"You're welcome," he said, and smiled, "but I'm not done."

Adam watched the young officer. He seemed to be getting more comfortable around Adam. Less awkward. Perhaps a glimmer of personality coming through.

Adam rolled his hand in an effort to get Young to continue.

"I found Jimmy Bell."

That was good news. "Do tell."

"I was able to find the cab Mr. Bell took from the restaurant on the night of the twenty-second. I spoke to the driver, Antoine Kesh."

"And did he remember our Mr. Bell?"

"He did. Turns out Bell was just as belligerent with Kesh as he'd been at the restaurant, cursing and threatening the driver to let him out, told him he was going to get his gun and shoot him, along with other pleasantries."

Adam chuckled. He hadn't expected the kid to have a sense of humor. Young's cheeks went bright red, but he continued.

"Kesh doesn't have the same kindhearted nature Ms. Tavich seemed to have, and drove Bell straight to our front door and left him there. The boys downstairs booked him for D&D, and tossed him in the drunk tank, where he stayed until approximately ten thirty the next morning, when his blood alcohol level was back to reasonable."

"And where did Bell go after that?"

"Home. Packed a few things, got into his Mercedes, and drove to a 'spa' in Green Mountain Falls for some R&R with a side of rehab. According to the intake nurse, who happens to be a friend of my family—so this is strictly off the record—"

Adam nodded and waved him on.

"Bell is a frequent flyer there. Shows up every few months, dries out, and goes back to his life of drunken folly."

"And how long was he there?"

"Still there."

"Hasn't left at all?"

"Nope. Turned over his cell phone and car keys, and is in self-reflection communing with Mother Earth."

"Huh," Adam said. If Bell had been in jail and then went straight to rehab, he wasn't Gwen's killer. As much as Adam wanted solid leads as to who killed Gwen, he would take being able to scratch one suspect off the list.

"Well done, young man. You get a gold star."

43

THE GROCERY STORE was busier than Kendall had thought it would be. Her few necessities took an hour to load into the cart, check out, and load into the Land Rover she had recently purchased to replace the BMW. Even though there had been no damage to the SUV, there was no way Kendall would be able to drive it—or a vehicle similar to it—ever again.

Her phone buzzed as she was returning the cart. A number she didn't recognize. "Kendall Beck."

"Hi, this is Sandra, from the restaurant."

"Hey, Sandra. What's up?" The woman had never called Kendall before, and she wondered how she had her number. And, more importantly, why she was calling.

"Um, so, not sure if this is a big deal or not, but I wanted to give you a heads-up since you and Gwen shared a place—"

"Okay," Kendall drew out. "What's going on?"

"I'm at the restaurant, doing some inventory. Ty was here, tearing through the office like a man possessed."

"Why was he doing that?"

"He was looking for something. But he was yelling obscenities. Basically ransacked the place."

"Do you know what he was looking for?"

"No, and I don't think he found it."

"What makes you say that?" Kendall scooted behind the steering wheel and started the engine. The call switched to hands-free, Sandra's voice now coming through the stereo speakers.

"He was muttering about going through Gwen's shit. He said something like, 'It has to be somewhere' or something like that. I asked him if I could help him find whatever he was looking for, on account I often did work in the office for Gwen, but he just kind of glared at me and said no and left in a huff. I swear, Kendall, I have never seen him like this. I mean, he's been belligerent in the kitchen, but there is definitely something wrong with him. He had this look in his eye—unhinged and panicky."

She paused. Kendall tried to imagine what Sandra was describing. In all the years she'd known Ty, starting from their last year in college, when he and Gwen had first started dating, he had never been the type to be anything other than laid back. Fun. Just plain *nice*. She had always attributed his outbursts in the kitchen to something chefs did. Ty was just Gordan Ramsey with a shaved head and darker skin.

"I think he might be on his way to your house—what with Gwen having a home office, and all," Sandra said. "I just wanted to let you know, since he seems to be in a bad place."

"Thanks, Sandra. I appreciate the call."

What the hell could Ty be looking for that had him in such a frenzy?

When Kendall pulled into her driveway, Ty's car was parked along the curb in front of the house. No one inside.

"Bastard," Kendall said under her breath. *How dare he use the key Gwen gave him to just let himself in.*

She opened the center console and took out her service weapon. If he was as agitated as Sandra portrayed, Kendall wanted to make sure she was protected. Too many things had happened lately, and Ty was becoming less predictable. It was not a time to let down her guard simply because they were once friends.

Tentatively approaching the front door, she carefully turned the knob and pushed it open. She peered around the corner into the living room and kitchen. Empty. Everything in its place. She had half expected the living room to be ransacked. She silently padded down the hallway. Gwen's door was closed. She put her ear to it. No noise coming from inside.

The sound of a chair rolling across the wood floor came from overhead. Kendall quietly ascended the stairs, keeping to the outsides of the treads to avoid any squeaks that would alert Ty. She wanted to make sure he was not in a rage. Or armed.

And she didn't want to have to shoot him. No one else was going to die.

At the top of the stairs, she butted up against the wall and slowly poked her head around the corner. File cabinet drawers were pulled out, the floor littered with their contents. Ty stood at the desk, head down, shuffling through a stack of papers. Completely oblivious to her presence.

In jeans and a T-shirt that hugged his muscular frame, there was no place to hide a gun. One less thing to worry about. She lowered the gun to her side but didn't holster it. "Ty, what the hell are you doing?"

He whipped his head around, his eyes wide. "Looking for something."

"I can see that." She pushed her gun into the waistband of her jeans at the small of her back. "What the hell are you looking for?"

"None of your business, Kendall," he snarled.

"And, see, I think you're wrong."

He snorted. "And I don't give a hairy rat's ass what you think. Now, how about you leave me alone so I can look through this . . . *shit*."

"How about you tell me why you didn't call before showing up and using a key to get in here. A key, I might add, that you need to turn over to me before you leave."

"Gwen gave me the key."

"Gwen's not here. I'm the only one living here now."

He continued to look through documents, letting them float to the floor as he rifled through the pile in his hand. "Just leave me the fuck alone, Kendall. I'll be out of here as soon as I find what I'm looking for."

"You have no right to be here, Ty."

"These are business records." He shook a handful of documents at her. His jaw was clenched tight, bitterness seeping from his pores. "For *my* business."

"Then you should've called me. Coordinated a time to stop by and get them."

"Fuck you. I have just as much right to be here as you do."

"Wrong. I have a lease that gives me the sole right to be on the property. You're trespassing and refuse to tell me why you're here."

"None. Of. Your. *Business*."

"Then I'm going to have to ask you to leave until it does become my business."

"And if I refuse?"

Kendall retrieved her gun and glanced at it without any expectation of using it.

Ty laughed. "What? You going to shoot me, Kendall?"

She pulled her cell phone from her back pocket with her free hand. "No, but I will call the cops if you don't leave now."

He stared at her for what could've been an eternity, releasing the papers in his hands, and took his keys out of his pocket. Removing the house key, he took a step toward her. She put her hand out, and he intentionally dropped it out of her reach.

"Oops," he said, a shit-eating grin on his face, his eyes as hard and dark as granite.

She followed him down the stairs and to the front door. He turned to her partway out. "I'll have my attorney get in touch with you to collect my business records."

"You do that."

She locked the door behind him and watched as he peeled away from the curb and took off down the road.

What the actual fuck was that all about?

Kendall had never seen Ty so angry, dismissive, and rude. Had she ever really known him? Had he duped her into thinking he was a nice guy? How could she not have seen this side of him before now?

After retrieving the groceries from the SUV, she filled a wineglass, not looking forward to the mess awaiting her in Gwen's office. She climbed the stairs to the attic, setting her glass and cell phone on the window ledge, which seemed to be the only clean spot in the room. It looked as if a cyclone had passed through. Papers littered the floor and desk. Gwen's chair was on the other side of the room. Usually Gwen's laptop would be in the center of the desk, but the police had taken it.

Ty had been looking for something at the restaurant. Something that made him determined enough to come here and ransack the place searching for it without informing Kendall he was coming. That told her he didn't want to have to explain what he was looking for.

So, what was Ty so desperate to find?

Whatever it was, he hadn't found it in the filing cabinet or the desk. Kendall stood in the center of the room, and slowly turned in a circle. Had Gwen intentionally hidden whatever Ty was looking for? If so, where?

And why?

The answer would most likely be apparent if Kendall could find the elusive document. Removing the desk drawers, she lifted them overhead. Taped to the bottom of the center drawer was a manilla envelope.

Bingo!

Kendall carefully removed the envelope and sat back. In very precise, neat, and distinctive handwriting was Kendall's name scrolled across it. Gwen had wanted her to find the document. Unclasping the flap, she extracted the papers inside. One was a letter. The other a form.

Not just any form. A change of beneficiary form for a life insurance policy. Kendall set it aside, and returned to the letter from the Hinton Small Business Insurance Company. It read:

Dear Ms. Tavich;

Enclosed please find the Change of Beneficiary Form you recently submitted. Since the policy is owned by the business, and not you, personally, any change in beneficiary must be agreed to by all owners of the business. Therefore, please have the co-owner, Tyson Butler, sign where indicated and return in the enclosed envelope.

The above regulation also pertains to your request to change the policy benefit amount. In order to decrease the amount of the payout, you will need to fill out the Change In Policy Payout Amount. Again, as with the Change of Beneficiary, we require signatures of both business owners in order to execute a change, in this case, a decrease, in the policy payout amount.

So . . . that's what Ty was looking for—the life insurance policy for the business. Did he know Gwen was attempting to change the beneficiary on the life insurance policy? And wanted to lower the benefit amount?

Bigger question—why was Gwen trying to make those changes? Had she been able to get Ty to sign off on them?

A sick feeling swirled in her stomach. Bile rose in her throat. Was the fact Gwen wanted to change the policy the reason she'd been killed?

Had Ty killed Gwen before she could make the changes?

Anger lit a fire in Kendall's belly and scorched through her veins. She had to find that policy. If Gwen had hidden this letter, she must also have hidden the policy.

That's what Ty was looking for—he was planning on cashing in on the policy.

Was the payout substantial enough to kill for?

She checked under the other drawers. Nothing. Likewise, zero paperwork tacked to the back of the desk. On her hands and knees, she used the flashlight on her phone to peer underneath. Only a few dust bunnies.

She rocked the filing cabinet away from the wall. Nothing taped to the back of it. No wall panels that could've been removed. Taking down the two framed Monet watercolor knockoffs from the wall, she envisioned a hidden wall safe or some other type of cubby. Zilch.

The rafters were exposed, so there was no way of secreting anything there.

A three-shelf bookcase, about five feet long, fit snuggly where the roof sloped and met the wall. Kendall knelt before it, grabbing books out, leafing through the pages for anything placed in between. When that didn't yield anything, she scooted the bookcase away from the wall.

A piece of drywall had been cut away. She pushed against it, and the drywall fell into a hole. Kendall grabbed her cell phone and shined the flashlight into the darkness. At first, all she could see was insulation. Carefully peeling it back exposed a hard-sided, zippered folder flush against the exterior wall. A trifolded legal document was the only thing inside. Kendall initially thought it was Gwen's will. But why put it in a spot where it was unlikely to be found? It didn't make sense.

Kendall moved out from behind the bookcase and cleared a spot on the floor. Unfolding the pages, she smoothed them out. "Hinton Small Business Insurance Company" was printed in big letters across the top. She quickly read the first few lines. The life insurance policy for the business. Gwen had told Kendall about it when she had renewed the policy. Kendall had no idea at the time there was such a thing—or a need—for business life insurance. But Gwen had explained the policy was so the surviving owner could keep the business running during the transition period.

Kendall gasped when she read the payout amount. Five million dollars. She flipped through the pages until she found what she was looking for: beneficiary name.

Tyson Butler.

When had Gwen placed the policy in the hidey-hole behind the bookcase? Did she believe her life was in danger?

She had to have suspected Ty might kill her.

The ache in Kendall's heart returned, nearly squeezing the life out of her. Why hadn't Gwen come to Kendall with her suspicions?

Her heart squeezed tight in her chest. The cold wave of grief engulfed her.

Delving into that was going to take more time, introspection—and alcohol—than Kendall could devote to it now. The main priority was to find out who had murdered Gwen. Once that was accomplished, Kendall could ponder how she had failed her best friend.

One thing was for sure; with Gwen dead, Ty stood to gain a whole hell of a lot of money.

The kind of money that made people forget love existed.

44

Sunday,
March 8,
1:34 PM

THE SQUAD ROOM was quiet on Sunday afternoon. While detectives were always on call, Adam typically had a nine-to-five workweek, and wasn't required to work on the weekends. Two unsolved murders on his plate meant "typical" went by the wayside, and his workweek necessarily bled into the weekend. It wasn't a requirement, but an unofficial part of the job.

Patrol officers were three hundred and sixty-five days a year, twenty-four hours a day, seven days a week. The hum one floor down was the same as any other day of the week. The buzz patrol officers created in the building was constant. And, Adam often thought, somewhat soothing. Comfortable. Familiar. A little like home.

He typed an email to Fran at the ME's office, and asked her to look at the autopsies of the five victims Saul and Fletch had discovered. He was curious if she would be able to determine any consistencies between the Jenna Rose case and the other cases. Perhaps the ME at the time had missed something. Or, as Fran believed Nestor had done, simply misidentified something that would link the cases together.

Truth be told, Adam wasn't sure how he felt about potentially unearthing a serial killer who'd been killing undetected for several years. It was almost a win–lose sort of scenario. Not that it mattered—serial killer or not, Adam was going to do everything in his power to solve Jenna Rose's murder, along with the other victims'.

Email sent, Adam shifted gears—and cases—and opened the thumb drive with the pictures a plainclothes detective had taken at Gwen Tavich's funeral. Adam hadn't seen anything odd. Hopefully, the photos or video would shed light on who killed Gwen, and why.

In every photo Kendall was in, she looked visibly upset. Like she was struggling to hold it all together and failing miserably. She wore a black sweater dress with boots that came almost to her knees, and a simple strand of pearls. Kendall told him the pearls had belonged to Gwen and had been given to her by Darla Tavich just before the service.

The Tavich family seemed to consider Kendall one of them, which was going to make it easier in the months to come, when things settled down and a new normal kicked in. Life would go on for most everyone else at the funeral. But for Kendall and Gwen's family, life would never quite be normal again. And it would be difficult to see other people going about their business as if the most precious person in the world hadn't been horrifyingly ripped from their lives. They would need each other to get through those times.

And the realization that Adam would probably never see Kendall after this case was solved sucker punched him in the gut. He liked Kendall. Their relationship felt natural, as if they'd known each other for years. She was hot, yeah—and it wasn't that Adam hadn't wondered about what she would be like in bed; he was still a guy—but he didn't get warm fuzzy feelings from her. She was definitively in the friend zone, and Adam was okay with that.

He returned his attention to the pictures. Quentin Novak was never far from Kendall except for the period of time Adam had found him sneaking a smoke. Adam was pretty sure Quentin was in the definitive friend zone as well. Kendall didn't seem to have men in her life who were anything more than friends.

He picked up a photo of Ty Butler. The man was sullen. Alone. A hint of anger in his demeanor. He didn't appear to be interacting with the family either. That was interesting. Had they shunned him? Kendall and Adam had been vague about naming any suspects around the family.

Was he feeling guilty?

Flipping through more pictures of people Adam didn't know, and who probably had nothing whatsoever to do with his case, he came across a few photos of a man in gray slacks and a white dress shirt, no tie. He was leaning against a tree and appeared to be surveying the mourners. It was peculiar he never had anyone around him. Not one shot showed him interacting with another person.

Curious . . .

Queuing the video, he fast-forwarded until he found the man. Standing in the same spot for nearly twenty minutes. He spoke to no one. Adam tried to remember where the tree was in relation to the church to figure out what or who the man was looking at. Strike that—staring at—because as far as Adam could tell, the man's gaze never deviated from one particular area.

What the area was could tell Adam a great deal about this man who seemed so out of place.

Adam printed off one of the pictures and taped it to the murder board. Next to it he wrote:

MAN AT FUNERAL
NAME & RELATIONSHIP: UNKNOWN

Who are you?
And what was he doing at Gwen's funeral if he didn't seem to know a single person?

45

Monday,
March 9,
2:03 PM

KENDALL PARALLEL PARKED along the curb across the street
from The Oyster, and let the vehicle idle. She gazed at her
best friend's restaurant. It looked so odd. Felt wrong. Normally
she would've parked in the lot at the back of the building and
entered through the kitchen. Greeted the staff on her way to
the bar, where Gwen usually sat keeping an eye on things. But
it wasn't the same now.

The restaurant was closed. Gwen wasn't inside getting ready
for the busy night ahead. She was gone, and nothing would ever
be the same again.

A few minutes later, Ty's Lexus pulled onto the street, and
he passed her without a single glance her way. Of course, he
wouldn't have recognized the new Land Rover. Even if he had
taken note of it parked in her driveway when he stormed out of
the house the previous day, it was doubtful he would associate
this one with her. They weren't friends anymore. There was
really no reason, now that Gwen was gone, for Ty and Kendall
to spend time together. Sad how many lives and relationships
were affected when one person died.

But it wasn't only Gwen not being there. Ty and Kendall
were like strangers now. She would probably never see the people who used to work at the restaurant. Some of them she'd seen
on an almost daily basis. She hated it. Hated the person who

had done this to Gwen—to all of them. And she really hated that it might have been Ty.

Kendall edged into traffic and stayed a far enough distance behind Ty's little black sports car to not be conspicuous but still keep him in sight. The sun was out, but there was not enough heat to melt the snow from the ground. Luckily, the heavily traveled roads were clear. But more snow was in the forecast that evening. Kendall had never been one to put much stock in weathermen; there was a chance they would get a light dusting of the white stuff, or maybe five feet. It was basically a crapshoot during Colorado as winter transitioned to spring. Hell, there was no guarantee snow wouldn't show up in summer.

Ty took the exit for I-70 west, out of town. A well-traveled stretch of highway leading into the Rockies, so there was no problem keeping a few cars between them. About thirty minutes later, he took the exit for Blackwood. Three other cars did the same. Kendall brought up the rear.

Something was up with Ty, and she needed to know what it was. If he had killed Gwen, she was going to make sure he paid for it.

God, I hope it doesn't come to that.

Fifteen minutes later, she drove up in front of the Blackwood Resort and Casino, nestled into the side of the mountain. Finding a parking place, she hurried into the casino, praying she would catch sight of Ty again before he disappeared. Or saw her.

It would've been impossible to explain why she was there. Ty knew Kendall had a thing about casinos. Ever since driving home from the one she worked at on the weekends while in college, when she had rescued Amy Carrington from a madman, only to be shot and left for dead. She had never set foot in a casino again.

Until today.

Her stomach twisted into a knot. Her breathing sped up, and sweat trickled down her spine. The smell was the same. The atmosphere. She forced the memories back, reminding her wandering brain she was there for Gwen. That was more important than some inability to deal with the past.

The foyer led to a second-story balcony that circled the gaming floor below. From up there, she had a bird's-eye view.

Standing along the railing, her gaze darted around the slot machines. She had absolutely no idea what Ty's preferred game of chance would be. She hadn't even known Ty gambled.

Finally spotting him at one of the machines along the periphery of the room, Kendall made her way down the large staircase, weaving through the rows of machines until she found a place to stand and watch Ty, yet could remain low profile.

"Can I get you something to drink, honey?" A woman in a skimpy outfit, balancing a tray of empty cocktail glasses on one hand, stopped beside her.

"Um, no, I'm just waiting for my friends to get done so we can go to the pool," she lied, and sat on the tufted bench against the wall.

The waitress nodded and walked away. Kendall glanced back over at Ty just in time to see a large, bald-headed man in a suit approach him. They shook hands, spoke for a moment, then Ty got up and walked off the gaming floor, with the man close behind. They made their way down a hallway. The man held a door open for Ty to pass through and then stood guard outside.

About five minutes later, Ty came from the hallway, paused, and then headed in the opposite direction. He took the stairs two at a time and disappeared at the top.

Taking her phone out, Kendall took a quick selfie as the waitress stopped next to the bench again. "Sure I can't get you anything?"

"Um, Diet Coke, please." She needed something to keep from drawing the wrong eyes on her and having to answer questions about who she was and why she was there. If they checked her ID, they would discover she was an FBI agent.

And Kendall didn't want that cat out of the bag yet. If at all. Casinos tended to have a shady underbelly. Feds were rarely welcomed.

The waitress nodded and walked away. Kendall watched the hallway out of the corner of her eye. Before long Ty's large escort, along with two others of equal size, appeared. Another man, shorter and impeccably dressed in an Armani suit, stood in the middle of the threesome, guarded as they all walked toward her. She took her phone out and snapped a picture of the man, and then quickly pulled up the selfie she had taken a few minutes before.

One of the muscle halted in front of her while the others continued on their way.

"What are you taking pictures of? You can't take pictures of the gaming floor." His voice was low, deep, and threatening.

She showed him the selfie. "It was of me," she said, forcing her voice to be meek. "I'm sending it to my friends to tell them to hurry up. I'm tired of waiting for them, and I want to go to the pool. That's all." She forced her words to sound rushed, nervous.

The man's face softened a bit. "Okay, well, make sure you keep the camera this way and not toward the gaming area."

"Oh, I will. I promise."

He looked her up and down, a leering smile across his face, and walked away. Kendall shuddered. Why men thought women were there to create a sexual fantasy for them to revisit later and get their rocks off would remain one of the great mysteries of the world.

Kendall pulled up the picture she had taken, hoping to God the man in the middle wasn't fuzzy or out of focus. It was a pretty good pic, but she had no idea who he was. His hired muscle indicated that he was not someone who liked to be trifled with.

"What the hell have you gotten yourself mixed up with, Ty?" she muttered under her breath, and headed up the staircase to leave.

46

SUNNY AFTERNOONS WERE not the best time to find agents in the Bureau. Magically, they all seemed to come across new information they had to "check out" in the field, instead of sitting at their desks. Kendall knew it was going to be a long shot at finding her buddy who handled racketeering cases still in the office. But she really needed him to see this picture and tell her how much shit Ty was in.

Rounding the corner, she nearly plowed into Stuart Barnes as he was coming out of his tiny office space.

"Jesus H, Kendall. What the hell?"

"Sorry, Stu, wasn't paying attention." She glanced down at the brown leather attaché case in one hand and his keys in the other. "I know you're probably trying to get out of here, but I need you to take a look at a picture and see if you recognize a guy."

He sighed, forcing the air out his nose while grimacing.

She held up two fingers. "Two minutes, I swear, and then I won't ask anything of you for, like, a month. Promise." She was pathetically giving him her best sad, sweet, lost-girl eyes. She hated stooping to that level.

His shoulders relaxed. "Two minutes," he conceded. "And you will not harass me again for three months."

"I wouldn't say I really harass you—"

He stepped back out into the hall and took a step away as if leaving.

"Sorry, you're right. Three months, no harassing. Got it." She pulled the photo of the man in the casino up on her phone and handed it to him.

He quirked up a brow. "What do you have going on that you're messing in circles with loan sharks and mob bosses?"

"You know him?"

"Yeah, everyone in this division knows him. Stanislav Volkov. We've been trying to get someone undercover in his organization for damn near forever. Every time we think we've infiltrated them, we find an agent who lost limbs and body parts while hiking in the mountains."

Kendall's blood went cold. "He's Russian? What's he doing here?"

"Legitimately running a casino, if you ask him. It's the behind-the-scenes action that's the most lucrative, though." Stuart sat down at his desk, withdrew his laptop from his bag, and opened it.

"Loaning gamblers money is lucrative?" Kendall asked. "Seems like a poor investment in people who can't manage money."

Stu started typing on his keyboard and answered without looking up. "*Pfft*, that's not the lucrative part. That's the part where he feels he can legitimately break bones. No, the real capital is in money laundering, drugs, and whatever else he can get his hands on and sell on the black market back in the home-land. Russia is still pretty sheltered, and Volkov is capitalizing on that by selling drugs, stolen goods, and guns to people will-ing to pay big money back in Mother Russia."

He swiveled in his chair and faced her. "So, back to my question. Why are you interested in Volkov?"

"I'm not sure, but I think a friend of mine may have gotten mixed up with Volkov somehow. My friend was escorted into what I am assuming was Volkov's office at Blackwood, but I have no idea what went on. He came out a while later and left. Volkov and his henchmen followed a few minutes after."

"Well, if your friend came out of a meeting with Volkov in the same condition he went in, he should consider himself lucky. Volkov has a quick temper and doesn't have time for excuses. Of course, there's always the possibility your friend avoided a beatdown because he's on Volkov's payroll." Stu's eyes lit up briefly. "Any chance of that?"

Kendall thought about it. "Up until a week ago, I would've said no and firmly believed it. Now—I just don't know. He's acting strange. Lying to police investigating a murder—" Kendall didn't want to get into specifics about the case. She was using FBI resources on a case not only outside the purview of the FBI, but one she should not reasonably be involved in.

"Too bad. We could've potentially flipped him and made him a CI." *Confidential informant.* Kendall didn't think CIs had very long lifespans in the mob any more than undercover agents did. Stu closed up his laptop and placed it in his bag. "I sent you my files on Volkov and his organization. Don't share them or spread them around." He patted her shoulder as he left his cubicle and walked down the hall to the exit. "Anything interesting comes up, keep me in the loop."

"Thanks, Stu," she called. He waved his hand in the air over his head before the door closed behind him.

She pulled out her phone, intending to call Adam, when a notification popped up on the screen: *Meet Q—Telluride.*

"Damn." She pressed "Okay" and then called Adam. Quentin was bound to be bent out of shape if they had to leave for their grief-cation later than planned. But Kendall knew she would break the "no tech" rule they had agreed to if she wasn't able to bring Adam up to speed on the latest developments in Gwen's case.

"Hey," she said when Adam answered, "I need to go over some information I just discovered about Ty. Can we meet?"

"Yep, if you don't mind stopping over at my house. You can meet Bruno, and I'll even give you a beer."

"Big of you," she snorted. "What's the address?"

Kendall waited until she got into her SUV to call Quentin.

"You better not be calling to cancel on me." His voice was clipped, and he had no other greeting.

"No, just need about an hour to get some stuff cleared off my desk and grab a few things from the house." She pulled out onto the street and headed toward Adam's place in Lincoln Park.

"I thought you already packed."

"I'm packed, Q—calm your tits. I just remembered a couple of things I forgot to throw in my bag. I'll meet you at the house in an hour and a half, and we can take off, okay?"

"It's supposed to start snowing in three hours. I want to get ahead of it."

"I understand. Just give me a little extra time, and then I won't have anything diverting my attention while we're gone."

"Okay," he said, his voice softer. "Sorry if I'm coming off as an ass. I just really need to get away."

"I know, Q. Me too." There was silence for a moment between them. They really did need this time to grieve together. Both had lost someone they loved, and if Quentin was missing Gwen even a tenth as much as she was—well, they could both stand some quality healing time.

"See you in a bit," he said.

"Yep," she managed over a sob building in her chest. She clicked "End" and rolled down the window. *Air . . . I just need air*—and to push the sorrow and pain down, and get through this meeting with Adam without falling apart.

Falling apart would come later with Quentin. With someone who knew Gwen. Who knew her. Someone she trusted completely.

THE GATE SQUEAKED as it opened. Bruno dropped his ball and ran toward Kendall as she approached. She knelt down in front of him and grabbed his face in her hands.

"What a good boy." Her voice rose an octave as if she were talking to a baby. Bruno's tongue came out and lapped along her cheek over and over, giving his best face wash.

"Bruno," Adam admonished, but the dog was much too happy to stop, being egged on by Kendall's laughter. Adam walked over and grabbed the dog by the collar, yanking him away. "Get back, you dumb mutt."

Kendall stood up, wiping her face with her sleeve. "He's fine. I'm not afraid of a little dog slobber." She reached out and rubbed the dog's head. "And he is not dumb—he's a sweet boy." Bruno wagged his tail so fiercely Adam thought it might come flying off his body.

"Let me get him squared away so he'll leave us alone." He motioned with his head toward the table on the patio. "Make yourself comfortable. I'll be right back."

She nodded and started walking away. "You said something about a beer," she called over her shoulder.

"Red cooler by the back door." He found one of Bruno's favorite balls in the yard and tossed it toward the back fence. The dog took off after it, and Adam joined Kendall as she twisted the top off a bottle of Fat Tire.

"Do you always drink beer in your backyard on the eve of a new snow?" she asked.

Adam glanced up at the atmosphere. Thin cirrostratus clouds covered the darkening evening sky. "Dark ages disease." He glanced at Kendall, a quizzical look on her face. "The dark ages—January through whenever Mother Nature deems winter is over. I love Colorado, but I'm not a fan of winter starting in September and bypassing fall. The first three months of the year can be challenging, especially when the weather teases us with a taste of warmer temps, only to give us the finger by dumping five feet of snow." He took a long draw from his beer. "So, Bruno and I try to take advantage of any time we can be out here before the weather gods spin the wheel on how much snow will stick."

A small smile lifted one corner of her mouth. "The dark ages—appropriate."

He dropped into his seat. "So, whatcha got for me?"

She took a swig of her beer and plunked the bottle onto the table. After swiping the screen of her cell phone, she turned it toward him. "Know the short guy in the middle?"

He took the phone from her, looked at the man, and handed it back to her. "No, who is he?"

"Stanislav Volkov."

"The mob guy who owns the Blackwood?"

"So you do know him?"

"By reputation only. What's he got to do with this case?"

"Ty met with him this afternoon." Her face was stone, but he could tell she was tempering the excitement in her voice. Good investigators loved the thrill of the hunt, and coming up with a clue tended to bring on excitement even in the most dire cases.

"Really? What about?"

She took another drink, leaned back in her seat, and shrugged. "Don't know. I had an agent in racketeering ID Volkov. He said Volkov is in pretty deep with black market shit to Russia. I have no idea how that fits in with Ty or this case. If it even does."

Adam dragged his hand down his face. This case was getting more and more bizarre.

"Do you think Ty could be in bed with Volkov?"

Kendall inhaled deeply and released the breath in one long sigh. "God, I hope not. That adds a whole new level of shit to this situation I don't even want to consider. Opens up too many questions. How is Ty enmeshed with them? Did he get the mob involved with the restaurant?"

"If so, how much did Gwen know?" Adam asked.

"If she knew anything." Kendall's eyes darkened with a protectiveness for her friend's reputation. "Or did she find out Ty had gotten their business entangled with a very dangerous criminal organization?"

"And she was killed because of it?"

Kendall closed her eyes and shook her head. "It's almost too much to contemplate."

She was getting overwhelmed with the possibility the mob had killed her best friend, when there was no proof. Adam would check out the theory while she was gone, and hopefully put it to rest. Or solve the case and have all the answers for her when she returned.

And maybe the lottery fairies will sprinkle fairy dust over me and make me a billionaire overnight.

Time to switch gears. Adam pushed the cell phone records over to Kendall. "Take a look at those, see if you find anything interesting."

She picked them up and went through both pages—one with the notation that Ty had called Gwen's cell after two in the morning and the other showing the cell towers. She finally looked up at him, her eyes a bit larger than they'd been a moment ago.

"This can't be right. She was by his place?"

Before he could answer, Bruno let out a couple of barks as the gate latch clicked. Kendall lifted her eyes to the gate and then back to Adam.

"You have company." She bobbed her head toward the gate and looked back down at the two pages.

Adam turned his head and met the icy stare of Sheri as she stalked across the lawn toward them.

Aw, shit! What the hell is she doing here?

When she made it to the table, he smiled up at her and tried to gauge her mood. She stared at Kendall, who was still engrossed in the cell records, and then swung her eyes to his.

They were narrowed, and for the life of him he couldn't figure out what her deal was this time.

"Hey, Sheri," he said. "What's up? Do you want a beer?"

"No." She practically spat the word out and then narrowed her eyes at Kendall.

Fuck me . . . she thinks Kendall and I are involved. Just shoot me now . . .

"Uh, Sheri, do you know Kendall Beck? She's with the FBI . . . she's collaborating on the Tavich case."

Kendall finally looked up and smiled at Sheri, putting her hand out to her.

"Sheri's a forensics specialist," Adam said, and took another swig of his beer, wishing it was vodka. Or hemlock.

"It's nice to meet you," Kendall said.

Sheri smiled back, but her jaw was clenched and the vein in her neck was throbbing. "The FBI? Why are you involved in this case?"

"The FBI isn't officially involved," Kendall stated, not seeming to notice the icy nature of his ex. Or not giving a shit. "The victim was my roommate, so Adam is graciously allowing me to butt in on his investigation. Are you the one who came up with these phone records?"

"Yes, that's part of my job." There was a slight twinge of defensiveness to her tone.

"Excellent work. These are golden."

For the first time in months, Sheri smiled in Adam's presence. Of course, it had absolutely nothing to do with him, but at least some of the awkwardness was subsiding.

"Well, if you like that, you'll love this." Sheri's body relaxed. She shifted so Adam was blocked from the conversation, and spoke directly to Kendall. He was being left out of his own investigation by these two pushy women—and in his own backyard.

Sheri pulled up a voice recording on her phone and turned up the volume. Ty Butler's voice filled the air.

"Baby, please talk to me. I'm so sorry you had to find out this way. I know you don't trust me, but you have to believe that I never meant to hurt you. Please, Gwen, call me back so we can talk about this. I need for you to understand why I did this . . .

I was going to tell you. I swear, I was going to come clean and make it right—for everyone. I'm . . . I'm so sorry."

The mechanical voice announced there were no other messages.

"Is that from Gwen's cell phone?" Kendall asked.

Sheri nodded. "We were finally able to get to her voicemail. The call originated from a cell phone belonging to Tyson Butler."

"Son of a bitch." Kendall fell back in her chair, looking like a kid who just found out Santa and the Easter Bunny weren't real.

"Can you email that recording to me?" Adam asked Sheri. She glanced over at him and nodded. No smile, but she wasn't scowling or burning holes into him either. He was counting that as a win.

"Well, I just stopped by to give you that bit of information. I'll leave you to mull it over," Sheri said.

Kendall sat forward. "Yeah, I have to get going in a minute also. Quentin and I are headed up to Telluride for a few days."

A smile spread across Sheri's face. *Guess she thinks Quentin is Kendall's boyfriend or something,* Adam thought. Although, why she would care if he was involved with Kendall baffled him. After all, Sheri hated him. With a deep passion reserved for someone looking to nail another to the cross. What the hell would she care if he was dating someone else?

"It was nice meeting you, Kendall," Sheri said, shaking Kendall's hand once again. She turned to Adam. "I'll give you a call later. Maybe we can get a bite to eat or something?"

He froze. Head dizzy. More than a little terrified. He barely remembered hearing the gate latch when she left. *What the hell just happened?*

"Hey! Earth to Adam." Kendall snapped her fingers in his face. "Want to come back to this plane of existence and talk to me? I don't have much time."

"Uh, yeah, sorry," he stammered like an idiot.

Kendall smirked. "Got the hots for the forensic expert, Taylor?"

"No, that ship sailed a while back. I have no fucking idea what that was all about."

Kendall shook her head and made some sort of snorting sound. "You're an idiot."

"Do we actually know each other well enough for you to say that to me?"

"Well, she either had a change of heart, hasn't had sex in a while, or is wondering if there is something between us and wants to put a stop to it." Kendall drained her beer and placed the empty bottle on the table.

"Nah, she hates me."

"So? Just because *she* doesn't want you doesn't mean she wants another woman to have you. Think of it as the female version of the pissing match. She's marking you, reminding you she's still around, in case you decide to go find something else before she is secure in another relationship."

"That makes no sense."

"Most human mating rituals don't, but I don't have time to educate you on the male and female libido and the mind games accompanying them. Let's talk about the phone message. I'm already going to be late meeting Q."

"What's to talk about?" Adam got another beer from the cooler, sucking down half of it. "Seems pretty clear to me. Gwen was on her way over to confront Butler. He obviously knew she had found out about him taking the money—or the mob connection—"

"We don't know there is one—"

"Where there's smoke."

She rolled her eyes.

"Hear me out. She gets to his place, they argue, things get out of hand. He kills her and tries to cover it up by dumping her in the lake."

"It's circumstantial. You have no proof he killed her."

"People are convicted on circumstantial evidence all the time." He leaned across the table and looked her straight in the eye. "Anyway, I have probable cause to obtain a search warrant for his apartment and get the crime scene unit in there to check for blood."

"I need more." She said. "I need the smoking gun."

"Who are you? Perry Mason? Cases aren't solved by confessions alone. And you'll never get the perfect case and all the evidence falling neatly into place and answering all the questions. Ty keeps lying, Kendall. He's had every opportunity to come clean, and hasn't. He stands to gain multiple millions of dollars with the life insurance proceeds and the sale of the business. I'd say that's a pretty strong case."

"Do what you have to do, Adam. Get CSU to go through his apartment. I just ask that you wait until I get back to arrest him. I need to wrap my head around all of this. Can you do that for me?"

He peered at her for a moment. "You know I can't make any promises. This is a murder investigation. *My* investigation. You're involved only because you also happen to be law enforcement. But you don't dictate how I run my case. And I don't have the luxury of putting things on hold while you go out of town."

She wrapped her arms around her chest and glared at him. But there was also a distinctive tinge of sadness in her eyes. He'd been too hard and now regretted what he'd said. And the veracity with which he'd said it. He leaned back in his seat and took a cleansing breath. "I'll try to stall as long as I can."

48

Q UENTIN STOOD WITH his arms across his chest as Kendall pulled into her driveway and met him at the front door. He was seriously pissing her off. They were delayed leaving by half an hour. *So what?* She understood he was a planner, and once a plan was made, he stuck to it—and expected everyone else to, as well. But he needed to get over his OCD planning bullshit and grow the fuck up. This was going to be hard enough on her without having to deal with his petulance the next few days.

The trip to Telluride was quiet. She turned onto the desolate winding road leading to the Taviches' cabin in the woods. Night engulfed them, which sucked. Now she would have to contend with Mr. Happy bitching about unloading in the dark.

They managed to get everything into the cabin in a couple of trips. Quentin was taking the bags to their rooms while Kendall unloaded the groceries in the kitchen.

"What do you want to eat tonight?" she called out to him. There was no response. "Yo, Q! What do you want to eat tonight?"

He came out onto the second-floor balcony overlooking the kitchen and great room, and stared at her for a moment.

"Seriously, are you really going to be a dick all week? 'Cause I'll take my shit and go home." She tossed a bag of potato chips into the cabinet and slammed the door closed.

"Not all week," he said. "About five more minutes, and then I'll be good."

She shot a death glare up at him and was met with his signature shit-eating grin. "And sandwiches are fine for tonight." He turned around and walked back into his room.

"Asshat," she muttered under her breath.

Grilled ham and swiss cheese sandwiches and tomato soup in the great room in front of a roaring fire was just what Kendall needed. Hanging with Quentin meant she didn't have to entertain him. He was content reading up on the latest computer tech crap while she read mysteries and thrillers. It was easy and comfortable.

The room had grown dark, making it impossible for her to see the print any longer. The cabin had taken on an eerie vibe as darkness settled in around them, without the benefit of city lights to provide any ambient light. Her chest tightened with each indrawn breath.

Closing the book and placing it on the table next to her, she let her head drop back against the couch cushion. A ton of horrible crap had happened in a short amount of time. It was hard to believe any of it was real. How she wished she could close her eyes and wish it all away. Wake up in the morning and find everything back to normal. But the burning in her chest reminded her that wasn't going to happen.

Quentin put his hand on her knee, turned sideways on the couch, and faced her. "It seems weird, huh? Being here . . . without Gwen. I feel like we're intruding or doing something behind her back. It's fucked up, I know, but—"

"Yeah, I feel it too. Not like she's here. It's the lack of her presence that's so disquieting. I'm overwhelmingly aware of her absence, and it feels all wrong." She stared straight ahead, visions of the three of them trying to start fires in the fireplace, laughing and joking about freezing to death, played like a comedy reel in her head.

It wasn't until tears hit her hands as they rested in her lap that she even realized she was crying. "God, Q, I miss her so much. I can't do this without her. She was my sister. How do I survive without her watching out for me?"

Quentin scooted closer, wrapping her up in his arms. He kissed the top of her head as she buried her face in his chest. "We do it together, Kendall. Like we have from the very beginning of our friendship. She would want us to be here for each other, to be what she would've been for us. We have to remember her strength and her love for us. It's the only way we get through this."

Kendall drew Quentin closer, clinging to him with every ounce of strength she had left. "I'm so glad you're here with me. I couldn't do this without you. It's just us now. Promise me you will always be here. Promise me you will never leave."

"Kendall, you're all I have . . . it's just you and me. And I'm not going anywhere."

Sobs filled the night air. She let go of everything she'd been holding back. All the pain. All the sorrow. All the guilt of not having been a better friend. All the anger and frustration.

They purged their souls. It was mentally, emotionally, and physically draining. They finally trudged up the stairs to their rooms in the wee hours of the morning. Hours had ticked by while they were reminiscing, laughing, and crying. It hadn't taken away all the pain and sorrow, but it was the first time in a long time Kendall felt she could breathe.

C H A P T E R

49

Tuesday,
March 10,
7:09 AM

FORENSICS WENT THROUGH Ty Butler's house on Tuesday morning. There was a long list of personal items—bills, receipts, entries for marathons he'd run. Nothing noteworthy. Preliminary chemical reports were devoid of anything significant. No blood. No chemical bleach smell. No new flooring to replace blood-soaked carpets pulled up and discarded. Since Gwen had been a frequent guest, finding her DNA was to be expected. The only evidence that would be substantive was the discovery of a considerable amount of blood.

It was beginning to look as if the search wasn't going to yield much. The lack of evidence didn't progress the investigation, but it also didn't clear Butler as a suspect. The lies were the sticking point with Adam. If Butler had nothing to hide, and everything was legit, why the deception?

There was also the big fat paycheck he was getting when the death certificate came in and he could sell the business and collect the life insurance.

"Detective?"

Adam walked into the bedroom. A crime scene tech had laid various items out on the bed. "Thought you might like to see these before I bag them."

Various items Adam recognized as BDSM devices sat on top of the comforter. Not that Adam had any personal experience with any of these accessories, but he'd been on enough crime scenes to know what they were. He just didn't know how they were used. Except for the butt plug. That one was pretty self-explanatory and made him want to clench at the thought of using one.

The items resting on one of the pillows garnered most of Adam's interest. A set of nipple clips and handcuffs. The ME had stated Gwen died as a result of electric impulses applied to her breasts, and had concluded it was through the use of metal clips attached to the nipples.

Gwen also had ligature marks around her wrists and ankles. The fact that there was only one set of handcuffs wasn't a disqualifier. He could've gotten rid of the other pair for some reason. Or used zip ties on her ankles and the handcuffs on her wrists.

Either way, this was damning circumstantial evidence. Along with all the other evidence, Ty Butler was looking awfully guilty.

Because Gwen had been nearby Butler's house just after two in the morning meant she could've stopped by and had an argument with him, and then he killed her to get the insurance money. Maybe he'd planned it all along. Perhaps having sex with her was just an added bonus.

Obviously he was having money issues—why else was he taking large sums from the business? They'd have to confirm that against his bank accounts and credit card statements, yeah, but Adam was certain there was something untoward going on financially. The appeal of having a few million dollars might've been more than Ty could pass up. And he'd done the unthinkable.

There was also Butler's association with the mob guy.

Adam needed to talk to the DA and get an arrest warrant for Mr. Butler. He couldn't risk Butler getting nervous and fleeing to some country without extradition laws while Adam waited for Kendall and Novak to finish up their getaway to the woods. Butler might already have a copy of Gwen's death certificate and just be waiting for the payout to hit his account.

Kendall would understand, eventually, but he needed to move on Butler. Immediately. Getting the man who murdered her best friend seemed more important than waiting until she was back in town.

*   *   *

Adam drove past The Oyster Grille. Butler's sporty Lexus sat in the parking lot next to an older -model Camry. He parked around the corner and dialed Sandra Bennett's number.

"Hello?"

"Ms. Bennett, this is Detective Taylor. If you are with Ty Butler, don't let on it's me on the phone."

"One moment, please." She held the phone away from her mouth. "Ty, I need to take this—it's my kid's school." Adam heard the squeal of a heavy metal door. "Okay, I'm outside. What's this all about?"

"Where is Mr. Butler?"

"He's going back and forth between the kitchen, the office, and the bar."

"Is anyone else in the restaurant?"

"No, just the two of us." She let out a heavy sigh laced with exasperation. "Detective, are you going to tell me what's going on?"

"I need for you to go back inside and leave the back door unlocked, and then get out of the kitchen. Do you understand?"

"Yes, I understand." She didn't ask any further questions.

"Okay, we'll be coming in in about three minutes." He hung up the phone and jogged toward the restaurant, texting one of the uniformed cops sitting in a van adjacent to the parking lot.

We are a go.

He met the cops, all wearing black tactical gear, next to Butler's car. Adam tightened the Velcro on the body armor covering his chest. The cops moved into the restaurant, Adam bringing up the rear. Sandra slipped out of the kitchen and into the dining room. Butler looked up from where he stood behind the prep table.

"You're supposed to go through my attorney if you want to talk to me, Detective."

"I'm not here to talk, Mr. Butler. You're under arrest for the murder of Gwen Tavich."

CHAPTER

50

Wednesday,
March 11,
10:42 AM

EARLY WEDNESDAY EVENING, Quentin and Kendall headed back to Denver. The few days at the cabin had been exactly what they needed. Once the Monday night bereavement purge occurred, they were able to enjoy the cabin and all it had to offer. They hiked the Jud Wiebe trail and had a picnic lunch above the Cornel Falls. The trail had been a favorite of Gwen's, and memories of her were everywhere along the nearly three mile hike. It was both tranquil and somber as they said a final goodbye to their best friend.

They agreed to remember past visits to the cabin without the extreme heartache weighing on them. It was inconceivable to think of Gwen being gone, but they could at least smile at some of the memories, and even laugh a bit, without the grief strangling them.

But at night, as Kendall was drifting to sleep, she couldn't shake the feeling of being watched. She had awakened the previous night sure she'd heard breathing inside her room. She flipped on the lamp, but the room was empty. When she investigated out in the hallway, no one was there, either. She crept down to Quentin's room, listening at his door for any noise indicating he was awake. But all she could hear were his snores. She chalked it up to her own paranoia over all the unanswered questions in Gwen's case. Somewhere, a murderer was roaming the streets. Free. Living a life Gwen had been robbed of.

And Kendall had never seen it coming. And that was making her uneasy. Seemed somewhat ridiculous—she was used to people's lives being taken at random moments. But this was different. This particular death hit a little too close to home. The unknown made her feel unbalanced and on edge.

She hadn't felt this way in a long time. Not since the Reaper shattered the glass bubble she lived in—the one that allowed her to think bad things happened to other people. Not to anyone she knew. Not to herself.

She had worked so hard to move past feeling the Reaper was waiting just around the corner to finish the job and kill her. But Gwen helped her manage her feelings and find a way to channel the fear and pain into helping other victims.

God, I miss her.

Kendall dropped Quentin off at his house, hauling his bags from the back while he grabbed their cell phones from the center console.

He handed Kendall's to her and smiled. "Well, that was an illuminating experiment," he said.

Her head cocked to the side. "Meaning?"

"We didn't die without our cell phones. We didn't even cheat. No sneaking off to check email or a quick glance at Facebook. Not once did we need these little pieces of technological mastery." He turned the phone over in his hand before looking up at her again with a lopsided grin. "Who woulda thought?"

"Who, indeed. I didn't even miss it." She hugged him and gave him a quick kiss on the cheek. "Must've been the company."

"Well, that goes without saying."

She punched him in the arm.

He rubbed his bicep. "Ow." Once his bags were gathered, he lumbered up the stairs to his front door. Climbing behind the wheel, Kendall turned her cell phone back on. Two messages, both from Adam.

"Kendall, hey, I wasn't sure if you'd have reception out in the woods or not. If you get this within the next hour, give me a call back. There's been a new development in the case. I need to talk to you about it."

The phone beeped and the second message played:

"Kendall, call me as soon as you get this message. I need to talk to you immediately. If you can't get me on my cell, try my desk phone at the station."

Kendall pressed the callback button and listened to it ring a couple of times. *What the hell happened that has Adam nearly apoplectic to talk to me?*

"Kendall. Where are you?"

"Back in town. I just dropped Quentin off and am heading home. What the hell is going on?"

"I had to arrest Butler." Adam's voice dropped and softened. "I'm sorry, Kendall. There was just too much evidence against him. The DA wanted to move."

"Are you kidding me? When did you arrest him?"

"Last night."

"And you couldn't wait for me to get back? That's bullshit, Adam."

"More evidence came in. I couldn't wait, Kendall. It's my ass on the line if he leaves the state."

"Whatever." *Sonofabitch.* "When's his arraignment?"

"Tomorrow morning, nine."

She ended the call without another word. It wasn't Adam's fault, but she needed to rage against someone, and he drew the short straw.

The fireball in her stomach, which had lessened over the last two days, came roaring back in a mass of hot flames, tightening, and scorching her gut. Whatever evidence Adam had uncovered must've been big.

Which meant her best friend's killer was the man Gwen had loved most in this world.

And that was unacceptable.

51

Thursday,
March 12,
9:24 AM

KENDALL STOOD IN the back of the courtroom, watching Adam talk to the prosecutors. She was still pissed he hadn't waited until she got back before arresting Ty, but also understood why he did it. The ability to be selfish at times was not an unknown to Kendall.

She just didn't want to believe Ty could actually be responsible for Gwen's death. And for what—money? Gwen would have given him everything she had. That's just the kind of person she was. She might bitch and moan for a while, but she would've gotten over it and given him whatever he needed.

Which was why none of it made sense. There had to be something Kendall was blind to. Her heart wanted desperately to find the missing link. Her head was telling her it was all in vain. The evidence against Ty was mounting. It was becoming more difficult to find reasonable doubt. Which just about broke her heart.

How could she have been so wrong about him? How could she not have seen what a danger he posed to her best friend?

The door next to the judge's bench opened and six people in orange jumpsuits, all shackled at the wrists and ankles, were led to the jury box and told to sit down. Ty was at the end of the line.

He looked as if he hadn't slept all night. His eyes met Kendall's, a mix of scared and pissed off. She gave him a slight head nod, but he just looked away.

She was the enemy now. And Kendall wasn't sure how to take that.

Adam leaned against the wall next to her. "Hey."

"Hey."

"You still pissed at me?"

"Yes." She glanced over at him. He had this injured puppy dog look. "No."

A shit-eating grin slid across his face.

"Don't gloat," she said.

"I'm not gloating. I'm happy . . . and relieved."

She quirked up one eyebrow.

"I was a little afraid you were going to kick my ass."

Kendall shook her head. *How are all the men in my life such pansies?*

About forty-five minutes later, Ty's case was called. His lawyer stood up and announced a plea of not guilty. The prosecutor requested no bail due to the serious nature of the charges and the large sum of money Ty would be receiving. Simmons argued Ty had never been in trouble with the law before and should be allowed to post bond.

The judge disagreed, and Ty would be transferred back to the county jail to await trial. All six inmates stood and were led back to the holding cell. As he left the courtroom, Ty glanced back over his shoulder. But he wasn't looking for Kendall. His eyes zeroed in on someone sitting in the front row. Whoever it was, was blocked from her view.

The morning court session was dismissed. Everyone seated in the gallery shuffled out into the hall. Kendall lingered, wanting to see whom Ty knew. An older man and woman got up and talked to one of the attorneys handling a different inmate's case. A woman in her early thirties was also there, but Kendall didn't recognize her. And an elderly man with a cane glanced up at Adam and Kendall as they stood along the back wall. He sneered at them as he passed, mumbling something she couldn't hear.

Adam glanced at her and shrugged. "Got time for coffee?"

"You buying?" she asked, as they headed toward the elevators.

"I guess, but if you continue to make me buy coffee and meals for you, people are going to think we're dating."

She squished up her nose and squinted. "No one would ever believe we're dating. There is no way I look desperate enough to go out with you, Taylor."

"Well, that's just mean."

Kendall laughed. She couldn't help it. Adam had the whole lost puppy dog eyes down, and it was just about the most pathetic thing she'd ever seen.

And it felt good, too. She rarely allowed herself to be happy these days. She had a death grip on her grief, never letting it get far away. It was the one constant in her life. The one thing she could control, and decide when to let it go. And it fueled her anger, which propelled her headlong into the investigation.

She had to find out the truth. Nothing else mattered beyond getting justice for Gwen.

CHAPTER

52

KENDALL WAS EASY to hang with. She drank beer, swore as much as the guys at the station, was not easily offended, and took her coffee black. There was a down-to-earth quality about her. Simple.

Adam needed simple and easy-going right now. He had arrested someone she considered a friend, for the murder of her best friend. And he felt as though he'd done it behind her back.

They took a table against the back wall. Away from everyone. She wasted no time interrogating him.

"So, what the hell happened? I thought you were going to wait until I got back before you made an arrest. What was so imperative you couldn't hold a few hours until I returned?"

"The search of his place uncovered a great deal of sexual paraphernalia, including nipple clamps and handcuffs."

"That's pretty thin, Adam." She took a large gulp of her coffee. "I have handcuffs. Am I a suspect?"

"We're law enforcement officers. Comes with the uniform, badge, and gun."

"They can be found at any sex shop in the area. It's not very strong evidence."

"By itself, maybe, but with all the other evidence, it points to him being the one who did this, Kendall."

"All of it is circumstantial."

"Which is an acceptable form of evidence to obtain a guilty verdict. We didn't always have DNA evidence for juries to drool over." He took a drink of his coffee, trying his best to quell the irritation blooming in his chest.

She shook her head, eyes down, her finger running along the rim of the cup.

"Look, we know Butler called Gwen and left a message. We know she was in the vicinity of his apartment building when she got the call. It makes sense she decided to go over and have it out with him about the money. She gets there, they argue, he loses it. Tortures her to make a point . . . or keep her in line. Things get out of hand, and he ends up killing her and dumps her in the lake. Intentionally or not, it's still murder."

Her eyes narrowed on him and she frowned. "And got back home, how? Walked all that way?"

"Why not? He's in good shape. According to the race tags in his condo, he's run a few marathons. A five-mile jog wouldn't be that big of a deal for him."

"I'm still not completely sold on it. Something feels off." Kendall finished her coffee and set the cup on the table.

"That's because you're too close to this. Your judgment is skewed. Maybe you feel guilty you didn't see this coming, you know, in your line of work and all."

Color flooded her face turning it a deep shade of red, and her eyes narrowed to slits. "Fuck you and your analysis, Taylor. Maybe you just can't stand to be wrong."

The chair skidded loudly along the linoleum and nearly toppled over when she stood up. She stormed out without another word before Adam had a chance to stop his head from spinning.

Well, that could've gone better. Adam Taylor, king of putting his foot in his mouth and continuing to talk while he suffocates. *Idiot.*

He sighed, drained his coffee cup, and walked out to the parking lot in time to see Kendall's SUV squeal onto the street and speed away.

CHAPTER

53

KENDALL ANSWERED HER phone as she crossed the parking lot of the Denver County Jail.

"Beck." A gruff male voice came over the line.

Brady.

"Yes, sir?"

"What's going on with the Scott Williams investigation?"

Kendall had been so wrapped up in Gwen's case, she'd nearly forgotten she needed to go back to the Williamses' house and take another look around.

"I interviewed the victim again. She mentioned Williams would take her to a secret room to molest her. Mother is convinced she means the storage room in the basement, but I thought I'd nose around a bit more. See if there's anything to Emily's statement."

"I agree. The storage room came back negative for any bodily fluids, so we need to nail down where the abuse took place. Won't hurt for you to take another look—a thorough look."

"Jake spoke to Williams's associates, but came up with nothing there. They all thought he was a model citizen, couldn't see him doing anything to harm his daughters . . . you know the BS," she said, tugging open the glass door.

Brady huffed. "See what you can find at the house. We won't get another bite at this apple, Beck. Once he's allowed back in, he'll destroy any evidence left behind. Leave no stone unturned."

"Understood. I'll let you know what I find out."

She disconnected the call as she entered the reception area and waited for the deputy on duty to get back from her break. The woman eventually waddled up and climbed into her high swivel chair. Kendall opened her mouth to speak, but the deputy's finger came up, halting her request before it even started.

Finally getting herself adjusted, the deputy hit the button to open the two-way mic between the thick bulletproof glass.

"Can I help you?" she asked, her voice as dull as her eyes. Kendall was tired of dealing with people who were so incredibly bored with their jobs they couldn't even muster a fake smile.

She held up her badge. "Special Agent Kendall Beck to see Tyson Butler."

The woman looked at the badge and the ID before scrutinizing Kendall with her beady little eyes. Turning her attention to the computer, she stared at the screen for a moment. "He has a visitor already. You'll have to wait until they leave."

"Is it his lawyer?" Kendall didn't want to wait for an hour or two while Ty and Simmons discussed strategy.

"No, the name is RaeLyn Volkov."

Her heart stopped beating for a second and then took off like a shot from a gun barrel. "RaeLyn Volkov?" *The Russian mob boss's wife?* Kendall had read about her in the file Stu sent her.

The deputy looked back at her screen. "Yeah, that's what it says here."

"Thanks." Kendall moved to an empty corner of the room, where she could still see the door leading to the visiting block of the jail. Within ten minutes, a woman exited and walked up to the reception window to check out.

When she turned around, Kendall saw her face—the woman from the courtroom. What the hell was she doing there? And why was she visiting Ty?

Kendall contemplated following her, but it really didn't matter where she went. Kendall had her name, knew who she was. What Kendall needed to know now was what RaeLyn Volkov wanted with Ty.

"Agent Beck, you can go back now," the deputy called over the mic.

After getting signed in and turning over her firearms, Kendall walked down the hallway to the visiting room, seated herself on a plastic chair, and gazed through the thick glass at Ty.

He looked tired. And despondent. She couldn't help but wonder if he was sad because of Gwen or because he got caught.

She picked up the receiver when he did. "Hey, Ty."

"Hey." His voice was gravelly and rough.

She just stared at him for a moment, this man she'd thought she'd known so well. Who was he? What was he capable of doing?

"What the hell, Ty?" Her voice was a scratchy whisper. She forced her emotions back to the pit of her churning stomach.

"Kendall, I didn't do this. You have to know that—I would never hurt Gwen. I have never raised a hand to her. Ever." His eyes darted back and forth between hers and the small desk in front of him. Desperate. Afraid. "How could you think I would kill her?"

"There's just so many lies, Ty."

He dropped his head and let it hang there. Kendall wasn't going to get him to talk about it. She was sure his lawyer had laid down the law of not discussing specifics while in here, especially to law enforcement of any kind. Of course, Kendall wasn't there as a member of law enforcement, so there were no rules being broken.

"Why was RaeLyn Volkov visiting you?"

His head snapped up and his eyes were wide and wild. "How do you know about RaeLyn?"

"I don't, but I know you had a meeting with her husband, Stanislav. I know he's not the type of friend you want to have if you want to keep all your body parts intact."

His eyes never left hers, but she noticed his chest rising and falling expeditiously. His lips clamped shut, free hand curled into a fist on the desk.

"I know you won't tell me what your dealings with him are, but why was she here? Did her husband send her to deliver a message? Is he threatening you, Ty?"

He made no attempt to speak, just held her prisoner in his gaze.

"Ty, let me help you."

"Leave it alone, Kendall. You can't help me."

He slammed the phone down and motioned to the guard that he wanted to leave. He never looked back at her. She sat there, watching him walk away and trying to wrap her brain around what had just happened.

One thing was clear. Ty was involved in some pretty scary shit, and Mrs. Volkov seemed to be at the center of it all. Time to find out what her role was and what the hell the real story was behind Ty, the Volkovs, and Gwen's murder.

54

Friday,
March 13,
1:36 PM

KENDALL OPENED THE file Stu had sent her with all his information regarding the Volkov organization. Clicking on the folder marked "RaeLyn Volkov," she scrolled through, not sure exactly what she was looking for until she came across it: "Comings & Goings."

A spreadsheet listed all of RaeLyn's usual activities during the week. The undercover cops who tailed her had done a fantastic job gathering intel. When she went out with friends, took tennis, golf, and swimming lessons. It looked as if her newest hobby was running, and she'd enlisted the help of a personal trainer.

Kendall ran through the list to see if RaeLyn Volkov was doing anything typical at that time. Manicure and pedicure at Wanda's Nail Emporium.

Kendall had never been one for getting her nails done. Gwen always tsked disgustedly whenever Kendall would pick at a hangnail or rip off a nail with her teeth. Gwen went religiously every week to the nail salon. "I work with the public," she'd said. "People notice my hands and will judge the restaurant based on my appearance."

Kendall believed Gwen was correct, but Kendall also didn't need to worry about what the people she worked with thought of her nails. The last thing she was trying to do was impress a bunch of pedophiles and sex traffickers.

RaeLyn had a standing appointment with her nail tech from two to four. Kendall glanced at the time. Two thirty. Enough time to get across town and catch RaeLyn before she left the nail salon. But just in case, she took down RaeLyn's address in town. Apparently the mob boss and his wife led separate lives— him in Blackwood, Vegas, Miami, and Russia; her in Denver.

Gathering her stuff, she signed out, adding a notation on the sign-out sheet: *In the field for the rest of the day.*

Kendall's cell phone buzzed. *Adam.* Christ, third time since she'd stormed out of the coffee shop the day before.

She had nothing to say to him. Yeah, maybe it had been childish. Maybe she should've let him off the hook after he apologized for being an ass. The truth was, she was more than a little concerned he was spot-on with his analysis. It cut a little too close to the heart of the issue.

And she desperately needed Gwen's killer to be anyone other than Ty. The consequences could be more far-reaching than the horror of being killed by the love of one's life. For Kendall, it would mean she had once again failed to save someone. And had been blind to the evil lurking so close to her and her best friend.

She didn't have the fortitude to delve into what it all could mean at the moment, especially if it was true and she had missed a murderer practically living with them.

She let the call go to voicemail. Deal with him later. Right now, confronting RaeLyn Volkov on what she was doing at the hearing and the jail was the priority.

Half an hour later, Kendall polished off her second extra-large Diet Dr. Pepper from the convenience store two doors down from the salon where RaeLyn was getting her nails done. She tossed the empty cup onto the floorboard behind the passenger seat—virtually zero chance she would remember to grab it and throw it away when she got out again.

Her biggest issue at the moment—she had to pee. Bad. She was assessing the risk of running to the bathroom, when Mrs. Volkov emerged, blowing on her nails.

Peeing would have to wait.

Hurrying over to RaeLyn's car, Kendall approached just as the locks beeped and disengaged.

"Mrs. Volkov?"

The woman looked up, but Kendall couldn't see her eyes through her dark sunglasses. She was tall, blonde, thin, and looked as if she'd had some work done on her breasts.

"I'm Kendall Beck."

RaeLyn glanced at Kendall's outstretched hand, didn't attempt to shake it. "I know who you are. What do you want?"

Okay, so this was going to be a less than cordial talk.

"I'm curious why you were at my friend's arraignment and then went to visit him in jail."

"Your *friend*?" RaeLyn snort-chuckled without any humor. "Don't make me laugh. You're no friend of Ty's." She jerked her door open and tossed her purse across to the passenger seat. "I'm sure you asked Ty these same questions already. If he didn't give you any information, what makes you think I will?"

"I *am* his friend, Mrs. Volkov. But I can tell you, as an FBI agent, if you were there to give him a message from your husband—or threaten him, in any way—I will make sure federal charges are brought against both of you."

RaeLyn threw her head back, a laugh bursting from her throat. She looked at Kendall, a wide grin across her face. "You really have no idea what you're talking about, Agent Beck. Do yourself a favor: look elsewhere for your killer. Ty didn't do it, and your roommate's death did not involve my husband or his business. But if you keep snooping around where you don't belong, you'll end up getting yourself and Ty killed."

She slid behind the wheel and began to close the door. Kendall grabbed the door and wrenched it back open.

"Thanks for the warning. Now, hear this: Ty is very likely going to go to prison for murdering his fiancée. I'm not sure where you fit into any of this, but if you have information that will exonerate him, I suggest you talk to me." She tossed her business card into RaeLyn's lap. "My cell phone number is on the back. I'm available twenty-four/seven. If it's true your husband's business was not involved in Gwen's murder, then there should be no problem with giving me information that could help Ty. Do the right thing, Mrs. Volkov."

Kendall stepped back as RaeLyn slammed the door, started the car, and screeched out of the parking lot. Twenty-four hours. That was all Kendall would give the woman. Then she'd show up at Mrs. Volkov's condo—maybe with a few buddies from the racketeering division—and press her harder. Kendall would use whatever means available to get information on Gwen's murder. And she didn't care if she ruffled a few mob feathers while doing it.

RaeLyn was hiding something. She could shed light on Gwen's murder. Kendall wasn't sure if RaeLyn was telling the truth about Ty not being involved, or if she was just desperate to divert attention away from any connection to her husband and his business.

Kendall's cell rang. She yanked it out of her pocket, hoping RaeLyn had changed her mind about talking to her. Adam's name flashed on the screen.

Groaning, she pressed the answer button. Adam was already talking by the time Kendall got the phone to her ear.

"Just answer the damn phone, Kendall."

"Christ, Adam, you're becoming a fucking stalker. What's with all the phone calls?"

"Holy shit, is that really you? Or did you change your voice-mail message just to insult me?"

"Do you have something you need to discuss or are you being a pain in my ass for no reason?"

She unlocked the Land Rover and got in.

"I have video from the night of the murder—of the parking garage, lobby, and exterior of the apartment building where Ty Butler resides."

Okay, that got her attention. "Have you started going through it yet?"

"Nope, waiting on you to answer my calls and get your ass over here so we can get moving on it."

"On my way—order pizza, extra pepperoni." She turned the SUV onto the highway and sped up. Traffic was going to be shit at this time of day. Could she legitimately use her flashing lights and drive on the shoulder?

"Pizza . . . right. Anything else, Your Highness? Something to drink?"

"No," she said, squirming in her seat. "No drink. Be there in about thirty." She hit "End," tossed the phone into the cup holder, and wove through the traffic.

The video could exonerate Ty. Or cement his fate and send him to prison for life. Either way, she had to know.

55

T HE PREVIOUS NIGHT had been a bust. Adam and Kendall
had started watching the security footage from the apartment building, only to discover the manager had sent video of
the wrong day. Adam left a scathing voicemail for the man and
received an apology in the morning, along with a promise to get
him the correct footage.

But the morning was shaping up differently. An email from
Fran Ward at the Medical Examiner's Office was sitting in his
inbox when he started up his computer.

Det. Taylor,

*This is in response to the cases you requested I take a closer
look at, to see if there is a forensic link between them and
the Jenna Rose case. My findings are as follows:*

*I reviewed all autopsies and photos of the victims. In
each case there appeared to be marks on the victim's back
similar to the marks found on Jenna Rose. As with Jenna
Rose, the marks on the other victims first appeared to be
scratch marks not connected to their murders.*

*I was able to blow up the pictures and had them
enhanced. To me, it appears the marks are very similar,
that is to say, they appear to create a similar pattern. Not
exact, which may be a byproduct of several scenarios (i.e.,*

difference in device used to make the marks, etc.). But the similarities are remarkable and, in my opinion, were made by the same person.

I hope this helps. As always, feel free to contact me with any additional questions.

Fran Ward, MD

Head Medical Examiner

Adam's head reeled. What did this mean? He forwarded the email to Saul and Fletch, and wandered into the Jenna Rose war room. He looked at the picture tacked to the murder board of the scratches on Jenna Rose's back, feeling a small sense of vindication. He knew there was something about those marks. Now, that had been confirmed.

However, what did it really do for his case—except add more victims of unsolved murders. Yes, it confirmed a serial killer was responsible for all of their deaths, but it didn't get him any closer to discovering who the serial killer was.

Fletch came swaggering into the room, eyes wide, smile on his face. "Holy hell! So, we were right—they were all linked."

Saul sauntered in behind Fletch, his face grim. Fletch was still young. He hadn't had as much time on the job as Saul. Good news in an investigation didn't get the same reaction from veterans. Where Fletch was ecstatic, Saul was morose. "So, what the hell do we do with the information?"

Adam dropped into a chair. "We pull the files and go through all the evidence from the cases to see if we can find anything to lead us to the killer. I'm on my way to talk to the boss."

Lu lifted his gaze when Adam rapped on the doorframe to his office. "What the hell do you want, Taylor?"

"We think we found some unsolved murders connected to the Jenna Rose case. Saul and Fletch uncovered potential evidence linking all of them. I had the ME take a closer look at the autopsies, and she agreed the cases are linked."

"Linked how?"

"Each woman had unexplained cuts on her back. Fran concluded the marks are too similar to be a coincidence."

"So, your murder case is now a multiple murder case?" Lu removed his reading glasses and rubbed the bridge of his nose.

"Yes, sir. There are a couple of issues, however. Some of the cases are not in our jurisdiction. I'm going to need to get in touch with the other police departments and see if they can send us their murder books on these cases."

"Shouldn't be a problem taking the lead on this since I assume the majority of the deaths occurred in our jurisdiction?"

"That is correct."

"Let me know if you need me to make a call to any higher-ups at these other departments to smooth the way. What else?"

"This confirms we have a serial killer on the loose."

Lu took a deep inhale and released it. Sitting forward in his chair, replacing his glasses, and picking up the document he'd been reading, he said in a flat voice, "Then you have some work to do. Get on it. I don't want this guy killing anyone else in my city, Taylor."

"Yes, sir." Adam turned to walk away.

"And, Taylor, the media better not start connecting the dots and report we have serial killer in our midst before we can find this fucker."

Adam nodded. That was just what he needed. The press getting a hold of this story and scaring the shit out of the city. The amount of calls the department would receive requesting information—where and when had the murders happened? Are the neighborhoods safe?—would be overwhelming enough. But the false leads were what Adam was trying to avoid. For whatever reason, there were people who wanted to be involved in investigations and would provide inaccurate information that sent investigators running in circles.

There was no time for that. It had been months since Jenna Rose's death. Was the killer getting ready to strike again?

56

INCESSANT BUZZING YANKED Kendall from sleep, pissing her off. The bedroom was flooded with sunlight. The clock was screaming at her in dayglow green. Eight thirty AM.

"Fuck!" She was usually up and moving around by this time, not rolling out of bed. The vodka tonics she had consumed the previous night, which ended up being more vodka than tonic by the time she'd crawled into bed—had been a good sleep aid. Maybe too good.

The buzzing continued while she searched for her cell phone. The screen indicated the call was from a private number.

She tried to force the lingering sleep from her voice. "Kendall Beck."

"Agent Beck, this is RaeLyn Volkov. I need to see you."

Holy shit! For some reason, Kendall jumped out of bed, as if that would be more professional for this conversation.

"Okay, I can be at your place in half an hour," she said, heading to the closet to grab a clean suit. Dry cleaning was fast becoming a necessity and not an option.

"No, it's not safe there. We need to meet somewhere else. I have a key to Ty's place. Can we meet there instead?" Her voice was soft, meek.

How and why does she have a key to Ty's place?

"Uh, yeah," Kendall stammered, trying to get dressed while not dropping the phone. "Half an hour?"

"Yes, that's fine." There was a pause, and then she said, "Thank you, Agent Beck." And the line went dead.

57

ADAM RECEIVED A call from the Denver County Jail. Ty Butler was requesting to see him. For what reason, Adam had no idea. As he signed in at the reception desk, he noticed a now familiar name—RaeLyn Volkov had visited Butler the previous evening.

Was she the reason Butler wanted to chat?

The prisoners meeting room was small. Ashley Simmons, Butler's attorney, sat next to her client, who was shackled to the table. Adam pointed to the restraints and directed his comments to the guard standing by the door.

"You can remove those."

The guard nodded and unlocked the handcuffs. "Be a good boy, Butler. If I have to come back in here and break anything up, I will not be gentle."

Ty nodded at the guard. "Understood."

CHAPTER

58

KENDALL PULLED UP in front of the Vistage Apartments and parked. Ty lived on the tenth floor of the twenty-one-floor building. Kendall knocked on his apartment door and was greeted by RaeLyn Volkov. Dark circles rimmed her bloodshot eyes. She backed out of the way and let Kendall pass. Kendall had been there a few times with Gwen. But, much like everything Gwen had been associated with, it didn't feel the same anymore.

And it felt downright wrong that RaeLyn seemed so at home there.

They sat on opposite ends of the couch. RaeLyn's fingers twisted nervously in her lap.

"Ty didn't kill Gwen." Her eyes were resolute, yet soft.

"You seem pretty sure," Kendall said. "Care to elaborate how you know this?"

"I was with Ty the night Gwen died." She paused, looking Kendall straight in the eye. "The entire night."

Kendall's heart raced. Her brain momentarily seized. She didn't like where this was headed. There was a sense of betrayal surging through her. She closed her eyes and tried to concentrate on the questions she needed to ask.

Be professional.

"Perhaps you should start from the beginning." Kendall pulled up the note app on her phone. She also managed to get the voice recorder started without RaeLyn noticing. Colorado is a one-party consent state, and while Kendall might be pushing the ethical bounds in other areas, it was at least legal to record the conversation without Mrs. Volkov's actual consent. "How do you and Ty know each other?"

RaeLyn grabbed a pack of cigarettes from a pack sitting on the coffee table. "I quit smoking a few months ago." She removed one from the pack, placed it to her lips, and clicked the lighter until a flame burst forth. "I live in the building too—in the penthouse. I met Ty in the elevator one day. I was coming back from a run, and we got to talking. He asked me if I was planning on running the 5K that was two months away. I told him I'd been thinking about it, and he convinced me to do it. When I said I wasn't sure how to even train for it, he said he would train with me."

She took a long, deep drag off the cigarette, held it in for a moment, and then artfully blew the smoke out the side of her mouth, away from them. "I swear to you, at that time, we were just friends. He helped me train, we ran the 5K together, and I was hooked. He started telling me about other races, and we decided to continue training together. It was probably six months into our relationship when things became more . . . intimate."

Kendall's heart sank into her stomach. She would bet her right arm that was the same time Ty had started acting strange.

"We went to Arizona for a 10K and spent a week down there preparing. That's when we first slept together. I never thought it would turn into anything more than two friends seeking comfort from each other. I never expected to fall in love."

Heat seared through Kendall's veins. "Explain 'seek comfort'—for what purpose?" Kendall looked at her, wishing she could drill holes through the woman's perfect blue eyes and light her platinum-blonde hair ablaze.

"Well, as you can imagine, being married to Stan is not a bed of roses. He's rarely here, and when he is, he stays out at the casino. We have a penthouse in the hotel there. He bought the penthouse here for me after I complained about being so far away from civilization. My husband is not really a one-woman kind of man. He prefers women who satiate his more deviant sexual appetites. I made it clear I was not that woman. So, he stays there, and I stay here, where I don't have to have his other women flaunted in my face every night. But it's a lonely existence."

"So why not just divorce him?"

RaeLyn stared at Kendall as if she'd grown a third eye in the middle of her forehead. "There is no divorcing the mob, Agent Beck."

"And Ty? What did he need comfort from? A fiancée who loved him? Adored him? Would have given him the world if he had asked her for it?" Kendall knew she had taken a giant leap from the impersonal investigator to overprotective best friend, but she didn't care. Ty had had no reason to treat Gwen badly, the way he had. To sneak around on her. Cheat on her. If he'd wanted out of the relationship, he should've manned up and broken things off before having an affair with a married woman.

"I can't really speak for him, but I know there were problems with the business that were seeping into their relationship. Ty wanted to keep the restaurant small, but Gwen refused. She wanted to expand, open another place across town. They argued about it a lot, apparently. The business seemed to take over their relationship, became the focal point, and he felt very alone. You can judge him for how he responded, but I know he felt guilty about—"

"Cheating on her?" Kendall didn't want to hear how horrible Ty's life had been with Gwen. How he was trapped in a relationship with her and couldn't help falling in love with the mob boss's wife. Her face burned hot. She needed to ratchet it down. Flying into a rage when RaeLyn was talking would only make her clam up. Which was the last thing Kendall wanted.

"He was going to tell her about us . . . before she went missing. The next day, actually. We had a plan. We were going to leave right after Ty told Gwen it was over. Escape before my husband returned from his trip overseas. But the plan fell apart."

"Yes, I'm sure Gwen's death put a damper on things." It slipped out, but Kendall was having a hard time biting her tongue.

To RaeLyn's credit, she was taking Kendall's hits with a certain amount of grace. "It was more than that. My husband returned early from his business trip. He came here, to our apartment, which he never does. It made it impossible for me to leave, and then when Ty discovered Gwen was missing—and then had died—we knew he had to stay."

Deep, controlled breathing was the only way Kendall could calm down and get her head back into investigator mode and away from being the grief-stricken friend. "Did your husband suspect you were leaving him? Did he find out about the affair?"

"No, we were careful. In fact, that's what initiated taking money from the business. Ty and I were in the lobby one day, discussing how to get money so we could get away. I was waiting for Stan to pick me up for a business party. He was running late and instructed me to meet him in the lobby so he wouldn't have to come all the way up to the penthouse. He showed up earlier than I expected. When he walked in, he looked at us. Stan is jealous by nature. He may not want me, but he will never let anyone else have me either."

Kendall stopped taking notes, sat back, and let the recorder take over. She no longer cared if RaeLyn had a problem with their discussion being recorded. The woman didn't have a choice, as far as Kendall was concerned.

"I knew I would never be able to steal money from Stan. That's when Ty told me he had taken money from the business and had used it to gamble. He thought he could use it to make more money so we could get out before Gwen discovered it was gone. But he lost it all. Anyway, when my husband came into the lobby and saw us, I introduced Ty as another resident in the apartment building. Ty said he was a regular at the casino and had recognized me as Stan's wife. He was hoping I would introduce him to Stan so they could do some business. One thing led to another, and before I knew it, Ty had managed to get a loan from Stan."

Kendall sighed and pinched the bridge of her nose to quell the pounding in her head. "So, Ty was using Stan's bookie services?" What an incredibly stupid move.

"Unfortunately, yes. In a way, Ty felt as if Stan owed me the money after all I had gone through in the marriage—not anything I wish to discuss with you. It was stupid. When I talked to him about it later, I made him promise to return what he owed Stan immediately. It was one thing to take from the restaurant. Ty was at least entitled to that money. To steal from Stan—that was a surefire way of getting beaten, possibly killed. But then Gwen found out Ty had taken the money from the business, so he used the loan from Stan to repay it."

"How long before your husband started threatening him to repay what he owed?"

RaeLyn sucked on the butt of her cigarette. "A couple of months. That's when Ty took the money from the business again. He didn't want to, but it was better to face Gwen than to face Stan and tell him he didn't have the money.

"That night, the night Gwen went missing, she called Ty and said she was coming over to talk to him. He told her he didn't feel well and would stop by her house the next day. He decided he was going to tell her about me, tell her he wanted out of the restaurant. He hoped he could get her to buy out his half so we could get money and leave town. Her family has money, so maybe they would help her pay him his share of the business—something like that."

"Why didn't Ty just do that to begin with?" Kendall asked. The pounding in her head was getting louder, and she felt as if her brain was bumping up against her skull with each thump.

"He thought it would lead to too many questions. We couldn't risk Stan putting the pieces together and discovering I was about to leave him. It would've been a death sentence for both of us."

She took a final drag on her cigarette and crushed it into a makeshift foil ashtray. "But Gwen showed up here after she closed the restaurant that night."

"And she found you together." Kendall had moved past rage and was uncomfortably numb. The emotional roller coaster she was on was shifting faster than she could acknowledge her feelings. Her heart physically ached. And she wasn't sure she could handle what was to come.

RaeLyn nodded her head. "She used her key to get in and found us in bed together—you know, not exactly sleeping. As you can imagine, she was really upset. She flew into a rage, cussing at Ty. Screaming at him, screaming at me. Ty tried to get her to calm down, but she stormed out before he could get clothes on and talk to her."

"Did he go after her?" Kendall was getting a mental picture of the events. She could see Gwen, upset, trying to drive away, wondering what the hell had just happened to her perfect life.

"No, he called her, tried to get her to come back so they could talk and work things out. She wouldn't answer, so he left a message, begging her to come back. He tried to call her once or twice—I can't remember. She finally answered and agreed to meet him. But when he got there, she was gone. He came home and decided to give her some space and time to calm down. He thought she would call him the next day, and they would figure out what to do with the business and stuff."

Kendall's heart was a lead ball in her chest. *This must be what it feels like to die of a broken heart.*

"So, why tell me all of this? Why not talk to the detective running the investigation?"

"I want you to help me convince him to get the charges dropped against Ty and get him released from jail."

Kendall chuckled dryly. "Oh, is that all? Sure I can't find a cure for cancer and create a time machine for you while I'm at it?" She sat back, arms tight across her chest. "What makes you think I want to help you and Ty have a better life?"

"Because, no matter what you think of us and what we did, you know Gwen wouldn't want Ty to spend the rest of his life in jail for killing her when his only crime was falling in love with me."

Heat flushed through Kendall's body, and her muscles quivered with rage. "Don't you dare pretend you can lecture me on what my friend would want. My guess is she would want to be alive. Spend time with her friends and family. But she can't because she's dead. And so far, you're not making a compelling case for me advocating on Ty's behalf."

"Please." RaeLyn reached across, as if she were intent on grasping Kendall's hand, but she thought better of it and returned her hands to her lap. "I need Detective Taylor to convince the district attorney to talk to me. He's the only one who can help Ty and me escape."

"Escape what?"

"My husband. Once he finds out about my affair with Ty, he'll kill us."

"Yeah, probably," Kendall agreed. "Perhaps you should've thought about your husband's strict code of gangster ethics before you fucked around on him."

Kendall wanted to scream she didn't care what RaeLyn's husband did to her. That RaeLyn didn't deserve to live while Gwen was dead. Maybe RaeLyn's death would be justification for the lives she and Ty had destroyed with their selfishness.

But Kendall knew grief and sorrow were overriding common sense and devotion to justice. RaeLyn and Ty had carried on an affair. That didn't equate to a death penalty as punishment.

She took a deep breath and switched gears. "What do you know about your husband's business?"

"A lot. I was his bookkeeper until we started fucking and got married."

"Can you still access information?"

"If I need to."

Kendall took in a deep, shaky breath and held it for a ten count before slowly releasing it. The truth of the matter was Gwen was dead. Nothing Kendall did or didn't do was going to change that fact. But Kendall could make it mean something. Justice could be served in more ways than finding Gwen's killer. Gwen could help bring down a criminal organization.

"I have to make a few phone calls and get some people over here. Then you're going to tell them what you just told me, and answer any questions I forgot to ask."

"Will they protect me? Protect Ty?" She started twisting her fingers together again, and her voice dropped to a low whisper.

"That's the plan."

"DETECTIVE," ASHLEY SIMMONS said, and gestured across the table to the open chair.

Once Adam was seated, Simmons began her version of an interview opening statement, because lawyers just loved to hear themselves talk, and laid down the rules of engagement.

"We are here as a courtesy and are under no obligation to disprove these ridiculous charges against Mr. Butler. That said, after consulting with my client, I have advised him to clear up the misconceptions surrounding the night Gwen Tavich disappeared, in an attempt to move the investigation forward and find the *actual* perpetrator of this heinous crime."

Adam wanted to roll his eyes but was more interested in hearing what Butler finally had to say than in getting into a pissing match with Simmons. He just hoped this wasn't another round of bullshit, lies, and cover-ups.

"I'm all ears, Mr. Butler."

Butler glanced at his lawyer, who gave a head nod to proceed. "I did talk to Gwen at midnight, as I said, and we agreed not to see each other that night. We'd been drifting apart for some time, so neither of us was upset about not seeing each other."

"And you know this—"

"Gwen said she didn't want to come over. I didn't try to persuade her to change her mind. I knew she was pissed at me for not going into work that night. And I admit I've been less than an exemplary copartner in the business recently."

"Okay." Adam leaned back in his chair and folded his arms over his chest, hoping to hell this was going to get somewhere interesting before his headache turned into a migraine. He'd only managed one cup of coffee so far, and this stroll down the lane of already-known facts was grating on him more than it probably should.

"Something must've happened between midnight and two that changed her mind—not sure what, but she used her key to come into my apartment." He looked down at his hands as they rested on the table. When he looked up again, he said, "She found me in bed with another woman."

That pretty much confirmed Martin Griffin's statement, even if he had a hard time believing Butler would ever cheat on Gwen. Adam drew his notepad closer and clicked his pen to start writing. "This other woman have a name?"

"RaeLyn Volkov."

"Jesus." So, Mrs. Volkov hadn't been sent to pass on a threat from her husband to Butler, like Kendall thought.

"Yeah. Well, as you can imagine, Gwen was upset and stormed out. That's when I called her cell phone. At first she didn't answer, and I left a voicemail."

The one Sheri had played for Adam and Kendall. Completely different context, if Butler's story was to be believed.

"When I tried her cell again, she answered. I begged her to come back so we could talk, but she refused."

"Can't really blame her. Kind of awkward with the mistress hanging around."

Simmons sighed. "Detective, please keep your opinions, and sarcasm, to yourself."

Adam raised his hands in surrender. "Please continue."

Butler inhaled deeply, dragging his hand over his face as he exhaled. "Gwen told me she was stopping to get gas, and if I made it down to the gas station before she left, she would talk to me. So, I got dressed and headed over there, but she was already gone by the time I arrived."

"Which gas station?"

"The Conoco about a mile from where I live."

"What did you do after that?"

"Went home."

"Why didn't you try to call her again?"

"I think she made her feelings pretty clear. I figured I'd give her a couple of days, let things cool down a bit, and then try to talk to her."

Adam quirked up an eyebrow. All of this was easy to come up with after the fact. But how much of it was true?

"Look, I know I was a grade-A prick and should've ended things with Gwen as soon as I realized I had feelings for RaeLyn. You have no idea how much I regret that now."

"You weren't worried about where she was the following week?" Adam asked.

"No, I really did believe she had wanted to get away and come to terms with everything. Gwen was a planner. When things went astray, she tended to lock herself away until she could come up with a new plan and get order back in her life."

"Weren't concerned even when Kendall came to talk to you about where Gwen might be?"

"To be honest—and looking back on it now, it seems absurd—I thought it was some sort of powerplay she and Gwen had cooked up to see if I would go after Gwen. Sort of a damsel in distress that would convince me to end things with RaeLyn and marry Gwen."

"Seriously?" Adam hadn't known Kendall long, but that seemed about as far-fetched an idea as he could imagine. And Gwen didn't seem to have been the type to play the woman who needed to be saved by a man.

Adam just shook his head. Did Butler even know either one of these women? Or was he so self-absorbed he could only see what his ego would allow?

"So why not come clean about your affair with Mrs. Volkov after Gwen's body was discovered?"

Simmons sat forward. "Surely you can comprehend the gravity of this information, Detective. RaeLyn's husband is a well-known organized crime figure. If he found out about his wife's infidelity, both RaeLyn and Ty would be in grave danger."

"How do you know Volkov didn't find out," Adam asked, "and killed Gwen as a message to stop fucking around with his wife?"

Butler shook his head. "Not his style. He doesn't love RaeLyn. She is his property. There's only one way Volkov deals with disloyalty. And trust me, he would not lose sleep over it. There's always plenty of future Mrs. Stanislav Volkovs waiting in the wings. And he never would've let me live and killed Gwen as some sort of message. The only message Volkov sends is 'If you cross me, you die.' Plain and simple. No deviations."

"So, if it's so dangerous for you and Mrs. Volkov, why are you coming clean now?"

"To clear my name and get out of here. As distasteful as it may seem, the money I will get from the sale of the business and the life insurance—RaeLyn and I can start a new life together."

"I'm sure Ms. Tavich can rest easy in her grave knowing she is providing you and your mistress a way out of a crappy marriage."

"Detective—"

Adam put his hand up to stop the attorney's admonition. Adam had just about had enough of Butler's "poor me" story. It made him sick to think Butler had deceived a woman Adam could now only admire and respect in death. Gwen Tavich had deserved so much better than what she got. So much better than Ty Butler.

And it made Adam want to pound Butler into the next life.

"Aren't you worried Volkov will hunt you down, even if you buy a new life somewhere else?"

"No."

"Such confidence, Mr. Butler. Why not?"

"RaeLyn is working her own deal."

Adam stood, wanting as far away from the man as possible. It was men like Butler who gave good men a bad rap.

Adam knocked on the door and waited for the guard to let him out. "Just so you know, Mr. Butler. The reason Gwen came to see you that night was because she discovered the money you

had taken from the business. She was most likely there to confront you about it, not rekindle whatever flame had gone out
between the two of you."

He didn't wait for a response—just left. Once outside, Adam
wondered why he'd told Butler about Gwen's discovery. Maybe
because he refused to allow Butler to think Gwen wanted anything more than to kick his ass for stealing from the business
she'd worked so hard to make a success.

60

A DAM SWUNG BY the Conoco station where Butler was supposed to meet Gwen the night she disappeared. It was an
old station with a small convenience store attached, almost lost
among the bigger, flashier gas stations along Sheridan Boulevard.
A small local business. No wonder Gwen stopped here to get gas.
As a small business owner herself, she would've wanted to support a business going toe-to-toe with the big conglomerates.

Adam noticed a security camera above the single island of
two gas pumps. Inside the store were two more cameras: one
at the back and one by the front entrance that also caught the
action at the cash register. Adam wondered if there was also one
behind the counter. If so, it wasn't visible.

A woman with long, brown hair stood behind the counter, her gaze glued to a small black and white TV that looked
older than Adam. Back when TVs still had tubes. She caught a
glimpse of Adam and stepped closer.

"What can I do for you, sugar?" Her shirt was embroidered
with "Hal's Conoco" over the left breast, and "Connie" over the
right. Connie had the deep, gravelly voice of someone who had
been smoking since emerging from the womb.

He showed her his badge. "I was wondering if I could see
the security video from two weeks ago?"

"Have to check with the boss," she said to him, then cupped
her hand to her mouth and yelled to someone obviously in the

back of the store. "Hal, someone here to see you." She smiled. "He'll be with you in a sec, sugar."

Hal was all of four feet eight inches, with a belly that made him waddle down the aisle. He was breathing heavy as he approached, as if the long ten-foot walk had been tantamount to a workout. Raking his hand through his greasy black hair, making sure his combover was in place, he wheezed, "What can I do for you?"

Adam flashed his badge. "I'm interested in taking a look at your security video from early Sunday morning, February twenty-third."

"Sure, sure," Hal said. He turned back in the direction he had just come. "Always happy to help."

Adam followed Hal through the door marked "Employees Only" and into a small office that was just barely big enough for the old metal desk and Hal. "Let me just bring it up for you, and you can take over." His fingers moved quickly over the keys, probably the only thing Hal did fast. "What time are you interested in looking at?"

"I guess from around two fifteen, just to be safe."

Video footage filled the computer screen. Hal rocked himself back and then forward, creating enough momentum to lift himself out of the chair. "Have a seat," he said, and moved out of Adam's way. Once Adam was sitting, Hal placed his hand on the mouse. "This view is the camera at the gas pump." He scrolled to the bottom of the screen. "To see the other camera views, just click on the thumbnail at the bottom. We have a camera at the front door, one at the back aisle by the beer, and another behind the cashier—gets the faces of the customers when they come up to pay."

"Thanks so much," Adam said.

"I'll leave you to it then." Hal duck-walked out of the back storeroom, the swinging door squeaking as he went to the front.

Adam pressed "Play." At 2:17:59, Kendall's BMW pulled up to the gas pump. He could barely see Gwen behind the wheel. The driver's side was closest to the entrance to the store, but not completely visible from this camera view. She exited the vehicle and walked around to the opposite side, where the gas tank was located, and started the pump. Engaging the lock on the handle, she stepped over the hose and opened the passenger-side door. Reaching inside, she emerged with a cell phone to her ear: 2:19:48.

The call with Butler, no doubt. Tears streaked down her cheeks, but her face was stern, her lips a tight line across her face. She was speaking, but there was no sound, so Adam couldn't hear what was being said. She tossed the phone back onto the seat and returned to the gas tank, watching the numbers tick away. But Adam would guess her mind was a million miles away. Maybe trying to figure out if she should stay or go. Trying to decide if she should give Butler a chance to explain himself or tell him to fuck off.

It was all speculation. And no one would ever know what her last thoughts were.

At 2:23:36, Gwen returned the gas pump to the holder and screwed the gas cap back into place. She walked around the back of the vehicle and out of sight. Adam could see movement near the driver's side, the headlights came on, and the vehicle moved away.

So, by 2:24 AM, Gwen had left the gas station without speaking to Butler in person. So far, the video was supporting Butler's story. Adam kept the video running until he saw headlights enter the parking lot behind the camera. The time was 2:27:04.

Adam switched to the interior camera at the front door of the convenience store. He fast-forwarded to 2:22, mesmerized by the accelerated movements of the people coming in and out of view in the small store. What the hell were so many people doing there at two o'clock in the morning?

He heard his mother's voice in his head. "Nothing good happens after midnight." It made Adam chuckle, then the truth of the statement sunk in.

If Gwen Tavich had just gone straight home from the restaurant, chances were good she would still be alive.

Adam thought he might be able to see the SUV from the inside camera. The vehicle was parked next to the nearest pump to the entrance of the store. It wasn't the clearest picture, but it was better than nothing. At 2:23, he watched as Gwen climbed behind the steering wheel and sped away.

At 2:27, a small black Lexus sports coupe pulled into one of the spaces to the right of the store entrance. Adam watched Ty Butler step out of his car and look around the area. He closed the car door and walked toward the entrance of the store. His face looked haggard, his eyes drooping. He stepped inside and walked up and down the only three aisles in the store. Looking for Gwen. Realizing she had left without waiting for him. Was that when it first occurred to him Gwen didn't need him? That she wasn't going to allow him to manipulate her into thinking he had no other choice but to cheat because they were both so miserable and neither was able to end it?

Hell, Adam figured Butler was the type of guy who would actually turn the fact that Gwen had caught him in the act with another woman into a good thing—forcing both of them to accept what they'd refused to believe about their relationship.

Prick.

Butler left the store and walked back to his car. At 2:32:15, he was backing out of the parking spot and merging onto Sheridan, turning in the opposite direction Gwen had taken, and back toward his residence.

So far, Butler's story had a ring of truth to it. The video backed up the claim he'd been at the store. Although it didn't completely exonerate him. That would come once Adam was able to view the security footage from Butler's apartment building.

Adam backed up the footage from the front door camera to just before Gwen arrived. He saw her pull up and exit the vehicle. Then she was out of sight. Adam knew what happened next. But just as he was about to move to a different camera view, he noticed a dark figure walk up to the vehicle. His head was covered with a black hoodie. The door behind the driver's seat opened and the man slipped inside, closing the door behind him. Within a minute, Gwen came into view, got inside, and drove away.

Never realizing someone was in the back seat.

Holy fuck!

Adam huffed, a feeling of helplessness rattled through him as he watched the SUV pull out onto the street. Not "someone."

Gwen's killer.

Adam checked the time the man got into the SUV: 2:21:03. Exactly six minutes before Butler showed up.

"Well, Kendall," he muttered, "you've got your smoking gun."

Except it proved she was correct. It was looking less and less like Butler had killed Gwen. All Adam needed was to verify it with the security from the apartments. If Butler returned to the building within a few minutes of leaving the gas station—he was not their man.

Which meant they were even further away from finding Gwen's killer.

Adam's phone buzzed. *Kendall.* "Hey, I was just getting ready to call you."

"Get over to Ty's apartment," she said. "And bring the DA with you."

CHAPTER

61

THIS WAS NOT the day Adam had expected. RaeLyn and Kendall had orchestrated a major coup that still had him shaking his head at how it'd all worked out. He'd picked up a reluctant assistant DA on the way to Ty Butler's condo and filled him in on what he'd uncovered. Tim Smith agreed the new evidence clearly pointed to Ty Butler not being Gwen Tavich's murderer. Smith had been on the phone the entire drive, getting the charges against Butler dropped.

When they arrived at Butler's apartment, it was filled with so many law enforcement officers, it looked like a cop convention. Some other feebs from the FBI racketeering division were also there. Everyone sat around the living room and waited for Kendall's show to unfold. RaeLyn Volkov started spilling the beans about her husband's business. When she finished, Kendall and Adam stood back and let the vultures pick at her with their questions. Not long after, one of the FBI agents approached Kendall.

"Okay, I owe you. I don't know how you managed to get her to turn, but if she can deliver even half of what she says she can regarding her husband's organization, we'll be able to shut him down and put him away."

Kendall nodded but didn't smile. She was stoic, unemotional, but Adam could tell there was a storm raging inside her. To her credit, she was keeping it together pretty well.

"So what happens now?" Adam asked, glancing over at RaeLyn Volkov talking to the assistant DA.

"Well, the DA has agreed to work with us since it appears Mr. Butler did not kill Ms. Tavich. They're going to get him released from jail so we can get both Ms. Volkov and Mr. Butler into protective custody by the end of the day. How they are going to accomplish that, I have no idea."

Adam nodded and headed over to the DA. RaeLyn smiled meekly at him and walked away.

"Need me to do anything?" Adam asked Smith. They were about the same age. Smith appeared to be a pretty straight shooter—for a lawyer.

"I need Mr. Butler to get a heads-up about what is going on. Out-processing is already underway, and you can bet Volkov's minions on the inside will start passing information to the outside that Butler has been let go. There's no telling what Volkov actually knows about the relationship between Butler and his wife, but I'm not taking chances. Let's get him out and handed over to the FBI. They can worry about his safety after that."

"I'll head over to the jail and wait around for him to be released and get him back here." Adam glanced over at Kendall and noticed RaeLyn walking toward her.

"Good," Smith said. "I'll talk to his attorney and let her know what's happening, but I would rather hold off as long as possible. Simmons may convince Mr. Butler to hold out for a better deal or something—who knows? The less Simmons is involved on the front end, the better the outcome on the back end."

"I hear ya. Can you find a way back to your office if I take off?"

"Yeah, I'll have one of the feds give me a lift."

RaeLyn was talking to Kendall when Adam approached them. "I can't thank you enough. I'm not sure what will happen after I testify against my husband, but at least we will be away from here. Have new identities."

"Well, you'll have all the money from Gwen's death. I'm sure you'll be able to live happily ever after on that." Kendall's tone was flat, eyes glazed over, and she was staring at something— or nothing—on the wall directly across from her.

"I know it must look bad to you. Even though Ty didn't kill Gwen for the money, he took advantage of her death to collect on the life insurance proceeds and profit from selling the restaurant. He only did that to help us start a new life, to hide from my husband. We just want to be together."

Kendall didn't speak. Her jaw was clenched shut, and her eyes never strayed from the spot they had been trained on since RaeLyn had approached her.

RaeLyn finally turned and walked away, leaving Kendall and Adam alone. He stood for a minute, silently watching her. She was fighting something internally, most likely trying to stay in control of her emotions and not break down in front of everyone. He knew that feeling. Had been there before.

He cleared his throat. "I've been tasked with escorting Butler from jail. You good?"

She swung her eyes over to him, but he wasn't sure she actually recognized him. She blinked a couple of times, and then her shoulders sagged as the muscles finally relaxed. "Yeah, I'm good. Probably step out on the balcony and get some fresh air."

"Just don't jump off."

She snorted softly. "I won't." She glanced around the room. "But I'm not promising one of them won't be tossed off at some point."

"I'm good with that." Her smile widened, and it helped to release some of the anxiety he felt being in her presence. Even sad, she had a great smile, and something hard inside Adam cracked, warmth spilling from the fissure. Somehow, working together on this case had made them more than fellow law-enforcement compadres. They had become friends. And Adam wanted his friend to be okay.

"All right, I'm out. I'll see you when I get back."

She nodded. "Bring me coffee."

62

I T TOOK A few hours, but Adam finally returned with Ty. RaeLyn rushed into his arms, and Kendall felt her heart sink into her stomach. How many times had she seen Gwen in Ty's arms, gazing adoringly into his eyes? Smiling at him. Happy. In love.

Alive.

It felt as if Kendall had been sucker-punched in the gut, and all the air had been forced from her lungs. It wasn't fair. Ty was getting a second chance. RaeLyn was getting a second chance. Gwen, who had done nothing, always honest and true, had suffered at the hands of a madman. She was the one who'd died.

Ty's eyes met hers, and he stepped away from RaeLyn and walked over to her. At least he had the decency not to touch her or try to hug her.

"I'm so sorry, Kendall. I know this must be hard for you, seeing me with RaeLyn. This is not the way I wanted it to work out. I handled everything so poorly. I hurt you. I hurt Gwen. And for that, I am truly sorry." He ran his hand over his face, letting out a long sigh before looking at her again. "At least you know I wasn't responsible for Gwen's death."

A ball of fire scorched Kendall's chest and radiated to every part of her body. He might as well have doused her with lighter fluid and tossed a lit match.

"You may not have been the one who physically killed her, but don't think for one minute you're not responsible for her death. She came over that night because you took money from the business without telling her. She found you in bed with another woman. Can you imagine how she felt? Can you imagine her state of mind as she drove away? Can you see the tears blinding her, making it nearly impossible to drive? Someone saw, Ty, and they took advantage of the situation."

Ty dropped his head, and refused to look at her.

Coward.

"It was a slow, tortuous death. Did you know that? Can you even comprehend what must've been going through her mind at that time? It wasn't hours. She was tortured for days. Taken to the brink of death over and over again until she died. Her final visions were of you screwing another woman. The betrayal of someone she loved. Someone she cared about more than anyone. Tell me, what do you think caused her more pain? Her heart finally giving out from one too many jolts of electricity, or the knowledge that the man she loved had completely betrayed her trust and pissed on everything she thought was real and true?" Kendall stepped closer to him, forcing him to look into her eyes. "Don't you dare stand there and tell me you weren't responsible for her death. You're every bit as responsible as the sack of shit who actually killed her."

She pushed past him, unaffected by the tears streaming down his face, and stalked out of the apartment, never looking back. She wasn't interested in how Ty felt. Didn't care if he was destroyed by what she'd said, by the truth of her words. Couldn't stand the thought of him being comforted by his mistress. She wanted to be blind to the relief he felt knowing it was all over and that he could live a long and happy life far away from anything reminding him of what he'd done to Gwen.

As far as Kendall was concerned, Ty Butler was dead.

She didn't remember going down the elevator or crossing the street to her Land Rover parked along the curb. It was all a blur. So many disparate feelings. She was numb. And cold. Sadness invaded her body, reminding her of how alone she was.

"Hey," a voice called from behind her. Adam stood, hand outstretched. "Keys," he said.

"No, I'm all right." She wasn't. She had no idea where to go or what to do.

"Keys," he said more forcefully. She dropped them in his hand and walked to the passenger side.

He got behind the steering wheel and started the engine. They pulled out into traffic and made their way back across town.

"I can't go home," she mumbled, unsure if he'd even heard her. "I can't go back there right now."

She wanted to explain there were just too many memories of Gwen and that she couldn't face the overwhelming loss of her amid all her stuff. But the words were stuck in her throat. Tears rimmed her eyelids and trickled down her face. Gwen was gone. Ty was gone.

Happiness and faith in love and humanity—gone.

They passed her exit and got off two exits up. Weaving through the residential area, Adam pulled into his driveway. Bruno bounded up to Kendall—tail wagging, whole body squirming—as soon as they entered the kitchen.

Bruno nuzzled his nose into Kendall's hand, inviting her to love him. She dropped to her knees and buried her face into his neck. The tears came unhindered, rolling down her cheeks, soaking Bruno's fur. Adam's cell phone rang. He moved past her into the next room, giving them both privacy.

After a couple of minutes, she pulled her face away. Bruno's tongue lapped her cheeks, cleansing her of grief. She smiled at him, scratching his ears as she stood. "What a good boy you are."

63

"I HAVE SOME NEWS for you in the Jenna Rose case," Fran Ward said when Adam answered his cell.

Adam glanced back into the kitchen where Kendall sat with her face buried into Bruno's fur. "What news is that?"

"When I went through Jenna Rose's autopsy to find links to the other cases you mentioned, I remembered another case where the victim had marks on her back—a recent case. Gwen Tavich. You're working that one, as well, correct?"

Sonofabitch. How had Adam not made that connection before? "Yes, that's my case. Did you compare the marks on Gwen's back to the marks on Jenna's?"

"I did. And, as with the others, they are not an exact match, but similar enough."

"So, Gwen Tavich was murdered by the same person who killed Jenna Rose?"

"And the other victims."

This day was shaping up to be one for the books. When the day started, Adam had been convinced he had a slam-dunk conviction against Ty Butler for Gwen Tavich's murder. Now Ty had been exonerated, and it was looking as if Gwen had been murdered by a serial killer.

"There's more," Fran said. "I don't believe the burns on Jenna Rose's genitalia were from the barrel of the gun after it was fired. On closer inspection, they appear to be electrical burns."

Gwen had electrical burns on her breasts. "Have you checked the other victims for electrical burns?"

"I'm up to my elbows in dead bodies at the moment, with the bus accident on I-25 last night."

Adam had heard about the accident when he was leaving the PD the previous night, and had been relieved not to have been called out to assist at the scene. A tractor trailer had jack-knifed on the interstate. A bus filled with people returning from one of the casinos had slammed into it, only to be rear-ended by another tractor trailer. The bus caught on fire, and several of the elderly passengers had perished in the flames.

Fran sighed. "Once I get a break, I'll dig into the other autopsies and let you know."

64

A DAM STOOD IN front of a wet bar, pouring himself a drink. He glanced over at Kendall when she entered. "Something to take the edge off?"

"Please." She sank onto the couch, rested her head against the back, and closed her eyes. *What a shit day.*

"What's your poison?"

"Not picky."

Ice clinked against the side of the glass in front of her face. She opened one eye and peered at the caramel-colored liquid, then took a generous sip. The spirit burned a path down to her stomach. "Oh, that's just what I needed."

"Figured." He moved to the seat not far from her and let out a long sigh. They sat there. Quiet surrounded them. Cocooned them. Kendall's mind raced in a thousand different directions. She would have one thought, follow it, and become sidetracked by something completely different. Too much was happening. Ty arrested. Ty having an affair with a mob wife. Ty exonerated of Gwen's death. Ty gone. Everything changed.

Only one thing remained the same. Gwen was dead. She was not coming back. Things would never change for her.

Her killer was still out there. And now they were starting over in the investigation, weeks behind where they could've been if Ty had come clean up front.

Shit, if Ty had come clean months ago, we wouldn't be investigating Gwen's murder at all.

"Who was on the phone?" It was none of her business, but she needed a distraction from thinking about Gwen and who had killed her.

"ME. Called with info on another case of mine. She confirmed my killer was likely responsible for some past unsolved murders." He pointed to files laid out on the coffee table between them. "Take a look, if you want."

Kendall picked up a couple of files and flipped through them. She didn't recognize the first victim, Isabelle Kenyon. Murdered in 2007. Kendall had been a freshman in college. Doubtful she would've paid much attention to anything happening outside her Denver University campus sphere.

The next file took her breath away. "Amy Carrington?" A name she knew well. Her heart seized. Someone else Kendall had failed.

"You familiar with the case?" Adam asked.

She stared at him for a moment. "Are you kidding?"

"What?"

Kendall shook her head. "You don't watch the news much, do you?"

"Hell, no. It's too damn depressing. Why?"

"There was a story recently you may have found interesting."

"And what was this *interesting* story about?"

"Me." Kendall held up the file in her hand. "And Amy Carrington. While I was in college, I was shot by a guy on my way home. I worked weekends at a casino in Cripple Creek. He ended up killing the girl in the car with me."

Adam sat up in his seat, nearly spilling his liquor in his lap. His eyebrows were scrunched together. "Wait, you were shot? What the hell happened?"

"I stopped to help what I thought was a stranded motorist. Turned out to be a young woman who'd been kidnapped and raped. I was trying to get to the police station, but the guy chased us down and eventually caught up to us. He shot me and took the girl. Luckily, a cop found me and got me to the hospital before I bled out."

"Holy shit!" Adam bolted up, sloshing his drink all over his hand and onto the carpet. "Jesus H, that was *you*?"

She nodded. "More to the point—the murdered woman was Amy Carrington."

"No, Kendall, you don't understand." He placed his glass on the table and wiped his hand on his pantleg. "Unbelievable," he muttered. "Kendall, *I'm* the cop who found you!"

"What?" Her world went a little wonky for a second. Adam was the cop who'd saved her life? " No . . . fucking . . . way."

"I swear to God, it was me. You gave me the license plate number of the vehicle he was driving." He dropped back into his seat.

They sat there, mouths gaping, staring at each other. She'd never known who had saved her that night. He'd never visited her during her recovery. She'd never gotten his name. Had never gone searching for it. She'd locked everything about that night away for a very long time. Eventually, she'd started dealing with it, thanks to Gwen and her family. But she'd never sought out the man who had held her hand and told her she would be okay while they waited for paramedics to arrive.

Kendall looked at Adam. Her heart raced with the memories of that night. But then she remembered the calming effect he'd had on her. The same calming effect he had now, and ever since they had met. And she could see it clearly and wondered how she hadn't made the connection earlier.

"Thanks," she said, raising her glass to him. It was long overdue.

He picked up his glass and tipped it toward her. "You're welcome."

They both slammed the remainder of their drinks back. Adam got the bottle from the bar, refilled both glasses, and set it on the table between them.

Kendall leaned back into the couch cushions. Her head was pounding, ears buzzing.

What a small fucking world.

65

Monday,
March 16,
8:55 AM

KENDALL DROPPED ADAM off at his vehicle as the sun was just beginning to break in the east. They had both been slow to get moving that morning. The empty bottle of Jameson sat mockingly on the coffee table and was the reason they were both bleary-eyed and not quite bushy-tailed.

Adam hadn't told Kendall the ME was tentatively linking Gwen's death with the other Reaper victims. There were too many things which didn't quite line up with the MO in the other victim's cases. Adam wanted time to go through everything before he hit Kendall with that news.

He'd wondered, somewhere around two in the morning, if Kendall had been the target. What if Gwen had been in the wrong place at the wrong time?

Now that the murder investigation was back in full swing, it was time for Adam to revisit some suspects who might have slipped under the radar while he was focused on Ty Butler. Adam wasn't convinced Gwen Tavich was a victim of the Reaper. Too many things didn't line up. For one, all of the Reaper's victims had been young and blonde and Caucasian. Gwen had been in her late thirties and clearly looked it, and she was African American. Additionally, unlike the Reaper's victims, Gwen had not been brutally raped with a foreign instrument. She hadn't been raped at all. A big deviation, in Adam's opinion.

Which meant there was a loose end to tie up. Martin Griffin didn't seem a likely candidate as Gwen's murderer, but even a person with the slimmest potential to be the perpetrator had to be eliminated. The last two weeks had been a waste, focusing attention almost solely on Butler. Adam wasn't going to be as myopic in the investigation, going forward.

Everyone was a suspect until they were satisfactorily cleared.

He drove down 46th Street, next to Rocky Mountain Lake Park, and turned onto King Street. Another two blocks down, and a right on 45th. He checked the address again. Sure enough, Martin Griffin lived two blocks from where Gwen's body had been discovered. It was also along the exact path the killer took from the park after dumping her body in the lake.

Could Griffin really have been upset enough over his lack of fair compensation to kill Gwen? Or was there more going on than anyone knew about? Martin wasn't a fan of Butler and how he had been treating Gwen. Had there been more to the relationship between Gwen and Martin? The possibility existed the infatuation was all on Martin's side—Gwen could've been clueless. What if Martin had made an advance and Gwen had turned him down? Could the rebuke of his affections have enraged Martin to the point of killing Gwen?

According to the security cam footage from the restaurant on the night of Gwen's disappearance, Martin got into his car and drove away a full fourteen minutes before Gwen even left the restaurant. Had he parked somewhere and waited for Gwen to come along? Ambushed her? Taken her back to his place and murdered her after a few days of torture via brink-of-death electrocution?

Full-on speculation without a scant trace of evidence to support the theory, which meant there was no way to obtain a search warrant for Griffin's apartment.

On top of that, Griffin lived with his mother, which made torturing and killing a woman for days a bit of a long shot. But you could never tell what went on in families. Adam had seen some bizarre shit over the years. To some families, there was no bond stronger than blood. And that meant protecting their own, no matter how vicious the crime.

Sheila Griffin's house was a one-story, redbrick, Tudor-style home. A long driveway stretched down the side of the house.

Adam took a walk down it before ringing the doorbell. He wanted to get a feel for the place before he went inside.

A four-car garage sat behind the house. Above it was what looked to be an apartment. Decent-sized one too. At the end of the structure was a small side yard with a grill and a seating area.

"Can I help you?" a woman's voice called to him.

He turned to find a woman in her late fifties, early sixties standing at a side door to the main residence. Adam pulled his badge off his belt as he walked toward her.

"Yes, ma'am. I'm Detective Adam Taylor with the Denver Police Department." He showed her his badge as he approached. "I'm investigating the death of Gwen Tavich."

The woman tsked and shook her head. "That poor woman. Martin is just torn up about it. He loved working at the restaurant." She gazed at Adam. "But what does her murder have to do with Martin?"

"We're questioning all the employees as part of our investigation."

Her arms wrapped around her chest, and her eyes narrowed a bit. "Martin told me you already questioned him at the restaurant. So what are you doing here, Detective?"

"I have to verify some information he provided." He took out his notepad. A stern look locked Sheila Griffin's features. "It's routine but has to be done."

"What would you like to know?"

"Martin lives here with you?"

"Well, yes, in a way." She pointed to the apartment over the garage. "He lives up there."

"I heard he was upset about not getting paid enough for the work he was doing. Did he talk to you about that?"

"Yes, and I agreed with him. Supported him talking to Gwen about it."

More like screamed and yelled at her after nearly getting himself fired, but whatever. Martin might not have told her what actually happened the night he claimed Gwen agreed to give him a substantial raise.

"It's a shame he waited so long to do it," she said. "The restaurant is closed, and he's trying to find another job."

"That means moving out of here will take longer."

Her eyebrows drew together, and her mouth dropped to a frown. "Why would Martin want to move? Rent is low. Utilities are low. The apartment has a state-of-the-art kitchen designed by him, for him so he can practice cooking. He won't find that anywhere else in the city, for what he pays."

"But he's a young man. Maybe he wants a place of his own?"

She laughed. "Detective, I can assure you. While it is true that Martin and I are close—we are all that each other's had since his father died twelve years ago—we stay out of one another's business. He comes and goes as he pleases, doesn't have to check in with me before he goes out. Or has visitors over." She gave him a knowing wink. "Trust me, there are some times when a mother doesn't want to know what her son is doing with his guests. I keep my nose out of his business."

"So, you don't pay attention to when he comes and goes, or who may be with him?" If she intentionally avoided checking up on her son, would he be able to get a possibly struggling Gwen out of his car and up to his apartment without her knowing?

"Well, I didn't say that, exactly. It's hard to avoid noticing a vehicle coming up the driveway. And I'm of an age I like to know who is coming onto my property."

"Did you happen to hear him come home from work Saturday night? February twenty-second?"

"I did."

"And what time did he get home?"

"It was around 1:40 in the morning."

"And you're certain of the date and time? That was over two weeks ago."

"Yes, Detective. I was up chatting with a friend in Hawaii when Martin drove up. I saw his headlights as he came down the driveway, and I checked the time. I was shocked I had been Skyping for so long, so I wrapped up my call and got ready for bed."

Adam glanced down the driveway toward Martin's apartment above the four-car garage. "Does Martin usually park his car in the garage when he's home?"

"Yes, we both do. No use leaving them out. The neighborhood is pretty safe, but it still has its share of car break-ins and vandalism."

"Is there access to Martin's apartment from the garage?"

"Yes." She stepped off the small cement porch and crossed to the opposite side of the driveway. Pointing toward Martin's apartment, she said, "See that doorway?"

Adam stood next to her. There was an exterior door to the left of the first garage door.

"That leads to a small foyer. There is also a door that goes to the garage. The stairs to his apartment come off the foyer. We use it as a sort of mudroom. Both of us hang our keys there when we come in. Martin also takes off his shoes and hangs his coat up before going upstairs." She faced him. "I typically wait to get into the main house to do that."

"I assume there is access to the main house from that foyer?"

"Yes." She smiled and looked up at the gray sky. Snow was in the forecast. Again. "I don't like trying to maneuver down the driveway on ice. I've made it sixty-one years without having a broken bone. I'm not getting one by slipping on black ice."

He smiled and nodded his head in agreement. "As far as you know, did Martin stay in the remainder of the night?"

"As far as I know. He's usually exhausted after a Saturday night shift, especially if he is running the kitchen on his own. I can't imagine him going anywhere after he got back."

"And as far as you know, he was alone."

"Yes. But as I said, I don't keep tabs on him. If he had someone with him, I didn't hear anything."

"Would you have—if he was making noise?"

"No, there is a door at the top of the stairs into the apartment. Saves me money not heating the stairs."

If Martin had had Gwen in his apartment, there was a good chance Mrs. Martin would have been clueless. And the ingress and egress was, for all intents and purposes, separate from the main house.

"Was Martin interested in Ms. Tavich romantically?"

"No."

"You seem sure—"

"He's in a serious relationship and has been for going on three years."

"People have been known to cheat—"

"With a very nice young man."

Ah...

She smiled. "Martin hasn't had a girlfriend since the seventh grade, when he figured out he was gay and started going out with boys."

"Okay," Adam said. "Thanks for your time."

Martin Griffin had seemed like a long shot when Adam arrived. The fact that he was gay didn't absolve him of the crime. It just closed the door on Martin killing Gwen over anything amorous. By the time he got in his car to head over to Quentin Novak's house, Adam was less sure Griffin was a dark horse. Until someone better came along, Martin Griffin was still at the top of the suspect list.

The drive to Novak's was short. He lived three-quarters of a mile away from Griffin. Farther south of Rocky Mountain Lake Park.

Still, a mile walk was not out of the realm of possibility.

Motive was still the big sticking point for Adam when it came to Novak. There didn't seem to be one. From what he could gather, Quentin was close to Gwen.

Although, if he had been in love with Kendall... love could make a man do stupid things. Adam had a hard time believing the relationship between Kendall and Novak was anything more than friendship, especially from Kendall's view. Or had Quentin been romantically interested in Gwen and she shot him down?

Novak was walking down the front path from his house to his car when Adam pulled up behind him.

"Quentin," Adam said as he got out of the car and walked toward him. "I'm glad I caught you before you left."

The color drained from his face. "Is something wrong with Kendall?"

"No, she's fine."

His shoulders relaxed, and he shoved his hands in his coat pockets. "Then what can I do for you, Detective?"

"I was just driving by—was over at Martin Griffin's residence, checking some things out. I knew you lived close by, so I thought I would wander over since I was in the area."

His eyebrows lifted, and his mouth quirked up on one side. "So, am I a suspect?"

Adam grinned. "Everyone's a suspect."

"Ah, I see. You're just going to go through all of the people closest to Gwen and start accusing them? When should I expect to be arrested? Maybe I should put in for vacation time, so I don't miss work until you discover I'm not the killer. Like Ty."

Whoa, Novak is a bit touchy.

Adam chuckled. "Yeah, Butler was an unfortunate waste of investigative time, for sure." Adam wasn't going to take shit from Novak on how he'd handled the investigation and subsequent arrest of Butler. All the evidence had pointed to him as Gwen's killer, at the time. "Of course, if he had just come clean about his affair, we could've moved on a lot earlier."

"And when you decide I'm not your man, will you then accuse Kendall?"

Time to set a trap for Novak, see if he bites. "I haven't decided anything about you. Besides, I don't think Kendall would kill Gwen."

"Because you know her so well?"

"Feels like I've gotten to know her pretty well over the course of this investigation. We've spent a lot of time together." He shrugged and kicked at a rock on the road. "Gotten close."

Novak stared at him. His face stone but his breathing rapid. He did not like Adam being friends with Kendall.

Or more.

"I mean, we had a good talk last night at my place. There's just no reason I can see for her to want Gwen dead. They were like sisters."

"Kendall was at your house last night?"

Adam knew it was going to bother Novak. He'd tried calling Kendall, but Kendall had ignored the calls at first, telling Adam she couldn't deal with "Q" at the time. By the fourth call, she let out a long sigh and answered it. Then lied to him about where she was, telling him she was home and going to bed early.

Adam felt a little bad about outing her, but figured she'd forgive him if he solved the murder of her best friend.

"Yeah, she was pretty upset when we left Butler's place. But she seemed fine when I left her this morning."

Novak's face and neck went a deep red. He removed his hands from his pockets and balled them into tight fists at his side. Adam took a wider stance in case Novak actually threw a punch. The man's entire body seemed to be vibrating with rage.

"Are you in love with Kendall?"

"What?"

Adam shrugged. "She's hot—and smart—easy to fall for."

Novak stared at him, but kept his jaw clenched tight.

"Or are you gay?"

"I'm not gay," Novak said through gritted teeth.

Adam kept going. Truth be told, he was actually having fun pushing Novak's buttons. "It's just, well—you're a decent enough looking guy—how come you don't have a girlfriend?"

"None of your damn business who I date, Detective. But to answer your question—K and I are best friends. So, yes, I love her."

"Romantically?"

"No. And for your information, we have both had relationships with other people during the course of our friendship. Hell, Kendall was engaged at one point."

"Okay," Adam said. "What about Gwen—anything there beyond friendship?"

Could that have somehow been the catalyst for him to kill Gwen?

Novak snickered, a cocky grin sliding into place as he dug his keys from his pocket and hit the unlock button. "I have to get to work."

He didn't wait for a reply, just got behind the wheel and confidently closed the door. Adam watched as the silver Prius drove away.

Quentin Novak had a temper. At least according to the bartender at the restaurant. And while he seemed to have controlled it pretty well with Adam, he wondered how much further Novak could be pushed before the tenuous hold he had on it slipped from his grasp.

Had Novak been jealous of the tight sisterhood between Kendall and Gwen? Would that have been enough to push him to get rid of her?

There was nothing to indicate any tension between the three friends, but Adam hadn't really tried to pull the veil back on the relationship either. He had been too short-sighted, focusing on Ty Butler.

Maybe it was time to take a closer look at Novak's alibi the night Gwen went missing. Long shot, yes. But Adam was going to track down every lead, no matter how implausible it might be.

Gwen Tavich deserved no less.

66

THE WILLIAMSES' HOUSE was part of a new trend in some of the older Denver neighborhoods to get rid of the mature, dilapidated, outdated homes and replace them with modern European-style houses. It was all different planes of dark, textured brick along sleek, light-colored, smooth stucco.

Kendall walked through the Williamses' beautifully decorated home and thought it was perfect for a young yuppie couple. Hardwood floors, white walls, and lots of windows. There was nothing rounded in the entire house. It seemed to be all sharp edges and corners. One of those new glass-front, blue-flame fireplaces that looked more like a picture hanging on the wall sat in the center of the living room. The stairs had sleek iron railings. There was a wine rack in almost every room on the first floor, and two wine fridges in the kitchen.

An entertainer's dream. But for a family with two small children, it felt more institutional. Even when Kendall had visited after Emily first went missing—when she was investigating a possible abduction—there hadn't been many signs of children residing in the house. A playroom in the attic was the only place where it was moderately apparent children lived there. Even then, the room was clutter-free when Kendall had taken a tour of the house. Kathy must've seen Kendall's reaction, and she explained that Scott insisted all toys were put away as soon as Emily and Sadie were done playing with them.

It was cold. Unwelcoming. And once again, Kendall was incensed over the loss of the carefree childhood Emily and Sadie deserved.

She descended to the basement. A huge sectional couch sat in front of a large-screen TV. Off to the side was another built-in bar area with a wine rack, mini fridge, and a sink. There were no toys in the basement. This was not a place for kids. Judging by the framed Colorado Avalanche jerseys hanging on the wall, this was indeed Scott's lair. The idea made Kendall shudder.

The storage room Kathy believed was the "secret room" was down the hall. The forensics team had done a thorough job of going through the room, but hadn't found anything. Walking around inside was a challenge with the amount of stuff stored in the room. Lying down was not an option, even with a small child.

Kendall closed the door and returned to the main floor. Perhaps Emily was confused about the secret room being in the basement. What if it was in another part of the house? Kendall looked around the first floor. The space was open. Not even a coat closet by the front door.

The bedrooms were on the second floor. She entered Emily's room first. On the bed was a small teddy bear. Kendall picked it up, wondering why it hadn't been taken. It was clear Kathy had gone through the place and removed everything of importance. Had this been left behind on purpose? Maybe a toy from Scott to his daughter?

Opening the closet door, Kendall stepped inside. Like the bedroom, it was nearly empty. Only a few empty hangers were left on the rod. She paced the perimeter of the walk-in closet, knocking on the walls, searching for anything to indicate there was space behind. On the ceiling was a door to the attic storage space. Kendall dragged a plastic child's chair into the closet and stood on it. Maybe there was a ladder that allowed access into the attic.

Nothing.

Sadie's room was next, followed by the Jack-and-Jill bathroom she shared with her sister, and the hall closet. No indication of a hidden door anywhere. Scott and Kathy's room seemed an even bigger long shot. It would've been difficult to get into a secret room with Kathy so close by, but Kendall checked it anyway. Empty. Pictures with the shattered glass were strewn across the bed. Every picture had Scott in it.

Kendall figured Kathy would like to do much worse than destroy pictures of her husband. She hoped it had at least been somewhat cathartic.

They had converted part of the attic into a playroom for the girls. All four walls were exterior walls. No secret rooms.

Emily had been adamant Williams had taken her to a secret room to abuse her. Kendall knew a child's mind under extreme conditions could morph reality, but couldn't shake the feeling Emily was not mistaken about this. So far, the CSU team had been unable to find any place in the house indicating Williams had done anything untoward to his daughter. No bodily fluids. No excessive amounts of hair or other DNA.

But it was there somewhere. Kendall knew it. Deep in her bones, she knew Emily was telling the truth. And Kendall was determined to prove the little girl correct. And then they could put Scott Williams away for good.

The basement was the key.

CHAPTER

67

ADAM WALKED INTO the conference room, phone to his ear. On the way back to the department from Novak's house, he had called Oren Mitchell, the restaurant's accountant, from his car. He needed to know if Gwen had discussed Griffin's raise with him.

"Yes, she sent me an email requesting he receive it for the previous pay period as well. The raise went into effect at the beginning of the month."

"So, he'll get backpay to make up for the difference from the last pay period?" Adam asked.

"That is correct. He is going to be receiving quite a substantial paycheck. Although that might not be much consolation since the restaurant is being sold."

Adam thanked the man and disconnected the call. Officer Young was sitting in front of Adam's laptop going through the video from Gwen Tavich's funeral. Adam had figured he could use a fresh set of eyes. Maybe Young would see something Adam, Saul, and Fletch had missed. At this point, Adam was willing to try anything to generate new leads.

Especially since his number-one suspect was all but cleared with that call from Mitchell. It wasn't likely Griffin would kill Gwen when she had not only given him a decent raise but also backpay. Just wasn't plausible. And because Griffin "pitched for the other team," unrequited love didn't seem to be a credible motive.

Quentin Novak. Really, the only suspect left. And he was highly questionable. Even if he'd realized Gwen didn't really like him, would that be enough of a catalyst for murder?

Didn't seem likely, but he was going to remain on the suspect list until Adam could verify Novak's alibi for the night Gwen disappeared. It was possible he'd been waiting for Gwen to leave the restaurant, and had followed her. Had he been the one to slip into the backseat of the SUV?

"Be right back," he said to Young, and returned to his cubicle to fetch his notepad from his jacket pocket. The television was on in the squad room, and several detectives were gathered around, watching the news of the day. Adam stopped to see what was so interesting.

The insane case of Scott Williams had taken over the news cycle, which had probably been why there was not much press on Gwen's case. It'd been nice not having to contend with the media hounding him at every turn.

"I hope they throw the bastard into a cell with a really big, hairy dude who will give Williams a taste of what it feels like to be used for sex," one detective said.

Other detectives voiced their agreement and made a few crude statements, jokes only acceptable inside the walls of the police department. Adam knew Kendall had been the one to break the case. She'd also physically assaulted Williams when she'd found out he was the perpetrator, so her role in the investigation was diminished. Now, though, she was at Williams's residence, doing another search of the place. They had discussed the case the previous night.

A picture of Williams popped up on the screen, followed by a chorus of boos from the detectives. Adam stilled. He recognized the man. But from where?

"No fucking way." He bolted into the Tavich war room and yanked a picture from the murder board. Returning to the TV, he held it up and compared the two men.

"Motherfucker."

Scott Williams was the mystery man from Gwen's funeral. The one who didn't seem to know a soul. Who stood away from everyone. No wonder he'd looked out of place. Adam burst through the conference room door, causing Young to nearly come out of his seat.

Adam held up the picture. "This man was at the funeral. Find him in the video."

"Yeah, I remember him," Young said. "I was going to point him out to you. He just didn't fit in. I thought maybe he was a loner, but no one paid any attention to him. As far as I could tell, not a single person gave him so much as a head nod of recognition."

Adam watched the video. Sure as shit, Scott Williams stood by a tree. Staring at Kendall. "Pull up the footage from the gas station the night Tavich disappeared."

As soon as the footage came up, Young found the man sneaking into the back of the SUV. "Switch to the view of the rear of the store, and back it up. Let's see if he's there. Maybe get a shot of his face."

Young went back to the 2:15 mark, and pressed "Play." After a couple of minutes, a man in a dark coat and pants walked down the aisle toward the coolers. As he came closer to where the camera was positioned, his face became more recognizable.

"I'll be damned," Young mumbled.

"Switch back to the front interior camera," Adam said. "Go back to around 2:10. Let's see if we can get this asshole coming in the door."

Young did as he was instructed. At 2:14, the man walked through the entrance. "Pause," Adam commanded.

The face was unmistakable, now that Adam knew who he was looking for. The man in the video had unknowingly obliged them by glancing up at the camera. There was absolutely no question: it was Scott Williams.

Adam wasn't sure whether to feel relieved he had another viable suspect in Gwen's murder case or terrified Williams had kidnapped and killed Gwen as retribution for Kendall being the one responsible for his future life behind bars.

If that were true, Kendall might never forgive herself. Chances were good she would blame herself for her best friend's death. Drive herself crazy with scenarios and options, "what if's," and "I should've picked up on . . ." It was a never-ending game. It would fuck with her mind. And she would question how she had missed something she could never have seen coming.

Adam knew. It's what he would do if the roles were reversed.

Picking up the phone receiver, Adam pressed a button and was connected to a dispatcher. "Put a BOLO out for Scott Williams. Wanted for questioning—and a suspect in the murder of Gwen Tavich."

68

KENDALL ONCE AGAIN made a slow walk around the finished part of the basement. Scott Williams had spared no expense on gaming systems, pool and air hockey tables, and autographed sports memorabilia. But nothing indicated an entrance into another room.

It had to be in the storage room somewhere.

Kendall opened the door and flipped on the switch. This part of the basement remained unfinished. At least drywall was up. Kendall had seen basements in some of the newer houses where the basement walls were just studs and insulation. But the floor was cement, and the room was a good fifteen degrees colder than the rest of the house. Kendall made another pass of the room, only this time, she concentrated on the floor.

She fished out her cell phone and opened the flashlight app. Sweeping it slowly back and forth, she looked for anything that looked off. Not that she had any idea what *that* might be. But she would know it when she saw it. She hoped.

Her cell phone buzzed and she glanced at the caller ID. Adam. He was going to have to wait. She declined the call, and then changed her phone setting to Do Not Disturb. Being distracted by Gwen's case did not absolve her of her responsibilities to the Williams investigation. Kendall was determined to give all her attention to Emily's case. She owed the little girl that much. Kendall would not be the cause of Scott Williams going free.

Without a conviction, there was a chance Williams would be able to get visitation with the girls. Continue to abuse both of them.

Over my dead body . . . or his.

She had made it toward the back of the room. Along the row of stacked boxes, a barely discernible scrape in an arc came from under the boxes. Like the kind a door would make along an uneven floor. Kendall shoved her cell phone into her back pocket. The boxes had to be moved. She just hoped they weren't filled with books weighing a hundred pounds.

Deep inhale. She grasped the top box and lifted. To her surprise and delight, it was light. Too light. She set it on the floor at her feet. She ripped the tape and opened it. Empty. She grabbed the next box. Also, empty.

"Well, logic would dictate—" Kendall murmured.

As she suspected. The bottom box was also empty.

"Fucking decoy boxes."

Grabbing her cell phone again from her pocket, she shined the light on the wall. "There you are." A white, flush-mounted door handle almost completely blended into the wall. In fact, Kendall would bet if she hadn't been intentionally looking for it, she might have overlooked it.

Placing two fingertips under the metal semicircle, she felt for the latch. The lock disengaged. Kendall opened the door and felt along the wall for a light switch. A floor lamp turned on. Emily had been right. Kendall had found it.

The secret room.

69

ADAM WAS ALREADY on his way over to Scott Williams's house. He knew Kendall was there, but she wasn't answering her phone. His heart pounded in his chest as he turned left onto Pecos Street. He needed to tell her about Williams. Warn her of the danger of being in his house alone when they hadn't been able to locate him. Apparently, no one, not even Williams's defense attorney, had heard from him in a couple of days.

Adam's cell phone rang.

Please let it be Kendall. "Taylor."

"Detective, this is dispatch. Be advised, there's been a report of a man identified as Scott Williams in the vicinity of 40th and Wyandot."

Shit, right by Williams's home.

"The caller is a neighbor of Williams and said he noticed the suspect sneaking down the alley behind the houses. He thought it was odd Williams was not in his vehicle. With the recent arrest and media attention, the caller felt he should alert the police."

"Text me the make and model of Williams's vehicle. And send backup to Williams's residence. I have reason to believe he intends to harm an FBI agent who is performing a search of the suspect's house. As of now, I have been unable to get in touch with the agent to warn her of the potential danger. Williams should be considered armed and dangerous."

Adam slowed to a stop at a light and hung up with dispatch. He looked through his call history, found Quentin Novak's number, and called it. It rang six times, then went to voice-mail. Adam clicked "End" and redialed. This time the call was answered on the third ring.

"Hello," came the hushed voice.

Adam didn't waste time with pleasantries. "Novak, it's Taylor. Are you with Kendall, by any chance?"

"No," he whispered. "I'm at a work. Why are you looking for Kendall?"

"We believe Scott Williams killed Gwen." Adam paused. "Kendall may have been his original target, and now he's attempting to correct his mistake. He was just seen near his home."

"What?" Novak whisper-yelled into the phone. "Are you fucking kidding me? She better not be hurt, Taylor. This is all your fault. You wasted all that time—"

Click.

Adam didn't have time to listen to Quentin Novak's tirade.

70

KENDALL FROZE IN the doorway. It seemed almost irreverent to barge in and start taking inventory of everything in the room.

A little girl had been brutalized here. There should be some sort of acknowledgment of the pain and sorrow Emily had suffered at the hands of her father. The death of innocence and unconditional love and blind faith. Too soon Emily was having to face harsh realities that life wasn't fair. Monsters do exist. And some don't stay under the bed.

The evil perpetuated in the room was still palpable.

In the center a mattress lay on the floor. A blue tarp was folded on top of it. Metal shelves, like the ones found in garages all over the city, stood along one wall. Plastic bins with lids lined the shelves. On the bottom shelf was a car battery, a set of jumper cables next to it.

Kendall pulled a pair of latex gloves out of her pocket, slipped them on, and grabbed a box off the shelf. Inside were a collection of sex toys. Anal beads, dildo, a cock ring, and alligator clips. Bile rose in her throat. She forced herself not to imagine Scott Williams using the implements on his daughter.

Replacing the lid, she opened another box, steeling herself for what she would find inside. Various types of lubricants. Condoms. A box of baby wipes exactly like one Kendall had seen in Sadie's room two floors up.

She wasn't sure if she could go through another box. Sweat rolled down her spine, the cold of the room chilled her. She quelled an overwhelming urge to run from there. A heaviness weighed her down as she peered into the next box. A Polaroid instant camera. And pictures. Lots of them.

Kendall grabbed a handful and set the box down. Tears sprung to her eyes. Emily, naked, lying on the mattress less than two feet from where Kendall stood. Sadie and Emily in the bathtub. A sleepover Emily must have had with friends. Seven little girls, fast asleep on top of sleeping bags laid out in the family room, *Shrek* still playing on the giant TV screen. Close-ups of genitalia covered only by thin cotton panties.

Kendall dropped the pictures back into the box and turned away to retch.

Scott Williams was a sick motherfucker. Death was the only punishment appropriate for the selfish, depraved man. And she wanted to be the one to kill him. Watch the blood flow from his body. His life extinguished. Never again able to harm another little girl.

She pulled her cell phone out of her back pocket. Time to make sure Scott Williams paid for what he'd done. She hit the speed dial for her boss.

"Brady, send ERT to the Williams home. We got him."

71

Scott Williams's Audi A4 was parked at the corner of 40th and Umatilla, two blocks from his house. The doors were locked. Adam had called Kathy Williams, and she was able to remotely unlock the vehicle from an app on her phone. Since her name was on the title, she also provided authorization for the police to search the car.

Young went through the interior of the vehicle. Adam drew on latex gloves and popped the trunk. On the side, tucked into a small cargo area, was an emergency roadside kit. Adam spread it out along the bottom of the pristine trunk. The usual things were in it: space blanket, tire inflator and sealant, triangle reflectors, and a small tool kit. The kit had a screwdriver, pliers, adjustable wrench.

And an exacto knife. Razor sharp.

The kind of thing Fran said could have created the cuts on Gwen's back.

Adam plucked an evidence bag out of his coat pocket and dropped the knife in.

"Sir," Young said, coming around to the back of the vehicle. He held out a large manilla envelope. "You need to see this."

Adam extracted items from the envelope.

A map of Telluride.

And photos. Kendall leaving her office. The exterior of Kendall's home.

Kendall's SUV.

But the most disturbing was a picture of Gwen, with a red "X" over her face.

CHAPTER

72

KENDALL FELT THE sensation of someone else in the room with her a split second before an arm wrapped around her neck and squeezed. Her hands grabbed at a muscular forearm, trying in vain to wrench it away from her windpipe. She couldn't breathe. Panic set in. She twisted her body. The arm tightened around her neck. The ability to inhale and exhale was gone. If she didn't do something quick, she would pass out.

Getting her feet under her, she pushed back with everything she had, her feet moving fast, propelling them both backward. They hit the wall hard. Air whooshed from the assailant's chest. The arm dropped from around Kendall's neck. She pushed off the man's body but was only able to take two steps before a hand wrapped around her ponytail. Her head snapped back, sending a stinger through her neck and shoulders.

She ducked under and hit the man's arm, forcing it up. He released his hold on her hair.

Kendall didn't give him an opportunity to reestablish his bearings. She balled up her fists, and drove them hard into his solar plexus. The man doubled over. Taking advantage of his position, he rushed Kendall, his head ramming into her stomach. All the air burst from her lungs, but she maintained her balance. Hands on his back, she held him down, and brought her knee up into his face.

"Fuck!"

She pushed him away, and backed up, instantly in a fighter's stance. The man swiped blood from his nose and mouth. A small ball of warmth filled Kendall's chest, elated she had made the fucker bleed.

He charged her. She blocked the backhanded punch with her forearm, but was knocked off kilter. He hit her twice in the upper body, in quick succession. On the third pass, she wrapped her arm around his, and hyperextended the elbow.

He dropped to his knees, but drove his fist up between her legs.

Sucking in air, she released his arm, and stepped back. *Fuck, that hurts!*

Before he could stand, she kicked him under his chin. His head snapped back. When it dropped forward, she kicked him again in the same spot. He fell to his back, his arms covering his head. When she stepped away, he wrapped his hand around her ankle and yanked. She dropped to her knees, but scrambled to get on top of him before he could stand. Straddling him, she punched at his head and face—wherever she could connect and get in a blow, until his eyes closed. His head flopped to one side. She stood and stared at him.

Scott Williams.

She kicked him in the side a few more times before turning away and whipping her phone out of her pocket.

There was a crackle in the air behind her. Something cold touched her neck. Pain emanated from the spot, so intense Kendall cried out. She dropped to her knees, placing her hands against the floor to keep from falling face-first onto the cement.

She had felt this before . . . when? FBI Academy? She was tingling all over, her muscles fatigued.

Stun gun.

She turned her head to the side just in time to see a boot seconds before it connected with her rib cage. Kendall wasn't sure if she actually heard the crack of her ribs or just imagined it. Pain shot through her upper body. Rolling onto her back, staring at the ceiling, she reached for her gun. She needed air. Couldn't breathe.

She had to remain calm, but her heart was beating so rapidly she felt it was trying to escape her chest. *Focus on your surroundings.* But her head was a foggy, jumbled mess. Where was her gun? Why couldn't she feel her fingers?

"Kendall Beck. FBI agent extraordinaire." Scott Williams hovered over her. "Not such a big shot now, are you? Thought you were all tough shit attacking me in the hospital."

Kendall reached under her arm and removed her Sig from the holster. She swung it toward him. Without aiming, she fired the weapon. The shot went wide.

"Nice try." He kicked the gun from her grasp. It skittered across the floor, barely out of her reach. "You know what I've been doing since being released from jail? Research. You have a very interesting past, Agent Beck."

He dropped to his knees, straddling her. She squirmed to get away from him, but he shifted his weight. She couldn't move.

"You were almost a hero in your youth. Getting ready to graduate from college when you came across a woman in the road who had been kidnapped and raped. You made it all the way to the police station—"

Amy Carrington's face flashed in front of her. Tears stained the young woman's face. Blood streaked her thighs. Fear like Kendall had never seen was etched in Amy Carrington's features. The memory now forever etched in Kendall's mind.

"If only you had run a little faster. But shot in the middle of the street in front of the police station—" Williams shook his head, feigning pity and sadness. "It must've been so horrible for you. And then to have poor Amy Carrington, the woman you were trying to save, be taken right in front of your eyes."

Kendall shut her eyes as tight as she could to get the visions to stop. She had fallen short of saving Amy Carrington that day. The first in a long list of people she had failed to protect.

"Is that why you became an FBI agent? Because you couldn't save her? Fat lot of good it did. Couldn't save Gwen either. Your best friend. Taken while driving your vehicle. That has to be especially poignant. Another person who was taken. Tortured. Killed."

He grasped her face and squeezed, forcing her to look him straight in the eye. "Do you know why Gwen Tavich is dead, Kendall?" He leaned close to her ear. His breath hot. She squirmed, desperate to get away. She didn't want to hear the answer. But she already knew.

"Because of you."

His hands slid around her neck. His face contorted as he tightened his grip. She reached up, tried to rip his hands from her neck. Clawed at his skin. She concentrated all her energy on her lower body. Raised her hips to buck him off. But he was too heavy. And she was still too weak from the electric shock.

Blackness rimmed her periphery. Her lungs were on fire. Her brain was telling her to take a deep breath, but her airway was blocked.

And the blackness continued to close in around her.

She was suddenly completely aware of what was going to happen next.

She was going to die.

73

COPS SWARMED THE Williams house. Adam threw his body armor on and ran inside without any idea where Kendall was. Or if she was alive. The thought took his breath away. He was no stranger to death; it was his job. He was around it every day, along with the evil people who killed. The one thing he had been able to avoid was the brutal murder of someone he knew.

Someone he had become close with over the last few weeks. A person he considered a friend. As he followed a cop in full tactical gear through the front door, he shook the fears of finding her dead body. He needed his head clear. Williams might still be in the house. Kendall could be injured. This could turn into a hostage situation.

Adam knew she had gone to the house to search the basement for the secret room the little girl had told her was there. The cop in front of him peeled off to the left and went up the stairs. Adam strained to see down the stairway leading to the basement. Slowly, each foot deliberately placed, as quietly as possible, he descended. Williams could be waiting to ambush them. Fear—and being boxed in a corner—made people do stupid things. Like shoot first. Take out as many people as possible, as soon as possible.

Adam was determined not to leave this house in a body bag. And no one else would either, with perhaps the exception of Williams.

Peering cautiously around the corner, he scanned the large family room. Empty. A door was open at the end hallway. Stealthily, he slipped down it, his back to the wall. He stepped into the storage room filled with boxes and other shit. A really good place to hide. And this was Williams's home court.

Adam had no doubt Williams had killed Gwen. He also knew from the evidence in the car that Kendall's life was in danger.

Guardedly, he walked so his shoes wouldn't squeak against the cement floor and alert Williams to his presence. He made his way down a makeshift aisle between stacked boxes toward the back of the room. At the end of a row of boxes, he stopped. Listened. No sound.

Leading with his gun, he poked his head around the corner. There was a hole in the wall. No, it was a door. Partially open.

I'll be damned. She found it.

The room was lit, but he couldn't see around the door. He waited outside of it for what felt like a year, focusing on any sounds coming from inside.

Silence.

No voices. No scuffling sounds. No breathing sounds.

Warily, he pushed the door open. A body was on the floor. Adam approached it.

Williams's body swam in a pool of blood. Adam squatted, placed two fingers against his neck. A thready pulse. He was barely holding on, very close to death. He needed medical attention immediately if he was going to survive.

For a split second, Adam considered letting that very thing happen. Williams had molested his daughter for years. Killed Gwen.

Had he killed Kendall?

He scanned the room. She lay a few feet away. Not moving.

Fuck!

Bile rose from his stomach. He scrambled over to her, and ran his fingers along her throat, desperate to find a pulse.

"Down here," he yelled. "Storage room. Two down. Need EMTs. Now!"

74

RAIN POURED. THICK. Heavy. Kendall could barely see. Her foot slipped on the muddy edge of the river.

Where am I?

She could make out two figures on the opposite shore. She shielded her eyes from the rain, concentrating on bringing them into focus. Two women. She knew them. Her heart nearly burst through her chest. Warmth and love radiated around her, creating a safe haven from the bitter cold of the rain and wind.

One raised a hand and waved. So familiar and comforting and Kendall knew instantly who she was.

"Mom?"

A smile spread across her mother's face. She brought her hand to her mouth and blew Kendall a kiss. Unconsciously, Kendall lifted her hand to catch it. It was their thing, might be one of the first memories Kendall had of her mother.

"No matter how far away," she would say, *"I will throw you a kiss straight from my heart. When you catch it, all my love will be with you."*

Her mother wrapped an arm around the other woman's waist and drew her in close. Into focus.

Gwen!

The black water raged and swirled at her feet. Kendall had to get to the other shore. Her heart was beating fast. Her breathing matching the pace. The water pulled at her. Tried to drag her into the rapids. There had to be a way across the river.

She tested the water. It was cold and angry. She snatched her foot away. Her legs tingled. Her hands and feet were numb.

What's happening to me?

Gwen and her mother were waiting for her. Just across the river. She swiped the rain from her eyes. They went in and out of focus. One minute she could see them perfectly. The next they were gone.

She had to get across. Wanted to be with them forever. Maybe she could wait out the storm. Let the river calm. Then she could swim to them. She was a good swimmer.

"Best in her class," her mother had bragged to her father at the conclusion of the six-week lesson at the Y.

She was still a strong swimmer.

And they were right there. So close to her, yet impossible to get to them. Touch them. Wrap her arms around them, and never let them go. Never let anything happen to them.

This time, she would protect them. She had failed them once. But never again. She had a second chance to fix things. Make them right. Bring them back.

If she could just get to them.

The shore gave way. Kendall eased into the water. She gasped for breath. The rapids pulled her under, wrapped icy arms around her. Held her beneath the surface. She could see them—Mom and Gwen—they were calling to her. She tried to fight the water. Force it to release her.

I have to get to them.

But the more she fought, the more the watery arms fixed around her. Her lungs burned. She needed air. Why was the river so intent on taking her?

Why couldn't she get to them?

The water pulled her farther away from them. She wanted to yell to them. Scream at them to save her. Tell them she loved them. But the words were strangled in her throat. Forced to remain inside of her forever.

Darkness closed in around her. Her mother and Gwen grew smaller and smaller until they were gone. And Kendall succumbed to her fate.

The water displaced around her, taking it and her by surprise. A hand grasped her arm and yanked her from the water's deathly grip. She was dragged onto the shore. She could feel the mud as she slid across it. Smell the earthiness of the ground. The sweet smell in the air after the rain cleansed everything.

She inhaled deeply, her lungs filling with air.

"Kendall?"

Her eyes opened. She coughed, rolled to her side, coughed some more. Pain radiated across her chest. *Fuck that hurts!* She rolled to her back.

Where the hell am I?

She scanned the area. The floor was cold. Cement. Low light. Something heavy was in her left hand.

"Hey, you with us?"

Kendall stared at the man sitting at her side.

Adam.

"Yeah." The word came out as a squeak. Her throat felt raw. She nodded and reached her hand out to him. He grasped it and helped her sit up. Her ribs throbbed, the pain in cadence with her heartbeat. And the pounding in her head.

"Williams?" she whispered.

"Barely hanging on. He's on the way to the hospital."

"What happened?" Jesus her throat hurt.

"Shot."

Kendall pointed at Adam.

He shook his head and pointed to her left hand—wrapped around the grip of her gun, finger on the trigger.

How the hell?

Adam took the weapon from her. "How about I take the loaded gun away from the crazy lady?" He secured the weapon and placed it on the floor next to him. "What do you remember?"

"I found the room."

"I see that. Congratulations."

"Williams . . . attacked me . . . strangled . . . stun gun." She made a motion with her arm to indicate she'd gone down. "I reached for—" she pointed at where her gun lay.

"Your gun?" Adam asked.

She nodded and lifted her arm, her fingers bent to form a gun, and aimed it at Adam.

"Good shot." A wide grin spread across his face.

She shook her head. Big mistake. The throbbing went into full-timpani-drum mode. "Missed." She pointed at the spot she last remembered seeing her Sig. "Knocked it out of my hand." Every word was a struggle to get out. "Choked me . . . passed out."

"And you don't remember shooting Williams?"

Gingerly, she wagged her head to the side.

Adam released a long, low whistle. "Well, that's too bad, because it was one helluva shot. One you want to recall when you're an old lady bragging to your grandkids about what a badass you once were."

The EMTs moved in, pushing Adam out of the way, asking her where she hurt. She pointed to her ribs on the right side. Her throat. Her head.

Memories of the dream returned—two women standing on a shore, one of them blowing her a kiss. And then they were gone.

And my heart . . . my heart hurts.

75

Thursday,
March 19,
2:00 PM

K ENDALL WAS SITTING on the couch, laughing at something her partner, Jake, had said as Adam entered the house. He'd practically had to barter any future children to get past the guard dog—aka Novak—at the front door. Novak had made Adam promise to stay only a few minutes and not to stress Kendall out by talking about the Williams case.

"She needs her rest," he said as he passed by Adam. Adam offered him a two-finger salute in response, garnering a huff from the man.

Kendall chuckled, then grabbed her side. She looked decent, considering.

"Jesus, you look like shit," Adam said.

She flipped him the bird.

The bruises around her neck were a nasty progression of red, blue, and purple. She had pillows around her, but he could see her right arm tucked in close to her body. Adam unconsciously ran his hand along his side, remembering when he'd been in her position. Broken ribs were a bitch.

He nodded his head at Jake, sitting in the chair Adam usually occupied. He and Jake had gotten to know each other in the hospital, waiting to get news on Kendall's condition. He was a good guy. Adam liked him. Had a sweet wife and adorable baby. Adam was envious of the wife. Not so much the baby.

Sitting sideways on the couch, Adam faced Kendall and set a paper grocery bag between them. "I wasn't sure what to bring someone who had come back from the dead with broken ribs," he reached into the bag. "So I brought you ice cream."

"Good call." Her voice was better than it had been, but he could tell it still hurt to talk.

He reached back into the bag and pulled out a bottle of bourbon. "And alcohol."

"Better call," she said, reaching for the bottle.

Novak snagged it before she had a good grasp, and picked up the carton of ice cream. "Not until you're drug free." She stuck her tongue out at him. "Love you too."

Jake chuckled. "I didn't do much better. The enchiladas Felicia made were acceptable. The six pack of beer was not."

"Beer?" Adam asked.

"Help yourself," Kendall said, pointing into the kitchen.

Adam considered it but was not in the mood to be one-on-one with Novak. The guy was Kendall's self-appointed sentry, and Adam wasn't about to butt heads with him.

"So, any new memories?" he asked.

She shook her head. "What happened to Williams?" she asked.

"Died on the table."

The news was bittersweet. Not that either of them would grieve for the man, but there had been a certain satisfaction in thinking he would spend his remaining days in prison, getting the same treatment from his fellow inmates Emily had gotten from him.

But the world was a better place with him gone.

"So, what's happening?" she asked.

"Essentially, both cases are closed. The Denver PD and DA are both satisfied with the evidence and have hung Gwen's murder on him."

"And the other victims'," Jake added.

"What do you think?" Kendall asked.

"I think it's the right call. Williams apparently recognized you from years earlier—when he shot you." He didn't add *"and killed Amy Carrington."* Kendall had already spent her adult life regretting that part. "When you showed up to investigate his daughter's disappearance, he was apparently afraid you might make the connection between the two of you, and he began stalking you. Knew where you worked, where you lived, and who your friends were. He had a schedule of comings and goings for both you and Gwen."

"All wrapped up in a nice, neat box," she said. That had bothered Adam, as well. From the look on Jake's face, he was wondering the same thing. *Too nice and neat?*

"Do you think he targeted Gwen or mistook her for me?"

Adam knew where she was going with the question. If Williams had been gunning for Kendall that night, and Gwen had been killed because she was in the wrong place, at the wrong time, and in the wrong vehicle . . .

"No, it's pretty clear he knew she was driving your SUV. We went back and looked at the restaurant security video. Two other cars drove by the restaurant at the time Gwen left. One of the cars belonged to Williams. He waited for her to leave the restaurant and followed her. We speculate he thought she would go home, and he could take out both of you. When she went to Butler's instead, he had to improvise. When he saw the opportunity at the gas station, he took it."

"And you're sure it was Williams who got into the SUV?"

Adam nodded. "Security video verified it was him. We identified him in the store—he was wearing all black—same as the man who snuck into the vehicle while Gwen was pumping gas."

Jake shifted in his seat. "Did they find any of Gwen's DNA in the secret room?"

"No, only for Emily and Williams. But that doesn't mean she wasn't there. The forensics guys think he had her on a tarp that covered the mattress, and wrapped her in that. She was electrocuted, so there wouldn't have been blood."

"Except for the cuts on her back."

Yeah, that had been what Adam had asked. "The ME says he could've used rags to wipe up blood as he went along. There was a firepit in the backyard. They think he burned the blood evidence in there."

"And the knife from the trunk?" She arched her back to stretch, arm tight against her side, a grimace on her face.

"No DNA, but the ME confirmed it was altogether possible they made the cuts on Gwen's back."

"I just can't believe Scott Williams was the Reaper."

"It doesn't follow any known pattern for serial killers—or pedophiles—that I've ever come in contact with," Jake added. "Pedophiles are not usually interested in women. Only children."

"All of the women were in their late teens, early twenties," Adam said. "But all of them looked much younger."

"Not Gwen, though," Kendall said.

"She was never supposed to be a 'victim.'"

Kendall cringed. He regretted the words as soon as they left his mouth.

"So, it's over," she said.

"Yeah." He reached across and squeezed her hand. "It's over."

EPILOGUE

K ENDALL RANG THE doorbell of the home in Highlands
Ranch, just south of Denver. It was almost country living,
as close as you could get and still be within a reasonable distance of the city. Kathy Williams opened the door. Gone were
the lines that had creased her forehead since Kendall had met
her. She had on a light sweater and jeans. The sun had made an
appearance and had warmed the day to nearly seventy degrees.

In typical and unpredictable fashion for Colorado, there was
snow in the forecast the next day. Snow was a possibility year-round
in the state. The savings grace was it never stayed around long in
the spring. Often the snow would come in the morning and be
gone by the afternoon, making way for a sunny end to the day.

"Come on in," Kathy said, a singsong quality to her voice.
She seemed to be standing a little taller, her confidence making
her almost regal as she led Kendall through her new home. The
soft cream colors of the walls, along with all the windows letting in the sun, warmed the place. The family room had a huge
overstuffed sectional couch with even more big, fluffy throw pillows in reds and teals and bright yellow. Family pictures filled
the walls. Scott was not in a single one. The kitchen had earth
and wood tones, the stove and vent hood looked like a hearth.
Pictures colored by the girls, Emily's strictly within the lines,
Sadie's a mass of scribbles, were displayed proudly on the fridge.

Comfortable. Cozy.

Home.

French doors at the back of the house led onto a deck over-looking the backyard. Kathy pointed to a chair next to a round brick firepit and lowered herself into one next to it, drawing her legs up. She inhaled deeply, briefly closing her eyes to the sun.

It was good to see her so relaxed.

"It's beautiful here," Kendall said. She set the carrier on the deck at her feet and sat.

"It really is," Kathy said. "Peaceful."

The girls were playing on a wooden playset in one corner of the yard. Emily launched herself down the slide, then bolted around to the back, climbed the ladder, and repeated. Sadie sat in a sandpit, fistfuls of sand in each hand, mesmerized by the grains slipping through her fingers.

"They look happy," Kendall said.

"Yeah, I think they are. Emily still has nightmares, but those will be a part of life for a while. For both of us." Kathy inhaled again and smiled. "But, yeah, we're happy here. Emily has made friends with some of the neighborhood kids. I've been accepted into the mothers' Wine Club. It's good. Tranquil."

Kendall chuckled. "Sounds like fun."

"It helps take the edge off, for sure," Kathy agreed. "I legally changed all of our names—took my maiden name back. I just didn't want anyone to associate us with . . . *him*."

"I think that was a wise move. Start over fresh. There's no reason the past has to continue to darken your future, and that is an excellent step in the right direction."

"I felt like a weight was lifted from my shoulders as soon as I got the orders. So much relief just in that one simple act."

"Do they know what happened to Scott?" Kendall's head dipped toward the girls.

Kathy nodded. "They know he died. They don't know you killed him." She stared at Kendall, her gaze intense. "It's sounds horrible, I know, but . . . thank you."

It was an odd thing to be thanked for, taking a human life, but Kendall completely understood the sentiment behind it. "You're welcome."

"So," Kathy glanced at the playset, the smile back in place on her face, "shall we do this?"

"Yep." Kendall unlatched the carrier door.

"Emily, Kendall's here. Come say hi," Kathy called to the girls.

Emily stood at the bottom of the slide for a second and then burst into a run across the grass. Sadie rolled onto her side and hoisted herself up, waddle-running to catch up with her big sister.

Kathy laughed and went to retrieve the toddler. Emily hit the deck and launched herself into Kendall's embrace, wrapping her arms around Kendall's neck.

"We have a new house and I got to pick the color in my room and we're gonna paint it purple 'cause that's my favorite color and I have a really big bed 'cause I'm a big girl now"—she wriggled from Kendall's lap and stood in front of her, never missing a beat—"but Sadie still has a crib, but it's brand new and her room is yellow 'cause we don't know what her favorite color is yet—" She stopped to take a breath.

Kendall felt out of breath just trying to follow everything the girl was saying.

"Honey, Kendall has a surprise for you," Kathy said before Emily could begin speaking again.

Emily's eyes grew as wide as her smile, and it melted Kendall's heart. She reached into the carrier and brought out a fluffy gray kitten.

The girl's hands covered her mouth and her feet stomped against the deck. "Ohh, is he mine?"

Kendall placed the kitten into the girl's hand. "Yes, but 'he's' a 'she.'"

Emily drew the kitten to her chest and placed her lips tenderly on its head.

"Kitty," Sadie said, her hands thrust toward her sister, squirming to get off her mother's lap.

Kathy tightened her hold on the child. "What do you want to name her?"

Emily looked straight into Kendall's eyes. Into her heart and soul.

"I'm going to name her Kendall."

ACKNOWLEDGMENTS

I WOULDN'T HAVE COME this far without my wonderful agent, Stephanie Phillips, at SBR Media. Thanks also to Terri Bischoff at Crooked Lane Books for taking a chance on this book and loving it as much as I do. Massive respect and kudos for the team at Crooked Lane Books, who took my little story and made it even better than I dreamed it could be. So excited to be a part of the CLB team!

I am so grateful to have found Deb Nemeth and Joan Turner (JRT Editing), who helped me make sure very early on that the story made sense and that I had all my ducks in a row, and pulled me out of rabbit holes.

Thanks to Jill Bastian for running around Denver, checking out the best places to dump bodies (and take pictures!), and answering questions, no matter how weird or disturbing.

Thanks also to Matt Beers, my Colorado law enforcement expert. And I'm grateful to Nick and Noah Harmon for loaning me their names. You are both a shining example of what is possible regardless of what obstacles are placed in your path. Keep up the great work, young men—so much promise ahead!

Many thanks to Lisa Regan, who supports a sister author whenever I ask for a helping hand. And to my author happy hour gals—Melinda, Kendra, Toni, Amy, and Loreth Anne—who made facing a pandemic more fun than it should have been, and who inspire me to be better at all things, not the least of which is my writing and my alcohol consumption. Love you ladies!

Big hugs to Helen Hardt, who read a very early version of this and told me this was what I was meant to be writing. You gave me the nudge I needed to make a change, and I'm forever grateful.

Chuck, there are no words for how much I appreciate all you have done for me. You have never told me to go find a "real" job, even when it took years for me to figure what I wanted to do when I grew up. My kids—you had to grow up in this crazy business and then learn how best to approach Mom based on how close I was to a deadline. Love you so much!

LeighAnn—you are my sister by choice, and I couldn't love you more if we shared blood. Love you, SB! Drue, your friendship and encouragement and swift kicks in the ass are more appreciated than you will ever know.

Thanks to Courtney Klute at Sol Virtual Assistance, for making branding and building a social media presence look easy and for getting my name out there!